"YOU ~~I~~

He leaned cl~~ose~~ ... ~~a hard breath that~~
until he reache~~d~~ ... caught in her throat while a knot of confusion twisted her insides.

"I warned you not to toy with me, Josette, but since you insist on doing so, I intend to return tomorrow evening with another bottle of rum. Can you prove to me you can drink that much on your own?"

His words, husky and raw, touched the side of her neck and sent a quivering through her. She swallowed a moan. "I could and then some."

What was wrong with her? Instead of gaining control, she was losing herself in him, and she'd just accepted a challenge she had no way of fulfilling.

He drew back in one fluid movement, and as he did so, his mouth seared her flesh, sending a hot pulse pounding low in her belly. She glanced down. Just long enough to catch sight of proof that he was as aroused as she was. He didn't miss her glance.

"You feel it too, don't you?"

Josette

Kathleen Bittner Roth

ZEBRA BOOKS
KENSINGTON PUBLISHING CORP.
http://www.kensingtonbooks.com

ZEBRA BOOKS are published by

Kensington Publishing Corp.
119 West 40th Street
New York, NY 10018

All Kensington titles, imprints, and distributed lines are available at special quantity discounts for bulk purchases for sales promotion, premiums, fund-raising, educational, or institutional use.

Special book excerpts or customized printings can also be created to fit specific needs. For details, write or phone the office of the Kensington Sales Manager: Attn.: Sales Department. Kensington Publishing Corp., 119 West 40th Street, New York, NY 10018. Phone: 1-800-221-2647.

Zebra and the Z logo Reg. U.S. Pat. & TM Off.

First Printing: October 2015
ISBN-13: 978-1-4201-3532-9
ISBN-10: 1-4201-3532-5

eISBN-13: 978-1-4201-3533-6
eISBN-10: 1-4201-3533-3

10 9 8 7 6 5 4 3 2 1

Printed in the United States of America

To Terri Bittner Abbas

You will always be my "little sister,"
a button-nosed, darling little blonde
with an infectious smile
who would snuggle up to me while I told you stories,
only to have you fall asleep before I'd finished.

Mornings, over breakfast, you'd ask for the endings,
but I had no idea since they were made-up tales
that had vanished during the night.
Do you remember the amusement in Mom's eyes?
Those precious moments will live in my heart forever.

Chapter One

San Francisco, 1857

Once he reached China, Cameron Andrews didn't give a bloody damn where he ended up.

He stood on the dock in front of the Andrews Shipping Company offices, one booted foot perched atop a stubby mooring, eyes fixed on the *Serenity*. The sleek clipper tacked back and forth, gracefully working her way into the harbor on the first leg of her journey since departing New Orleans. She'd tie down long enough to drop off mail and cargo, then refill her stores and head to the Orient for another load of goods. He'd be aboard her when she set sail.

Born in New Orleans's Vieux Carré to a French mother, and educated at Cambridge like his English father, he was used to the very best. He and his cousin had inherited the family business, had worked their arses off to turn the shipping line into an empire that maintained the largest fleet in the world. He was a wealthy man who could afford just about anything.

A soft snort escaped him. Anything, that is, except a modicum of peace. No amount of money could buy his way out of the misery that threatened to suffocate him.

Somewhere behind him a church bell pealed the noon hour, and like clockwork, his stomach growled. A glance down the street at the Morgan Hotel, and any desire for food left him. He'd taken his noon meal there every day without fail since his arrival four years ago—that is, until recently. Even though it had been two years since his wife's passing, facing her parents, the owners of the hotel, was growing more tedious by the day. Lately, he'd been skipping luncheon altogether.

The sun escaped the cover of a billowy cloud and turned the gray waters of San Francisco Bay into a hard sparkle of blue. The air lost a bit of its briskness. He shielded his eyes from the glare and watched the *Serenity* glide silently through the water. Good Lord, she was magnificent. The fastest ship on the seas. *Merde*, but it would feel good to gain his sea legs again.

The *Felicité* and the *Celine*, two more of the company's elegant clippers, rode low in the water harbor-side, both laden with goods from China and India. In a few days, one would head to New Orleans, the other to Boston.

As the *Serenity* tacked eastward one last time before coming into port, Yerba Buena Island appeared behind her like a backdrop, an emerald oasis in the middle of the bay. A familiar hollowness ate at him. His wife and stillborn son lay buried on the western slope of that island. His chest grew taut. Would Dianah forgive him if he left? Lord knew how many times he'd stood beside her grave begging permission to leave without guilt.

"Ho, there, Mister Andrews," Davey, his dockhand, shouted. "*Serenity* heavin' to. The wind's shifted, so she'll be coming 'round port-side. Best ye step back, sir."

Seagulls swooped and squawked, wheeling and diving into the choppy waters like pirates after buried treasure. The sleek clipper, her sails drawing in, glided silently to the dock. Sailors tossed a couple of ratlines. Davey grabbed one, while Cameron slipped the other over the mooring post he'd just vacated. The vessel came to a complete stop in the water.

The gangplank lowered. First off the ship was a scowling, red-cheeked captain, the ship's log tucked under one arm, as he dragged a scruffy boy by the neck.

Cameron stepped forward. "Looks like you got yourself a stowaway, Hallowell."

"The little bastard is all yours now, by God." The captain gave the boy a hard shove.

The lad, his face smeared with dirt, stumbled to a halt in front of Cameron, shoulders scrunched in an exaggerated wince as he rubbed at the back of his neck. "Why you be draggin' me like dat? I was damn glad to be off dat boat, don'cha know. *Merde!* I would've come down on my own without you trying to rip my head off.*"

Bloody hell if it wasn't a no-account Cajun straight out of the bayou. "Ship," Cameron drawled. "*Never* refer to my fine line of vessels as boats."

The breeze kicked up and swirled around the boy, shooting an acrid scent up Cameron's nostrils—sweat, dirt, and frayed clothing that likely hadn't seen a washing the entire trip. If ever. "Christ, you smell like Napoleon's army after a forty-day march."

"Probably worse," Hallowell responded. "He refused a bath the entire journey. Can't figure how a body not used to the sea could find so many places to hide. Whenever I mentioned even a little water around the ears, the guttersnipe vanished so fast I had to scratch my head and wonder if he wasn't an apparition. I finally gave up and stuck to my duties. It was either that or toss him overboard and forget I ever saw him. Can't tell you how many times I was sorely tempted to do that very thing."

The boy shot a fiery glance at the captain and muttered a French profanity so foul, Cameron was glad Hallowell didn't understand the language. "Take your leave, Hallowell. I'll see to the scalawag. Is my replacement aboard?"

"Aye." The captain jerked his thumb in the air behind him and headed for the company offices.

"Mr. Andrews!" Joshua Cooper, carpetbag in hand, stepped smartly off the ship, but when his feet hit the deck, he weaved from side to side like a drunken sailor.

Cameron chuckled. "Still got your sea legs, I see."

Cooper managed to stick out his hand and, with a grin, grasped Cameron's and pumped it up and down. "Much as I love the sea, and everything about the shipping business, sir, I still end up thinking I'm afloat for a good three or four days after we've docked."

He glanced around at the gray clapboard buildings lining the bayside wharf and at others branching out behind and along narrow streets. "Isn't this a sight different from New Orleans?" His eyes narrowed at the new clouds forming overhead. "Not to mention the cooler weather."

"It takes time, but you'll get used to it. Whatever the conditions are at the moment, they can change fast. You'll soon learn to carry an umbrella with you as a matter of course." Cameron gave a nod toward a large white building emblazoned with a green roof to his left. "That's the Morgan Hotel. Go ahead and get yourself settled in. We'll meet over dinner there and discuss permanent lodgings for you."

"Thank you, sir. Until this evening, then." Cooper trotted down the street.

Cameron folded his arms over his chest and turned to the boy standing beside him. He stared at the top of a cap-covered head. "What's your name?"

"Alex."

With the way he cast his eyes to his boots and scuffed a toe against the dock, Cameron would bet the scamp was lying. "Straighten up and look me in the eye, boy. How old are you?"

The lad lifted his head and, with a cocky attitude that nearly made Cameron laugh, folded his arms across his chest, arrogantly mirroring Cameron's stance. "Old 'nuff."

"Is that so?" What the devil was he supposed to do with this ne'er-do-well until the clipper destined for New Orleans set sail? He surveyed Alex, from his threadbare clothing, to his worn shoes, which appeared a few sizes too large. A shaft of compassion shot through him. "Were you looking for a little adventure? Is that what made you stow away? Or was the law after you?"

"*Non.*"

"Were you running away from someone who mistreated you?"

"*Non.*" Alex assessed Cameron in the exact same manner as he'd been surveyed, slow and easy. Completing his mock appraisal, his gaze settled back on Cameron's, where it held steady. A smirk curled one corner of his mouth. "I had a fair good reason for hoppin' aboard your fine vessel asides finding me a good time."

He spoke in that lyrical Cajun French that made even the most evil of epithets roll off a tongue like a sweet lullaby. Unease spread through Cameron. Was he in charge or had the boy just taken over? Wily little thing.

"Since my stomach is playing fiddle with my backbone, the sooner you tell me why you stowed on one of my ships without a never-you-mind, the sooner I can get a meal. Are you hungry?"

"*Oui.* I could use me a bite."

He'd have to take Alex to the public baths before they'd dare venture into the hotel. "Not until you wash away that stink and get into some clean clothes. There's a mercantile down the street where we can pick up a change of clothing.

And then you can bloody well have a bath before eating. Got any money?"

That smirk again. "*Non*, but you fair do."

Cameron grunted. "Brilliant. After a free trip halfway around the world, you expect me to supply you with clothing as well?"

"Sumpin' like dat."

Bloody hell, he couldn't just leave a lad this far from home to wander. "Is San Francisco where you intended to land?"

"*Oui.*"

"So what was your purpose in coming here?"

Alex grinned, flashing a set of fine white teeth, but the look in his eye turned flinty. "I came lookin' for my papa." The boy rocked back on his heels, his arms still crossed over his chest. "And it looks like I done found you."

"Me?" A bark of laughter left Cameron's throat. He peered into sharp, amber eyes fringed top and bottom with dark lashes. A chill snaked through him. If he looked in the mirror, he'd see the same damn thing. But that was impossible.

"You're coming with me." He dug his fingers into the boy's dirty jacket and headed him toward the mercantile. "Davey, I'm off to lunch. Tell the captain I'll see him and Cooper at eight, over dinner at the Morgan."

"Aye," Davey called back.

In less than ten minutes, Cameron and Alex were in and out of the mercantile and in front of the public baths.

Alex twisted away. "I ain't goin' in there to get buggered by some lusty sailor who can't wait to be slidin' his wiggle worm into some doxy."

Cameron halted, his neck hairs bristling. "Is that why you refused a bath aboard ship?"

A slow turn of Alex's head away from Cameron's eyes, and he let go a soft, "*Oui*."

By now, Cameron had moved beyond hunger and frustration, and was fast working his way into full-blown anger. "Then it's to my home we'll go, but if you so much as slip a candlestick inside one of your pockets, I'll have your head on a platter."

"*Oui*, Papa."

"Don't call me that!" Hell, the boy could belong to his cousin, Trevor. No, those were definitely Cameron's eyes. But still, the idea was preposterous. "How old did you say you were?"

Alex shrugged. "Didn't."

"Well, do so, now," he roared.

Alex only grinned. "I'll be needin' dat bath first, don'cha know."

Bates, a miner-turned-butler, met Cameron at the door to his California Hill mansion. Cameron shoved the paper-wrapped clothing at him. "See to it Alex here gets a decent bath, and have Cook fix a couple of plates."

"Jambalaya would suit," Alex piped in. "But I ain't takin' no bath with your man here tinkin' to scrub me clean an' bugger me at the same time."

The butler's cheeks flushed, but he made no comment. Cameron fought a grin. *That must have curled the old boy's toes.* "There's no jambalaya to be had in San Francisco, and you can bloody well take a bath alone, but I'll be checking your pockets when you come down, you hear?"

"*Oui*," Alex said, and jauntily climbed the stairs behind Bates. "You got yerself a peculiar accent, Papa. Sometimes you sound like a right good Frenchman out of Nawlins oughta, but other times you sound like a proper Englishman. Just saying so you know I pays attention."

"Christ." Cameron turned on his heel and made his way

into the library, where he dropped onto the sofa with an exaggerated exhale. How the devil could a predicament like this have popped up out of nowhere? And now of all times, when he was about to embark on an endless journey to nowhere.

A Cajun bastard? Not likely. Cameron had been just seventeen when he left New Orleans. He and Trevor had been hell-raisers, which was why Cameron had ended up in a private school in England and later at Cambridge, but the last thing he could've done was leave a child behind.

An hour later, when Alex failed to appear, Cameron went looking for him in the guest quarters. He gave a quick rap on the door.

"*Entre*, Papa. I be all cleaned up and dressed in my new clothes, now."

"Haughty little fool," Cameron mumbled, and helped himself inside.

And nearly fell over.

Gone was the dirty, disheveled boy with a worn cap pulled over his head. Long, black hair, as shiny as a crow's wing hung about the face of a beautiful young girl heading straight into womanhood. They stood staring at each other while Cameron collected his thoughts.

And she smirked.

"What did you say your name was?"

Soft laughter rolled out of her. "Alexia, dear Papa. Alexia Thibodeaux. From Bayou St. Laurent."

Her sweet, silken voice sounded too old, too wise for a young girl. She stepped forward, bold as you please. "You remember my *maman*, don't you? Solange?"

"I . . . I can't say as I do. How old are you?"

"Near thirteen, Papa." She tilted her head. "My *maman* was Solange Thibodeaux. Oh, wait. She was Sally to you."

Well, he had her there. Even in his misdirected youth, he had known better than to have anything to do with a woman out of the bayou. The idea that they could be even remotely connected was absurd.

"*Non?* Then you must remember my uncles, René and Bastièn? They near beat you to death for lovin' my *maman* in Madame Olympée's whorehouse."

Dear God! The young woman who'd squired him into manhood was this girl's mother? He'd forgotten about her, hadn't a clue at the time that she might be a French Cajun. She'd told him she was an orphan from the Quarter. "It can't be . . . you can't be. You're lying. I wouldn't trust anyone related to René or Bastièn to give me the correct time of day. Who put you up to this, your mother?"

"I never knew my *maman,* Papa. She died when I was born." She sauntered forward. "Do you like my eyes, Papa? Family been tellin' me all my life dat I look just like my papa. I wanted to believe I was more like Maman, but now I see dey was right."

What the hell was he supposed to do now? "I was only seventeen when that fight took place at Madame Olympée's. I was shipped off to England immediately afterward. There's obviously some mistake."

"There be no mistake." Her eyes hardened. "Maybe you only be seventeen at the time, but you done slid dat big snake of yours right up inside my *maman* and let loose a powerful poison."

She took another step closer and shoved her chin in the air, her eyes flashing crude determination. "And dat poison you let loose turned out to be me, Papa. Now, wach'ya tink?"

Chapter Two

New Orleans

Cameron marched Alexia past the clipped lawns of the mansions in the new, ostentatious section of New Orleans, wondering if she wasn't leading him on a wild goose chase. He'd challenged the unruly child, had told her to go ahead and run off to her family in the bayou. But if she was serious about proving she was his daughter, then there were to be no games or he'd board the next company ship and not give her another thought for the rest of his days.

Lord, she'd been a handful aboard ship. Hallowell had been right. How could she disappear for days at a time only to wander into his cabin sporting a mischievous grin?

More like the devil's spawn than his.

The rapscallion could think up more mischief than any ten monkeys, then laugh as though everyone should laugh with her. She carried the ship's cat around wherever she went—even slept with the little mouser. Like Hallowell, Cameron finally gave up and left her to her own devices.

As if on cue, Alexia hopped off the banquette, the raised boardwalk that prevented shoes and hems from collecting dirt or mud, and strutted through a pristine lawn. Cameron scowled at her. "Get back here before you ruin your new dress."

"It be the color of grass, so no matter."

"You heard me, get over here. I ought to put a bit in your mouth and lead you by the reins. I've never seen a wilder filly."

Alexia's gay laughter filled the air. She hopped on one foot, removed a shoe, and then did the same with the other. "Betcha wish you could make me mind with a mere snap of yer fingers."

"Get off the grass, and put your shoes back on."

"They pinch."

"Why didn't you tell me?"

"Ya didn't ask."

He snatched one from her, but before he could flex it to test its suppleness, she already had her stockings off and was traipsing barefoot through the wide grassy lawn again.

"You, Alexia Thibodeaux, are a fibber. These are the best shoes money can buy. Now put them back on."

She giggled and tossed him a stocking. "What's the matter, Papa? You ain't never walked barefoot in grass before? Once you wiggle your toes in the coolness, ain't no goin' back to shoes." She pointed her finger. "There, dat be *ma tante's* house."

Cameron practically stumbled to a halt in front of a white-columned mansion. Like the grand lady she was, the house sat in pristine splendor, taking up half the city block, surrounded by an ornate wrought-iron fence and bedecked with flowers looking like so many jewels scattered around. "Liar. That's Louis Leblanc's residence."

"*Oui.* She be his widow, don'cha know."

"No, I didn't know. Now put your shoes and stockings back on."

She giggled. "In dat exact order?"

"Do as I say. And try acting like a girl for once."

"Whatever dat be meaning."

"Do you always have to get the last word in?"

"Do you?"

Josette Thibodeaux LeBlanc, widow of one of the wealthiest merchants in the history of New Orleans, stood in the shadows of the open doors leading to the second-floor balcony, her heart pounding a wild rhythm. She watched her niece struggle into her stockings and shoes and then face her father, both of them with their arms folded across their chests, engaged in animated conversation.

So, here he was, after all these years. And even more handsome than she remembered. He was taller now, broader in the shoulders. But where his midnight locks had once been clipped short, they now reached his collar. They looked soft to the touch, those curls.

Seeing him in need of a trim after weeks at sea, wondering what it might feel like to run her fingers through his hair, felt like an act of intimacy. She shouldn't indulge in such nonsense, but sweet heaven, he was a sight to behold, even more so than when she'd secretly followed him around in her youth. While he'd obviously inherited his size and breadth from his English father, he'd clearly taken on the looks of his late mother, a French beauty who'd never failed to turn heads whenever she strolled through the streets of the Vieux Carré.

A faint smile—anything but affable—touched Josette's lips. While her memories of Cameron Andrews remained crystal clear, he hadn't even known she existed. Oh, as a young girl, she'd fallen desperately in love with him from afar, but by the time she'd turned thirteen, she'd hated him with a passion. That was when Solange, her older sister, had decided Cameron was her ticket out of life in the swamps.

As if hearing her thoughts, Cameron glanced at the

house. Josette moved away from the curtain a few inches. Vivienne, her cousin, slipped in beside her.

"No mistaking those two be cut from the same cloth. *Oui*, dat be her daddy, a'right."

"*That is* her daddy, Vivienne. Do remember to drop the Cajun patois or we'll never get Alexia trained right."

"*Pardon*. Seems I fall back into old habits whenever I get excited. What a lovely frock Alexia be . . . is wearing. Do you suppose it's one of Madame Charmontès's creations?" She squinted. "But of course. Look at the fabric. Same as one you have in your wardrobe. Do you think that crafty little woman did that on purpose?"

Josette noted the emerald-green dress draping Alexia's slender body as being of a design only that particular dress-maker could manage. "Would clothing such as that come from anyone else?"

"How did monsieur manage to get her into a dress, I wonder?"

"I would imagine he used a threat or two."

Cameron grabbed Alexia's hand and, with a little yank, headed for the front steps. Josette and Vivienne moved deeper into the upstairs landing.

"What a foolish girl, running off like she did," Vivienne said. "It's a wonder she managed to return at all, let alone with her papa in tow."

Josette shuttered her mind against the dreadful worry she'd endured after Alexia had stowed away on one of Cameron's ships. "If only the little snoop hadn't run across the letter I'd written to her father before I had a chance to post it. Had I not penned the blasted thing, she wouldn't have known where to find him."

"And we wouldn't have had to suffer so many sleepless nights."

"What was I to do, Viv? I couldn't handle her any longer, and my brothers are the worst kind of father figures. I don't want to lose her to bayou life or worse, have her follow in Maman's footsteps. I felt I had no other choice but to try to contact her father."

Vivienne bit her lip. "You worry about your *maman*, but I worry about my brother. I don't like the way Lucien looks at her now that she's beginning to show her loveliness."

Which was one of the prime reasons Josette had written the note to Cameron. She hadn't mentioned anything to Vivienne, but if rumors were true, and Maman was training Lucien up to be her *Hougan*—her voodoo priest—then he was more dangerous than ever, because the path Maman walked seemed to be growing ever darker. Josette's stomach curdled at the idea that he might try to include Alexia in his lascivious initiation into the priesthood.

Vivienne's brother wasn't the only man who concerned Josette—all those unruly men up and down the bayou had their carnal sights on Alexia as well. The girl had no concept of her beauty, nor was she aware of the attention she garnered. Even dressed as a boy with her hair tucked under a cap, she attracted men's eyes. Her days of wandering around on her own, of slipping away in the middle of the night to play amongst the stars, were over.

"See Mister Andrews in, then send Alexia to me. I'll be down in a quarter hour."

"*Oui*." Vivienne limped toward the staircase, her day gown hiding her disfigured hip, but not the hitch in her step the condition produced.

One of the double doors set with beveled glass swung wide, and Cameron found himself staring into the face of a fairly handsome, dark-haired woman dressed in gray and white.

"*Tante* Vivienne!" Alexia tore loose from Cameron's grip and fell into the woman's arms.

The woman gave a slight bow of her head. "I am Mademoiselle Vivienne Thibodeaux, first cousin to Madame LeBlanc and once removed from Alexia. She only refers to me as her aunt because of my age."

"I see." But what of it? Who was to say they both weren't in this together, thick as thieves? They had a long way to go to convince Cameron that Alexia was his daughter. A twinge ran through his gut at the thought, as if his conscience took hold and shook him. If Vivienne truly was a cousin, that meant she could be related to that scourge of the earth, Lucien. God help her if she was his sister.

Vivienne gave Alexia a quick hug, and then a little shove. "*Tante* Josette awaits you upstairs, *pouchette*."

Alexia took off at a run up the wide staircase. Cameron watched her go. At times, she seemed far too old and wise for her years, while at others, she seemed much younger. But whatever the case, that joie de vivre she carried with her at all times was infectious—he couldn't seem to remain angry with her for long.

Vivienne turned to Cameron. "Come in, Monsieur Andrews. Madame LeBlanc received Alexia's note and is expecting you."

Cameron stepped inside the graceful mansion. Vivienne walked ahead of him down the wide hallway and directed him into a large room he guessed to be the formal parlor meant for receiving guests. He recognized goods from around the world—an expensive étagère from France, exquisite Chinese carpets, a small Greek statue in one corner of the well-appointed room. Whether it was the widow's good taste or LeBlanc's, he didn't give a bloody damn. He just needed to get this matter resolved and be on his way.

As he moved to the window facing a lush rose garden, a bead of perspiration ran down the back of his neck. He swiped at it. Barely noon, and already the heat and humidity were stifling. Too many years in England and San Francisco had changed his blood. All he could think of right now was getting back to the hotel, stripping down to his underwear, and lying about in his room sipping minted lemonade until the sun went down and he could venture outside. Surely this aunt of hers would take the girl—at least until there was proof of her parentage.

Truth be told, the longer he was around Alexia, the harder it became to deny his fatherhood. As often as she deliberately mimicked him, there were other times her mannerisms were unconscious and natural—and just like his. Even the turn of her hand when she set about explaining something mirrored his movements. Bloody hell, if this wouldn't undermine his plans to disappear into oblivion for a few years.

"Monsieur Andrews, welcome to my home."

At the smoky, velvet sound, Cameron swung around. Every function in his body—heart, breath, blood—ceased to function.

She was lovely.

More than lovely.

Tendrils of raven hair framed a face so exquisite, it disarmed him. Her mouth, a soft, dewy pink, as though she'd pressed rose petals to her lips, parted. And those eyes, as dark as Creole coffee, intelligent and assessing, roamed over him and then back to take hold of his. But it was her complexion, as flawless as a newborn's, and with a soft glow to it that mesmerized him, that made him want to step closer and stroke her skin.

He turned back to looking out the window while his scrambled thoughts found some semblance of order. He cleared his throat. "It seems I am being accused of begetting a child some thirteen years ago. An incorrigible, uneducated, and as-wild-as-the-bayous-are-thick-with-mosquitoes child."

A soft chuckle sounded behind him. "You mean to describe a Thibodeaux, don't you, monsieur?"

God, yes! He clasped his hands behind his back, and

turned to face her again. *Merde*, but she was lovely. He'd guess her age to be three or four years younger than his thirty-two. And she was Louis LeBlanc's widow? Egads. LeBlanc had been middle-aged even before Cameron had left for England. "And you are a Thibodeaux as well, Madame LeBlanc?"

"*Oui*." She glided into the room, the hem of her pale blue gown whispering across the floor. "Removed from the bayou to a lovely home in what people are referring to as the exclusive Garden District, yet no one in New Orleans has forgotten where I came from, or worse, that I am Odalie Thibodeaux's daughter. Thus, I am considered even lower than Cajun bayou trash. I want something different for my niece."

At her frank honesty, Cameron caught a glimpse of fleeting pain, replaced by a calm demeanor and benevolent smile. Oh, there was anger in this woman. And he'd not get within ten feet of it.

She moved to a table holding a rather large box. She lifted the lid and withdrew a folded garment. "Do you remember this, Monsieur Andrews?"

She shook out a diaphanous peignoir the color of the moon and held it up. "Even though you were but a youth, you had fanciful dreams more befitting the man you are now. You gave this to my sister. Do you remember? She loved it."

His chest constricted. "I do recall, Madame LeBlanc." He swiped a hand over his damp brow. *Blast the humidity.* "I was a foolish young man who never questioned if a woman might get with child while in Madame Olympée's strict employ. I suppose it does happen. But that piece of fabric still does not prove the child is mine."

She studied him for a long moment with eyes that seemed to see right inside him. A flush of heat settled low in his belly. Had she felt it, too, that indefinable *something* that had passed between them just then?

For a telltale second, she cast her eyes downward and a slight flush washed over her cheeks. "Please, call me Josette." She took in a visible breath, and when she glanced back up, the façade she'd let slip was back in place. Elegantly so. "Madame LeBlanc is far too formal for what and whom we are discussing. I'll be most honest with you, sir. My sister tricked you."

A jolt ran through him. "Tricked me?"

"Oui." Her incredible fathomless eyes seemed to peer into him once again. "She intended for a babe fathered by you to be her escape from the low life she lived along the bayou. In her frivolous youth, she thought to wipe out the social rejection she'd endured by bearing your child. Your family does have a reputation for being honorable."

"How do I know Alexia is mine and this isn't just another trick?" As if some magnetic force pulled him to her, he took a step closer. A buzz ran through him. His gaze fell to her luscious mouth, and for a brief moment, his only thought was what those lips might taste like. He stepped back, confused at his strong physical reaction to her. What the devil had gotten into him? She'd been speaking of her sister, for God's sake.

Josette gave a soft laugh and extended her hand toward the dark blue velvet sofa. "Be seated, *s'il vous plaît.*" She sat in a chair several feet from him and smoothed the fabric of her gown. Humor danced in her eyes. "Would you care for some lemonade? You suddenly look . . ." She shrugged. "Somewhat parched."

She knew damn well what he'd been thinking; it was written all over her face. And did the vixen intend to make him squirm? Well, she'd not play him for a fool. His gaze locked with hers. "If it pleases you, Madame."

She lifted a brow and matched his half-smile with one of

her own. "Indeed, it would. Please me, that is." She called
for Vivienne.

Before Cameron had time to think up a clever retort,
Vivienne appeared with a tray, serving first him and then
Josette before disappearing as silently as she had entered.
Thank God for interruptions. His mouth was so dry, he
forced himself to drink slowly and not guzzle the cool drink
laced with mint. "If your sister was planning to trick me,
mightn't you be as well?"

Josette sighed. "I suggest you pay a visit to Madame
Olympée and consult with her. If you recall, she keeps a
tight rein on her ladies. Solange, who called herself Sally
when with you, went to Madame with an offer to become
her virginal goddess, but only with you as a client. After
Madame Olympée schooled my sister in how to take care of
a man in the most sensuous of ways, Solange dispensed with
any and all methods taught her to prevent a child from
coming into the world. She then went about sweeping you
off your feet. Unfortunately, my brothers found out—"

He raised a hand. "Please, that part I recall quite clearly.
I still carry a scar on my leg from René's knife." He should
take his leave before his growing discomfort became apparent. "I'll speak with Madame this evening."

"And if you decide to accept your daughter, what then,
monsieur?"

He pinched the bridge of his nose. "I don't know. She's
quite the handful. Send her off to school somewhere, I would
suspect."

Josette's dark eyes grew even darker. "She'd only run
away. Back to her *maman*."

"*Maman?* I thought your sister was deceased."

"I speak of my mother, monsieur. Alexia's grandmother."

"*Merde*, the voodoo witch!"

"Please, Monsieur Andrews. She is my mother, after all."

"Your pardon." He leaned back and studied the woman

before him. An ethereal scent floated around her whenever she shifted—something so enticing as to make him want to draw closer yet again, study her breathtaking beauty up close. Blast it all, what was he thinking? She was René's and Bastièn's sister, for God's sake. And her mother was Odalie. Some called the woman a witch while others referred to her as a healer. Whatever she was, he'd only laid eyes on her once, after the melee in Madame Olympée's. He hoped to never run into her again. There was something very dark and very wicked about her he'd never forgotten.

"Your mother raised Alexia? With Bastièn and René lurking about? No wonder the girl is the way she is." He scowled. "Why didn't you try your hand at turning her out in a proper manner?"

Josette stood and began to pace, but even her strides appeared elegant and filled with grace. "I was barely Alexia's age when she was born, monsieur. I was as wild as she is today, if not more so."

She paused in front of him, her scent captivating him once again. "What good was I to her? And after my sister died, Maman took fierce control of what was left of Solange—her babe. No one was allowed near Alexia those first few years but Maman. Now we have a problem, you and I, because Alexia is turning into a woman of exceptional beauty. But she is headed in a very bad direction if we do not intervene and help her change her course."

He gave a tilt of his head. "We?"

She gave a slow nod. "She does not comprehend the exquisite beauty she is becoming. And her spunk and intelligence wreak havoc. I, alone, cannot handle her, nor can I shield her from Maman's or my brothers' influence. I am calling on you to act as her father and help her before it is too late."

"Then I suggest a school. A far-away school. England has some wonderful institutions out in the middle of nowhere.

I should know," he muttered. "She won't find too many pockets to pick out there. Are you aware she picks pockets? There wasn't a sailor aboard ship who didn't have something or other go missing. She gave it all back at the end of the trip, laughing her fool head off, as if she'd pulled off the greatest feat since the Egyptians built the pyramids."

He felt around his vest pocket. "Bloody hell! She stole my gold watch. Must have done that on our way over here." He cursed again. "That's the second one I've lost to a pickpocket."

"Today?"

"No. I had one stolen from me years ago. My father gave it to me when I turned fifteen. I had the one Alexia lifted off me made as an exact duplicate so he wouldn't know I'd been running wild and lost it. Brilliant. Just brilliant."

Josette broke into quiet laughter.

"You think this funny?"

"Your pardon. I'll see to retrieving it for you. It was your reaction that I find rather humorous, not Alexia's thieving. Your watch is likely intended for Maman. Alexia takes everything to her. It's deceitful and sinful, and something I want to break her of before it's too late."

"Madame, it may already be too late."

She turned to him, her lovely features suddenly a portrait of peace. "I was stealing at that age, monsieur," she said softly. "And I reformed. It only takes the right man to steer Alexia onto a higher path. Though I married a good man, your daughter has not had a decent male around to act as a father. Now that you have discovered her, I would think you would take pride in seeing to her well-being and upbringing. Alexia is incredibly intelligent and learns very easily. She is not entirely uneducated, merely unrefined."

Cameron snorted. "That's rather like throwing a coat of whitewash on a black horse and calling it an albino."

Josette sat back down, this time very close. Something in

her nearness set his nerves on edge. He wasn't quite sure he liked it—but his body did, blast it all. It wasn't right to be reacting to another's beauty, not when he'd once thought his wife the most beautiful woman in the world.

Josette tilted her head, and there was that discerning look again. "I would dearly like to know your thoughts, just then, monsieur. You seemed troubled for a moment."

As if I would confess my indecent thoughts to you. "Well, I am troubled. This is a disturbing predicament. Wouldn't you agree?"

"*Oui*, but I beg you. I cannot manage your daughter alone, and I am seeking your word that you will help me find a way to turn Alexia in a different direction. To force her, to send her off somewhere she doesn't wish to go, will only bring disaster. She has to want the finer things in life. She has to want to better herself. Right now, she idolizes Maman, the voodoo witch, as you call her, and that could prove perilous."

"And where is our darling reprobate at this moment?"

Josette shrugged. "Likely going through my things. Either that or sitting quietly on the edge of my bed and watching your timepiece tick away. Whatever she's up to, you could pull all her teeth and she wouldn't give up your watch." She laughed again, light and airy. "Oh, you scowl at that. Such an expression ruins your handsome face."

He raked a hand through his hair. The last thing he needed to hear was that Josette Thibodeaux LeBlanc found him attractive. He was tired and aching, and he needed to announce himself at the company offices before the day was out. Lastly, he had inquiries to make at Madame Olympée's. He needed to hear what she had to say; there was little in this town that escaped her.

He stood. "I'll get back to you, but I must be on my way."

Josette did the same and escorted him into the hallway.

"Vivienne, will you fetch Alexia? It's time for her to take her leave."

"Take her leave?" Bloody hell, she didn't expect him to take Alexia back with him! "She's to remain with you. I've arranged for Madame Charmontés to have a wardrobe sent over so she'll be well dressed and—"

"Take her with you, monsieur. Leave her here and within the hour, she'll only run off to Maman's and to bayou life."

"And what's to keep her from running off if she's with me? She can pick a lock or a pocket in the blink of an eye, seems to make no difference to her. But you would know that."

Josette lifted her chin and folded her hands in front of her. "Take her with you to your workplace. She's a bright girl and she might like it. She delights in new things. When she was above stairs greeting me, she told me she had a devil of a good time while on her voyage."

Cameron stepped closer to Josette, her scent licking at his nostrils and sending a curl of excitement through him he didn't care for. Not at all. "And has she yet told you of her sail around Cape Horn, where the winds howl and water washes over the entire ship, so cold as to freeze a man's moustache right off? Did she tell you she was tied to her bed so as not to be washed out to sea?"

Josette paled. "*Non*. She did not tell me of such things. She only told me of her good experiences."

A dawning took place in Cameron. "Tell me something, Madame LeBlanc. If you are so concerned about your niece, and if you try to keep her out of trouble, how did you react when she disappeared?"

Josette took a step back. Her lovely hand went to her breast. "She left a note."

"Did she now?"

Her gaze flicked from his eyes to his mouth and back again. And then over his shoulder, seeming to stare at nothing. "*Oui*. A note. She said she'd return once she found you."

"I don't believe you." He took another step closer. "Why do I have this sneaking suspicion that you did what you suggest I do—find something that interests her—such as locating her so-called father by sneaking aboard one of my ships? Did you pack her a lunch? Enough food so she wouldn't starve until the ship traveled into waters too far out to turn back?"

Her face flushed. "I . . . well, that's preposterous."

Cameron tucked a curled finger under her chin and lifted. "Why, Madame LeBlanc. I do believe you have your own game to play. You'll understand my reluctance to participate?"

"Take her with you," she whispered. "If you don't she'll just go off to Maman's and . . ." She stopped in midsentence, walked to the door, and opened it, her jaw set. "I have more pride than to beg, Monsieur Andrews. Good day."

When Josette closed the door behind him, she peered through the beveled glass, watched his broad back and fine set of shoulders until he disappeared down the street. What was wrong with her? She should have told him about the letter she'd written to him that never got posted. Just because he'd stood close enough to surround her with his essence, setting every nerve in her body on edge, was no reason to act like the besotted fool she once was. A part of her still hated Cameron. No part of her loved him any longer—that young, passion-filled girl and her fanciful dreams had died a long time ago. Still, there was no denying how the sheer presence of this dark-haired, amber-eyed man unlocked something inside her that had been hidden away since Solange had stolen Josette's dreams.

She turned and made her way upstairs, trying to remind herself that guilt served no good purpose. She'd written the letter to Cameron out of desperation. She wasn't about to explain to him how Alexia had found it and hied off in pursuit of him. Let him believe what he wanted. What did she care?

Hearing Alexia and Vivienne in her cousin's room, Josette strolled in. "Alexia, change your clothing. I'm taking you to Maman's before you run off there on your own. And if you have on your person a gold timepiece you filched from your father's vest pocket, you had better hand it back to him the next time you see him."

Alexia lifted her defiant nose in the air. "Why, I don't know what you be speakin' of."

Their gazes locked for a long moment, and then before Josette left the room, she said, "You do not fool me, *pouchette*. I am your *tante* who knows you inside and out, and does not pretend otherwise, not like Maman. And don't you forget it."

Josette retreated to her own chambers. Locking the door behind her, she went directly to the étagère and the mother-of-pearl inlaid box sitting on a glass shelf. Opening it, she removed the few sundry articles that would prove of interest to Alexia's quicksilver mind, and lifted out the false bottom. Inside the black velvet recesses, she retrieved the gold watch she'd stolen from Cameron some fifteen years ago, along with his diamond stick pin from that first night he'd bedded her sister. He'd not even noticed that particular item had gone missing when she'd bumped into him accidentally on purpose after spying him and his cousin leaving Madame Olympée's bordello.

Josette had been an excellent pickpocket back then.

Even better than Alexia was now.

Chapter Three

What an unholy mess! Cameron turned onto St. Charles Avenue, slowing his pace in an effort to keep perspiration at bay. Had he been in San Francisco, he'd be moving at a near trot, using speed to release some of this god-awful pent-up frustration. He glanced around at the mansions lining the street. Not a soul in sight. Not even a trolley to hasten his journey to the shipping offices. No wonder—it was high noon. Only idiots wandered about in heat and humidity so stifling it muddled one's brain. At least the branches of the tall oak trees lining either side of the walkway met overhead, creating a leafy, sun-dappled canopy.

Solange. After so many years, he could not conjure up her features, though their feverish couplings still haunted the perimeter of his mind. He doubted any man forgot his first sojourn into the exquisite mysteries of woman. In the past, he'd occasionally reveled in those passionate memories, but no longer. Of late, they had become specters in the night, robbing his soul of sleep. He wanted them gone.

He swept the back of his hand across his damp brow. What had Madame Olympée been thinking, allowing him and Trevor to run loose in her establishment at such tender ages? No sense blaming her; she was an astute businesswoman. He and Trevor had dropped so much coin night after night, they'd probably bankrolled her for a good ten years. *Merde*, but they'd been reckless fools, feeding off each other's daring escapades. Good that they'd finally turned their energy into productive measures and built the shipping empire—that is, after turning the better part of France and Italy upside down in their waywardness.

But a father at seventeen? And what of poor Solange? To hell with her deliberate intention to trick him, she'd been just as young and foolish. And no matter whom she was related to, she hadn't deserved to die as a result of her fanciful and misguided imprudence. His gut clenched. "Christ."

And then there was Josette—lovely, ethereal, strong-minded Josette. Why the devil had he crossed the line and reached out and touched her? One curled finger beneath her chin, and her very essence seeped through the layers of his flesh, dipped into his blood and heated it. He shoved a hand through his hair and cursed aloud. He had no business contemplating anything of a salacious nature with the sister of the woman who might have borne his child.

Tell that to his brain . . . and body.

He looked to the sky, through the branches of the great oak boughs hovering above him like a lacy emerald umbrella. "Tell me this isn't true. Tell me this is merely a nightmare from which I shall shortly awaken."

Returning his focus to the lane in front of him, his feet pounded a path to his destination. Lost in thought, he didn't glance up again until he approached the offices of Andrews Shipping Company Ltd. He sucked in a breath and halted. There, heavy in the water, floated the *Dianah*.

God, he'd not expected to see his late wife's name emblazoned on one of his vessels. He'd changed the shipping routes after her death so he wouldn't have to be reminded of his loss every time the ship sailed into port. The clipper must have recently docked, arriving from the east, but why so many guards? What the devil was she carrying?

"Cameron!" a male voice bellowed.

Jerked out of his reverie, Cameron turned and spied a tall, broad-shouldered man eating up the banquette with his long legs. Cameron squinted. Good God, was that Trevor's younger brother? His cousin had grown into manhood and, in doing so, changed so much as to be barely recognizable. "Michel?"

"The very one." Michel's words carried that soft Southern but educated drawl. He clasped Cameron's outstretched hand and, with a slap on the back, gave him a quick hug. "Abbott told me you'd arrived yesterday on the morning tide."

"*Merde*, I wouldn't have recognized you in passing," Cameron said.

Unlike Trevor and Cameron, who resembled their respective mothers, Michel was the very image of his English father, tall and brown-haired. His prominent nose suited him better than it did the patriarch. Michel grinned. "Just when I thought I was doomed to remain skinny as a vine, I filled out until I can boast that I now stand head and shoulders beside you and Trevor."

He turned and, with a sweep of his arm, guided Cameron into the company offices. "I can't tell you how good it is to see you. It's been what, four years since you passed through here on your way to San Francisco? I thought you'd gone off to China on the *Serenity*."

Cameron walked around a large, waist-high table situated in the center of the room, filled with maps and journals. His trained eyes missed nothing. "A temporary change in plans. Very temporary. Abbott said you were in Baton Rouge on business."

"I was. I returned a couple of hours ago. We've got a new sugarcane contract up there. Abbott's out to lunch, but need I tell you what a valuable accountant he is? The San Francisco office may have lost him to us, but we couldn't be more delighted. He's the best there is when it comes to numbers. Are you staying at the family town house?"

Cameron shook his head. "No. I figured you'd taken up residence there since you now work for the company, so I checked into the St. Charles rather than intrude."

Michel settled into a chair in front of a massive desk covered with paperwork. He picked up a pen and twirled it between his fingers, humor tracing fine lines about his eyes. "I bought a place of my own. Since my looks don't have a chance of attracting a comely wife, perhaps my fortune and a mansion in the Garden District might. Are you here to stay, then?"

"God, no. I have every intention of sailing off into the sunset, even though it looks like it'll be on something other than the *Serenity*."

"Back through the wretched Horn to China?"

"*Non*, likely in another direction. The Caribbean or back to England to pay respects to my father, and Trevor and his family, before heading out again." He shrugged a shoulder. "Not that it matters much where I go. Any direction will do." He stared through the window at the ship, and at his wife's name painted on the bow. That familiar sense of having been kicked in the gut shortened his breath.

Michel shifted in his chair. "I'm sorry for your loss, Cam."

"Indeed." Lord, but he would be glad when condolences had run their course. The last thing he needed were reminders of the life he no longer lived.

"For what it's worth," Michel said, "I'm glad you're here. I'm too new at all this to meet the level of excellence you and Trevor have achieved. Now that Cooper's gone to San Francisco, I could use any advice you might have to offer."

"You're likely doing a fine job as manager. You don't need me interfering, but I'd like to take a look at the books, general business, that sort of thing, as long as I'm here."

"Of course. I'd rather you did, as a matter of fact. Two sets of eyes and an excellent accountant. You've made my day."

"I was surprised when I learned you wanted to take over the New Orleans offices," Cameron said. "I thought you meant to throw your hat into the political arena after university."

"I had no idea how much I'd take to the business. I despised it growing up. You know how it was with both our fathers always gone, late nights over the books when they were here. Then, when Mother died and Father remained home with us, his somber mood only added to my idea that the business wasn't for me. As for politics, I came to the conclusion that I can do as much good sticking my nose into things around here as in Washington." He grinned. "Nawlins is in my blood."

Cameron wandered around the office, his peripheral vision filled with the clipper bearing his wife's name across her bow. "What's your cargo on the *Dianah* that requires so many guards?"

"Rum."

"An entire load? Egads. That's literally playing with fire."

Michel frowned, his pen paused in midair. "She arrived late yesterday from the Bahamas. Didn't you get the missive telling you I signed a five-year contract with Gosling Brothers to ship to both Nawlins and San Francisco?"

Cameron took a bead on Michel. Something wasn't right. "No, and no wonder the extra guards. A shipment of gold wouldn't have drawn this much attention in these parts. But that much rum is a mighty volatile cargo."

"That's the problem, I'm afraid. There's already cargo missing."

Cameron unbuttoned his jacket, spread it apart, and set his hands on his hips. "How did that happen?"

Michel shrugged. "I wasn't here last night, so I can't say, but the guards saw nothing."

"Sounds like maybe one or more of them might be involved?"

"We're looking into it, and any insight you have will be appreciated." Michel picked up a stack of papers. "Look at these. Orders from every good restaurant in town. And there are others. Some are from private individuals, and there's even one from Madame Olympée. Every one of these orders is for what's aboard the *Dianah*. Word travels fast in this town."

"Did those doing the requisitioning know a shipment was due prior to its arrival?"

Michel shook his head and laid the pile down. "I only intended to supply our sailors their daily rations, here and in San Francisco, but it looks like we've stumbled upon a new line of business."

Cameron strode to the desk and picking up the orders, sifted through them. "There's no finer rum than what Gosling Brothers produces. If I resided here or ran any kind of decent establishment, my order would be among these. Do you have a secure storage area?"

Michel tossed his pen down and leaned back in his chair, fingers steepled. "I certainly thought so until now. How the devil did someone manage a theft right under our noses?"

"Any idea what Bastièn and René Thibodeaux are up to nowadays?"

"You don't think those two are capable—" Michel sprang from his chair. "René, yes. Bastièn, no."

"Why not Bastièn?"

Michel let go a burst of laughter. "That scoundrel is currently employed in the position of his dreams."

"Meaning?"

"Meaning, Madame Olympée has him servicing young and lonely widows, and some not so widowed, I hear."

"The devil you say. When did Madame start hiring males?"

"About a month ago. Bastièn is a veritable swamp alligator turned into a sleek panther. He's been seen on the streets wearing the finest cut of cloth and acting the perfect gentleman. It seems he has been well-trained by Madame, and his—ahem—schedule is full. As far as thieving rum, I'd leave him out of the mix."

And he happens to be Alexia's uncle. Cameron pinched the bridge of his nose. "What of Lucien, their cousin?"

Michel raised a hand. "That good-for-nothing has his own stills. I doubt he'd know the difference between moonshine and quality rum. If you intend to look to that family, I'd lay my odds on René."

"Then we shall."

A black cat curled in one corner of the office stood, hunched his back, and stretched slow and easy. Flicking his tail, he arrogantly walked to the map and charts table. In one leap, he landed there and sauntered across the sailing chart, where he curled up and stared at Cameron through yellow eyes.

"Unusual cat with those yellow eyes and that tip of white on his tail as though it's been dipped in paint. It looks familiar. Any others like him around?"

Michel shook his head. "That's Midnight. He's one of a kind. Everyone on these docks knows Midnight."

"He looks like a miniature of one of those panthers that roam the bayous."

"Doesn't he, though? Fierce-looking critter, but he's gentle enough. Until he sees a rodent. Best mouser in the parish. I swear, he can walk in front of a ship and send any rat within a hundred yards scurrying upriver. Abbott's fair attached to the thing, and was a bit unnerved when it went missing yesterday. Thought he'd lost him, but the little beast is back. Odd, though. He said Midnight isn't inclined to wander far."

Bloody hell, if that wasn't the same little beast Alexia had sneaked into the hotel suite last night, the little thief. Cameron perused the room. "Do you keep everything locked up good and tight when you leave for the day? What about any cash?"

Michel picked up his pen and set it twirling between his fingers again. "We have a guard on the docks, and since you and Trevor are charter members of the Bank of Nawlins, we get special privileges, so money is deposited every day no matter the time. Not a cent left in here after I lock up."

"Be sure to keep it that way." Cameron flipped a few pages of the log, then closed it. Distracted as he'd been, he hadn't a clue what he'd just read. "And double the guards around wherever you intend to store the rum."

Michel leaned back in his chair and studied Cameron. "You seem distracted, cousin. Anything you care to discuss?"

Cameron folded his arms over his chest and moving to the bay window, stared out at the *Dianah*. "As a matter of fact, there is something I'd like to run past you. If you have no plans for this evening, would you care to meet up at Antoine's?"

"Eight o'clock good for you?" Michel asked.

"That'll do."

Michel tossed his pen from hand to hand. "Have you eaten yet? If it's a serious matter, we could discuss it over lunch."

Cameron strode to the door. "Oh, it could turn out to be a very serious matter indeed, but it'll have to wait until tonight.

I'm in need of a little conversation with Madam Olympée beforehand."

Michel grunted. "Ah, barely noon and off to Madame's already. You've been aboard ship too long."

Cameron's gaze fixed on the clipper's bow and Dianah's name. The idea of spending any time at all with one of Madame's trained ladies curdled his stomach. "It's not like that at all. I think she has a history lesson in store for me."

Chapter Four

Josette sat at one end of the flat-bottomed pirogue while Alexia stood at the other end, deftly managing the long pole that eased them through the slow-moving bayou waters, guiding them deeper into the swamplands. Alexia looked as if she'd been born to the task.

An alligator slid off the muddy cypress-lined bank and disappeared under water. Another rose up near the boat, only its green eyes and snout visible. The beast stared at them as though contemplating its next meal. Josette shuddered, but Alexia merely ignored it and, like the expert she was, guided the boat silently past. She took in a deep breath and sighed, her cheeks flushed with joyfulness.

Alexia's obvious good cheer at being back in the bayou tightened Josette's chest until she could barely breathe. Ever since she could remember, she and Solange had always wanted to escape life in these backwaters. But not Alexia. What would it take to change her mind? To make her want something more, something better, before Maman's ways settled too deep in her granddaughter's bones?

Cameron Andrews had to see the truth sooner or later. He had to take Alexia out of here before it was too late. At the thought of him, something low in Josette's belly heated.

Well, she'd have none of that. "You aren't to come here alone any longer, Alexia."

"You be meanin' at night, because it's broad daylight, and there ain't no one in dese parts can handle a pirogue better than me. Exceptin' maybe René and Bastièn since they's the ones taught me."

"Oh, for heaven's sake, Alexia, stop with your Cajun talk. You don't fool me. You've been speaking like that to get under your father's skin, haven't you? And you've likely managed to drive him nearly insane with your belligerent patois. Save it for Maman and your uncles. I'm thoroughly sick of it. I've worked far too hard and long with you to listen to your drivel."

Alexia's lips pursed as if fighting a smile. She said nothing, merely skimmed the surface of the brackish water with those shrewd amber eyes of hers while she guided the pirogue around a wide bend.

A weathered wood shanty, set back from the bank in a nest of pines, appeared, its tin roof overhanging a deep porch running the length of what most likely was a one-room house. A barefoot, shirtless man sitting in a rocker stood, a jar of what appeared to be moonshine in his hand—probably Lucien's brew if the man hadn't concocted it himself. He squinted first at Josette, then settled his gaze on the figure clad in boy's clothing with a long black braid hanging down her back. Something low and wicked sounding rolled off his tongue.

Josette waited until they were well past him. "Did you catch that, Alexia? He wanted you, not me."

"Seems like I might need to be carryin' a good knife, then. I lost mine at sea. Maman will have one. Or René."

"At any time, Alexia, day or night, you are not to travel alone. You've grown too big, and too many men are taking notice. You travel with me and no one else."

"Not even with René?" A pout formed on Alexia's lips,

yet her eyes still danced with humor. "*Merde, ma tante*. He's your own brother. He won't be botherin' me none. Not in the way you mean."

Josette would be damned if she'd let Alexia see her lose her temper at the girl's refusal to drop the Cajun patois. "Don't be silly. René loves you as if you were his own daughter, but he has no common sense with regard to your personal welfare."

"He is a smart man, *ma tante*. He takes fine care of me."

Josette adjusted her hat and narrowed her eyes at Alexia. "You'd find yourself smack in the middle of something before your uncle realized the predicament he'd landed you in. He knows you're growing into womanhood, and he thinks you can handle yourself, but you cannot. If you found yourself surrounded by ten drunken men determined to steal your virginity, Alexia, you'd have no chance to save yourself, and there would be little René could do to rescue you. Another one of his '*pardonne-moi*, I didn't see it coming,' excuses would do little good if you were dead or sold upriver."

Alexia pushed the pirogue toward Maman's shanty, her eyes scouring the landscape. "See them bubbles?"

"Where?"

Alexia laughed, light and airy. "Bubbles show me where crawfish hide in the mud."

"I know very well what they mean, Alexia. I was born and raised here, too."

"*Oui*, but you didn't see them and I did. That's my point. Soon's we get to Maman's, René will take me out to dig 'em up for tonight's étouffée, which Maman be fixin'."

"Who says she will?"

Alexia's jaw twitched. "She will."

"You are to remain with me or with your papa. But not here, Alexia. Never here, again."

This time, Alexia's pout was real. "What I'm supposed to be doin' at your house, huh? I may as well be stuck in the graveyard with Maman Solange for the nuthin' that goes on in your home. You tell me, what I'm to do? Get out of bed, eat breakfast, read a book, eat lunch, go down to your shop and smell the pretty smells, and then walk back home. Eat dinner, take a bath, and go to bed. That is some kind a day what whips me into a fair frenzy. So excitin' as to steal my breath."

"You left out the part about your education. You like learning new things."

Alexia leaned on the pole and halted the pirogue in the middle of the muddy water. "You don't think I gots me a good education out here? Look around. There's not a tree in sight I don't know about. Not a root in the whole of here I don't know how to pick and use to heal a body, just like Maman shows me. I can out-fish, out-hunt any Thibodeaux, and when Maman takes to the heavens, I'll become the healer." She pounded her thumb on her chest. "And Lucien taught me how to make moonshine. Now ain't that some-thin'?"

"Dear Lord." Josette closed her eyes and waited for the shock running through her to clear. "When did he start teaching you this?"

"Going on six months, thereabouts, before I went to San Francisco."

"Does René know of your little *education*?"

Alexia rolled her eyes, as if she was talking to an imbecile. "Never thought to ask."

Josette sprang to her feet. The boat swayed.

Alexia jammed her pole into the mud and steadied the pirogue. "Careful, or we'll both end up gator bait." She grew serious. "No need to go worryin' over me, *ma tante*. I know how to take care of myself."

"Then why not start speaking the way I've taught you?"

"Doan know what you mean."

"Damn it, Alexia!"

Silence fell upon the pirogue, until only the sounds of the bayou rustled through the air. Josette closed her eyes, muttered a short prayer, and let the rhythm of her heart return to normal.

She sat back down. "You don't have to be bored living with me. Why not take interest in my shop? All the mixing and inventing of new products should intrigue you. Look at the herbs we can gather together that will make a woman's complexion remain youthful until the day she's laid to rest. You could do well to begin using my products, anyway."

"Exceptin' for the roots I could collect, the rest of what you do is more boring than guttin' a squirrel."

"What of your father and his business?"

A hardness fell over Alexia's countenance. "What of him and his business? He don't want me none. Besides, he'll be sailin' off soon enough. That's all he ever said to me the whole trip from San Francisco to here." She scrunched up her face. "'Do this, Alexia, do that, Alexia, or I will sail off into the sunset and you will never see me again. And I won't even give you another thought.' That man has no more heart for me than this pole I hold. He's on his way to nowhere, so he says, an' I won't be going nowhere with him, don'cha know."

Josette's chest constricted again. So it mattered to Alexia what Cameron thought of her, after all. A little ray of hope filtered through the darkness in Josette's heart. If she could only find a way to connect father and daughter, make them inseparable. Alexia was loyal beyond words, but her loyalties were misplaced. Time. Josette needed more time, and that was something she didn't have if Cameron intended to leave soon. She had to think of something to hold him here until a couple of hearts connected.

"Here we be." Alexia angled the pirogue to the end of the dock and held it steady while Josette lifted her skirts and removed herself from the craft. Alexia tied a rope onto a wooden mooring and jumped out, agile as a deer. "You don't even look like you were raised in the bayou or that you ever stepped foot in this house before." Not waiting for a response, Alexia ran up the steps. "Maman, your Alexia, she be home!"

At the sight of her mother rushing through the door, arms stretched wide, and Alexia flying into them, Josette squared her shoulders. She didn't approve of Maman's questionable ways. But then, her mother didn't favor Josette's choices in life, either. She certainly hadn't taken to Josette marrying a man more than three times her age. That hadn't been all of it—there had always been one kind of hurt or another between them. Josette had felt it as far back as she could remember, even though she couldn't put a name to it. Now if she could only convince her mother to give up her hold on Alexia, along with her nefarious plans to turn her granddaughter into another voodoo witch.

A shirtless and barefoot René stepped onto the porch and shoved a hand through his wayward black curls, his grin as wide as Alexia's and just as fetching. No man had a right to be so handsome—and so equally worthless.

"*Pouchette*," he said, giving Alexia a quick hug. He tugged the cap off her head and rubbed his knuckles over her scalp.

"Will you take me crawfish huntin', Uncle? If we get a bucket full, we can have us some étoufée. Where's Bastièn?" Alexia scampered into the house, not waiting for an answer and leaving Maman and René staring at Josette.

Her mother's hands fisted on her hips. She settled an ominous gaze on Josette that raised the fine hairs along the back of her neck. "You done sent my Alexia off looking for her papa, didn't you? Now he's here, what you gonna do? Because I won't be giving her up to no man who murdered my Solange." Turning on her bare heel, she marched back into the house, not bothering to wait for a response.

René leaned a shoulder against the door frame, hung his thumbs in the top of his trousers, and watched Josette through lazy lids.

Josette heaved a sigh, lifted her skirts, and climbed the steps. "And hello to you, Maman." She turned to René. "And to you, as well, dear brother."

René gave a soft snort and a corner of his mouth turned up. "I love you, don'cha know."

She gave him a quick kiss on each cheek. "But why I love you, I haven't a clue. You are a sister's nightmare, and a town's worst disaster. What are you doing with yourself these days besides giving the ladies about town the vapors?"

He rolled his shoulder off the frame, sending him back into the house. "That attribute belongs to . However, I am about to become gainfully employed. Come inside, little sister."

Josette no sooner stepped through the door when Bastièn padded barefoot from the back of the house and into the one room that served as an open living and kitchen area. He, too, wore only trousers. "You talking love here? Must be my sister done arrived, 'cause everyone knows Alexia's here." He shoved a shock of black hair out of his eyes, then with a mischievous grin, bumped his shoulder against Alexia's.

She had her nose over a pot and was waving her fingers through the fragrant steam, breathing it in. "Look, *ma tante,* étoufée. Maman knew we was coming 'cause she got the second sight, and went to cookin' up my heart's desire." She rushed over to her grandmother and gave her a hug.

Maman pressed her cheek against Alexia's chest. "As if I don't know your favorite, *chère.* You cut your teeth on it."

Josette regarded her mother, who sat at the table in a brightly painted chair, a cup of ever-present coffee before her and dangling a rabbit's foot on a chain that first turned in slow circles, then paused and began moving sideways, like the pendulum of the hall clock in Josette's home.

Whatever message Maman intended about her unique ability to know what was going on at just about any time, or anywhere, Josette ignored, as she sat in a chair opposite her.

Perhaps it was because her mother didn't smile much, or perhaps it was the result of the creams she concocted, but nary a trace of crow's feet edged her eyes. Her hair fell in a loose French braid down her back, and light through the window danced off a crown of shiny, black hair. It struck Josette that she had no idea of her mother's age, but she must have been a stunning beauty in her youth. Whatever Maman's past, she kept it to herself. With René at age thirty-two, if Maman had given birth to him when she was fifteen, then perhaps she might be around forty-seven, but no matter her age, she could easily pass for Josette's sister.

Bastièn poured two cups of the strong café noir and, setting one in front of Josette, slid onto the chair next to her, his blue eyes—the only feature that set him apart from the others—still sleepy-looking. He grinned, a slow and easy smile that Josette imagined had stolen more than one female heart.

René poured a cup, as well, and sat at the head of the table. In the silence that followed, Josette took a sip of coffee and set the cup back down on the pristine woven mat that sat atop an equally pristine white tablecloth, its center embroidered in a bouquet of colorful flowers. Maman had likely spent hours bent over this cloth, working her needle in intricate floral patterns, much as she had so many times in the past. Josette glanced around the room. Not a thing out of place. But there never was.

Why had she never felt as though she belonged in this family? Why had she never taken to this kind of life? She took another swallow that went down hard, wishing the hour she'd planned on staying would fly by.

Poor as they were, Maman always kept a tidy home, even though Josette wasn't quite sure where pieces of furniture or knickknacks came from when they mysteriously appeared. While they had never gone without food, shoes were another matter. Maman didn't believe in wearing them, said feet belonged connected to the earth. She couldn't have had an easy life raising four children, along with Vivienne and Lucien after Maman's sister had passed away. But what made this shanty along the bayou feel like a real home was the tangible camaraderie that existed within this tight-knit family—herself excluded.

So in the long run, had Josette truly bettered herself by marrying Louis? Did she live a richer life alone and lonely in a mansion that saw only Vivienne and another cousin cross the threshold? She couldn't think such thoughts. Not now, not when Maman watched her with that penetrating, all-knowing gaze that had seen God-knew-what over the years.

Maman's eyes narrowed at Josette's study of her. "Alexia, bring me Benoit."

Damn it! Josette's skin crawled. She had to get out of there. Immediately. God, she hated that so-called pet Maman was known to use in her rituals. *Li Grand Zombi*—her reptilian deity. On any given day, Maman treated that disgusting creature better than she'd ever treated Josette.

Alexia scampered to the rear of the shanty and quickly returned with the albino snake coiled heavy in her hands. She set it on Maman's shoulder, where it slithered around her neck and trailed along one arm. A faint grin passed over Maman's lips.

Alexia headed for the front door, calling out as she disappeared. "Will you help me ride Satan standing up again, Bastièn?"

Josette gasped. "Again?"

With a roll of his eyes, René rose to his feet. "Not to worry, *chère*. Bastièn will be on one side of her and I'll be on the other."

Josette stood. "I'd better come along."

"Sit," Maman said, the single word filled with authority.

Josette fisted her hands in the folds of her skirt and did as she was told, watching René walk out the door. "You obviously have your reasons for asking me to remain behind, so you may as well have your say."

Maman balanced the fat snake's head in one hand, its beady red eyes staring at Josette, its equally red tongue flickering in and out. With the other hand, she held the rabbit's foot by its chain and watched it move slowly about in a clockwise manner. Then it stopped and began circling in the other direction. So she was using the blasted thing as a pendulum, no doubt asking it questions regarding Josette.

Just when she thought she could take no more, and made to stand, Maman looked up. "You intend to sleep with the man who killed your sister? Produce yet another one of his bastards?"

"Oh, for heaven's sake, Maman, don't be ridiculous. He had nothing to do with Solange's death, nor did giving birth to his child do her in. She stopped eating—that's what killed her."

"*Non*, that is not why she died." Maman lowered the snake to the table and let it slowly slither toward Josette. "I'm warning you. Leave Alexia to me or you will suffer the consequences."

Josette stood and backed away, relieved to hear the sound of multiple footsteps coming along the porch.

Alexia ran in ahead of her uncles. "Satan didn't want to do anything but stand there, Maman. You been bleedin' that good-for-nuthin' horse again?"

"*Oui*," Maman said, drawing the serpent onto her lap. "For my medicine."

Josette's insides shook so hard it was a wonder her bones didn't rattle. She turned to René. "Might I have a moment with you outside?"

He scraped her skin with those dark, penetrating eyes. "*Oui.*"

Once on the porch, she sat in one of the four rockers lining the deck. "I'm concerned about Alexia, René."

Her brother settled into the one next to her and gave a little grunt. "You got something new to tell me, because I do believe I've heard this from you before."

"I doubt it. Lucien has been teaching Alexia how to run a still."

She felt, rather than saw, René stiffen. "She told you this?"

"Not a half hour ago. She said she was at it for six months before she went to San Francisco."

"And you believe her?"

"Wouldn't you if she said something like that to you?"

René took in a long slow breath, and let it out with the same slow precision. "I'll be takin' care of this."

"I'm forbidding Alexia to come here any longer, René."

He lifted a brow. "You mean to keep her from her family? I do not think that a wise decision, sister."

The way he said it, his words low and dripping with veiled warning, made Josette fight to maintain control. "I mean what I say, René. I do not want her under Maman's influence any longer."

"She is under mine."

"You know full well that her father has arrived in New Orleans."

"*Oui*, but she is a Thibodeaux, and always will be. I'll be lookin' after her."

"René, please. She belongs with me until her father takes over. You are the very person who can convince her of her place in this world. At least give her the chance to achieve the dream our sister wanted but never got. Doesn't the fact that Alexia took the risk of stowing aboard a ship in order to find her father tell you something?"

He turned his head until he looked her squarely in the eyes, his gaze growing hard. "You wish her to live with you in a cold home that has no soul until her papa takes her under his wing? And what will you be up to, Josette? Will you be fallin' under his spell and openin' your arms wide to him? Like your sister did?"

Josette sprang to her feet, her composure disintegrating. "If you must know, there are rumors about that Maman is grooming Lucien to become her *Hougan*, and that he intends to initiate Alexia as his *Manbo*. René, we're talking about a virgin priestess he means to deflower during his initiation. You know Maman's intention is to have Alexia eventually take her place as the voodoo queen."

Something shifted in René's eyes before his cold gaze swept past Josette's shoulder and landed on the murky bayou waters. His jaw clenched, but he said nothing.

"I swear, René, if you cannot see that Maman has gone far afield from what Marie Leveau taught her, then you are blind as well as a fool. Maman's wickedness is worsening. I don't know how you and Bastièn can remain living here with her. Oh yes, I forgot. While she treats Alexia as her princess, you two are her knights in shining armor who can do no wrong."

Thoroughly disgusted, Josette rose from her chair and headed for the door. "We need to leave. Alexia will see us home."

He grabbed her wrist, preventing her from going inside. "Alexia remains here for the rest of the day. She be needin' family right now, somethin' you never did catch on to."

His lips moved a couple of times as if he intended to say one thing or another but changed his mind. After a long pause, he said, "I am no fool, little sister. Did it ever occur to you that Bastièn and I stay with Maman so we can watch over her? See to it she does no harm to anyone, especially Alexia?"

As she stared down at her brother, the backs of her eyes

pricked with tears. "I do not want her here overnight, René. On that I will fight you to my last breath. You think you watch after her? Then tell me how she's managed to slip over to Lucien's for months on end without anyone the wiser? Give me credit for knowing what is best for her."

René studied her for a long while. "I'll see her home by nightfall. Leave her here."

There was no mistaking the power emanating from her brother. She'd lost this round. "Then who is to see me home?"

"Bastièn will." A slow smile lifted a corner of René's mouth. "He has business to attend to in Nawlins."

Chapter Five

Beneath the soft glow of a gas wall sconce, Cameron seated himself on a red velvet chair opposite Madame Olympée. Crossing one foot over his knee, he discreetly swiped his thumb across a tiny smudge on his otherwise spotless shoe.

A smile worked one corner of Madame's mouth. "Ever the fastidious one, aren't you, Monsieur Andrews?"

Merde, but her accent was horrid. She was about as French as he was East Indian. "Since it's just the two of us, feel free to call me Mister Andrews. Trying to wrap your tongue around the word *monsieur,* or any other French word for that matter, must get tedious at times."

She tapped a slow rhythm on the ornate desk with her scarlet lacquered nails. "I know quite well what to do with my tongue, *Mister* Andrews. Don't tell me you intend to cause trouble again. Since Trevor is not with you, my security detail would find it rather boring having to grapple with only you. Still, I surprise myself allowing you in here."

He raised a hand. "You know full well the Thibodeaux brothers started that fracas back then. Might I add, you were more than handsomely compensated for damages. As for the mess four years ago, that was Trevor's doing. But we won't discuss the amount of absinthe you so generously supplied him that corrupted his brain, will we? I'm here for a reason other than availing myself of your gentlemen's club."

"Oh my, Mister Andrews. Whatever happened to that young man filled with joie de vivre?" She lifted her champagne flute to rouged lips. "Something sucked the life out of you."

Cameron took in a slow breath while he picked a speck of imaginary lint off his trouser leg. If he was going to get the information he needed, holding back was not the thing to do. "You knew Judge Morgan and his family moved to San Francisco and built a successful hotel business there?"

A faint expression Cameron couldn't identify passed over Madame's countenance. "I was sorry to see him leave Nawlins. He was a fair and decent man."

"I married his daughter, Dianah."

Madame arched a manicured brow. "That, I did not know."

"She passed away."

The liquid in Madame's glass quivered. "When?"

"Two years ago. She died in childbirth." His mouth went dry. Oh God, uttering the words still hurt. "I came this evening to speak to you of something else—something that occurred here nearly thirteen years ago."

He cleared his throat. "It seems the young woman I spent all my time with back then might have held a hidden agenda. Do you know of this?"

Madame studied him for a long moment, taking tiny sips of her bubbly. A clock ticked somewhere behind him, growing louder by the second. Damn her, she knew. Not much occurred in this town without her catching wind of it.

"Ah," she said at last. "It seems Solange Thibodeaux tricked the both of us."

"Then you know why I am here." Despite his parched throat, he didn't dare touch the drink sitting before him—if he did manage a swallow, his unsettled stomach would likely toss it back up.

"I assume you seek verification of what has recently been presented to you?"

His jaw clenched at her deliberate game of drawing out the inevitable. "You are obviously aware she gave birth to a child. I have come to ascertain if I might be the father."

Madame took her time setting her champagne glass down. She shuffled a few pieces of paper on her desk and then set them aside with a flick of her fingers. "Solange gave birth to a little girl about eight months after you were shipped off to England. Are you here to stay, this time?"

"No." The walls were closing in on him, and an ache crept along the back of his skull.

"A pity."

"Why is that, Madame?"

"Too bad for a certain young girl, I should think."

"Can you swear this child is mine?"

Madame slid her gaze to his grasp on the chair's arms. His knuckles had turned white. "You were Solange's first and only lover, Mister Andrews. I am certain as the rising sun the youngster in question is yours. But I suspect in your heart you already know that."

Cameron shifted in his seat and eased his tight grip, which only served to increase the tension pummeling his insides. "How can I be certain?"

"Solange came to me with a business proposition. If I would train her, she'd agree to become my prime courtesan, so long as she was able to have you as her only client until she got you out of her blood. Since that particular Thibodeaux family is possessed of extraordinary beauty, she would have been a great prize, to be sure. Unfortunately, she lied, which destroyed her."

"I need the truth, Madame. All of it. I take very seriously the notion that the child she left behind might be mine."

Madame leaned over her desk, and clasping her hands together, took aim with her searing gaze. "Solange came to me some time after you'd sailed away. We had many long talks, the two of us. She was intent on keeping the child, begged for my help. She was afraid to eat her mother's food, drink from her mother's cups for fear she'd lose the child, so I took her in until it was too late for Odalie to work her herbal magic."

Good God! "You know of Odalie and her way with herbs?"

"I do. Although I am particular in my business affairs, and a physician visits once a month, there are rare occasions when certain, shall we say, accidents occur. Odalie may be evil as the night is black, but she serves me well in that regard. So, yes, I know of her and some of what she is capable of doing."

Madame shifted some papers on her desk again, then eased her gaze somewhere over Cameron's shoulder. "I have my thoughts as to what actually happened to Solange."

The pain lingering at the back of his skull sliced through his brain like a hot knife. "What are you getting at?"

"I have no proof, so I would rather not say. However, what I do know is that Odalie did not take kindly to her daughter losing her innocence to you before she could make her a voodoo priestess. Since Solange's birth, her mother meant for the girl to follow in her footsteps. Giving birth to babies comes after the initiation, not before. You should watch your step around Odalie, by the way. She's not forgotten how you ruined her plans. The same goes for your daughter."

"My daughter? What the devil is that supposed to mean?"

"Odalie likely has her mind set on Solange's offspring taking her dead mother's place." Madame went back to sipping her champagne and rifling through papers.

Cameron's foul mood worsened. "But now, after all you endured with regard to Solange, you insist on employing her brother, who is about as honest as a riverboat gambler."

Madame laughed. "As a matter of fact, Bastièn was tossed off the *Marie-Thérèse* for that very thing. He was supposed to cheat for the house, not line his own pockets."

Cameron shook his head. "You've got your hands full, then. But you must figure he's worth the price, since you're as shrewd a businesswoman as I've ever come across. But why him, of all people?"

"Oh, you've not seen the man he's become—a veritable Adonis. When he took to privately servicing some of the young widows in the parish, trouble soon followed. Rumor has it there were a number of hasty exits made through windows rather than doors, and more than one gunshot fired. Since it became apparent he was not about to cease his latest business venture, I figured I could at least train him properly, perhaps keep him, and some of the higher-ranking members of this town, a bit safer. In many respects."

Cameron grunted. "And you collect what, half his pay, now?"

"Oh, he earns far more doing things my way than when he was on his own. He's also an excellent student. In fact, the entire family is quite intelligent. Wayward for the most part, but clever. Have you met your daughter's aunt, Mister Andrews?"

"I have."

"Madame LeBlanc is the youngest of the Thibodeaux clan—even lovelier than was Solange. But untouchable to men like you." She shrugged and sipped again. "Or any man for that matter. The two sisters looked nothing alike, by the way."

An odd sensation—something he didn't care to dwell on—wended through Cameron. He nearly squirmed when Josette's exquisite face swam before him. He needed to end this little meeting and get to his appointment with Michel. "I have no interest in this part of the conversation."

"A shame. She's beautiful, wealthy, and the only straight-

shooter of the lot. Runs a legitimate business next door to
the dressmaker, Madame Charmontés. Madame LeBlanc
creates all manner of skin preparations, and the ladies swarm
to her shop hoping to obtain her flawless complexion."

"She's Louis LeBlanc's widow, so of course she'd be
wealthy. But why run a small business when she doesn't
have to?"

Madame took up her champagne flute once again and
pressing it to her lips, gave a little shrug. "Boredom, I would
suspect. Oddly enough, she sold off all her husband's
holdings to that viper Émile Vennard. Very strange, that
transaction."

Cameron stood. "What LeBlanc's widow did with his
holdings is none of my concern. If you'll excuse me, I'm
past due in meeting someone."

Madame leaned back in her chair and looked up at him.
"Tell me something, Mister Andrews. Have you been with a
woman since your wife died?"

Good God, what a question. "If you are offering to
provide me with one of your ladies, I have never been less
inclined." He headed for the door.

"That's not what I asked, Mister Andrews. I now understand why you aren't the carefree spirit I've known you to
be. Your joy has been swallowed up by grief. There is a certain part of your misery that will remain with you until you
eradicate it. And the only way to do so is through intimacy
with another woman."

Too startled to move, he paused at the door, gripping the
handle. "I came here to discuss Solange's daughter, nothing
else."

"You mean *your* daughter, don't you? Solange is dead."
She tapped one sharp nail on her chair's armrest. "When you
married, did you take the vow of 'till death do us part'?"

His throat tightened and the air left his lungs. "We did."

"Those are merely empty words, sir. In truth, the sacred

ceremony of marriage itself is what binds a couple together. And that pledge goes beyond the grave, endures until the remaining spouse has sexual congress with another."

Chills raced up and down his spine. "That's nothing but drivel."

Madame shook her head. "I've studied the ancient mysteries, Mister Andrews. Until you break the tie between you and Dianah by making love to another woman, you are still bound to her, whether she is dead or alive. It will be bittersweet, this undoing, but it must occur or, inch by inch, you will wither away."

He was beginning to wonder if his legs would carry him out the door.

"You don't have to say anything. Just let the thought roll around in your head awhile."

He had to think of something to say while he collected himself. He sure as hell didn't want her knowing how badly she'd ruffled his feathers. "Tell me, Madame, why continue with your line of work? Surely it's not for the coin. You must be quite wealthy by now."

"If I don't keep this place running, someone else will, and I doubt they could manage as fine a job as I do."

She had a point. "I often wondered what got you into this sort of business in the first place. Even now, you're still an attractive woman."

"My mother died in Whitechapel, Mister Andrews."

"Whitechapel?" At her shocking words, his grip slipped off the handle. He planted his hand squarely against the door for support. "Bloody hell, I didn't know you were from England, let alone that squalid place."

"She died a horrid death, I might add." Madame folded her arms around her stomach and rubbed at them as if chilled. "Although I was able to distance myself from such a sordid environment, I came to realize that it doesn't matter where one lives, or how high the social ranking, there will always be men seeking women of the night. And a good many of them bringing home disease to an innocent wife. I thought I could at least do my share in preventing some of those occurrences."

"But how did you end up in New Orleans?"

She laughed, deep and throaty. "Your father-in-law rescued me."

"My what?"

"Judge Morgan. He was a magistrate in London's East End back then. When I was dragged before him for stealing food, he and his young bride took me in, gave me a decent education. When they emigrated to America, they brought me along. I opened this gentlemen's club when Dianah was only a few months old, so she knew nothing of my connection to her parents."

There went that eyebrow of hers, arching upward. "Allow me to shock you even further—Judge Morgan funded me. He, too, wanted a certain kind of traffic off these fine streets."

"*Merde.*" He shifted about in his chair. "I had no idea."

"I doubt anyone does. Now then, Mister Andrews, if you should change your mind and wish to break the invisible bond tying you to my dear friend's daughter, come see me. I can promise you a woman who won't bamboozle either one of us."

Cameron managed to yank the door open. "Thank you, no. I'll be on my way."

He stepped outside and into the night, only to have a lit cigarillo fly past his nose and hit the ground in a shower of sparks. He jumped back. "What the devil?"

From out of the dim-lit shadows, a well-dressed man lifted a shoulder off the wall he'd been leaning against. "Good evening, Monsieur Andrews."

"What the bloody hell was that about?"

The dark-haired stranger separated the panels of his finely tailored jacket and rested his hands on lean hips.

"There may be little I can do about you being Alexia's father, but there is something I can do should you ever think to engage yourself with my only surviving sister."

So this was Bastièn all grown up. Madame was right about the Adonis part. He also cut as fine a figure as any London dandy. "What the deuce makes you think I'd have any interest in your sister?"

Bastièn slid his hands into his trouser pockets and took a casual stance. Apparently there'd be no attempt at physical altercation—at least not tonight. "Just thought I'd let you know we Thibodeaux watch out for our own." He lifted a brow. "You understand, *oui*?"

Cameron stepped forward, the frustration boiling in him all evening threatening to blow into white-hot fury. "Beware, Bastièn. I'm not the skinny seventeen-year-old you and your brother once pounded into the ground. You wouldn't want to risk having that pretty face of yours spoiled, would you? I don't think the wealthy ladies you service would appreciate it if I battered it into the shape of a pie tin."

Bastièn grinned, slow and easy, then turned on his heel and disappeared into the night. Cameron headed in the opposite direction, to Antoine's, where he was about to give Michel the shocking news that Cameron had sired a daughter—a Cajun bastard from Bayou St. Laurent.

It was late when Cameron exited Antoine's and turned onto Royal Street. Midway down the block, he reached the family town house where he'd been born and grown up. He slid the key into the lock of the wrought-iron gate leading through the porte cochère and into the darkened courtyard. The scent of roses filled his nostrils.

The grating turn of the lock, the chink of the gate closing, the lock turning again echoed in the silent enclosure. Such a hollow sound. It left an equally hollow feeling inside him.

How his life had changed. With only Michel around and his uncle Justin squirreled away on his plantation upriver, Cameron's solitude burned like acid in his stomach. That two women had died because of him caused the burn to chew its way up his throat.

Once inside, he made his way through the darkness and into the parlor. Removing his jacket, vest, and cravat, he plopped onto the divan, and with a heavy sigh, leaned his head against the sofa's back. He shoved his legs out in front of him and rubbed at his shoulder where Trevor had put a bullet through him when last they were in town. It still ached whenever the weather took a turn, or if he was bone weary, like tonight.

Merde, Cameron had asked for what he got, but thankfully, not even the duel had broken the bond the cousins forged as youngsters. What foolishness, instigating a battle over the woman who was now Trevor's wife. Damn. It took getting shot to realize that as an only child, Cameron hadn't known the difference between a form of sibling love and the love for a woman he wished to be bound to. It wasn't until Dianah came along that he'd finally understood.

He groaned, and the sound echoed back to him in the utter silence. God, he missed her. Theirs had been a robust blending of two strong-willed people who thought nothing of disagreeing one minute and settling their differences in bed the next. Or on the floor. Or at the seashore. It made no difference where they landed if the moment was right. Life had been good back then. Better than good.

With another heavy sigh, Cameron rose from the divan and mounted the stairs to his chambers. He was growing damn tired of climbing into bed alone every night. And what did he have to look forward to when he got there? More tossing and turning? Only now he'd be burdened with a new problem to mull over—a daughter he didn't know what the hell to do with.

Odd, but the door to the master suite stood partially open. He distinctly remembered hearing the soft click when he'd closed it earlier. He mentally shrugged. The housemaid had probably turned down his bed. He made his way into the room and to the fireplace, where a spill and candle always stood on the mantel. Setting the candle aflame, he took it in hand, turned, and nearly stumbled. There on his pillow, candlelight glinting off its golden chain, lay his pocket watch.

"Damn you, Alexia!" He crossed the room and swept it up. Still ticking.

How the hell did she know he'd moved from the hotel? She had to have broken in sometime after dark, when he'd left for Madame Olympée's. It was one thing to have her steal the blasted thing, but now that he'd acknowledged her, the idea of her being out so late at night did more than rankle him. He burst into a litany of curses. Candle and watch in hand, he dashed down the stairs and back to the parlor. Moving the table in front of the sofa aside, he rolled back the rug, lifted a loose board, and opened the hidden safe, where he deposited the timepiece.

"She'd only steal the blasted thing again," he muttered. He'd keep it there until he left New Orleans for good. He replaced the board, the rug, and the table, then grabbed his jacket, cravat, and vest. On second thought, he tossed them back down. The hell with it. He didn't need them where he was headed.

Chapter Six

Josette sat in a parlor chair opposite her brother, wishing he would call it a night. Using a long-handled spoon, she went about the mindless task of crushing mint leaves and slices of lime in the bottom of her glass, muddling the juices with the iced, dark liquid. She breathed in the heady scent, then took a sip. "This had better be my last one or I'll never make it up the stairs. I'm already a bit light-headed."

A slow smile curled a corner of René's mouth. "I should like to witness you having to crawl up the steps as a result of enjoying yourself. You lead far too dull a life."

She ignored his comment and took another sip. "There's something different about the taste from what you've made in the past."

"Such as?"

"This has—oh, I don't know—there's a subtle elegance to it, if one can describe liquor in such a manner. In any case, it goes down far too easily."

"It's Gosling Brothers rum making all the difference." A cut-glass decanter sat nearly empty on a low table between them, along with a carafe of the iced concoction. Rivulets sweated down the outside of the latter, disappearing into a folded cloth beneath it. "A supply arrived from Bermuda just yesterday."

"Bermuda? Why all that way when plenty of rum is brewed right here in America?"

He took a long swallow. "Ah, but this happens to be the finest in the world. Even you notice its superior quality. We couldn't get any here until now."

Lifting his glass to the lit chandelier, he studied the rich, dark liquid. "And since you keep a nice supply of ice buried under a pile of straw in that hutch out back, I thought you might appreciate a sampling of the very best, *oui*?"

She barely managed a half-smile. "So you gifted me with this fine brew for your benefit as well as mine?"

René chuckled, but then he tilted his head and grew serious. "What be the matter, *chére*? You're off somewhere in your own world tonight."

She fought a heavy sigh. "Nothing's wrong. I'm merely fatigued. I had a rather taxing day after I left Maman's. I was also concerned you wouldn't keep your word. Thank you for returning Alexia to me."

"Have I ever not kept my word?" He made a clicking sound with his tongue. "You should know better."

"Your pardon." She didn't dare let on that Émile Vennard had paid her a visit. Why in the world would that louse want to purchase her shop and run her out of business? What would he want of her after that—her home? Ask her to leave town? She'd been through this before with him, knew what was coming next if she refused his offer. At first, there would be veiled threats indicating Bastièn and René might meet with a series of unfortunate accidents. If she still said no, then her brothers would eventually lose their lives altogether.

The man was a formidable presence in New Orleans, with more clout than any ten men. She'd sold her husband's holdings to him after Bastièn took a mysterious beating in an alley, and a runaway horse nearly trampled René to death. Both had taken weeks to heal. But what would she do without her business? It was the only thing she cared about in her sorry life besides Alexia—and one way or another, her niece would soon be gone—to Maman or with her father. Much as Josette would like to, there was no holding on to Alexia forever.

"You're biting your lip, Josette. What's the matter?" René's voice had grown cold and his words fell hard on her ears. "Are you concerned now that Alexia's father has returned to Nawlins?"

"Don't be silly."

"Perhaps you're sorry you sent Alexia after him, *oui*?"

Shock waves ran through Josette. "What makes you think I had anything to do with her running off?"

A low grunt left René's throat. "Alexia takes to chattering when we float along the bayou. Have you forgotten I am closer to her than her flesh-and-blood papa?"

Josette pressed two fingers against her temple and rubbed in circles. "Please. I'm in no mood for a debate. Besides, I really do need to retire."

René sat back and studied her beneath heavy lids. "Do not forget that it was I who practically raised you, not Maman. I changed your drawers and combed the knots from your hair. I know you better than anyone, *oui*? Enough to know you are not being honest with me."

He was right. He knew her better than anyone, and that idea tugged at her heartstrings. Only four years her senior, and a child himself, he'd acted the part of the father she'd never had. He'd seen to dressing her until she was old enough to do so herself. He'd made certain she got enough to eat before he took a bite off his own plate. It was he, barely ten years old, who'd pushed a pirogue through thunderstorms to see she went to school.

"In due time, René. In due time."

Bang. Bang. Bang.

Josette jumped at the loud pounding on the front door.

René stood. "Who be that at such a late hour?"

Oh God, she prayed it wasn't Vennard. How could she explain?

The pounding increased.

"I'll see to it." René made to step past her.

She sprang to her feet and grabbed his arm, her heart in her throat. "This is my home, and since Vivienne is not present, I will see to answering my own door."

René scowled. "*Non*. You are dressed in a flimsy robe and your hair is down."

"Do you think I give a damn about propriety when society shuns me for being bayou trash trying to better myself? Did you know they still whisper ugly rumors that Louis died either by my hand or Maman's?" She released his wrist and walked away.

"Then I will wait right here, you stubborn woman. But at the first sign—"

"Oh, hush with your nonsense." She reached the foyer and paused when she saw movement through the door's beveled glass side panels. Vennard was not as tall as that. She squinted. My God! Instinctively, she tugged at the panels of her red silk robe, as if they'd somehow separated.

He pounded again.

She turned on her slippered heel and fairly sailed back to the parlor. "It's Cameron Andrews. You need to leave."

"*Merde*, what is that cur doing here at such an hour? Even more reason to stay."

"Probably wanting to check on Alexia—how should I know? In any case, he's about to break down the door, so go."

"*Non*. I will remain for your safekeeping."

"Oh, for God's sake." She planted her hands on his chest and pushed. "Do you think he is here to do me harm? He might be finally acknowledging his daughter and I will not have you mucking things up by making a scene. Leave."

René stepped back and, amid the pounding, studied her for what seemed an eternity. "*Oui,* I shall leave then." He headed down the corridor toward the rear of the house as the pounding increased. "The door, she is about to be split in two."

"And don't merely pretend to leave. I'll not have you slinking about."

He spun around, hand on heart. "You do not trust me?" He advanced toward her, mischief outlining his features. "Then I shall see myself out another way."

Oh Lord, no! "Not the front door, you mindless fool. You'll only take a punch at him, if he doesn't manage to lambaste you first."

René strode into the parlor, guzzled the remainder of his drink, set the empty glass on the table, then hiked open the window and slid through it as effortlessly as though he'd done it a thousand times. "*Au revoir, ma petite soeur.*"

Josette swept a mass of curls off her cheek and grabbed René's glass still full of ice, limes, and mint leaves. It wouldn't do if Cameron happened in and saw another person had been here this late. Especially his alleged enemy. After the way he'd reacted to the news that Alexia had been raised around René and Bastièn, let him think her brothers didn't visit much. The last thing Josette needed was to have Cameron decide his daughter wasn't worth the trouble and sail off again. By all the saints, if this wasn't bad timing!

She turned in a circle. Where to hide the blasted thing?

Bang. Bang. Bang.

"I'm coming." She shoved the glass behind a pillow propped in one corner of the sofa, made her way through the corridor and opened the door.

One look at Cameron Andrews standing there in shirt-sleeves, leaning one hand against the door's frame, his hair mussed as though he'd run his fingers through it a thousand times, and everything around her melted into the night. It was only him floating before her, his angry amber eyes burning into hers.

He took in a deep breath and exhaled.

Was it her imagination or did something just shift in him? His gaze slowly traveled down the length of her, then up again, pausing briefly at the pulse pounding wildly at her throat. Then his scrutiny took in her face, her hair, before settling once again on her eyes. Was it surprise or puzzlement washing through him that caused his cheeks to color, the anger in his gaze to dissipate?

Those eyes.

At once, she was back in the Vieux Carré, a young, besotted girl following him around, stealthy in her escapades so he wouldn't take notice of her. But then there was the one time when they'd encountered each other. She'd knocked over a merchant's barrel she'd hidden behind, and there they were, face-to-face, this close. Instead of running her out of the French Quarter as others had done, he'd bought her a *cala*, that sugary sweet cake only the rich enjoyed—unless one managed to steal one, that is. He'd handed her the *cala*, tilted his head for a moment while he studied her with those incredible whiskey-colored eyes, then sauntered off alongside his cousin.

Oh, how she had loved that sweet cake—and him more than ever. But that was back then, she reminded herself. She'd learned to despise him soon after.

Josette's head cleared until she had sense enough to collect herself. Did he intend to stand there all night? Say nothing? Bitterness crept in once more. "Oh no, you're not bothering me at all, Monsieur Andrews. I am always prepared for company in the middle of the night. Do come in."

"Where's Alexia?" he growled.

His voice rumbled through her, making her feel tipsier

than the rum she'd imbibed. Lord, she wanted to fold her arms around herself and disappear into the woodwork. But no, he'd only see the unsettling effect he had on her. Instead, she flipped her head and swept her hair off one shoulder. "In bed. Where she belongs."

The fire was back in his eyes as his gaze swept the length of her and back up again. "Show me."

She stepped aside and bid him enter. A bit of wickedness bubbled into her strange mix of emotions. Boldly, she returned his overt perusal of her. "Far be it from me to deny her papa *any* privileges."

Cameron let loose a soft snort, then strode through the door, a good head and shoulders above Josette. She caught his scent, and something else coalesced with the amalgam of emotions stampeding through her like a herd of wild horses.

Heaven help her.

He stood in the corridor, hands on hips and looking up the staircase. But oh, she'd caught him taking another glance at her as he passed by.

"If you'll follow me, I'll take you to your daughter. But please, don't wake her. I took her to her grandmother's today and she is worn out."

He turned, a look of disgust setting his mouth into a thin line. "You took her to Odalie? To your brothers?"

She sighed. "Monsieur Andrews, Alexia would have run off on her own had I not taken her there. Your daughter was far safer with me." Josette wasn't about to tell him she'd left Alexia at Maman's and René had brought her home barely three hours ago, dirty and exhausted.

She indicated the stairs. "It's late, and if I know Alexia, she'll be up before the rooster crows, while I will not have had a bit of rest. See her, then leave, *s'il vous plaît*."

Lifting the skirts of her dressing gown, Josette climbed the stairs ahead of him. His eyes were on her; she could feel the heat as surely as if a fire had been lit. Despite the static in the air between them, sinful amusement settled in. She nearly laughed. Let him ogle, for all she cared. Hadn't she done enough staring at him in her youth to make things even?

She turned right at the top of the landing and led Cameron to Alexia's room. Opening the double doors, she stepped aside and bid him enter first. Despite his size, he moved silently across the Aubusson carpet and halted at Alexia's bedside. The light from the gas lamps in the corridor sent a pale stream of light in his wake.

He folded his arms over his chest and stood beside his daughter's bed for a long while.

Once Josette's eyes adjusted to the dim light, she took her time studying Cameron from behind. He wore no jacket or vest, and when he stood with his arms crossed in front of him, the fine fabric of his shirt stretched tight across broad shoulders and a well-muscled back. His trousers fit snug around his hips and for a moment, she had the terrible urge to step forward and touch his bottom. Only to see if it was as taut as it appeared. Curiosity. That's what had caused the whim. But of course, mere curiosity.

She stepped into the room and moved to stand beside him. How odd it felt being this close, yet at the same time, a kind of comfort settled in. It had to be because Alexia's father had come at last. For Alexia. What else? A slight breeze found its way through the open window, lifted the curtains, and filled the room with a floral scent, not unlike the handmade soap she'd used to scrub Alexia clean.

Alexia lay sprawled on her back, covers in a tangle, one foot hanging over the edge of the bed, her pillow on the floor. She breathed in a steady rhythm through parted lips, her pristine white night rail a beacon in the dim light.

"She seems so innocent," he whispered. "Looking at her now, one could hardly guess she could send a person to Bedlam with her chatter alone."

"If she babbles, it means she likes you, Monsieur Andrews. And in her own way, she is quite innocent. I hope to keep her that way."

He turned his head toward Josette, so close she could feel the heat emanating from his body in waves—hot waves that washed right through her. "You may as well call me Cameron."

Even in the near dark, his mesmerizing gaze raised the hairs on the back of her neck and left her feeling as though she'd fallen under some dizzying spell. Control. She needed to take command of unruly emotions that seemed to be flying around in every direction. "Then you may call me Josette since we're going to have to spend a bit of time figuring things out."

He shoved a hand through his hair. "She's thirteen, nearly grown. I don't know what the devil I can work out. And according to you, she has a fondness for your mother's ways. In all likelihood, it's too late."

"On the contrary. You may be just in time to save her from the kind of life I so despise."

His gaze swept the room. He regarded the crystal chandelier hanging overhead, the soft blues and creams covering the windows and walls, the pastel-colored Aubusson on the wooden floor. "I wouldn't have guessed she'd have a room like this. Why in the world would she prefer a shanty in the swamp?"

He shifted his weight, shoved his hands in his pockets, and took in a deep breath. "Look . . . I need to tell you right out that I'm sorry for what happened to your sister. I had no idea—"

Alexia flopped over and gave out with a little moan.

"Shush." Josette hadn't intended to touch him; she'd only meant to raise her hand to stop him from speaking. But in the dim light, she hadn't realized how close they were standing and her hand landed on his chest—his hard, muscled chest, hot beneath the thin layer of his shirt. She dropped her hand as if burned. "We need to leave or we'll wake her," she whispered.

He nodded and stepped aside for her to exit before him. Side by side, they descended the staircase. "What brought you here so late?" Josette asked, though she knew darn well what had brought him. "Would you like something to drink? My bro . . . I have a cool drink in the parlor if you'd care for anything before leaving."

"Thank you, I will." He followed her into the parlor. "I moved into my town house in the Vieux Carré today. When I returned from dinner at Antoine's about an hour ago, I found my fob watch on my pillow. How the devil did the little thief know I'd moved from the hotel to there?" He shoved his hand through his hair again. "But that's not the point. What set me off was that she'd been out after dark, wandering the streets."

Josette bit her bottom lip to keep from grinning and indicated a chair as she moved toward the armoire opposite him. "Please, sit."

Instead, Cameron seated himself on the sofa, too near the pillow where she'd hidden René's empty glass. Her heart skipped a beat. Now why had she gone and done that in the first place?

Cameron leaned forward, his hands draped over his knees. "Is that ice I see in that decanter?"

"I have it shipped down from up north. There's a shed out back covered in hay that holds it for the better part of the summer. There's not much left by now, but it gets me through the worst of the heat."

"Interesting. My uncle Justin keeps it on his plantation upriver, but since we only have courtyards in the Vieux Carré, there's no place to hold ice."

His voice, smooth and deep, ran along her spine like warm honey. But when she closed the armoire doors and turned to face him, she was startled to see he had in hand the cut-crystal decanter holding what was left of the rum, an odd look on his face.

"You drank this all yourself?"

Her heart would give out before the night was over. She just knew it. "There's not much left, but you're welcome to it."

He gave a nod and reached for the glass she held. He poured what remained, and took a sip. "This is Gosling Brothers rum, isn't it? A shipment just came in on one of our clippers, and either the count is off or some has gone missing. How did you come by it?"

Oh, dear God. She was going to shoot René. "It was a gift delivered to my door."

If a look could lay one bare to the bone, his did. "And you drank this all alone, or do you entertain men with my daughter in the house?"

"It's not like that."

"One of your brothers then?"

She didn't know what else to say. "I think it's time for you to leave. You've seen your daughter is soundly asleep in her bed, and I need my rest. Now please don't give me cause to be rude."

He stood to pass her, but then paused and turned. With one slow step and another, he backed her up against the wall, caging her with an arm on either side of her head. "Don't toy with me, Josette."

His breath fell on her mouth and she swallowed it. Her knees went weak.

He leaned closer and the look in his eyes shifted.

"What do you want?" she whispered. "You've seen your daughter."

"Where's your cousin Vivienne?"

Josette turned her head aside, giving him her cheek. "She

is seeing her brother for the night, just as she does once a week. Now let me go."

"You are trying to tell me you drank that entire bottle alone?"

"So what if I did?"

"Then you should not be taking care of my daughter in your condition."

Not only did he surround her, he had her backed into a mental corner. "Fine, I'll send her to you tomorrow, since that's where she belongs anyway."

He leaned closer and his mouth brushed across her cheek until he reached her ear. She sucked in a hard breath that caught in her throat while a knot of confusion twisted her insides.

"I warned you not to toy with me, Josette, but since you insist on doing so, I intend to return tomorrow evening with another bottle of rum. Can you prove to me you can drink that much on your own?"

His words, husky and raw, touched the side of her neck and sent a quivering through her. She swallowed a moan. "I could and then some."

What was wrong with her? Instead of gaining control, she was losing herself in him, and she'd just accepted a challenge she had no way of fulfilling.

He drew back in one fluid movement, and in doing so, his mouth seared her flesh, sending a hot pulse pounding low in her belly. She glanced down. Just long enough to catch sight of proof that he was as aroused as she was. He didn't miss her glance. "You feel it too, don't you?"

"Feel what?"

He leaned closer. "That kind of undeniable tingling running through you. Clear to your toes. Do you know what it is?"

She could feel his heat, smell the scent of soap, skin, and a hint of rum. "What?"

"That's common sense draining from our bodies. I need to leave." He pushed away from the wall and walked off. "I'll see myself out. But I'll be back with another bottle of rum tomorrow night, Josette. I want to see what you can do with it."

Cameron's feet pounded a steady rhythm on the wooden banquette, loud in the dead of night. What in blazes had he gone and done? This was insanity. One look at Josette when she'd opened the door and something stirred deep inside him that he'd thought long dead.

This couldn't be happening.

He couldn't want her.

Not Josette Thibodeaux LeBlanc.

But he did, and his groin still ached.

There was no denying how the sight of her hit him like a fever dream, all wrapped up in red silk, hair flowing in wild disarray, and smelling sweet and feminine. That mouth. He wanted a taste of it, but he'd dared not, and so he'd brushed his cheek across hers, alongside her neck. She was like an opiate—one slight taste, and he was addicted.

He had enough problems without getting involved with Alexia's aunt. And those goddamn brothers of hers. The rum-stealing bastards. The last thing he needed was to get near Josette Thibodeaux LeBlanc again.

Chapter Seven

Cameron stood before the table in the center of the shipping offices, scanning architectural renderings of the warehouse where the rum was stored. Michel sat in front of a desk piled high with papers, while Midnight, the cat, sat hunched in a corner cleaning body parts Cameron didn't care to dwell on.

"Why only another two barrels missing and not more?" he asked. "It's the thieves sending a message that they can come and go at will."

Michel swung around in his chair and leaned back, clasping his hands behind his head. "You're certain it's the Thibodeaux brothers?"

Cameron grunted. "René, at least. But with those heavy barrels, he can't be acting alone. Something tells me if we simply wait, we'll soon be privy to whatever cat-and-mouse game he's decided to play."

"Is he that clever? Or just taking whatever he can handle at the moment?"

"He's cunning. We'd be fools to underestimate him."

Cameron swiped at the back of his neck. Barely ten o'clock and already the heat and humidity chipped away at his mood and drained his energy. Removing his jacket, he draped it over the back of a chair and set his fingers to the buttons on his gold embroidered vest. Changing his mind, he left it and his cravat in place. At least he could show some measure of decency. He rolled his white shirtsleeves to his elbows to prevent ink from rubbing onto the fabric, and went back to perusing the drawings.

A breeze blew in through the open windows and door just then, offering a modicum of relief. He rubbed at his nape again, thankful he'd managed to get his hair trimmed so it didn't cling in wet clumps to his skin and collar.

"Feeling the heat?" Michel asked.

"I hope that blasted tailor manages to deliver the lighter-weight clothing today as promised. Between this wool, and the heat and humidity, I'm about done in. Why I didn't think of the difference in weather before I left San Fran . . . well, I had enough on my mind at the time, what with that little . . . with my daughter." He shot a glance at his cousin.

Michel's mouth took on a comical twist. "You were saying?"

Cameron gave a shake of his head. "Can you believe this bloody turn of events? How the hell am I going to manage all this? I ought to board the next ship out of here and pretend I bypassed New Orleans completely."

He returned to scanning the drawings. "Thibodeaux must have a key. There's no other way he could've entered without some kind of damage to windows or locks. And where were the guards that they heard nothing? Sleeping? Damn it to hell!"

Abbott winced and his pen skittered sideways across the ledger. He muttered something unintelligible.

A shaft of humor sliced through Cameron. He couldn't hold his tongue. "Aren't you happy as a duck in water to have me back in your life, Abbott?"

"Is it time for our noon meal?" Abbott responded in

a monotone. "I prefer taking mine outdoors today. In the hot sun."

Michel chuckled. "Admit it, Abbott, life was rather boring until a couple of days ago. Everything around here runs as efficiently as a greased wheel—your entire day is timed to the minute. How long could you expect that to go on without falling asleep on the job?"

With the teasing, some of the pressure in Cameron's chest eased. The droll accountant was a master of his profession, but his sheer blandness and severe work ethic screamed for disruption every now and then. How anyone could work day in and day out with nary a change in routine or a word uttered was beyond Cameron. The man had operated no differently in San Francisco. Somebody had to do him a favor and shake things up a bit now and then. "Come, Abbott, you've been here barely six months and already you're in the same rut as in San Francisco. And you know what they say about ruts."

Abbott set down his pen and slowly stroked his graying mutton chops with stubby, ink-stained fingers, his eyes devoid of emotion. "I had no idea I was in a rut, sir, much less knowing what *they* have to say about them."

Ha! Cameron finally had the round little man's attention. "A rut eventually turns into a shallow grave, Abbott. Then all you end up doing is waiting around to be buried. So there you have it, my man. Live a little. Spice things up. Try showing up for work once in a while at nine minutes to the hour instead of ten. But God forbid you should arrive a minute late."

The little man scratched his jowls again. "The way you two carry on, perhaps living in a rut is more comfortable and far safer."

"Touché." Cameron hiked a brow. "So how does Michel carry on? I thought he was a paragon of virtue."

Michel laughed. "I might not set the town on fire like my brother and you once did, but I do manage to get around."

A carriage rattled up to the office. Michel craned his neck. "What's this? Or rather *who* is this? Uh-oh, I'm afraid I already have the answer."

A high-pitched chattering caught Cameron's attention. "Good God, tell me it isn't so."

Michel grinned. "I'm afraid Miss Alexia Thibodeaux Andrews has arrived. Or am I premature in calling her such?"

Cameron raked his fingers through his hair. "Her aunt threatened to send her over. As if—"

"*Bonjour*, Papa!" Alexia eased through the entry, gingerly balancing a large oval tray filled with what looked like . . . could it be?

"Beignets?" The sweet, warm scent of the powdered-sugar-coated confection wafted through the room, filling Cameron's mind with a jumble of childhood memories. His empty stomach growled.

"*Oui*, Papa. And café au lait. *Ma tante* Josette, she be bringing along the coffee."

Michel, closest to the door, lifted the tray from her small hands, a quirky smile working his mouth. "You must be Miss Alexia."

She beamed and bounced inside. "*Oui*, dat be me."

Abbott, who usually remained in the background, wasted no time coming forth and setting his sights on the heaping platter. "Beignets, you say?"

Michel set the tray on a corner of the table next to where Cameron stood. "Did you make these yourself?"

Alexia giggled. "Cousin Régine cooked up the batch just for y'all. *Ma tante* calls her our chef, but she's really just a cook in sheep's clothing."

Michel shot a glance at Cameron and spoke through his

teeth. "Didn't your day just take on a new glow? No rut for you."

"Clever." Cameron automatically patted his vest pocket to check the time, then remembered his fob watch was hidden away in the town house floor safe. Damn. Collecting his lighter-weight clothing from the tailor wasn't an option now that Miss Sticky Fingers had descended upon them. He'd send word to have the order delivered to his residence.

Except for a blotch of the powdery sugar smudging one corner of Alexia's mouth—the scamp must have sampled from the tray—she could easily have passed for an angel. Her dark hair hung thick and shiny to her waist, swept back from her face by a ribbon that matched the pale blue frock she wore. Hard to believe this was the same ragamuffin who could out-curse a sailor.

She slipped her slender hand into Cameron's and offered up a dazzling smile that outshone the sun. "You like, Papa?"

For some odd reason, Cameron's heart gave a little lurch. "Indeed."

Without thinking, he reached out with his other hand and wiped off the dusting of sugar at the corner of her mouth. When it didn't come entirely clean, he licked his thumb and swiped again.

Alexia's eyes widened. She rubbed her fingers where he'd touched her. "You put your spit on me, Papa."

Christ, that's what his mother used to do when he was a lad—the very thing he'd detested with a passion. "Your pardon. I wasn't thinking."

She grinned and rubbed again. "It be good, though. I never had me a papa around to wipe spit on me before, don'cha know." With that, she spied the cat in the corner and rushed over.

Michel, arms crossed over his chest, chuckled. "Doesn't life have a way of offering up the most interesting of surprises?"

"Go to the devil," Cameron grunted.

Abbott licked clean the two fingers he'd used to shove a beignet into his mouth. "Where might I find the café au lait, Miss Alexia?"

"Right here," came a throaty, feminine voice.

Josette. Cameron's stomach did a flip. He turned. She stood in the doorway holding another tray, filled with two silver carafes, a small bowl, spoons, and several china cups. Dressed in the same soft blue as Alexia, her dark hair tucked beneath a matching bonnet bearing a wide rim, she looked a vision.

For several stunned seconds, Cameron let the sight of her pour through him. Then he moved forward in a rush and took the tray from her. "Please, come in."

His cousin and Abbott openly stared, and then Michel introduced himself and the accountant. Frustration welled in Cameron. How had he so crudely missed being the one to make introductions when he'd been raised with impeccable manners? He set the tray beside the other, holding the beignets.

"May I pour?" she asked, as if entering a business and doing so were an everyday occurrence. "Mr. Abbott, you look in need. One lump or two?"

"Two," he said, his cheeks taking on a slight blush.

So she gave little heed to hierarchy, did she? Cameron was beginning to see that it wasn't only Alexia with a bit of rebellion in her. Josette poured from both carafes at the same time, one filled with the rich black coffee blended with chicory, the second with milk. Her smooth-as-silk motions, her clean, fresh-as-a-breeze scent, her small waist . . . he stopped his thoughts before his body reacted in a way that could prove embarrassing. He focused on the tray in front of her, but his peripheral vision insisted on fixating on her . . . especially her lips, petal pink and dewy. Wouldn't he like a taste of such a kissable-looking mouth?

"Mr. Andrews?"

He glanced up, but she'd addressed Michel, who looked

as smitten as a schoolboy. *The fool.* But why should Cameron care?

She turned to him. "And for you?"

"One lump," he said and took a bite out of a beignet. And nearly moaned with pleasure. "Delicious. These are impossible to come by in San Francisco."

A small smile played about her lips. "It was your daughter's idea. She begged Régine to fry up her famous beignets for you."

Abbott emptied his cup, swiped another sweet confection off the tray, and scurried back to his work area while Michel took his coffee and fritter and moved to his desk, that smirk still plastered on his face.

Josette finished her task and backed away. "I'll leave you now, since I have a shop to run. Alexia, be a good girl and mind your papa. And please, be home by seven."

"*Oui, ma tante,*" Alexia said without looking up from the cat.

Cameron nearly choked on his coffee. "You intend to leave her here?"

Josette gave him a knowing look and smiled as sweetly as Alexia had when filled with the devil. "Didn't I say as much last night? I always keep my word."

She started to walk away and then paused. "Perhaps you'd care to join your daughter for dinner? Régine is making jambalaya."

"The brown kind," Alexia called out, her attention still on the cat, who now curled in her lap, bumping its head against her hand. "And shrimp gumbo."

Cameron waved a hand about the room. "You cannot leave her here. I . . . I have things to do."

"And your daughter can either help you or not interrupt you. She knows her place." Josette turned to Michel and Abbott. "It was a pleasure meeting you, gentlemen. Good day."

Cameron caught up with her at the door. "It appears your driver has gone off with your carriage."

"I intend to walk since it's good for my disposition. My driver will come for me at an appointed hour. He'll also drop by and pick up the trays beforehand." She stepped outside.

Cameron followed her. "Then I'll see you to your shop."

It was as though a cloud passed overhead, dampening her spirits and setting a faint line between her brows. Just as quickly, she recovered and the crease disappeared. "Thank you, but I much prefer my time alone. I have so little of it with a young girl around and having so many obligations."

What was that all about? He tilted his head and studied her. "Why is it I don't believe you?"

"All right, then. I don't care to have you walking with me because I don't like you so much. I'm only here to help Alexia make a strong connection with you."

Something hot and sultry shone in the depths of her dark eyes that made his pulse twitch. He took a step forward until they were standing so close he caught her lovely scent again. "Liar. I think you don't want me walking with you because you like me too much and you don't know what to do about it."

She looked him over with a half-smile. "Aren't you the arrogant one?"

She gave him her cheek and snapped open her umbrella, the same blue as her dress. "You didn't say whether or not you would join us for dinner. After all, you threatened me with a late-night visit and a bottle of rum, so you may as well arrive early and get to know more of your daughter over a bowl of the best jambalaya in town."

He stood there, staring at Josette, a riot of emotions he couldn't name battering his insides. God, she was beautiful. "The brown kind, is it? I haven't had good Creole cooking since I was here four years ago, and brown jambalaya happens to be my favorite."

Josette laughed, low and silky. "See you this evening, then."

Cameron watched the sway of her hips until she disappeared around a corner, his mind in a muddle. This was a dangerous sport he'd fallen into. He needed to figure out what to do with Alexia, stop the rum thieving, then get the bloody hell out of New Orleans.

Once out of Cameron's sight, Josette nearly burst into laughter. Oh, but that was delightful fun. And didn't she look forward to tonight?

Her thoughts turned to her shop and her good mood dimmed. Damn that Émile Vennard. He'd likely be waiting in her office, sitting on the edge of a chair in front of her desk, straight-backed and leaning on his gold-handled cane, one hand crossed over the other. Whenever she saw him on the streets of the Vieux Carré, twirling his walking stick, she wondered if there might be a weapon hidden inside. Perhaps a sword. Or a sharp blade.

Tall and wiry, the French Creole seemed agile enough without benefit of a cane, even for a man of his indeterminate age. Perhaps he was in his sixties. But then, perhaps not. Many dark-haired men went gray early. He had the kind of face that would never wrinkle, even if he lived to be a hundred.

And she knew this because she assessed everyone's skin, a habit she'd acquired at a young age when her grandmother had taught her how to gather and mix herbs. Even though Grandmere had been nearly as aloof as Maman toward Josette, she'd vehemently opposed Maman's relentless practice of voodoo. In retaliation, Grandmere had taught an eager Josette all she knew. Josette had long since gone beyond those teachings, constantly creating new and better formulas for the wealthy.

Cameron had good, clear skin. A bit of olive to his complexion. Age had not diminished his fine looks. Instead, the years only served to enhance them. What would it be like to run her fingers along his finely sculpted face? Over his body? To taste him? Something elemental and fierce shot through her. A small, breathless noise escaped her lips. She picked up her pace as if doing so would purge the erotic energy running rampant through her. *Good Lord!* Deliberating on such fanciful notions would only bring trouble.

She halted. Not a hundred yards in front of her, Vennard crossed the street, swinging his cane in a blithe manner, his top hat perched at an arrogant angle. Here was the very reason she'd refused Cameron's offer of escort. What difference would it make if Vennard had happened upon them? She did not know—she only knew her instincts loathed the idea.

He headed straight for her shop.

Keeping her head down, she faced the store window and pretended to study the displayed goods. Why was the man so intent on making her life miserable? She understood how buying up her husband's lucrative holdings had been beneficial to him, but this? Unless she misunderstood his signals, she doubted he was seeking her out as a mistress, as others had been inclined to do, so that couldn't be the reason. And from what she'd heard, he was faithful to his wife— a formidable woman who frequented Josette's business on a regular basis. So why would he want to buy her out and shutter the place? Nothing made sense.

Anger welled up and tears pinched the backs of her eyes. She waited a good ten minutes—at least she could control that much of her life at the moment—and then, head high, she marched into Belle Femme.

She greeted each of her workers by name. They were dressed alike in blue and white pinstriped gowns, the fronts covered by crisp white aprons complete with ruffles gathered along the outer edges of the shoulder straps.

Beneath each of their starched white collars hung a cameo pendant on a golden chain, the carved ivory a flawless profile of a beautiful woman.

Josette took great pride in offering her clients the finest quality in every regard. The floor was of white Carrera marble veined in gray and had been shipped in from Italy; the ceiling, painted a sky blue with billowy clouds and lovely little birds flitting about, gave one the feeling of being out of doors. Solid oak shelves and counters, lacquered white and trimmed in gold, held apothecary jars filled with all manner of creams and herbs, the name on each jar etched in the same gold. The light, airy fragrance filling the shop gave the impression of a spring breeze floating about. Three round tables draped in Belgian lace stood in one corner, a small vase of flowers topping each, the chair cushions a plush, rose-colored velvet. Sweet and delicate mignons and China's finest teas were served to her clients in that elegant but cozy corner.

Belle Femme was Josette's inspiration alone, born three years earlier out of a feverish desire to have something to call her own, something that came from no one but her. It was the child she would never bear, the husband she would never curl up next to at night. Here was the one place where she garnered respect in this town, despite the fact that her clients only acknowledged her within these walls and ignored her on the street.

After all, she was daughter to a Cajun witch who'd learned her sinful ways at the knee of the voodoo queen, Marie Leveau, then stepped across the line into a very dark world. And Josette's sister was a dead whore who'd left an illegitimate daughter behind. Then there was Josette herself—a seventeen-year-old low-life married to a fifty-two-year-old man who, the gossips said, died under mysterious circumstances within a year of the wedding. Very suspect, they whispered, what with all the herbs at her command. And then there were her two brothers and a no-good cousin to consider. They could turn New Orleans on its ear in a trice.

Josette knew her place. And it was here, in Belle Femme. The only place where she'd ever felt comfortable, the only place she dared to call her own, heart and soul.

And the man who'd entered the shop wanted to take it from her.

If—God forbid—he proved successful in turning her out, and Cameron would be willing to take full charge of his daughter, then there would be no reason to remain in a town where she was scorned. That familiar cinch tightened around her heart. She breathed deeply to try to break its hold. Wherever would she go?

"A Monsieur Vennard waits in your office, Madame LeBlanc. He said he had an appointment at ten and when you didn't show on the hour, I served him tea. I do hope it was the thing to do since he insisted on waiting."

"Thank you," Josette said to Elise, the head shop girl. "I'll see him at once."

She stepped into her luxurious sanctuary at the rear of the building, and there he sat, on the edge of a gilt chair, hands on his cane, just as she'd predicted. The anger she'd managed to keep under wraps went off like a bomb exploding.

She marched around to her desk and, leaning her fists on it, narrowed her eyes at him. "Why in the world would you want a business such as mine, Monsieur Vennard? It cannot be of any use to you. The bulk of my work comes from personal consultations and how would you manage that without me?"

"Oh, the sales price would include your tutorials as well. For a period of, say, three months?"

"Impossible. I refuse to sell." She sat and steepled her fingers, determined to win.

Vennard slowly rubbed his long fingers over the handle of his cane. "How are your brothers, Madame Leblanc?"

"They are fine and will remain fine, so don't start your veiled threats or I'll be forced to tell them what you are up to." That was the wrong thing to say. He knew she wouldn't do such a thing and risk her brothers tangling with the law after they took care of Vennard.

He merely smiled. "And have your volatile brothers hanged for murder? How is your niece, by the way?"

Good God! The hair on her nape stood on end, and it felt as though her heart had stopped. He wouldn't dare touch Alexia.

"She's turning into a lovely woman," he said. "Is it safe for her on the streets at night? Or even during the day?"

Josette clasped her hands together on the desk to keep them from shaking. "Alexia's father has returned and intends to raise her. I wouldn't threaten her safety or you may find you have a very angry and lethal patriarch on your hands."

He raised an eyebrow. "Oh, so Cameron Andrews has come forth to acknowledge his Cajun trash?"

It took everything Josette had in her to keep her voice calm. "I need to ask you to leave, Monsieur Vennard."

He arched a brow. "Oh, but we've not yet gotten to my reason for paying you this little visit."

She reached into the desk drawer and pulled out a pistol. "Leave, Monsieur Vennard. At once."

"Well, when you put it that way." He stared at the end of the pistol for a long moment, and then stood, his sharp blue eyes growing dark and dangerous. "But you and I are not finished, Josette."

"You do not have permission to use my Christian name."

He laughed. "Christian name? That's rich coming from someone like you."

Grabbing his gold-tipped cane with a snappy flourish, he started for the door. "No need to see me out. I'd like an answer in two weeks or—"

"Or what? Bastièn and René begin having accidents

again? I'm not the same grieving widow who gave in to you after my husband died." She cocked the gun. "Leave."

"Really, Madame. No need to go to extremes." He paused at the door and turned toward her, an odd look about him. "Have you ever wondered why things never seem to quite go your way, Josette?"

She pulled in a ragged breath and exhaled, trying to release the raw and primitive energy building in her.

When she refused to respond to his bait, he said, "It's because a curse was placed on you when you were very young. Your life is a pitiful one and will remain so until you die."

It was her turn to laugh derisively. "Poppycock. I don't believe in curses. Now leave."

"You, raised by a wicked voodoo witch, do not believe in curses?" He stilled while a cold, lethal look washed over his countenance. "You should, Josette, because it was Odalie who placed the curse upon your soul."

Chapter Eight

"Can I take a peek at the Gulf Stream flow charts one more time, Papa?"

Cameron closed his eyes and pinched the bridge of his nose. "This is the fourth time, Alexia. Why again?"

"Because Cousin Michel gave me some paper, and Monsieur Abbott gave me a pencil so I can bring me home a copy, that be why."

"As you wish." Once again, he fished out the rolled charts and spread them across the table. What the hell, it might keep her busy for the remainder of the afternoon.

Until today, Cameron only thought he knew what exhaustion was. Not only did he yearn for a quiet corner to disappear in, but Abbott, who usually left work looking as fresh as the moment he walked in, appeared disheveled, as well. Michel on the other hand, took obvious pleasure in Alexia's shenanigans. But it wasn't just her getting into things that tired Cameron, it was her curiosity and thirst for knowledge that none of them seemed able to quench. Between architectural renderings, ships' logs, and copious questions, she'd drained him. An unbelievably bright girl, she'd likely be able to make sense of Abbott's ledgers if put to the test.

He'd even had to step in between her and Abbott over who laid claim to Midnight. Alexia finally agreed that the cat was to remain in the office, but then she was caught hiding the little beast in a drawer for later transport.

"Let's call it a day." Cameron's brain felt like so much sludge. Why had he agreed to dinner when what he wanted to do was go home and crawl into bed?

"We've still a quarter of an hour until quitting time," Abbott said.

Pushed to the limit, Cameron clenched his jaw. "Since none of our bloody ships are due in for the remainder of the day, and since I happen to be head of this bloody empire, if I want to shut down fifteen minutes early, I bloody well will."

Alexia giggled. "Then we can bloody well go home?"

Merde. Cameron pointed a finger at her. "You are not to use that word. It is an Englishman's derogatory term, it's not ladylike, and I should not have used it in front of you. Forget you heard it."

A shadow fell over the table. Cameron glanced up and stood in stunned silence.

René Thibodeaux leaned against the door's frame, hands in his trouser pockets, a lazy grin on his face. "Your daughter, *oui*?"

"Uncle René!" Alexia rushed to him and threw her arms around his waist, hugging him tight.

He stroked the top of her head and bent to her ear. "Why don't you wait outside for me, *pouchette*?"

Without a word, Alexia turned to make her exit.

Cameron bristled and the floor rocked beneath him. *What the hell?* "Alexia, get back in here."

She paused with her foot on the threshold and looked to her uncle, question in her eyes.

Cameron clenched his jaw. "No, you look at me, Alexia. I'm the one giving orders."

René kept his eyes fixed on Cameron. "She should wait outside while we men talk. You understand, *oui*?"

"She's my daughter, and if I tell her to get back in here, she does. Alexia, do as I say, and come to your father."

Michel slowly rose from his chair, as did Abbott. The two men worked their way around to where Cameron stood with his fists clenched.

Alexia stepped back inside, looked to her uncle and then to Cameron, confusion rampant in her eyes. She whispered something low to René. When he shook his head, she slowly eased away from him and made her way to her father. Cameron set an arm around her shoulder.

"What are you doing here, Thibodeaux?"

He shrugged. "Since you have a new business, I thought I should come to work for you, *non*?"

Cameron shot Michel a knowing glance. So this was René's game. "Or not, and more of the rum goes missing?"

René continued to lean a shoulder against the door frame as though they were merely chatting about the weather. "You have rum missing?"

With a snort, Michel walked back to his desk and began locking drawers. "I'm going home. You can deal with this on your own, Cam."

"Not just yet, cousin." Cameron's anger clamored for a hotter conclusion, but instead, he forced calm. "Hire him."

"What?" Michel whipped around, shifting his gaze back and forth between René and Cameron.

In full control of his faculties now, Cameron's head was clear for the first time all day. "You heard me. Hire him or we'll only keep losing rum. Isn't that right, Thibodeaux?"

Michel turned and gave René a desultory once-over. "That's outright blackmail."

René grinned. "What be that old saying? 'Keep your friends

close, but your enemies closer'? I'll be back in the morning.
What time do you start work?"

"Oh, but wait." Cameron turned to René. "You are hired
on the condition that you tell us how the hell you got in and
out of the warehouse."

"*Très facile*, Monsieur Andrews."

"How easy?" Cameron asked.

René shrugged. "There was no need to break into your
warehouse when all we needed was a key to the building
next door. You see, there is a door connecting the two,
hidden on each side by stacks of old goods. One can go back
and forth with great and silent ease."

Cameron laughed. This was rich, so very rich. "Don't tell
me—the door to that warehouse is located on the other side
of the building, where even our guards won't hear you."

"*Oui*." René touched two fingers to his forehead as if tip-
ping an imaginary hat and rolling his shoulder off the door
frame, walked away.

Michel shut the door behind René and stomped over to
where Cameron stood. "What were you thinking?" He
covered Alexia's ears with his hands and spoke in a harsh
whisper. "That man is nothing but trouble, and he's bound to
bring even more trouble with him in the form of his thieving
relatives."

He dropped his hands.

Alexia rubbed at her ears.

"Perhaps," Cameron said. "But not as much misfortune
as if we refuse to hire him. Come, Alexia, I need a change of
clothing before we go to dinner. And by the looks of you,
you'll likely need to freshen up as well."

He tugged the drooping ribbon from her hair and shoved
it in his pocket. "You've been inside this clean establishment
the entire day, so how did you manage a tear in your dress,
and dirt from head to toe?"

"And a rapidly expanding ink stain on the side of her dress, I might add," Abbott called out. "My India ink has gone missing."

"Alexia?" Cameron held out a hand.

Without so much as batting an eye, Alexia dug into her pocket and fished out the small bottle of turquoise ink. She marched over to Abbott and set it on his desk. "I'd have brung it back tomorrow."

"You aren't coming here tomorrow," Cameron snapped.

She stiffened. And then she turned to him, looking as though she'd been slapped. But then the pain in her eyes vanished, and Cameron was left staring at a blank face. "If you say so, Papa."

He flinched. He'd had no notion how thin her defenses could be when struck just right. "I didn't mean how that sounded." For the hundredth time today, he drew in a long breath and shoved his hand through his hair. "What I meant was—"

What did he mean? Hell, he was only making things worse. And he'd hurt her. His own daughter. What had he done? She'd obviously enjoyed herself today. "I . . . I may not be here myself tomorrow, but if I am, you are welcome—"

She shrugged and headed for the door, any sign of being upset having vanished. "What do I care? I'll be off to Maman's tomorrow, seeing as how it's boring as bloody hell here."

Chapter Nine

The moment Josette opened her front door, Cameron knew he should never have accepted the invitation to dinner. She stood there, a goddess in peach silk cut so low a saint couldn't help but gawk.

One glance and his flesh rebelled against any resolve to remain neutral. Worst of all, his eyes failed to obey his command and flickered not once, but twice, over the top of her gown. And his mouth—curse the beggar for wanting a taste of that creamy-looking skin. Well, his traitorous body could bloody well go back into hibernation because laying so much as a finger on Josette was out of the question.

A flash of puzzlement crossed her features. And then that telltale light in her eyes flashed mischief. The one that told him she knew exactly what had crossed his mind.

Blast it all, how long had he been staring? He'd bet a small fortune she'd worn that dress on purpose, the minx. Well, let her play her little games now—she had no idea the one *he* had in mind. He cleared his throat. "Did you receive the note I sent ahead informing you we'd be a couple hours late?"

"Indeed." She stepped aside and bade him enter.

Her ethereal scent nearly did him in as he walked past her,

but then the spicy aroma of Cajun cooking hit his nostrils and precious childhood memories slammed into him so hard, he nearly stumbled. Darn, he missed that long-ago way of life.

"Your pardon for our delay." He handed her a velvet sack containing the bottle of rum he'd promised—or threatened her with—depending on how one viewed the matter. "It seems little Miss I've-Been-Into-Everything-Imaginable-Today needed a good scrubbing. We collected one of the dresses Madame Charmontès had at the ready. The remainder of the order should be here sometime tomorrow."

Josette openly perused the length of him. "You obviously made a stop at your tailor's, as well. You must feel more comfortable in your lighter-weight clothing. It becomes you, by the way."

He gazed into those luminous eyes as if they were magnetic, slowly drawing him near. He now stood too close; that was the problem. Either that or he shouldn't have added rum to his lemonade. Probably shouldn't have drunk three tall ones before setting out. Damn, she was beautiful. He managed a step back, as if doing so would set a new level of self-discipline. Odd, but this close, she somehow seemed familiar. Had to be because of her sister. No, Madame Olympée said the two looked nothing alike.

Alexia marched past them, a scowl furrowing her brow. "I got me a powerful hunger. I'll see you at the table."

"As do I have a powerful hunger," Cameron murmured.

A soft snort left Josette's lovely throat. "Aren't you the clever one?" She eyed the retreating Alexia and her new rose-colored dress. "Just because she wore ragged clothing when you first laid eyes on her, doesn't mean her closet is bare. We are not strangers to Madame Charmontès's shop, I'll have you know. What happened that left your daughter in such a foul mood?"

For whatever reason, Cameron's instincts told him not to mention that Alexia had been caught thieving again.

He glanced around the entry, at the gilded ormolu table festooned with flowers, at gold-framed oil paintings hung against pale, damask-covered walls, all in a vain attempt to ignore the essence of one stunning woman. "Judging by the incredible cooking smells in here, I'd say the girl is on a mission guided entirely by an empty stomach. Although I don't know how that could be since she talked both Michel and Abbott out of their lunches."

He gave a nod to Vivienne, who stood behind and to the side of her cousin, a vague smile tilting her mouth. "Evening."

Josette handed her cousin the bottle of rum. "Would you mind taking this into the parlor, then joining us for dinner?"

"*Oui*," Vivienne said, and disappeared.

Josette turned to Cameron. "My other cousin, Régine, has dinner at the ready. If you'll follow me."

He walked alongside her and tried like hell not to glance her way. With his height, even a brief glimpse meant looking down that blasted bodice. His nether regions saluted him and begged for a peek.

"Very nice," he said when they entered the formal dining room. Old Louis LeBlanc couldn't possibly have had a hand in this kind of decorating, not with the lace tablecloth, French chairs upholstered in velvet, and walls painted in a bold trompe l'oeil of green ivy, colorful flowers, and, hell, even butterflies that looked amazingly alive.

Alexia humphed at his dallying. "Food's getting cold."

He leaned over and boldly scrutinized the lower lip she'd just licked clean. A smattering of crumbs clung to the front of her dress. She slid her hand into the folds of the tablecloth, but not before he spotted a hunk of half-chewed bread. He nearly laughed. "And judging by the wonderful smells and Alexia's twitching nose, we'd best seat ourselves or there'll be nothing left."

He drew out a chair at one end of the table for Josette, but instead of properly seating himself to her right, he helped Vivienne into that chair and chose an empty one opposite Josette. He'd be facing her straight-on all evening, blast his lust-filled heart. Not even the bowl of fresh flowers sitting low in the center of the table was going to obscure his view.

Flickering candlelight from the chandelier danced across Josette's dark hair and played over a mouth tilted at one corner. What was that about? Did she have her own secrets? She glanced up at him, as though she'd read his thoughts. The woman was sultry as sin and didn't even know it.

"White wine or red?"

"Red," he said. A bottle, maybe two, would do.

She gave a nod toward the table. "As you can see, we have shrimp étoufée, brown jambalaya, and two kinds of gumbo. Despite the formal table setting, I'm hoping you subscribe to the casual dining this kind of food calls for."

He grinned. "Have you forgotten I grew up in the Vieux Carré?"

"Then do feel comfortable in helping yourself." She lifted a vessel of steaming étoufée her way and spooned a ladleful into her dish.

Cameron reached for the same glazed crock as Alexia. "I'm the guest," he said with a cocky grin and a wink. "Me first."

Despite Alexia's foul mood, her lips twitched.

He heaped his bowl full of the aromatic stew thick with chicken, andouille sausage, and tasso—the spicy, smoky Cajun pork that gave the dish its rich color—something else he couldn't come by in San Francisco. Would mannerly Josette abide by the tradition of dunking chunks of bread into the bowl?

She answered his silent question by promptly breaking off a hunk from a hot, crusty loaf, her supple fingers managing the act with graceful ease. She dipped the bread into the broth and popped the juicy morsel into her mouth without spilling a drop.

His groin hitched.

He tore off a piece and followed suit. Appreciation sounded at the back of his throat. *"La seule manière de savourer la nourriture des dieux."*

The only way to eat food from the gods. It was a tradition, this saying, meant to accompany the first bite of anything Creole or Cajun. How many times had he spoken that phrase? But somehow, tonight, the words uttered low in his throat felt more like a seduction meant for Josette. What the devil was wrong with him? His daughter sat to his right and Vivienne to his left, for God's sake.

He emptied his glass of wine and poured another to steady his nerves, then focused on a woman who'd quietly entered the room and set another basket of hot, crusty bread on the table. "You must be Régine."

She nodded and flushed scarlet.

"This has to be the finest jambalaya I've ever tasted. There's nothing like good Creole and Cajun cooking to bring back pleasant family memories, *oui*? *Merci beaucoup*."

Again, she merely nodded, then scurried out the door.

Candlelight reflected in Josette's dark gaze holding steady on him. He paused with the bread midway to the bowl, waiting for her to say something about what had just occurred.

Vivienne shot her a narrow-eyed glance.

Something odd flickered over Josette's countenance and, shifting in her seat, she went back to eating. A dichotomy, this woman. Strong and purposeful one moment, then apprehensive the next. Exploring her in all her naked glory would be a mesmerizing dance of wills, to be sure.

Where had *that* blasted thought come from? He'd be a damn fool to try to seduce her. He needed to do or say something to distract himself from his prurient thoughts. "Pass the étoufée, please."

Without a word, Alexia shoved the bowl his way.

"Do be civil," Josette warned. "What's gotten into you?"

Gads, one could cut the air with a knife between those two. A little levity might do the trick. Cameron speared a fat shrimp with his fork, and holding it up for examination, fell into his best clipped British accent. "I say, Miss Alexia, would it be considered a contradiction in terms to call this fat tidbit *jumbo* shrimp?"

Vivienne giggled while Josette smiled, but Alexia shoveled more jambalaya-soaked bread into her mouth. "I ain't heard dat word 'contradiction' afore, so ain't nuthin' funny about it, don'cha know."

"Brilliant." He grinned at her and bit off half the shrimp.

Josette placed her bread on the side of her plate. "Alexia, that's the thickest accent you've managed yet. I do believe you have an apology to make to your papa."

Cameron popped the rest of the shrimp into his mouth. "More like a hundred, but I'll take what I can get."

Alexia took another bite and mumbled, "When I be done eatin'."

Josette set down her spoon. "Finish what's in your mouth before you speak. If you don't wish to apologize, consider your meal finished and take yourself to bed."

Alexia swallowed with a big gulp. "But my belly's not full and cousin Régine made peach pie. Saying what needs saying can wait or I fear it'll sour my stomach."

She looked at her father and smiled sweetly. "You wouldn't want me going to bed with a bellyache, now would you, Papa?"

Cameron gave a low laugh. "After all you've put me through

today? I couldn't give a damn whether you end up in bed with an empty belly or an aching one. Your aunt has my curiosity piqued."

Alexia heaved a sigh, set her spoon to her plate with a *clink*, and kept her head down. "I apologize for lying to you about my manner of speaking. I only used the Cajun patois to irritate you."

Shocked, Cameron shot a glance Josette's way.

She nodded.

"Alexia," he said. "Look me in the eye when you speak to me or we'll be here all night until you do."

She glanced up and, without blinking, repeated herself, then added, "My jambalaya is getting cold."

"Don't be fresh," Josette said.

Alexia folded her arms over her chest and tapped her foot.

Oh, the little conniver. This was getting good. Cameron drained his glass of wine, poured another, then mirrored the toe tapping and arm crossing. "And I owe you an apology, as well."

Alexia's foot drumming ceased. "You do?"

He'd be damned if she was going off to Odalie's tomorrow as she'd announced when they'd left the shipping office. He'd take her back to his place and tie her to a chair if need be, but he wasn't about to let that voodoo witch get her hands on his daughter. "I should never have said you couldn't return to the shipping office. I have a few things to do first thing in the morning, but if you can manage to arrive at ten once again, I'd be pleased to have you."

A sheepish expression fell over Alexia. "But what of Monsieur Abbott? Won't he throttle me soon's I appear?"

Josette sat back in her chair and folded her hands in her lap. "Ah, so that's what's wrong with you. No doubt you have good reason for being concerned. Your change of clothing wouldn't have anything to do with Monsieur Abbott being irked at you, would it?"

There was a long pause while Cameron and Alexia stared at each other, silent messages passing back and forth. Could this be an opportunity to build a bond of trust by saying nothing? He had to do something to resolve her future so he could sail off wherever the wind blew.

Well, worth a try. "It was nothing. I'd had a long day and my temper was on a short fuse. Abbott is not used to any disruption in his precisely planned labors, and having a guest in house didn't sit well with him. He'll get used to having Alexia there."

The sigh of relief in his daughter's exhale filled Cameron with humor. She rubbed her eyes, shoved a hunk of gravy-soaked bread into her mouth, and, while chewing, stifled a yawn.

Vivienne raised a brow. "Finish your meal before you fall asleep in your plate, Alexia. Then let me ready you for bed."

Alexia thrust out her lower lip. "It wouldn't be the first time my face landed in my soup. I haven't had any peach pie."

Josette opened her mouth to respond, but Cameron spoke first. "How about you have it for breakfast, when you're up and full of energy?"

Alexia's eyes widened. Her gaze flitted from Josette to his and back again. Then she grinned as though she herself had pulled something over on her aunt. She rose and moved close to Cameron. To his surprise, she blew him a kiss on each cheek. "G'night, Papa."

For a moment, just for a moment, his heart folded over onto itself. When she made to walk away, without thinking, he reached out and pulled her back to him. "I rather like your lovely French accent. I'd hate to see it fall by the wayside altogether."

The moment of silence that passed between them while

she stood so close filled him with an odd guilt. What had she been like as a baby?

He gave her a nudge toward Vivienne and the door. "And every now and then, when you find me in a jolly mood, I doubt I'd mind if that Cajun patois snuck up on you. God knows I toss my British and French accents about like so many rocks having a tumble. Sleep well."

Without a word, Régine slipped into the room and set a slice of peach pie in front of Cameron and Josette, another at Vivienne's place at the table.

"Vivienne can take her pie in the kitchen," Josette said. "Who knows how long it will take to settle Alexia in?"

Régine nodded and retreated with the portion in hand.

Cameron watched the woman disappear, then turned to Josette. Their gazes locked. A current passed between them as if the air were suddenly electric with an imminent storm. A surge of pulsating heat shot through him. There was no denying that she felt it too. The brown in her eyes deepened to a rich, sultry shade, the color of the dark Creole coffee he favored—hot and bold.

He tore his gaze from hers and his eyes roved leisurely over her exquisite face and supple lips. It had been a long time since he'd kissed a mouth like that. An image danced in his head of her naked and sprawled across his bed, her hair a tangle of curls. "Is there a reason you sent everyone away and left the two of us alone?"

Her throaty sigh floated across the table. His eyes snapped back to hers. To his surprise, the passion he'd seen in them only a moment before was gone, replaced by humor.

She took a sip of wine and smiled. "Don't bother. It won't work."

Damn, she was something. "What won't work?"

"Your attempt to make me squirm in my chair. If you think my head is filled with fantasies of you, think again."

Oh, he was the wrong man to trifle with. "You're telling

me that delightful sigh was fake? My dear, is that the best you can manage?"

"I don't fake boredom."

He chuckled. If games were what she wanted to play, she just might enjoy the one coming up. "You amuse me."

He poured the last of the wine into his glass. When had he drunk so much? "I came here hoping for some honest conversation this evening, so please, do not disappoint me. Admit it—I do more than bore you. Far more."

She scoffed. "You are so puffed up with yourself, it's a wonder your buttons don't burst."

He lifted a brow. "Got any particular buttons in mind?"

She merely laughed.

Damn if he didn't want her.

He'd known that last night.

And he'd known it again this morning when she'd strolled into his office, a vision in blue and smelling all womanly. His body had been dangerously close to betraying him then, but once she'd gone, he'd kept his mind busy enough to forget about her. Not now, however. Every blasted muscle in his body had a mind of its own, and was about to betray him in truth if he didn't change the subject.

Holding the wineglass by the stem, he twirled it between his fingers, watching the slow swirl of ruby liquid, trying to keep his scandalous thoughts away from the opposite end of the table. He downed the rest of the wine while contemplating his next move.

"Tell me, Josette. Who delivered the stolen rum—*my* stolen rum—to you?"

She sat quietly for a moment, then said, "Would you care for another bottle of wine?"

So, she still refused to name her brother as the thief. Which meant she was either toying with Cameron, or René had not paid her a visit during the day and informed her of his new employment. Why she insisted on protecting him when she had Cameron's daughter sleeping upstairs, he didn't know. But she'd soon find out she played cat and mouse with the wrong person. With a grin that he knew bordered on wicked, he stood. "Henceforth, I'd rather drink rum."

He extended his hand to her. "Shall we?"

Chapter Ten

The heat in Cameron's hand as he guided Josette into the parlor seeped through her lower back and shot straight into her womb. Good Lord, would she get through this night unscathed?

A fresh, clean scent of having recently bathed still surrounded him, penetrating her senses and scattering her thoughts. She'd had the same reaction when he'd walked into her home earlier. Back then it had been worse—his hair had been slightly damp. That he'd been naked only a brief time before arriving had provoked all manner of forbidden images. Another wave of heat rushed through her.

He shut the door behind him and turned the key.

At the click of the lock, Josette's heart missed a beat. What in the world was he up to? "You require a locked door in order to ascertain whether or not I am able to imbibe a certain amount of liquor?"

Sharp, amber eyes fringed with thick, sooty lashes flickered over her, then back to her face with nary a change in expression. Had she just been judged and found lacking? What had she been thinking, wearing something so revealing? With a quick swallow to wet her throat, she reminded herself that she didn't like him much so his opinion hardly mattered. After all, she'd only asked him to share a meal because of Alexia.

Having retrieved the bottle of rum from the black velvet sack, Cameron collected the crystal decanter sitting on the table between them. "Tell me how much to pour. I want to make certain it's the exact amount you claim to have drunk while alone last night." He shot her a meaningful glance. "That is, unless you wish to tell me who delivered the rum, and I'll be on my way."

Since she couldn't very well give René away lest there be bloodshed, she took a seat in a chair, folded her hands in her lap, and watched what he was about, hoping her deportment sent him the message that she refused to be intimidated. "You can stop near the shoulder of the bottle."

He looked her way, then back to the decanter, as if checking to see if she'd been truthful. His long fingers held the carafe steady as he poured from the other bottle, his movements lithe and graceful.

Didn't he cut a fine figure, though? His dark jacket and charcoal trousers fit him to perfection. A snowy-white shirt and cravat, and a burgundy brocaded vest, made him look rather sin-filled with his mass of dark, wavy hair and sun-kissed skin. But it was more than fine clothing and a well-made form that caught her eye. He seemed always to be draped in a kind of dazzling charisma. And power. Lord, he must be a formidable force to be reckoned with when angry. Was her imagination playing tricks on her or was he growing more handsome by the day?

He filled two shot glasses and, handing her one, seated himself on the sofa with the apparent ease of someone used to being a guest in her home. He said nothing.

What a day she'd had, and now this. Until he'd shown up at her door this evening, she'd felt strangely empowered, having drawn Louis's old pistol on Émile Vennard. The shocked look on his face was worth the risk she'd taken. One of these days she ought to purchase a few bullets.

Cameron leaned back against the sofa, watching her. "You should smile like that more often."

She'd been grinning? "I do so often enough."

"Not like that, not with amusement in your eyes. Care to share your thoughts?"

His deliciously low, rough voice scraped across her skin. The fine hairs on her arms tingled. "I do not."

"You don't play enough, Madame. Therefore, you can't possibly be having enough fun in life."

"My brother René tells me the same thing. But since neither one of you lives my life, who are you to judge?" She finished the rum—because she desperately needed to—and set the shot glass on the table next to her. This was all she needed, a long, drawn-out evening. Well, so be it, because even though they both knew full well the name Cameron was after, she would not give him proof.

Cameron stood and walked over to where her glass sat empty. There was his wonderful, male scent again, rousing her senses. He picked up the glass but instead of refilling it, lined it up with five others alongside the decanter of rum. He proceeded to fill each of them precisely three quarters full, then set three on the table beside the sofa and three next to her.

Oh, dear. "What are you doing?"

"Since you refuse to give me a name, then we shall make a little game of this." He spoke in such a way that implied it wasn't little and was perhaps not so much of a sport.

She drew in a slow, deep breath and exhaled just as slowly. Wherever this was leading, she had to keep her wits about her. "And what would this game of yours consist of?"

"It's called the naked truth." He poured another shot of rum into the glass he'd held and returned to sitting on the sofa. His steady gaze, dark and powerful, settled on her as though it were a direct touch, sending another current of heat through her. "We used to play it at Cambridge. It was how we studied for exams . . . among other things."

"And just how does it work?"

"When it's my turn, I get to ask you a question, any question." He paused, letting his words sink in. "If you fail to respond, either because you do not know the answer or you refuse to give it, you are required to empty a glass of its contents and remove an article of clothing."

"What?" Shock cut directly into her veins. Had she heard him right? The idea was so bizarre, she couldn't help but laugh. "You cannot possibly be serious."

He held the small glass of liquor to his lips, watching her over the rim. "But I am, Madame. That is, unless you wish to tell me who stole my rum."

This couldn't be happening. This *wasn't* happening. "Your proposal is ludicrous, not to mention indecent. And you actually expect me to take a turn, then have you do the same, only to repeat the process until one of us keels over? And possibly naked at that?"

A lazy, confident smile turned up the corners of his mouth. "Just say the name, Josette, and I'll be out the door."

Oh, she couldn't have him go looking for René, she just couldn't. They'd once nearly killed each other. "Perhaps you should take your leave. I'll not play absurd games over a silly missing bottle of rum."

He laughed then, deep and low. "A great deal more than a bottle is missing, my dear. If I take my leave now, it will be to go directly to the police."

A shudder ran through her. Good heavens, what had René done? And was Bastièn involved? More than likely. They might be her brothers, but they'd gone too far this time, involving her. Come morning, she'd hunt them down and shoot both the fools.

"You seem to be considering my offer. Are we moving

closer to getting on with the game?" His gaze never left hers, but his lids lowered slightly and his voice had deepened.

Something coiled inside her that was wicked, yet strangely playful. Just once in her adult life, she'd like to feel free enough to do as she pleased. And René, bless his un-principled heart, had unknowingly set everything in motion.

Why not take part in this silly game? It would serve her brothers right for putting her in such a delicate position. She didn't have to let things go too far. Besides, Cameron would be gone from New Orleans soon enough, and she was in her own home. Who was around to start a scandal?

A delicious thrill shot through her. "You actually played this at Cambridge as a form of study?"

"That and . . . ah . . . at other times." He gave her that slow smile he'd given her before. "A bunch of foxed young men running around in the skin they were born in, letting off steam before a rigid exam. I must say, I thought it quite healthy and productive. I did rather well in my studies, by the by."

She choked back a bit of laughter. "And if I refuse to play?"

He picked a bit of lint that didn't exist from his trouser leg. "Then I shall call you out for being a coward." He glanced up from his task, and she noticed that his eyes had taken on a smoky aura. "Every time our paths cross, I shall remind you that you have no sense of humor, that you must have plenty to hide, and that you are a poor sport."

"And how will we know when the game ends?"

"When one person loses all of his or her clothing—"

She held up a hand. "I will *not* play your game to that extent. This is ridiculous as it is, and crude of you even to bring it to my attention."

His chuckle, low in his throat, told her he didn't care. "Then tell me who was drinking a supply of contraband with you while my daughter was in residence, and we can call it a night."

It would be so easy to tell him, get it over with, but she also knew that besides endangering René, Cameron would make his exit and she'd be left alone for yet another sleepless night. Alone to do what? Continue wearing out the floorboards in her room? "I'll play this little game with you, but only on the condition that you may not ask that particular question."

He lifted a brow. "You have a big secret, don't you?"

No, she didn't, because he knew full well whom she refused to name, but she would not supply the proof, and by now this was too much reckless fun to pass up. She hadn't felt so wayward since she'd ceased picking pockets. She couldn't help but grin. "You've forgotten something."

"Which is?"

"I wear far more articles of clothing than you, therefore—"

"Ah, but will you answer the questions I ask of you, or will you lose everything and become inebriated more quickly than you expect?" His eyes were filled with wickedness as his gaze cruised her body from head to toe.

"Who would go first?"

He lifted a brow. "Why, the lady, of course."

Her heart in her throat, she sat back and studied him for a long moment. Until he'd shown up at her door, her life had been as predictable as the rising sun. Bettering herself had turned out to be little more than a ritual of going between a house and a shop, and living her days devoid of anticipation. Or daring. She darn well deserved a bit of naughty fun.

As if Cameron had read her thoughts, that lazy, sensual smile touched his mouth again. A corner of her heart squeezed. Lord, he was beautiful. And here he was, her lifelong fantasy, not six feet away and urging her to join him in a bold and risqué activity.

For however long it lasted, she wanted this brief interlude with him. Wanted the magic of staring into those mesmerizing amber eyes while she asked him question after question of an intimate nature. Perhaps when it was all over, she'd have her fill of him. Her blood thickened, rolled through her veins like hot lava. Oh yes, she'd sip his rum and join him in this provocative game. No matter what happened, how could she lose?

"All right," she said. "Here is my first question. Have you ever before played this game with a woman?"

A pause, then Cameron stood, removed his jacket, spread it over the back of the sofa, picked up his shot glass, and emptied it. "Didn't you start out on a rather brazen note? My turn now."

He sat back down, his eyes glittering in the flickering light. "There are times I look at you and find something oddly familiar. Was I known to you before I showed up at your front door with Alexia in tow?"

"Yes."

"Did you—"

She lifted her hand. "Pardon me, but I do believe it is my turn, is it not?"

He laughed. "I suppose so."

"Have you ever spent time behind bars?"

His eyes locked with hers. Then he untied his cravat, tossed it aside, and emptied his glass, his movements seamless.

Her throat thickened. "Oh, so you refuse to answer? I'll take that as a yes."

Still holding the glass, he raised it as if in toast and pointed a finger at her. "That, Madame, is another question. I do believe it is my turn. Were you a virgin when you married old Louis?"

A buzz went through her brain. Despite the shock, she held steady. He was bound and determined to scare her into giving him René's name. Well, let him try. "Yes. And despite your feeble attempt to shock me as a means to get what you are after, I'm ahead in the game."

Cameron stretched a long leg out in front of him and leaned back, propping an elbow on one arm of the sofa and proceeding to rub his thumb slowly back and forth over his bottom lip. "I believe the next question is yours?"

A breeze blew in through the open window, sending the curtains rustling like leaves in a fall wind. The tension in her blood ratcheted upward while she struggled to think of her next question. "Were you ever in love before you married your wife?"

"No," he said quietly. "Are you still a virgin?"

A strangled sound left her throat. "You don't waste any time being impertinent, do you?"

"Uh, uh, uh, that's a question and it's still my turn."

Of course she wasn't a virgin, but why give him the satisfaction of an answer? She emptied her glass and slipped off a shoe. His lazy gaze shifted to her silk-stockinged foot. Just for spite, she wiggled her toes.

A half grin slid over his mouth and he licked a drop of rum from the edge of his glass. "Aren't you turning into the sassy one?"

"I do believe that's a question, Monsieur Andrews."

"Ah, we're back to formal names, are we? Trying to protect yourself?"

The low timbre of his voice raised goose bumps on her flesh. "That's two more questions, yet it is still my turn. Perhaps we should institute a punishment for breaking the rules."

"Then to keep us on our toes, so to speak, an out-of-turn question requires a drink and the forfeit of an article of clothing."

"Agreed." She studied him while pondering what question to ask. Despite the heat in the room, a chill ran through her at the hazardous game they played. Oh, but she'd hungered to spend time with him for so many years, and here he was, locked in a room with her and challenging her in a kind of play that would scandalize the entire town were they to hear of it. But who was to know? And who was she to care? Oh, this was really quite delicious.

"So, Monsieur Andrews, how many women have you bedded?"

He poured another shot of rum, tossed it down his throat, and removed his vest. He stood and moved to the low table between them, and after refilling his three shot glasses, reseated himself in that languid fashion of his.

"I take it the number is so large you cannot calculate, or you refuse to answer because it may be humiliating?"

Unmistakable amusement flashed over his countenance. "You asked a question out of turn, so remove another article of clothing and have a drink. You're down two."

"Nonetheless, I'm still ahead." She removed the other shoe.

"Madame LeBlanc." He paused.

She almost took the bait and mentioned he was now using her formal name. She closed her mouth and waited.

"Did you desire your husband in the most intimate of ways?"

She nearly choked on the question. Her cheeks heated. She slipped her hands beneath her gown and removed a pink ruffled garter. She tossed it on the table between them, and emptied the third glass.

His gaze flicked from the garter to her face and back. She knew hunger in a man's eyes when she saw it. Lord, but the rum was potent. Add that to the wine she'd drunk at dinner and she was beyond light-headed. How long did they dare go on with this sinful repartee? She'd never felt so much intimacy with another human being with just her shoes and a garter gone and him in his shirtsleeves. The space between them seemed to narrow, the spark in his eyes deepening. These questions ran along a very dangerous track, indeed.

Without saying a word, he moved to where she sat and retrieved the glasses beside her, hovering so close as to take her breath. God help her, she wanted to say something clever, but his very closeness deprived her of her voice. He refilled the glasses and set them back in place, then returned to his seat. "Do you wish to continue our game, or are you going to give me the name?"

Oh no, not after having retrieved a garter and sending it his way. "You just asked a question out of turn, Cameron. Please empty a glass and remove an article of clothing."

He tossed her a wicked grin, downed the rum, and kicked off a shoe.

She nearly laughed out loud at the scamp. Now it was her turn. "Since your wife, were you ever in love with anyone else?"

"No. What about you, Josette. Have you ever desired another man besides your husband?"

Oh Lord, yes, you! And right now, but she would go to her death before admitting it to him. Reaching beneath her skirts, she slowly worked the other garter down her leg and tossed it to him.

He was sitting back again with his elbow resting on the arm of the sofa and rubbing a finger across his full lower lip. "Do you ever get lonely?"

"That was two questions, one of which is out of turn, sir." Was that right? She'd lost count.

He emptied his glass, and kicked off his other shoe. "What of you, sir? Do you ever get lonely?"

He studied her for a long moment, and then he stood. In one swift movement, he whipped off his shirt and tossed it on the sofa behind him. Slowly, he downed the rum, his eyes glued to hers over the rim of the glass.

Her breathing stopped along with her heart.

He raked a hand through his tousled hair and a sultry grin

touched his mouth. Oh Lord, he could have just crawled out of bed, the way he looked. Instead of sitting down, he shoved his hands in his pockets and just stood there, his gaze heavy-lidded but steady. He tilted his head and a stray lock fell over his forehead. Why, the man was inebriated!

It was her turn to stare. After all, he was offering, wasn't he? She perused him in the same manner as he'd done to her, but if he'd found her lacking, she found him glorious. In the low light, shadows glanced across his cheekbones and lush mouth. His arms were strong and corded, his skin golden. Bands of taut muscle strapped across his smooth stomach and she wondered what he did to look like that. On his left shoulder, a thick, round scar bespoke a battle of some kind. Was that where his cousin had shot him over a woman? Everyone had heard of that scandal.

She let her gaze roam downward to a thin line of hair that circled his navel and disappeared beneath his trousers. Her cheeks heated at what lay beneath the fabric stretched tight across his pelvis by his hands in his pockets. She swallowed hard and glanced back to his face.

His mouth twitched. "Since I forfeited, and if you are through judging me, I believe it's my question, Madame." His voice, husky in his throat, set her heart pounding a double beat. "Have you ever . . . ?" He paused.

She focused on him and held her breath steady. "Are you trying to decide which question to ask or whether or not you dare ask what's on your mind?"

He picked up the crystal decanter and refilled the glasses. "I count that as two questions out of turn, so that's two shots and two articles of clothing." He handed her the filled glass and held his hand out for whatever she was about to remove.

"That was clearly a single question I asked out of turn, you cheater." She sacrificed a silk stocking.

"Ah," he said. "I need to even this out a bit. Can't leave

you with just one stocking on. "Have you ever made love and reached a climax, Josette?"

She jolted. "Dear heavens, stop it!"

"Have you?"

"Why would that interest you?"

He chuckled. "An out-of-turn question. Since you have yet to answer my question, and you tossed in one of your own, that's either two drinks and two pieces of clothing— and I do believe that would put you somewhere in the vicinity of petticoats or your gown—or you are relieved of one article of clothing while you down another shot of rum, and then give me an honest response to my question."

Lord, not only had she lost count of whose turn it was, she'd lost count of how many shot glasses she'd emptied.

He took a step closer. "What will it be, Josette?"

She removed the other stocking, slapped it in his hand, and replied, "No, I have not."

She forced herself to look up at him, trying to appear bold as ever. "Do you entertain fanciful notions about giving me one?"

Another step forward and he leaned over her, a hand on either armrest, caging her in, his breath hot against her mouth. "Oh, Josette. Even though you are a widow, you know nothing, do you? While I cannot give you an orgasm, what I can do is assist you in getting there."

"Merciful heavens," was all she could manage.

A soft chuckle left his throat. He leaned closer and brushed his lips ever so lightly over hers. "In the best ways I know how."

His strong arms pulled her to her feet and he held her in front of him while he studied her, his lips parted, his breathing erratic and heavy. "You could cause me to do things I might regret, do you know that?"

Her pulsed tripped. "Then let me go."

"I should, shouldn't I?" His gaze slid to her lips, and

while he spoke, his head dipped lower. "A taste," he murmured. "Just one."

His mouth, warm, supple, and flavored with rum, covered hers. Her knees turned to jelly and folded. One hand slid around her waist, fingers spread over the curve of her hip. Holding her upright, he pulled her closer until an unmistakable hard length pressed against her belly. With his other hand, he nudged her chin. "Open up for me, Josette."

The kiss deepened and she moaned. His tongue touched hers. Tentatively, she touched his back and this time the moan came from him, deep and guttural. Lord, she'd never been kissed like this. Never knew a mouth on hers could light a fire in her soul.

She had to stop this.

Had to push him away.

Her hands found the hard planes of his bare chest. His skin, so smooth against iron-clad muscle, rippled beneath her fingers. Glorious didn't begin to describe his body after all. God help her.

His gentle kiss turned hot and greedy, and his arms tightened around her. One hand cupped her buttocks and pulled her into him. These weren't the hands of a bumbling old man; these were practiced hands belonging to a man who knew where and how to touch.

"This is insanity," she whispered against his mouth and gave him a push. "We have a young girl to see to and I don't even think I like you."

"You're right." But he didn't let her go. Instead, his mouth traced her earlobe and she shivered. He groaned. "Why can't I keep my hands off you?"

"You're drunk."

He stepped back. Humor traced fine lines at the corners of his eyes. "Indeed, and jolly well glad of it. But I'm clear-headed enough to know that you're right. Not only is my daughter asleep upstairs, but you've relatives there as well.

So unfortunately, the game needs to end here, and I will bid you good night."

He moved to the sofa with a bit of a weave in his step and slipped into his shoes, then dressed as though he might have risen from her bed after a round of lovemaking. He tucked his cravat into his pocket and left the top of his shirt open. A dusting of dark hair peeked over the top of the fabric. "I apologize."

She tore her gaze from his shirt and gave him her back. "No need, I agreed to the game."

"That's not what I'm apologizing for."

Puzzled, she turned back to face him. "What then?"

He walked over to where she stood, studied her for what felt an eternity. Then his hand slid behind her neck and, leaning down, he brushed his lips lightly across hers. "You'll find out soon enough."

Cameron practically stumbled down the slick stairs leading to the wooden banquette beyond the house. When had it rained? The full moon lit a watery path to the tree-lined street, which he had a little trouble navigating in a straight line.

God in heaven, what had he been up to tonight? Josette would probably come looking for him when she found out he'd already known her brother had stolen the rum. Still, he chuckled to himself at getting caught in his own game. He rubbed at the back of his neck. What had he been thinking? He hadn't been thinking, only reacting. If it hadn't been for his daughter in a bedroom above stairs, who knew how far he'd have gone? Soul shattering, that's how Josette had felt in his arms.

His body ached and had yet to relieve itself of an erection that actually pained him. He weaved into a tree and cursed, as though it were the tree that'd gotten in the way and owed him an apology. He kicked at it, only to stagger back a few feet. Now more than his cock hurt. What the devil was he going to do? It had been over two years since he'd lost his wife and since he'd made love. He'd been dead inside for so long, he'd not given thought to anything sexual.

Until Josette.

Now his chest hurt. He rubbed at it. Damn it to hell. He wanted back the man he'd once been—filled with a lust for life and feasting on happiness. If it took sailing the seas until he found joy once again, that's what he'd do. And he couldn't set out too soon.

He had no idea how far he'd walked or where, but suddenly, there he stood, before Madame Olympée's front entrance, staring at the gaslights flanking the double doors. He heard his own snort. He'd been here so many times in his youth, all it took was too much alcohol and a hard cock and it pointed to his true north . . . a whorehouse. He couldn't do it. Sauced as he was, he couldn't bring himself to set foot inside.

A figure emerged from the shadows. "I used to stand in front of LaFleur's Sweet Shoppe in my youth, just like you be doin' now, lookin' for something I couldn't have because I had me no money. But you, Monsieur Andrews, you can have whatever's inside this fine establishment. All it takes is the coin in your pocket. And I hear you have plenty of that."

Cameron didn't bother looking the man's way. "Well, if it isn't Bastièn goddamn Thibodeaux."

Bastièn snorted. "You had yourself a real good time tonight, *oui*? Maybe too good, since you don't seem to be holdin' yourself any too steady."

Cameron tilted his head and tried to focus on Thibodeaux. "If I wasn't so bloody foxed, I'd beat the living hell out of you, just to top off my evening."

Bastièn laughed. "Oh, we'll be comin' to that sooner or

later if you cross a particular line I mentioned regarding my sister."

"Bugger off." Cameron turned and headed for Royal Street and his town house.

Once inside, he climbed the stairs in the dark. He tripped once and nearly fell, muttering to himself that he'd not drink so much again. After stumbling into his room, he lit the candle on the mantel and kicked off his shoes. He managed to remove his jacket, but that was as far as he got. To hell with it, he'd sleep in his clothes.

He headed for the bed and halted. On his pillow lay a voodoo doll. A chill ran the length of him and he sobered. Who the hell had been in his house? He picked the thing up and another chill skittered through him. A red heart had been patched onto the doll's chest with a needle run through it and red strings hanging from it like dripping blood. He gave a shudder at the sight of a circle of five needles protruding from the doll's crotch.

"Bloody hell."

Chapter Eleven

The old backyard rooster crowed, and from habit, Josette rolled out of bed. When her feet hit the cream and pale blue Chinese carpet, the room swayed.

"Oh, dear."

Head in a whirl, she flopped back onto the mattress and stared at the trompe l'oeil ceiling meant to mimic a morning sky filled with saintly beings. Now, however, the pink-tinged clouds seemed to waver while the angels fanned their wings. And were the little cherubs peeking down at her doing so with a measure of disgust?

She covered her eyes with her hand. Good heavens, how much had she imbibed to end up in such a pitiful state? Wasn't downing a good amount of water before retiring supposed to prevent this? After all, her hedonistic brothers swore by the practice after a night of carousing.

Sitting up, she reached for the water pitcher on her night-stand, poured a glassful, and drank it dry. She kicked back the blue counterpane, pulled a matching oversized pillow to her side, and curled up against the down-filled bolster as if it were a comforting body.

Her fingers splayed against the fabric, only to have the action remind her of how she'd pressed her hand against

Cameron's bare, muscled chest. Memories of the night before slammed into her with a force that made her moan—the hard planes of his body, so intimate against hers, his mouth covering hers, his tongue delving . . .

And—her breath caught—that sinful game.

What had possessed her to allow such a dangerous activity? Oh, but it had been a heady sport, one that could easily have become a prelude to greater immoralities had she not had the wherewithal to stop him.

What would it be like to lie night after night beside a man such as Cameron Andrews? To be held in his strong, sure arms while he made love to her in ways that would surely set her on fire? The man knew things, dangerous things that had likely stolen more than one woman's will. And he was bound to steal a few more before he left this earth.

She'd been nearly undone by the way he'd kissed her, the way he'd held her, the way his throaty words had simmered with a kind of potency that filled her with a desperate want from heart to womb. Knots of confusion tangled with the heat in her belly and the loneliness in her heart.

It had been one kiss.

Nothing more.

But oh, to the girl who'd loved him in her youth, then despised him after he'd taken up with Solange, the kiss had been an oasis to a parched soul. The young lad she'd once imagined as a prince rescuing her from life in the bayou had returned, a stunning, virile man who'd held her in his arms and kissed her senseless mere hours ago. While the taste of him was likely imprinted on her soul forevermore, he'd probably not give the incident a second thought. What memory had she given him in return? Inexperience so pitiful she didn't even know how to press her lips to a man's.

Her stomach lurched at the miserable idea that she'd been someone's wife but knew nothing about something as simple as a kiss. Her husband, a plump, shy man, had been her only lover, if one could even call him that. He'd showered her with all the finery money could buy, seen to her every comfort. But although he'd been desperate for an heir, no amount of herbs or voodoo spells her mother invoked could keep his flaccid organ stiff enough to do fathering justice.

Guilt flooded her chest. She would cast no aspersions upon a good man's soul by entertaining such thoughts. He'd been a kindly person, and she'd done all she could to see he'd not been humiliated, but the day had come when he'd quietly moved his things to a room down the hall. He'd told her the master chamber was hers to arrange as she pleased, and so, to try to alleviate her sense of being an orphan once again, she'd redecorated the room in shades of pale blue fluff—curtains, walls, chairs—as it remained to this day.

Even though their friendship had endured, and he'd continued to pamper her, she'd gone to bed each night feeling wretchedly alone. Then came that terrible morning when she'd awoken to the rooster's crow and made her way to his room for their usual shared breakfast, only to find he'd passed away during the night. Her loneliness had plunged to new depths after the funeral, when his friends shunned her.

Vivienne had come to live with her then, as had Régine. Her brothers had stopped by as well, bringing adorable Alexia along. But not Maman. Never Maman. Why she openly resented Josette was still something no one had figured out. Perhaps it was because Josette, being the youngest, was the final burden as Vivienne and Lucien joined the household, as well. All without a man around. Josette had somehow gleaned from a very young age that one did not question the whereabouts of their father. All she knew was that she, Solange, and her brothers belonged to one man only.

Old heartache mingled with the new. She punched the pillow, wiped away a tear that threatened to spill, and, feeling less dizzy, removed herself from the bed. She wandered to the balcony overlooking her beloved gardens. She'd remain at home today and labor in her backyard—that's what she'd do. Pulling roots and digging in the dirt until she dropped into bed exhausted could work miracles when it came to fixing a low mood. After that, she'd think about redecorating her chamber, getting rid of all this blue. Yellow, that would be a good color. Like the roses in her garden. She'd leave the ceiling looking like the sky, though. It made her room feel less like a suffocating coffin.

Turning with a heavy sigh, she made her way to the wardrobe, where she donned a simple sprigged cotton gardening dress with a skirt that rose above the ankles in order to keep her hem dry. Vivienne could take Alexia to Cameron's office. Josette would send a note along to be delivered to Belle Femme informing the girls she wouldn't be in today. Or the next, as a matter of fact. Why not take Vivienne, Régine, and Alexia into the bayou tomorrow to gather the roots Josette couldn't manage to grow out back? That should keep her well away from Cameron.

Leaving her room, she paused midway down the stairs. There was no mistaking Alexia's cheery laughter, but it mixed with a deep male voice. Pray don't let it be Cameron. But who else could it be since her brothers never rose so early? Her heart jumped into her throat. Alexia's father was the last man she wanted to face this morning.

When she reached the bottom of the stairs, Vivienne met her, hands wringing and brow creased. "What's wrong?"

"I told him no, Josette. He knows he's not allowed in your home."

"Dear God. Don't tell me it's your brother's voice I hear?"

"Believe me, I tried—"

Josette waved a hand in dismissal. "It's not your fault. Please, stay with Régine while I set Lucien straight."

Another round of light laughter mixed with a low chuckle, and fury burned in Josette's veins. She marched down the hall, but when she spied the parlor doors closed, she took off at a run. How dare the monster!

Flinging the doors wide, she spied Alexia leaning over the back of the sofa where Lucien sat. Josette descended upon him like a madwoman. "You . . . you leave here at once. Alexia, go to the kitchen for your breakfast."

"I done ate."

"Then see if Vivienne needs anything." She couldn't bring herself to mention Régine's name in front of the man. Régine still refused to speak of what had occurred that long ago day when she'd gone crawdad hunting with Lucien. He'd shown up hours later, alone, and with scratches on his smug face. From then on, Régine had refused further visits to her cousins in the bayou, and had withdrawn into her own world, distrusting all men. Lucien was pure evil. Even his sister was certain he was dangerous.

A lazy grin spread over Lucien's face. "Alexia and me, we be going to the bayou for a bit, *oui*?" He gave Alexia a wink. "I got newborn pups she be beggin' to see."

The blood that had heated in Josette's veins only moments ago turned to ice. Had he actually thought to entice Alexia away? Steal her out of the house right under their noses? Did Alexia not have a lick of sense?

"Alexia," Josette said through her teeth. "You'll be off to your father's workplace this morning, but if you don't take yourself to the kitchen this minute and stay there until I collect you, then you shall spend the next two days locked in your room."

A great frown settled upon Alexia. Nonetheless, she headed for the door. "*Au revoir*, Uncle Lucien."

Josette clenched her teeth together so tight, her jaw twitched. "He's your cousin twice removed, Alexia, not your uncle. Good uncles respect their nieces, recalcitrant distant cousins do not. Remember that."

With Alexia out of sight, Josette bore down on Lucien

again. "So help me God, if you ever set foot in this house again, or if you ever come near Alexia, I will shoot you."

Lucien pulled the faceted stopper out of the crystal decanter and held it up to the light streaming through the open window. He shoved his dark hair aside and, closing one eye and squinting with the other, twisted the stopper about, sending rainbows dancing around the room. "You mean to frighten me, *ma chère*?"

What possessed him to actually enter her home when she'd managed to avoid him for years? He knew full well he was to stay far away from her and Régine. But now he had his eye on Alexia, and the danger was even greater.

Lucien stretched a long, lanky leg out in front of him and tossed the decanter top from one hand to the other. "Alexia told you she be learning to make the moonshine, *oui*? That was to be our little secret."

So, Alexia had opened her big mouth, which was likely his reason for drawing so close, to tell her to keep it shut. "And that activity ceases as well, Lucien." Purchasing bullets for the pistol in her desk drawer no longer seemed a fantasy. She'd see to getting them tomorrow. "Leave my home now."

"Or what, Josette? You toss me out?" He laughed and took a swig of what was left of the rum. "This be some fine libation, cousin. Where you be gettin' it?"

"Where my sister obtains anything is of no concern to you," came a low, almost casual-sounding response. "Now do as she says and get out, or I will break every bone in your body."

Josette whirled and found René leaning casually against the doorjamb, as was his usual habit, but she knew him well. His body was as tight as a bayou cat ready to pounce. His dark eyes flashed an ominous warning at Lucien.

Her mouth dropped open. René was dressed in a proper suit of clothing. Custom-made, by the looks of it, and just as fine a fit as the suits Cameron wore. "What are you doing here?"

He gave a nod Lucien's way. "Rescuing you and my niece from *him*."

Lucien gave René a sneer and rose from the sofa with the air of someone who had all day. "I do believe the door is blocked, cousin, unless you would like me to climb out the same window I crawled through."

René stepped into the room, and Lucien strolled past, to the front door Vivienne held open.

Once he'd gone, Josette slammed shut the parlor door and gave her brother a shove. "You . . . you . . . you scalawag. You . . . you devil's servant."

René spread his arms wide in a defenseless gesture. "Why was I expecting a thank-you and not name calling? What's the matter, *ma soeur*?"

"You made an utter fool out of me with your thieving, that's what's wrong. Why didn't you tell me that rum was stolen? Why did you put me in a position—"

"You never asked me where it came from." He strolled over to the sofa, picked up the crystal stopper Lucien had left there, and replaced it on the decanter.

She looked him up and down. He'd always had a certain masculine assuredness about him, but now, in that fine suit of clothing, he appeared sleek and refined. And even more handsome. Which somehow made him all the more dangerous. "I suppose you stole those clothes as well."

He laughed. "*Non.* I had them made."

"When and what for?"

"Did I not tell you when you visited Maman that I was about to become employed?"

"Yes, but you always have something or other up your sleeve that never pans out, so what is going on that has you purchasing tailored clothing of the finest cut?" She ran a hand over her brow, as if the action would soothe her temper. "What are you up to, René?"

"I have permanent employment. Of the best kind. And I intend to keep it."

"Doing what?"

A grin slid from one corner of his mouth to the other. "Working for Alexia's papa, don'cha know."

It took a moment for his words to sink in. "You . . . you are employed by Cameron Andrews?"

"*Oui.*"

She stared at him while his bizarre words dizzied her. "Since when?"

"Beginning today, so I can't stay long, but I could use some breakfast. Is Régine up and about?"

The ramifications of his words sank in. "When did you have those clothes made?"

"When I heard the shipping company was bringing Gosling Brothers rum to New Orleans. That's when I decided there'd soon be some thieving going on. But should Michel Andrews employ me, the thieving would cease."

"So you had the whole thing planned before the ship ever landed in port?"

He shrugged. "Something like that. Didn't expect Alexia's papa would be doing the hiring, though."

"When did he do so?"

"Yesterday."

Rage poured through every inch of her, even her bones. "Did he hire you in the morning or in the middle of the night?"

René studied her through narrowed eyes. "Why would you think it would take place in the middle of the night?"

Cameron had known all this before he set foot through her door. Why, that deceitful, game-playing vermin. "And you are on your way to his place of business now? Is that why you stopped by, to show me your new uniform and tell me that you'd found decent employment?"

A moment passed while René studied the toes of his new shoes as if he'd suddenly gone shy. "*Oui.*"

"Then when you get there, please tell Mister Andrews I would like to see him. No, don't tell him I would *like* to. You tell him you have orders to see that he gets here. And take Alexia with you. You can look after her while he meets with me."

René shoved his hands in his trouser pockets. "Impossible. I have a job to do."

She planted her fists on her hips and went nose to nose with him. "Well, so do I, René. So do I."

His demeanor shifted, and he took on that fatherly look that, at her age, she despised. "What happened between the two of you when he was here last night?"

She folded her arms over her chest. "Nothing happened. And who told you he was here?"

"Bastièn informed me." Those assessing eyes of René's held steady on hers. "If nothing went on, then why are you so upset? Did he diddle with you like he did Solange?"

She could feel the heat run right up her cheeks. "That crude remark does not deserve an answer. And Bastièn needs to mind his own business."

"Ah, *chère*, by the looks of who I chased out of here this morning, I might need to watch over you myself." He reached into his pocket and withdrew a calling card. "I found this tucked in your door. What's this man doing here?"

Puzzled, Josette took the card. Vennard! Her stomach did a somersault. Why would he contact her at home? Her day was getting worse by the minute. "I don't know, René. I don't know."

"He's a married man with a grown daughter getting married today. You been messin' with him?"

"Don't be vulgar. I am not *messing* with anyone. For heaven's sake, his wife is my best customer."

"Then perhaps I should call on your Monsieur Vennard and learn of his purpose for the visit to your private residence, *oui*?"

"*Non*." Good Lord, she couldn't let René get within reach of Vennard. She had to think of something. "His daughter has been visiting the shop, as well. Since it's to be her wedding day, he might be seeking me out for something having to do with that. I am a businesswoman, in case you've forgotten. Even though Madame Vennard can be rude, and her daughter quite arrogant, they are my best customers, so don't go mucking things up."

He continued to study her through narrowed eyes. "As you wish."

Oh, she couldn't take much more. "Then see yourself out. I need my privacy. And take Alexia with you to the shipping company, and don't forget to inform her father I wish to see him at once."

Eyes flashing fire, René turned on his heel and headed for the kitchen. "I will do as you ask. But don't you forget who Alexia's papa is and who her *maman* was, and how those two came to be together."

Josette closed the parlor door and sat on the sofa Lucien had vacated. What the devil had gone wrong with her life?

Chapter Twelve

Cameron reached the shipping office at the same time as the errand boy. "Morning, Henri."

"A good day to you, monsieur. The *Dianah* sails for England on the next tide." He waved a sheaf of papers in his hand. "Everything's in fine order."

Cameron glanced over the boy's shoulder at the clipper floating heavy in the water. Sailors scurried every which way, readying for departure while the captain leaned against the ship's railing overlooking the whirlwind of activity.

Common sense told Cameron it was merely a vessel with a name painted on it, but his heart said otherwise. He and Dianah had given the beauty a second christening after its arrival in San Francisco. They'd taken the clipper to sea for a week—the devil with the cost—and sailed up and down the California and Oregon Territory coastline without a care in the world. At the memory, the band around his chest cinched tighter.

"Anything amiss, monsieur?"

Cameron pulled his mind out of the past and focused on the boy. "I was merely noting all the activity. There's always a bit of excitement at a time like this, isn't there?" He made to step through the door, but paused. "I'll take the papers to

Abbott. You go on back to Captain Croxton and tell him I'd like a quick walk-through before he sets sail."

Shaking off the odd impact the *Dianah's* imminent departure had on him, Cameron strode into the office and, bidding Abbott and Michel a good morning, set the bills of lading on Abbott's desk. "Any rum go missing last night?"

Michel leaned back in his chair and clasped his hands behind his head. "Not a drop."

Cameron grunted. "Fancy that."

"What do you have in mind regarding that questionable relative of yours?" Michel asked.

"Questionable relative? If you value your neck, cousin, you will never again refer to René as having any connection to me. As for his employment, how about we send him on a training voyage somewhere out to sea?"

Michel laughed. "A good long journey ought to give him a decent education in the business of shipping. China perhaps?"

"There's a thought." At the sound of a light rapping on the open door, Cameron turned. A dark-haired beauty stepped over the threshold, her pale yellow gown hugging voluptuous curves.

Michel jumped to his feet. "Felicité! Where the devil did you come from?"

His sister laughed and threw her arms around him. "From upriver. Weren't we born and raised there?"

Cameron squinted. "Felicité, is that you?"

"Cameron!" She pushed away from Michel and gave Cameron a hug, dropping a kiss on each cheek. "Why, I haven't laid eyes on you since Trevor shot you. He said you gave up the San Francisco office and sailed to China. What happened?"

Merde. "Obviously, I am not in the Orient, as you can well see."

Unwinding her hold on him, Cameron set her at arm's

length and looked her over. "I never would have recognized you as that same skinny girl of sixteen who used to follow me around and drive me to Bedlam. Too bad your manner of speaking hasn't changed along with the rest of you."

Dimples creased her cheeks and she did a slow pirouette. "I'll be twenty-one next month. You used to call me skinny ninny. Can you still say the same?"

Cameron grinned as the old urge to tease crept in. "I can leave out the skinny, but as for the ninny part, that remains to be seen."

Michel intervened. "Hold on, Felice. I knew you were on your way here from England, but how did you land at Father's and not here first?"

"I sailed to Boston, conducted some business for Trevor regarding the completion of a new ship, and then, rather than catch a clipper to New Orleans, I decided to take a train to the Mississippi, then a steamboat downriver to Papa."

"Why a train?" Cameron asked.

She shrugged. "Other than short jaunts in Europe, I've not traveled on one before. However, I do intend to sail back to England from here. One journey by rail was enough to convince me of the luxury of traveling on the Andrews shipping line."

Abbott introduced himself, and Michel asked where she was staying in the city and for how long.

She gave her brother a patronizing smile. "Why, I'm staying with you, Michel. Your butler let me in so my things are already in the guest room. Lovely home, by the way. I didn't know you had such good taste."

She turned to Cameron. "The years have been good to you. You resemble Trevor even more. The two of you appear more like brothers than do he and Michel."

Cameron laid a hand over his heart. "And hard as it is for me to admit, you've changed from a gangly young filly into a beautiful woman." A private memory took hold of Cameron. "You look like your mother, only taller."

"Which means I also look like *your* mother since they were sisters." Felicité's voice softened. "You miss her still?"

"Of course," Cameron responded. "How long will you be staying?"

"In New Orleans? Not long. I simply cannot pass up a visit to Madame Charmontès, so I'm here for a few days while I choose some designs, then I need to get back to Papa."

She turned to Michel. "Trevor sent me to try to talk Papa into selling the plantation since he won't pay you or Trevor any heed. If Papa agrees, I'll remain until everything is in order and take him back to England with me. If not, I'll stay with him about a month. I do miss England, along with its convenience to Paris."

Addressing Cameron, she said, "Our brother is still convinced there's trouble brewing between the North and South, and he wants Father safely in England. Do go see Papa, Cameron."

"I intend to."

"Good, and take Michel with you. Papa will like that. I'm afraid he's quite lonely, although he won't admit it."

Michel rolled his eyes. "You're not here five minutes and already you're ordering everyone around."

Alexia rushed through the door. "*Bonjour*, everyone. *Bonjour,* Monsieur Abbott!"

Abbott set his pen down and frowned. "Am I not considered a part of the *everyone* group, you little curmudgeon?"

Eyes wide, Alexia stumbled to a halt in front of Felicité. "You're almost as pretty as *ma tante*." She shot a wary glance back and forth between Cameron and Felicité. "Who you be?"

Felicité smiled at the girl. "I'm Monsieur Michel Andrew's sister. And who are you?"

Relief flooded Alexia's countenance. She puffed up her

chest and struck at it with her thumb. "I be Alexia Thibodeaux. Or mayhap Alexia Thibodeaux Andrews. I don't rightly know."

She turned to Cameron, her Cajun patois growing thicker with every word. "What I be, Papa?"

Felicité made a slow turn toward Cameron, her eyes glittering, her lips fighting a grin. She raised a brow. "Papa?"

Cameron sidestepped the answer and responded with, "Who brought you?"

"Uncle René. He be looking over the ship about to sail, says it's his job now." She beamed at Felicité. "My uncle and Papa, they work together now. Right nice, don'cha know."

At that, she rushed over to Abbott. "*Ma tante* gave me some coin to take you out for a beignet."

Abbott's bushy brows knitted together. "Why?"

"For causing disruption in your work yesterday. I truly am sorry, Monsieur Abbott. Truly, I am."

Abbott, still frowning, reached into a drawer and withdrew a fresh bottle of India ink and a pen. "Here. Now leave mine alone."

Felicité could have been watching a cricket match for the way her head went from Abbott and Alexia to Cameron and back again. *Papa?* she mouthed at Cameron.

He shot her a menacing look.

She laughed. "Oh, please, do let's have a family dinner at Antoine's this evening. I am simply dying for some conversation with a little punch to it."

Alexia whipped around. "Am I your family, too, mademoiselle? I never been to a fancy place like Antoine's. I only peek in the windows."

Cameron cringed while Michel observed the entire scene in obvious amusement.

Felicité made her way over to where Alexia stood, tapping the point of her parasol on the floor with each deliberate step she took. "Since you are Cameron's daughter, I do believe that would make us first cousins once removed, so certainly you should join us for dinner. How old are you?"

"Thirteen, but I have me a birthday next week."

Felicité touched a gloved finger to her cheek in a feigned moue. "Oh, I have always been so very good at mathematics, Cameron." She turned to Abbott. "If you should require any assistance with . . . ahem . . . addition, feel free to call on me."

"I'm Solange Thibodeaux's daughter if that's what you're getting at," Alexia said while studying the ink label. "She worked at Madame Olympée's and died when I was born, but that was after Papa got shipped off to England, so he didn't know nuthin' about it until a bit ago."

Michel chuckled and sat back in his chair.

Felicité pursed her lips in a futile attempt to hide a smile. "Aren't you the clever one? I have a feeling we're about to become the best of friends."

Alexia shoved the bottle of ink into her pocket and with a tilt of her head, studied Felicité.

Abbott stood and cleared his throat. "Come along, Miss Alexia. Let's see about those beignets."

The moment they were out of sight, Felicité marched over to Cameron. "Don't tell me Alexia's 'Uncle René' happens to be none other than one of the two brothers who nearly beat you and Trevor to—"

"I'll have you know, we didn't go down without a bloody good fight of our own," Cameron interjected. "It seems you haven't changed a bit. Once a ninny, always a ninny."

She laughed. "And now you've hired him, and . . . oh, this is so rich. What a very interesting life you lead, cousin. You're not only a father, but suddenly related to those bad boys from the bayou. Perhaps I won't be leaving New Orleans so soon after all. And since I took an instant liking to Alexia, and since I have learned we are related, perhaps I'll invite her back to the plantation for a spell." She gave an affected bow. "With her father's permission, of course."

At her words, something clicked in Cameron's brain. "Felicité, if you can manage to be serious for a moment, let me give you a few details regarding Alexia, because I think you might be on to something that could solve a rather ticklish problem."

"Oh, dear," Felicité said once Cameron finished telling her the entire story, including Odalie's plans to train Alexia as her successor, the dangers with Lucien, and Alexia's desire to remain in the bayou. The one thing Cameron left out was his growing attraction to Josette, and all that had transpired between them.

"Then see to it Alexia and her aunt join us tonight," she said. "Nothing draws people closer than a warm combination of family and food. I'll see what I can do. Michel, you'll be joining us, of course."

Michel straightened a stack of papers and set a paperweight atop them. "Is that an invitation or a directive, little sister?"

Felicité opened her mouth to say something, but her gaze traveled over Cameron's shoulder toward the doorway, and her breath was abruptly suspended.

He turned.

René stepped into the room. *"Bonjour."*

Merde! Had Cameron not known Thibodeaux and passed him in the street, Cameron would have guessed him to be a successful business owner of some kind. Obviously, the man had no intention of becoming a dock worker. It would seem René had a definite idea as to what his duties were to be, the rotter.

In the few seconds it took René to glance around the room, his gaze landed on Felicité, where it remained.

As did hers on him.

Lightning could have struck inside the office and Cameron doubted it would have created as much electricity as what snapped between René and Felicité.

Christ Almighty.

Michel, pen paused in midair, blanched.

Hell, this was Michel's problem, not Cameron's. Still, she was his cousin, so before Michel could rise from his chair, Cameron intervened. "Felicité, I'd like you to meet our newest employee, Monsieur René Thibodeaux. Monsieur Thibodeaux, meet Mademoiselle Felicité Andrews, Michel's sister, in from England."

René stepped forward, lifted Felicité's gloved hand, and kissed the top, then let it go and took a step back, as if to get a better view. "What a pleasure to meet you."

He turned to Cameron. "I've just come from my sister's home. She insisted I give you a message that she must see you at once." He paused, letting his words sink in. "I'm to look after Alexia, while the two of you talk." A small grin lifted a corner of his mouth. "I should warn you. She's in a temper."

Before Cameron could respond, Alexia bounded through the door, sugar coating the corners of her mouth. "We had beignets, Uncle René."

He grinned down at her, and retrieving a snowy white handkerchief from his breast pocket, swiped it across her mouth. "*Oui*, I can see that, *pouchette*."

Abbott walked past René and, in doing so, gave him a good once-over. "Should I be ordering another desk for the office, Mister Andrews? And isn't the day getting more interesting by the moment?"

Cameron shook his head. "Since I'm only here temporarily, there'll be no need." Besides, the damn fool probably wouldn't last a week. He'd likely fare better working alongside Bastièn. At least Michel wouldn't be there to skin him alive.

Michel sent a speaking glance to Cameron. "When you have a minute, I'd like to revisit our previous discussion regarding that certain shipment to China."

Cameron fought a grin and glanced at René, who now leaned a hip against the center table, crossing his arms and making no attempt to hide his study of Felicité.

Michel scowled at him.

Felicité glanced from Michel to René. Her cheeks were pink. She turned to Alexia. "I've an appointment with Madame Charmontès and then I'm off to lunch. Would you care to join me, or would you rather sit around in this stuffy office listening to men discuss shipping business?"

Alexia wrinkled her nose. "Except for the cat, nothing much interests me here."

"Good, then let's be off." She lifted a hand to adjust her hat, and paled. "Oh, no. My bracelet. It's gone—"

"Alexia!" Cameron and René shouted at the same time. Both stepped forward. One glance at Cameron and René went back to leaning against the table.

"Get over here," Cameron growled.

Alexia laughed and, lifting her wrist up for all to see the pearl and diamond bracelet, went instead to stand in front of Felicité. Alexia held her arm out to her.

Instead of erupting in a fit of anger, Felicité removed the bracelet and handed it to Alexia, before holding her own wrist out. "Put it on me, if you please. And do tell me how you managed that little trick. You must give me lessons."

Cameron grunted. "I do not think that a wise idea, Felicité."

She turned to Cameron and, with her back to Alexia, narrowed her eyes as if to send the message that she knew full well what she was about. "I'm off to mind my own business now. Come, Alexia."

René stepped forward. "I'll escort the two of you to Madame Charmontès."

Michel stood. "I think they can make their way safely down the street in broad daylight."

"Ah, but I am to look after Alexia while Cameron meets

with my sister. The fact that your sister happens to be along is not of my doing." René turned and presented his arm to Felicité.

She tucked her hand through the crook of his elbow. "How kind of you. See you this evening, Michel?"

As the three stepped through the doorway, René asked Felicité how long she planned to remain in New Orleans.

"I don't rightly know, Monsieur Thibodeaux. My plans seem to be changing by the minute."

"Please, call me René."

As soon as they were out of earshot, Michel let loose a mouthful of curses.

Cameron laughed. "Was that the cat growling?"

"What the devil are we going to do with him, Cam? I thought we'd have a stevedore train him on the docks."

Cameron shrugged. "Apparently, Thibodeaux is serious about becoming a part of our enterprise. As much as I dislike him, he's clever and intelligent. Given a chance, he may turn out to be just the man to replace Joshua Cooper. Either that or we can bring Cooper back here and send René to San Francisco, where he'll freeze his Southern balls off. That ought to take care of any worries you might have regarding your sister, twice over."

Michel grunted. "Aren't you the genius?"

"What was it someone recently said to me? Oh, yes. 'Didn't your day just take on a new glow? No rut for you.'"

"Go to the devil."

"Ah, that reminds me of something else you recently said. Let's see, what was it? Oh, yes. 'Doesn't life have a way of offering up the most interesting of surprises?'"

Michel tossed his pen down and, grabbing his jacket, headed for the door. "I'm following the bastard."

Chapter Thirteen

Cameron leaned against a sun-bleached dray parked along the dock and stacked high with cotton bales, his gaze fixed on the clipper *Dianah*. The last-minute discovery that cargo had yet to arrive from upriver—made because René had been sifting through paperwork, no less—had set the ship's departure back a good two days.

"She's quite the beauty, isn't she, sir?" Croxton removed his hat long enough to take a swipe at his damp brow.

"Indeed. You must be gnawing at the bit to get her into deep waters, Captain."

"That I am." With watchful eyes on the ship's activities, Croxton propped himself against the cart beside Cameron. "You've got quite the daughter, sir."

Cameron grunted. "She's only been here for a few days, yet everyone in and out of the office seems to know who she is."

"This isn't the first time I've seen her. She's hung around the docks on several of my trips here. Clever girl. Tried to sell me a mouser for the ship this morning."

"Not a black feline with a white-tipped tail by any chance?"

Croxton nodded. "Mmm. Abbott's cat."

Merde. "She'd have pocketed the coin, then stolen the blasted thing back before you had the anchor raised. She's attached to the little beast."

"But not above making a profit off it?"

Cameron shifted his stance. "You didn't climb off that ship just to tell me I have a shrewd daughter, did you?"

"Don't reckon I did, sir." Croxton paused long enough to signal to a sailor holding a fistful of rope. "When I reach Liverpool, do you want me to ask Trevor about changing this vessel's name?"

"No."

Croxton gave a brief nod. "I was a widower for two years. I know what losing someone special feels like. I remarried recently. This Missus Croxton doesn't take the place of the former, wasn't meant to, but she sure as heck managed to heal the hole in my heart. I don't love her any less than my first wife, just different."

"What are you trying to tell me?"

"That there's a limit to the amount of grieving a person can do. You shouldn't feel guilty about giving it up. I can remember when you laughed a lot and made others laugh along with you. I'd like to see that again."

"I'm getting there."

They stood in silence a while longer. Finally, Croxton heaved a breath and stepped away from the dray. "I suppose it's time I saw to my job lest I lose it."

He headed for the ship, then halted. "One thing I learned when I lost my Beatrice is that we're all given a blank book of life. When all's said and done, sir, you're the only one who can fill those pages with memories worth looking back on in your winter years."

Croxton's words hit Cameron like a punch to the gut. God, he wanted to be aboard a ship. He wanted nothing more than to glide across the seas to nowhere, stumble across an adventure or two. Most of all, he wanted to disappear until he managed to lift that blasted anvil off his chest once and for all. He'd grown damn sick of it weighing him down.

He wandered off the dock. Where to? One look at the shipping office with its door standing open, and he sure as hell didn't care to venture inside, not with René and Michel hammering out René's duties. Nor did he want to go home and listen to the echoes of his own footsteps. Alexia was still off somewhere with Felicité, which meant there was only one other place where things had been left undone today.

According to René, Josette was mad as a hornet, but Cameron had expected no less, and that was for the good. Her ill temper would serve to keep him at a distance.

No touching allowed.

And for God's sake, no repeating what had gone on last night. If his plans worked out, he'd be gone in less than a fortnight. Until then, he'd make certain any contact with Josette would be strictly held to the subject of Alexia, with Vivienne present.

When he reached Josette's front steps, the door opened. Vivienne and Régine, hats on their heads and parasols in hand, stepped onto the wide veranda. Both frowned at him.

"Ladies."

"We're on our way to the fish market for the late-day catch," Vivienne said. "Madame LeBlanc is in the gardens out back. Would you like me to announce you?" Despite Vivienne's perfunctory offer, she was obviously not inclined to do any such thing.

"No need, I'll come back another time."

He turned to leave. Oh hell, he still had to inform Josette about that bloody dinner at Antoine's tonight. Since Alexia's fate had been decided this afternoon, and without her knowledge, Josette definitely needed to be present to help convince his daughter of what was best for her.

There went his decision not to meet with Josette alone. But Vivienne said she was out of doors. What could possibly occur so long as he kept well away from her? "I have to give Madame LeBlanc a quick message. I can see you're in a bit of a hurry, so I'll pass it along and be on my way. Out back, you say?"

While Régine remained stoic in her usual silence, a look of relief swept over Vivienne. She nodded. "As you wish, but please lock the door after entering. We've had some unannounced visitors today."

"Do tell."

Vivienne hesitated, then said, "Madame LeBlanc's brother, René, for one, which left madame in a prickly mood." She gave Cameron a look that suggested she might know something about what had gone on last night.

Who else had shown up unannounced? An odd current passed through Cameron. Vivienne's thinned lips kept him from inquiring, so instead, he offered up a pleasant smile. "I fear Madame LeBlanc's foul mood might have something to do with me, so if you'll pardon me, I'll apologize while I'm at it."

He should have regrets for instigating that lusty drinking game. He really should. At least he'd see to it that it never happened again. However, devil take it, he'd not had such a rousing good time in months. No, not in nearly three years—which felt like decades. Suddenly, revitalizing energy shot through him. "Buck up, Vivienne. Your cousin could use a little shake-up in her routines every now and then."

While Régine looked askance, Vivienne flipped open her parasol and gave Cameron a sidelong glance. "I couldn't have said it better myself. You'll find the back door straight down the corridor after you turn off the main one. Good afternoon."

Now there was a response he hadn't expected.

Entering the house, he turned the lock behind him. Despite the vanishing daylight through the windows, the noiseless interior gave him pause. Silent as a cemetery at midnight, it was. A feeling that he'd trespassed snaked along the back of his neck. Well, what was done was done. He was here to discuss Alexia's future, inform Josette about dinner, and depart. He strode to the rear entrance, his boot heels clicking along the wide corridor.

Once on the veranda, he halted in stunned fascination. Whatever he'd expected, this wasn't it. A radiant display of flowers, vines, and all manner of greenery dazzled him. Was all this Josette's planning? The Tuileries would have a hard time competing with this splendor.

He stepped off the stairs and onto a cobbled path edged with a swath of colorful blossoms ranging from short-stalked jewels in the front to waist-high at the rear. He hadn't a clue what they all were, but as he soaked in the intriguing scents, his mood elevated.

The stone path veered in several directions. He wandered about, searching for Josette. He'd be damned if he'd call out to her.

The place was like a painting come to life. Ironwork benches curved around stately oaks; a swing hung from the overhead branch of a graceful magnolia tree. And there she was, wearing an oversized floppy hat and gardening gloves, bent over a row of something or other, pulling what he assumed were weeds and tossing them into a basket.

He stood there as if mesmerized, watching her toil. The late-afternoon sun shone at an angle, shaping the outline of her slender body against a thin layer of fabric with not much beneath it. The sight came as a seductive jolt to his senses, and his body rebelled against any determination to remain detached. What he wouldn't do to rush over, grab her in his arms, hug the hell out of her, then find some cozy spot and lay her down. Strip them both bare.

Damn it, this kind of madcap thinking had to cease. Wasn't it enough he'd tossed and turned the night through, imagining the impossible with her?

Not trusting his runaway impulses, he remained in place, willing his flesh to listen to reason until he felt in control once again. He stepped forward, his heel sounding against stone.

She glanced up, her forearm passing over her brow as if to wipe away perspiration.

His mood soared even higher. He grinned, as if doing so might make amends for the prurient thoughts warming his blood.

Slowly, she rose. "How long have you been spying on me?"

"I don't know, a month?"

Her brows knitted, and he swore flames shot out her eyes. She charged, waving some kind of gardening tool at him, her hat flying off her head, hair spilling about her shoulders. "Why, you miserable, lying cur. You knew damn well it was René who stole your filthy rum. Leave my home this minute."

Christ, he shouldn't laugh. The sight of her, barefooted, breathing fire, and barreling down on him as if he didn't outweigh her by a good ninety pounds had him wanting to kiss her senseless. His groin tightened. That wouldn't do. Not at all.

"In case you were too sauced to recall, I apologized last night."

She threw the tool at him.

He sidestepped.

It whizzed past his ear and landed with a *clank* on the cobblestones behind him.

"You're angry."

"You noticed?"

"Hard not to."

She yanked off her gloves and threw those at him. One missed, the other landed square on his chest, then fell to his feet.

He backed off, hands held up in surrender, but he couldn't help the grin that managed to escape. "Think, Josette. I never lied to you. I merely asked you to tell me who brought you the rum. I wanted to hear it from your lips."

The shift in her expression was as easy to read as a daily newspaper. She'd just gone from angry to hopping mad.

Sputtering, she came at him again, set her hands on his chest and pushed. "Out!"

He clasped her wrists and held her in front of him. She stared at him, unspoken thoughts churning behind her widened gaze.

Those eyes.

The expression in them held an odd familiarity. Some memory in the recesses of his mind crept forward, only to slink back and disappear.

She blinked and tried to pull away. When he continued to hold her firm, her eyes widened once more.

There it was again—that look that gave him pause. "Stop, Josette. Whatever you were thinking just then, think it again."

Puzzlement filled her countenance. She tried to wiggle her hands free, but he held tight. "No, don't. That's the third time I've had this strange feeling I knew you from before. Last night, during our game, I asked if you'd known me previously, and you said yes. Tell me."

She looked away. "I don't have a clue what you mean."

"Now you're the liar." *Merde*. He should let her go and get the hell out of here. He wanted her. Not just sexually. Oh, he wanted that part, there was no denying it anymore, but he wanted to touch her. He wanted to slide his arms around her and hold on tight. For a long, long while.

"Look at me."

She turned her cheek to him. "Let me go. You do not have the right."

He released her and, heaving a frustrated breath, shoved at the hank of hair that had fallen over his forehead. "You're right, and I do beg your pardon."

This wouldn't do. He had to cool off, put his mind to

what he'd come here for. He walked over to where her hat hung at an odd angle off a bush, gathered it up along with the gardening tool and gloves she'd tossed at him, and handed them to her. "I came about Alexia. I've figured out what's to be done with her."

"Which is?"

He studied Josette for a moment. "Walk with me while we talk. Show me your gardens."

Gone was the expression he couldn't place. Expression— of what? Fright filled with defiance? Whatever it was, not a trace remained.

She folded her arms over her chest and tapped her foot on the ground. "No more lies?"

He glanced down. He wished she wouldn't do that . . . draw attention to her bare toes. Cute little toes. He could massage those dainty feet and make her swoon. Damn it, there went his blasted groin twitching again.

"I told you I didn't lie. I am also not a man who makes excuses, so I won't tell you that I'd already had too much to drink before I arrived. Nor will I tell you that I drank more wine than I should have during dinner. I won't even tell you that I likely did so because when I am anywhere in the vicin- ity of Madame LeBlanc, I have trouble keeping my hands off the lady. Deuced wicked of me, isn't it?"

Her foot stopped tapping. Her cheeks flushed. She dropped her arms to her sides and her mouth opened as if to say something. Seeming to change her mind, she clamped it shut for a beat, then said, "Put my things on that bench over there and come along. I need to hear what you are up to with my niece."

He dropped the handful of her belongings on the nearby wrought-iron settee and matched her slow pace, clasping his hands behind his back, mostly to refrain from touching her again. They passed the wicker basket she'd been filling when he'd spied her. "Why do you toss weeds in there and not use them for mulch?"

"Those happen to be licorice roots, not weeds. I use them for healing purposes. Now, did you or did you not come here to inform me of your plans for Alexia?"

Blast it, she was still irritated. "You've met my cousin Michel, who runs the shipping office."

She nodded.

"His sister Felicité is home from England, only long enough to try to convince her father to sell the plantation up-river and relocate to his place of birth. Which is also where most of the family has settled, including my father and step-mother."

"What does this have to do with Alexia?"

"The two met today and hit it off like the long lost cousins they are. Felicité invited Alexia up to the plantation for a week. That's when it dawned on me that since the two connected so famously, perhaps Alexia could be convinced to travel back to England with Felicité. Alexia could settle in with my family, which is now hers, receive a fine education, and with the family backing, fit nicely into society there. Eventually marry—"

"Oh, *merde*." Josette's breath hitched, and she stumbled. Cameron grabbed her by the arm, steadying her. "I thought you were eager to have her gone from New Orleans?"

Her fingers shook as she tucked a curl behind her ear. "I was. . . . I am. It's just that England is so very far away—"

"But isn't that what you wanted? Having Alexia a good distance from Odalie and the bayou? Given enough time, and exposure to another world, she'll likely acquire a different mind-set."

"Yes, yes, I know." Josette took in a deep breath. Her exhale seemed filled with pain. "It's . . . it's just that Alexia has been like my own child, and I shall miss her terribly."

Her voice hitched, and Cameron struggled to keep from

reaching out to comfort her. "If it's any consolation, René was in on the discussion today. He's all for Alexia being sent to England."

"He actually said so?"

Cameron nodded. "While she was with Felicité, we men had quite a discussion. As much as your brother and I would like to tear each other's throats out, he's clearly intent on making something of himself in the shipping industry. He's eager to learn everything about the business, including the possibility of training voyages. This means he'll have occasion to sail back and forth to England, where he can meet up with Alexia every so often."

"Oh, my." She blew out a breath. "I see. That makes perfect sense."

"She has a grandfather there—my father. His wife is a kind person, as is Trevor's wife. He and Celine have three children, by the way, and with Felicité's youngest brother attending university there, Alexia will be surrounded by more family than I had growing up."

He offered her a small grin. "You'd be welcome to sail on one of our ships anytime you choose. It's not as if you'd never see her again."

Josette halted and studied him for a long moment. "And what of you, her father? Where do you fit into all this?"

"I'll set up a trust for her, ensure she wants for nothing."

She tilted her head and her eyes narrowed. "You said just a bit ago that you wouldn't lie to me. What are your plans?"

Christ. He forced himself to continue facing her. "I don't know the long of it, but if Alexia is agreeable to traveling with Felicité to England, I'll be taking a ship out of here in ten days on my own."

Something he couldn't decipher ran through her eyes. "Obviously not to England. So you intend to deposit her amongst strangers in a foreign country, and that's where your responsibility ends? How very noble of you."

Fresh guilt added more weight to the anvil on his chest. "Damn it, Josette, I need to disappear for a while. I'll head back to England once I'm ready. I've been through a bit of hell and—"

"And Alexia hasn't?" Fire flashed in Josette's eyes once again. "Can't you see she's all caught up in you, her in-the-flesh father? She calls Odalie *maman*, but don't think for one minute Alexia has not pined for her mother, hasn't felt like an orphan."

His throat thickened and every nerve went on edge. "I have all the guilt I can contend with, knowing my wife and Alexia's mother died as a result of my impregnating them. Have a care."

"You're asking me to have a care? I never had a father, Cameron. To this day, I don't know who he is or even if he's dead or alive. I have a mother who dislikes me and had little to do with me all my growing years. The only time she touched me was to punish."

Stunned by her words, he swallowed hard and found his voice. "The devil, you say."

She rubbed at her arms as if suddenly chilled. "I know the pain and emptiness of feeling like an orphan while living in the midst of an otherwise close-knit family. I don't want that for Alexia."

Without thinking, he reached out to comfort her.

She stepped back and returned to tapping her foot. "You may have been an only child, Cameron, and you may have lost your mother when you were barely fifteen, but at least you had a good and decent upbringing. You also had all those Andrews cousins living a life of luxury on an upriver plantation where you made your second home. Admit it, life for you was good, whereas it hasn't been so good for Alexia."

And obviously not so good for you either. "So what am I

to do? Move back to England with her and have her end up hating a father who is miserable because he doesn't know what to do with himself? Think about it, Josette. If she's welcomed into a large, warm family, not to mention having another country to explore, wouldn't she be better off? At least until I can figure out what I want to do with the rest of my life."

Josette rubbed at the back of her neck and let out a sigh. "I need some time to think, Cameron. Give me a few days to let this all settle in. I also need to speak with René."

"Which reminds me. Felicité insisted on getting together for a family dinner this evening at Antoine's. She invited Alexia."

"Really?"

Cameron nodded. "In Alexia's eagerness to become a part of the Andrews clan, the little vixen managed to finagle an invitation for René, as well."

Josette's hand went to her breast. "Lord love a duck."

"I expect this could turn into an eventful affair, seeing as how sparks started flying between Felicité and René the minute they laid eyes on each other. As a result, his newly minted superior is shooting daggers at your brother. But Michel is keeping his mouth shut at the moment since Felicité will be here only a few days, and your brother managed to save the company several thousand dollars by catching a shipping error."

"Mercy." Josette's fingers covered her mouth.

"We all decided that to gather in a respectable public place over excellent food mixed with a bit of conviviality might go far in bonding Alexia to her new family. We need you there to lend your full support."

"Impossible."

Cameron lifted a brow. "Why is it impossible?"

She shook her head. "You do not want to be seen in my

company. And you should think twice about being seen in René's. Though society ladies frequent my shop, I am scorned by them. And I've no need to remind you of my brothers' reputations."

"Do you think I give a damn what people think? Besides, the Andrews name has been known to carry a bit of clout around these parts. If anyone so much as ventures a glance across the room at you with anything less than mild curiosity, they'll hear from me. As for René traveling in our company, doing so is bound to give the arrogant ass some respectability."

To Cameron's surprise, she laughed. "You actually intend to assist my brother in garnering a measure of esteem in this town, and yet you still call him an ass?"

He grinned. "Worse if a lady weren't present."

She was back to studying him again. This time through narrowed eyes. "You trust him to work for you?"

"Hell, no. That's Michel's problem. I'll soon be gone."

Amusement flashed in those lovely eyes of hers. "Tell me if I understand you correctly. You were the one who insisted on hiring my brother, yet you intend to walk away and leave your cousin with the problem?"

Cameron shrugged. "When we were kids and I stayed at their plantation, Michel used to slip frogs and worms, or whatever else he could find, into my bed to antagonize me. René happens to be Michel's long overdue recompense."

Josette's mouth dropped open. And then she giggled. Hard. "You, Monsieur Andrews, are very, very wicked."

He couldn't help staring at that luscious pink mouth. God, he wanted to cover it with his own. Do things to her that would make her beg for more. His body buzzed with want. No longer wholly in charge of all his faculties, he stepped closer. "You should laugh like that more often." His words settled deep in his throat and he had to force them out. "It makes you even lovelier."

She tried to step back, but he slipped a hand around her waist and dipped his head until their lips were a breath apart. He held still, absorbing her clean, sweet scent until he was left with nothing but a tangle of emotions. His other hand came up of its own volition, and the backs of his fingers swept across her petal-soft cheek. "Why can't I stay away from you?"

"Don't do this," she whispered, but she leaned in nearer and, closing her eyes, touched her lips to his.

A low groan left him. He wrapped his arms around her and deepened the kiss. God, she felt good, so warm and willing.

He touched his tongue to hers, and her fingers clutched his hair, gripping and twisting, inflicting delicious pain. Sliding his hand low to her back, he urged her against him until his erection strained against her belly.

She gasped and pushed him away. "No. I . . . I cannot. I will not."

He opened his eyes and met her gaze, one that still flashed heat and longing. But there it was again, that familiar look he couldn't quite decipher. "You're right, and I beg your pardon. I should take my leave before Alexia arrives."

"Then do so at once."

He put distance between them. Only a fool would fail to notice Josette was both aroused and upset. Her fingers splayed across her stomach, her breath releasing in short little gasps.

"For Alexia's sake, will you agree to dinner at Antoine's?"

She nodded. "But I don't have to like it."

He turned and headed toward the rear of the house.

"Stop," she called out.

He halted and pivoted. She looked like an angel in the

fading light, her hair a halo in disarray, her bare feet peeking beneath the too-short dress. "What?"

Her gaze met his, held steady. "A part of me hates you. You should know that, Monsieur Andrews."

A muddle of knots tightened his gut. He resisted the urge to rush back to her. "And well you should, Madame LeBlanc. I can be a right bastard at times."

They stood staring at one another for a long moment. "Alexia will be spending the night with me at my town house, so pack a few things for her. Since she is quite taken with Felicité, my cousin has agreed to join us, which should please Alexia no end. I'll send a carriage at nine for the two of you."

He turned and walked away, wondering what the devil had just happened.

Chapter Fourteen

Of all times for Josette to venture out to Antoine's in the evening, it had to be the one night Émile Vennard claimed as his. With fourteen themed rooms of various sizes that held up to eight hundred people, every room but the one Cameron had reserved was filled to overflowing with a large wedding party—the Vennard-Laroque wedding party to be exact.

Cameron's entourage had to pass through the room where Vennard and his wife held court at a grandiose flower-and-candle-festooned table. It had been all Josette could do not to make a hasty retreat at the sight of the arrogant bastard.

By the time they neared dessert, however, Josette had relaxed and was actually enjoying herself. Still, just thinking about the man's viperous gaze burning into her made her flesh crawl. Whatever the pompous cur wanted, she could rest easy knowing he'd not bother her this night. Or for the next few days, with the largest wedding celebration the parish had seen in recent history going on. If ever.

René sat across the table, his dark, penetrating eyes fixed on her as if reading her thoughts. Was she that transparent? She ignored his quizzical lift of an eyebrow and sipped her sherry. The scamp had one arm slung casually along the back

of Felicité's chair, where, every so often, his fingers lightly
brushed her shoulder.

Michel had his eye on that hand.

And when Felicité wasn't casting furtive glances toward
René, her attention appeared to be squarely on Alexia, who
lapped up the kindness like a kitten with a bowl of cream.

Josette's heart pinched. However much it would hurt to
lose her niece, Cameron was probably right: sending Alexia
off to England had to be for the best. She'd have a future
beyond anything Josette had imagined when the girl went
looking for her father.

While Alexia chattered away to everyone at the table,
Cameron leaned over until his mouth nearly touched
Josette's ear. "Have you forgiven me for this afternoon?"

The deep rasp of his voice, coupled with his warm breath
against her neck, sent her pulse racing once again. What a
dilemma. If she ignored him, he'd only keep at it. If she
turned his way to respond, their lips would meet. But if she
spoke to him otherwise, René would likely overhear every
word.

Once again, René's sharp, assessing gaze swept over the
other guests in the room, then returned to her. She narrowed
her eyes, shooting him a message to leave her be, one he
should be thoroughly familiar with since he was the recipi-
ent of that glare nearly every time their paths crossed.

He smirked and leaned to whisper something in Felicité's
ear, mimicking Cameron's actions. Whatever the mischief-
maker said, Felicité laughed softly.

Was that a little growl coming from Michel just now? He
downed another glass of sherry and continued with the light
banter interspersed with verbal jabs that had floated around
the table all evening.

Josette leaned away from Cameron, just enough to miss
touching his lips when turning his way, but not enough to

end up with her head against Michel's shoulder. "I'm still working on forgiving you for your little game last night."

He chuckled. "Nice memory, that."

"René is watching us, you tease."

"And Michel has a bead on René. Clearly a round robin going on here, wouldn't you say? Oh, to be a mind-reader."

She couldn't help but laugh. "You're intent on stirring things up, aren't you? No wonder Michel put worms and frogs in your bed."

Michel sat back in his chair. "He told you that?"

Heat ran up Josette's neck to her cheeks. "You over-heard?"

Cameron gave a little laugh. "Of course he did, or he wouldn't have asked. Have you imbibed too much or have you been in Felicité's company too long? She's a known ninny."

Felicité raised her glass of sherry to Cameron. "Careful, cousin. I have sordid tales to tell."

Oh, wonderful. René clearly had his antennae up and wasted no time asking Felicité to elucidate.

Cameron's quiet laugh may have seemed innocuous to the others, but Josette felt the power in him shift to something slightly feral. Certainly Felicité wasn't fool enough to re-spond to René's inquiry?

Josette turned to Michel in an attempt to shift the focus. "Remind me to tell you why Cameron spilled those secrets."

Cameron's hand covered hers in her lap and he squeezed. "Now who's the scamp?"

She caught a glimpse of his warm, strong hand over hers. Her mind flashed back to the afternoon, and how his long fingers had caressed her, nearly causing her to invite him into her bed.

Nearly.

She didn't think it would take much to get him there. Not the way he acted toward her every time he was in her presence. So why didn't she? For heaven's sake, she was a widow, and he'd be gone in a fortnight. And unlike with the others in town, whose invitations to become their mistress sickened her, the very closeness of Cameron, the scent of him, heated her blood.

Antoine Alciatore, owner of the restaurant, approached their table, jarring her thoughts. To her surprise, he greeted each of them in the same gentlemanly manner, including René. While business was certainly business, Monsieur Alciatore made it known he catered only to the upper echelons of New Orleans. Why did she have a feeling Cameron had pulled a few strings?

"Monsieur Andrews," Antoine said. "May I have the privilege of serving you and your guests our special flambé dessert using the fine Gosling Brothers rum you sent over?"

"You may," Cameron said.

Antoine gave a slight bow and departed.

"Now I know why we Thibodeaux have been treated so well this evening," Josette whispered to Cameron. "You bribed the owner."

He splayed a hand over his chest. "*Moi?*" Then he leaned closer to her, his expression suddenly sober. "I would never barter your standing in this community with a lowly barrel of liquor. Your worth is well above that, and don't you forget it."

A breath of silence followed, and then, "You look lovely this evening, by the way. I like the way you've wound that string of pearls through your hair."

He'd done it again—sent hot little shivers racing up and down her spine only to have them land in her belly, where they curled into a tight, heated ball. Well, enough was enough. She had to put a stop to his flirting, however he meant it. "You are not looking at my hair. You are staring down my gown."

He chuckled, and lifting a flute of champagne to his lips, muttered, "That, too."

"You're impossible, and René is at the boiling point over there."

"Bully on him."

Thank goodness Madame Charmontès had talked Josette into updating a couple of her gowns some months ago. She had not ventured out to formal gatherings since Louis's passing, so she'd thought there'd be no need for evening wear, but madame, owning the shop next door to hers, had pestered Josette until she'd handed over several. What madame had managed to do with the silver beaded gown Josette wore tonight was sheer genius. Although in her opinion, it was cut too low in front.

Two white-gloved waiters entered the room, one carrying a China platter holding the special dessert Monsieur Alciatore had offered, while the other held a tray of *café brûlot*, coffee mixed with orange liquor, lemon peels, and a bit of sugar, cinnamon, and cloves—Josette's favorite. While one server poured rum over the white, fluffy confection and lit it afire, the other set the coffee to flame as well.

A collective murmur of appreciation rose up in the room. Josette kept her focus on the coffee and dessert, relieved that most of the crowd sat behind her.

Alexia clapped her hands. "May I have a coffee, as well?"

"*Oui*," René replied, but then glanced at Cameron, deferring to him for approval.

Cameron nodded.

A third waiter led a couple to the recently vacated table in front of Josette. Oh, dear, it was the flamboyant widow Robicheau, one of Josette's wealthy clients. She breathed a sigh of relief when one of the waiters blocked the widow's view, and was equally relieved when she saw the woman was about to be seated with her back to Josette.

She peered around the waiter, just enough to spy the

broad back of a finely dressed gentleman as he held the widow's chair for her. His movements were smooth and languid, his long fingers brushing the back of the woman's shoulders as he moved to his own chair. Who the devil was he?

As women were wont to do while Josette consulted with them in her shop, they talked. But Madame Robicheau didn't just talk; she bragged that she was exceedingly content living the widow's life. Much to Josette's discomfort, Madame often spared no detail regarding her private encounters, saying she much preferred younger, virile men to pleasure her.

It was also a well-known fact that the woman dined nightly at Antoine's, ordered the most expensive wines from the restaurant's vast vault, and generously gifted the wait staff at Christmas. No wonder Antoine allowed her companions of questionable rank inside his establishment.

The waiter serving the *café brûlot* stepped around Michel to serve Josette, blocking her view of Madame's companion entirely. Blast it! Surreptitiously, Josette peeked around the server, her curiosity growing as to who the escort might be.

At last, the waiter moved, leaving Josette with a full view of a darkly handsome man, his black hair swept cleanly back from his face and brushing over his collar, his bearing powerful, yet polished. It took a moment before recognition slammed into her. Bastièn! Her heart jumped to her throat. "Oh, dear God."

Everyone at the table turned to see what had caused her outburst.

"Bastièn," Alexia called out.

He glanced up. A faint look of surprise washed over him, then quickly faded.

"Hush," Felicité said, but when Alexia informed her the man was her uncle, Felicité's eyes flashed appreciation. "Oh my, isn't he a devilishly handsome one, though?"

"Bloody hell," Cameron muttered.

Bastièn rose, and in a graceful movement, bent to the widow's ear. She gave him a slight nod, but to Josette's relief, did not turn around.

He approached the table nearest Alexia. "*Pouchette*." He spoke to her, but his eyes, glittering like polished sapphires in the candlelight, settled on Felicité.

"Who is your *belle amie*, Alexia? Or is this *your* beautiful friend, René?"

Alexia stood and slipped her hand into Bastièn's. "This is Mademoiselle Felicité Andrews. She is here from England."

His sharp gaze slid over Felicité. His lids lowered, and a smoky smile played over his lips. "A pity we have not met before, *oui*?"

Felicité's lips parted, but she said nothing. She didn't have to—her countenance told Josette that Bastièn had the same effect on Felicité as he had on most women. As upset as Josette was, she couldn't help noticing how handsome he looked in his impeccable clothing, his manner so very refined.

René shifted in his seat. "What are you doing here, Bastièn?"

"Working."

Puzzlement filled Josette. "I don't quite follow you."

René snorted and shifted in his seat again, his arm still over the back of Felicité's chair.

"Bastièn works for Madame Olympée," Alexia piped in. "Doing what my real *maman* used to do."

Felicité gasped, but Josette didn't think it was from embarrassment, not by her awed expression.

Josette glanced from Cameron, whose jaw was set, to Michel, whose grip on the stem of his glass had grown dangerously tight, and back to Bastièn. A queer feeling wended its way through her, giving her brain a buzz. "Hush, Alexia. We don't speak of that place in public. Besides, he'd merely be positioned at the front door of the establishment were he to be employed there. Which, I doubt."

René's and Bastièn's carefully controlled expressions, along with their silence, told her otherwise. Her breath froze in her lungs. It couldn't be. Madame Olympée didn't employ men in that kind of position. Did she?

As her stomach sickened, and her throat grew parched, denial receded. Dear Lord, not another Thibodeaux working in a whorehouse. One more reason to be shunned. "Tell me this isn't true, Bastièn."

She sat there, light-headed, staring into those startling blue eyes that set him apart from his siblings. He held himself in a manner that spoke of self-assuredness laced with élan. Then he leaned over and very quietly said to Alexia, "*Pouchette*, this is a very respectable place. If you lifted anything off anyone on your way to your seat, kindly slip it into my pocket, tell me which person I should seek out, and I will return whatever you stole as having been dropped on the floor."

"Christ," Cameron muttered. "At least the din in the room covers this deplorable conversation. Alexia, if you have anything not belonging to you, give it over immediately."

She slipped her closed fist into Bastièn's pocket, whispered something in his ear, then went back to her dessert as though nothing had occurred.

Bastièn gave a nod to everyone. "*Pardon*, but I must make my *sortie* into another room where I shall note in passing that a certain lady's bracelet has fallen off her wrist onto the floor." He strolled over to his partner for the evening and spoke quietly to her before exiting the room.

Josette feared she was about to lose her entire meal. She braced her hands on her stomach.

Cameron touched her arm. "You didn't know?"

She shook her head, fighting the panic threatening to overcome her. "I had no idea."

What fools they were. A Thibodeaux family from the bayou in the finest restaurant New Orleans had to offer, and one of them was a whore, the other a thief. She needed to leave before Bastièn returned and she did or said something she might regret for the rest of her days.

"René, take me home."

Cameron set his serviette to the side of his plate and rose. "I'll see you there."

She gave her head a shake. "I insist René accompany me."

René rose and rounded the table to stand behind Josette. Tenderly gripping her shoulders, he helped her from the chair. "Come then, *ma chère.*"

An angry storm rolled around inside Cameron. He cursed to himself, lest Alexia hear and imitate him.

"Well," Felicité said in a whoosh of an exhale. "Whatever all that was about, they certainly had my attention. How incredibly interesting."

Cameron cursed under his breath again. "At least some-one thinks so."

Michel shoved his chair back and rose. "I think I can safely say our evening has come to a close." He shot a meaningful glance at Alexia, who was busy watching the door for Bastièn's return. "Perhaps not as we had intended, but nonetheless, to an end it has come. And since Felicité and Alexia are spending the night with you, Cameron, I'll be on my way. Lord knows I could use some fresh air and a quiet walk home after this calamity."

"We'll see you out, at least," Cameron said.

They were exiting the room just as Bastièn returned. He stepped aside to allow them passage, and in their leaving, said to Alexia, "You look lovely tonight, *pouchette.*"

She grinned up at him in adoration. "*Merci,* Uncle."

Cameron swallowed another litany of curses. Obviously,

she adored her blasted uncles, no matter what fool things they did.

Bastièn made no effort to disguise his blatant interest in Felicité. "Although I have not met you before this evening, I suspect you, Mademoiselle Felicité, always manage to look lovely." A sultry invitation touched Bastièn's countenance.

Cameron leaned a shoulder into him as he swept by, just enough to warn the *salaud* that Felicité was off limits.

Bastièn chuckled softly in response, then moved the short distance to his table, and seated himself across from the widow.

As Cameron's small party attempted to make their exit, they got caught up in the wedding crowd flowing out of the restaurant and into the street like a tidal wave.

Antoine approached Cameron. "I am so very sorry to cause you any delay, but we've six hundred people exiting, not to mention those waiting outside to enter for their late reservations. The wedding party will follow music makers along Rue Royale to a ball that will go on all night."

Alexia tugged on Cameron's sleeve. "That's your street, Papa. Can we watch?"

"You may. From an above stairs window overlooking the event."

"But Papa, we won't feel the excitement if we're not in the thick of it."

He bent down and grasped Alexia by the shoulders, forcing her to look him in the eye. "I am going to be quite frank with you, Alexia. I do not trust you in this crowd. If you were to get caught divesting any of the ladies of their jewels, you would cause more trouble than you can imagine. For all of us."

Enthusiasm left her eyes and a blank look crossed her face.

His gut clenched. "I speak the truth for your own sake, Alexia, but I'll have you know, I detest having to speak such words. I can no longer tolerate your thieving. In fact, I am so sick of not being able to trust you that I've a mind to . . . to . . ."

"Do what, Papa?" Her eyes had grown suddenly cold. "Get on the next ship out of here? Leave, and never set eyes on me again?"

He detested feeling guilty again. He pinched the bridge of his nose. "Alexia, I—"

Felicité stepped forward and laid a hand on Alexia's shoulder. "If your father didn't care about you, he'd already be gone."

Alexia blinked hard and fast.

Were those tears? *Merde.* For the life of him, Cameron didn't know what the blazes to do next.

While the crowd funneled out of the restaurant, Alexia stood staring up at him for a long while. Finally, her slender hand slid into his, feeling no larger than a babe's.

"You can hold my hand, Papa, and Felicité can hold the other. I promise to be good. Just for a while, Papa?"

He pushed away his unwanted emotions and nodded. Once out the door, he maneuvered them through the crowd and to the street behind Royal, where merrymakers rushed ahead and beat the parade to his town house.

A dozen violinists walked in front of an elaborately decorated carriage holding the bride and groom. Behind them, several other carriages held the wedding couple's parents while the remaining crowd followed on foot.

"Isn't this something?" Felicité said. "How beautiful everything is."

As promised, Alexia, her face shining with pleasure, held tightly to both Felicité and Cameron's hands. "I would be happy with the flowery hats the horses wear," she said.

Cameron chuckled. Leave it to Alexia to notice the little details. Good thing he was holding her hand or come the morrow, she'd be wearing one to breakfast.

The procession was nearing an end when René slid in beside Cameron and sent Felicité a speaking glance.

Cameron turned to her. "The parade is coming to an end. Please take Alexia inside. I'll join you in a moment."

Felicité's cheeks flushed, but she did as she was bade. As she brushed by Cameron, she muttered, "You are so transparent, cousin."

"We'll talk," he said and abruptly turned to René. "I take it Josette got home all right?"

"*Oui*. She has had a very bad day."

"Vivienne said your sister had uninvited visitors that put her in a foul mood. Do you know who?"

"Vennard was one of them, I'm afraid."

"Émile Vennard? The father of the bride?"

"*Oui*."

"What the devil did he want?"

"She wouldn't tell me, but I spoke to him this afternoon. It seems he would like to purchase her house for his daughter as a wedding present."

"Why?"

"He says it is because his daughter would like to live in this new area people are calling the Garden District and my sister's home is the finest of them all. When I assured him the idea was out of the question, he dropped the subject."

"Does Josette know of this?"

"*Non*. Tonight was not the night to tell her. But she is aware he wants to purchase her shop, and refuses him at every turn. Unfortunately, Vennard has a reputation for getting whatever he wants."

"Why the hell would a man like him want to own a shop for women?"

René shrugged. "I do not know, but I intend to find out. She hasn't a clue I am aware of his proposal so I cannot bring the subject up with her just yet."

"How did you come to know all this?"

A smile worked one corner of René's lips. "I am, shall we say, close friends with Josette's lead shop girl. Mademoiselle Elise has been known to press her ear to my sister's office door whenever that snake Vennard visits."

"Let me get this straight. You are sleeping with the shop girl with the intention of looking after your sister's best interests?"

"*Oui.*"

"How bloody chivalrous of you."

"Ah, but there are benefits to looking after my sister. I find long legs wrapped around me most satisfying."

Anger welled up in Cameron. He whipped around and shoved René against the brick wall. "You do what you will with that shop girl, but leave Felicité alone. You touch her, and I'll have my foot in your balls so fast you won't know what hit you."

A slow smile curled René's mouth, and his eyes filled with humor. "We make a deal, *oui*? I leave Michel's sister alone if you leave my sister alone."

Cameron muttered an oath and shoved harder. Why wasn't the bastard fighting back?

People on the street were stopping to gawk. Someone stepped forward and called out, "What goes there?"

He dropped his hold on René's jacket. "If that's your game, you're playing a dangerous one."

René merely brushed at his lapels and walked off. "Go to the devil."

"You first, Thibodeaux."

Cameron watched René stroll down the street and disappear around a corner. What kind of family had he gotten mixed up with? Seeing those two brothers together tonight, he realized they both had practiced their smirks with the intention of rattling their opponents, and Cameron had fallen for their game. He'd be damned if that would happen again.

He let himself in through the wrought-iron gate, locked

it behind him, and made his way into the town house. Hearing laughter coming from above, he climbed the stairs and strode to the room across the hall from his. He knocked.

"*Entrez s'il vous plaît*," Alexia called out with a giggle.

He opened the door and there she and Felicité were, curled up in bed, an open book on their laps. For some strange reason, the sight of them, their backs propped against a pile of shared pillows, reading together, touched him. He leaned a shoulder against the wall, and crossed one foot over the other ankle. "Now there's a sight."

"We've decided to share a bed," Felicité said. "I've never had a sister or female cousin to do such a thing, so I'm looking forward to it as much as Alexia is."

Alexia yawned and rubbed an eye.

He shoved his hands in his trouser pockets and watched his daughter. "I should warn you that when Alexia falls asleep, it can be on her feet or in her soup, so you had better be ready."

Alexia giggled. "G'night, Papa. I've had the best day of my life."

"You don't say?" He moved to the bed, bent and kissed her on the forehead. He glanced at Felicité. "As for you, I'll merely say good night."

"Papa?" How very innocent Alexia looked in her snowy-white nightgown, her hair in a braid.

"What is it?"

She slid her hand beneath a pillow and withdrew her fist closed around something on a golden chain. She dropped his pocket watch into his hand. "I don't want to keep it any longer. I don't want to steal things anymore because I don't want you to be ashamed of me."

He stared at the watch, his heart dropping to his feet. How the hell had she managed to find the safe under the floor? He ought to wallop her a good one. But not tonight. Not when she'd had the best day of her life. He'd confront her tomorrow and find out how the devil she'd tripped the safe's tumblers.

Making his way downstairs, he moved the table in front of the sofa, pulled the rug back, and exposed the safe. Opening it, he spied his pocket watch, right where he'd left it. "What the hell?"

He lifted it out and compared it to the one Alexia had handed him. The one from the safe had a deep scratch on the back, something that had happened right after his father gifted him the watch. But how . . .

A chill ran through him.

He remembered now.

Josette.

Those eyes.

That certain look in them.

Damn it!

He stuffed both watches into his pocket, and after putting everything back in place, he headed for Josette's.

She'd had a bad day, had she?

Well, what was left of it was about to get a hell of a lot worse.

Chapter Fifteen

God's saints, which brother was beating on her door at this hour?

Josette rushed along the gas-lit corridor and down the stairs, her mind jumping ahead to the cabinet holding bandages, tinctures, needles, and thread. Why was it always the dead of night when one or the other needed stitching?

The rapping turned into furious pounding.

"Blast it, I'm coming!"

Her pulse rate ticked up. With this racket, something had to be terribly wrong. What if both were injured? What in the world had possessed her to send Vivienne and Régine off for the night?

Yanking open the door, she stumbled to a halt. "Oh!"

"Invite me in, Josette." Despite Cameron's deceptively calm words, fire blazed in his eyes. It could have been Lucifer himself come to call.

She clutched at the opening of her robe and stepped back. "Where's Alexia? What's happened?"

"Alexia is safe with Félicité. Invite me in."

"Did one of my brothers get to you?" He didn't appear to have been pummeled—at least not externally.

He muttered a foul curse.

Good Lord, she'd sooner let a growling bear inside. She hiked up her chin and willed her heart to settle back in her chest. "I am not their keeper."

"Damn it, Josette, we need to talk. Invite me in, or I shall forget my proper upbringing and barge in without your consent. Should I be forced to do so, you'll find my mood even worse."

The fine hairs on her nape tingled, sending a shiver down her spine. She backed up a few more steps. "Then come inside before I have to fight off a swarm of mosquitoes. I don't need them biting at me since you seem to be doing a fair job of it on your own."

He strode in, anger pouring out of him like black rain. "How did you break into my town house?"

His town house? This was the last thing she'd expected to hear. Her mind reeled as she bought time. "I beg your pardon?"

His gaze cruised her length, from her tousled hair, down her red silk robe to bare toes, and back to her face. Something dark and hungry flashed through his eyes, nearly stealing her breath. The emotion waned, and wrath eclipsed whatever had sped through him.

He reached into his pocket and withdrew . . . dear heavens, the watch.

A muscle twitched in his jaw. "You recognize this, don't you?"

"Is it the pocket watch Alexia stole from you?" She knew better. He'd just asked her how she'd gotten into his home.

"Nice try." He flipped the watch to its backside. His finger traced a deep scratch. "Do you see this gash across the top, here? I managed to scrape it against something within the first week my father gave it to me. That would have been on my fifteenth birthday. Two years later, it disappeared by the hand of a certain pickpocket."

A derisive smile raised a corner of his mouth. "A very

clever thief since I never felt a thing. I wonder if that little bandit also lifted a rather expensive diamond stickpin off my cravat?"

Oh, her heart was in her throat again. Even though he knew, she couldn't bring herself to confess. Not with all the years and emotion banked behind the two deeds. How could she tell him she'd stolen both items because she'd been an infatuated girl? That she'd been furious with him for choosing Solange over her when Josette was clearly too young for what he and her sister had engaged in? How could she tell him she'd pilfered his things not to sell or bring back to Maman, but to have something of him to hold dear?

"This watch was removed from my person about a year before Alexia was born," he said. "I had a substitute made soon after. Which happens to be the one Alexia pinched."

He reached into another pocket and, retrieving the duplicate, let it swing hypnotically from its golden chain. "She returned this one tonight after telling me she had no desire to steal again. I wonder if I can believe her words."

Josette backed up.

She needed space.

Needed to catch her breath.

Needed to think.

Blast it, she couldn't manage to get her swirling thoughts to travel in a straight line. Not with him standing before her, both watches dangling from his hand. With deliberate and slow movements, he set the timepieces side by side on a small table next to him, careful to straighten the chains in equal measure. Finished with his little task, he folded his arms across his chest and met her eyes, that amber gaze of his seeming to strip her bare.

She had to get rid of him.

Gathering all the chilly composure she could muster, she turned on her heel and headed for the stairs. "This is ridiculous. It's after midnight, and you're here to shove a couple of watches in my face? Close the door on your way out. The night latch is on and will catch on its own. Good night, Monsieur Andrews."

She lifted the hems of her dressing gown and night rail, and hastened to the stairs.

The heels of his shoes pounded the floor behind her. "Not so fast."

She swallowed a squeal, and dashed up the steps. "Get out!"

"By jove, if you aren't the little bully."

She managed to clear the stairs and scamper halfway down the hall before he caught up with her. Grabbing her by the arm, he swung her around, his eyes burning into hers.

Shock sent a high buzz into her ears. "You are no gentleman. Unhand me and leave."

"Like hell, I will. We need to talk, and if I let you go, you'll disappear behind one of these doors."

His grip sent a rush of conflicting emotions running rampant—part of her grew so angry she saw red while another insane part wanted to kiss him. Her senses blurred, she fisted her free hand and struck out.

He blocked the blow with ease, curling his fingers around hers and holding them with a firm grip.

She tried to jerk free.

His fist tightened for a beat, then loosened. But only enough to let her know he was the one in control. Slowly, he backed her against the wall, and caged her in, his hands flat on either side of her head.

A wild sensation of wanting to pull him closer cleaved a drunken path through her anger, leaving her feeling even more perplexed. Good God, what was wrong with her?

Once again, she wrapped herself in a cloak of false self-assurance. "And you call me a bully?"

A beat of silence, then a short burst of laughter left him. "Christ Almighty, Josette. You're like a kaleidoscope the way you shift your moods to match whatever fits the occasion. You're guilty as hell, yet you're trying to make me look the fool. Do you think you can weasel out of this so easily? Didn't you tell me you picked pockets at Alexia's age?"

The rush of his breath against her skin sent wicked signals racing along her nerve endings. "Do you honestly think I'm going to have this discussion with you?"

He bent his head until he was so close, his clean, musky scent enveloped her. "Then I shall be forced to conduct a one-sided conversation with you, my dear."

Something shifted in his gaze as it roved her face. "When I found myself in possession of two watches, I suddenly recalled why you've seemed so familiar to me of late."

Her heart stuttered, but this time for an entirely different reason—his lips had parted and his warm, measured breaths were falling on her mouth. "Is that so?"

A tilt of his head, and he studied her with unnerving intensity. "By any chance do you favor those sugary *calas* the vendors in the Vieux Carré sell?"

His words stunned and left her speechless. Her gaze left his mouth and found his eyes. The day she'd knocked over those grocer's barrels while spying on him had been a pivotal moment in her life, but it had to have been an insignificant one in his.

She had to clear her throat to speak. "How could you remember such an event as that?"

He leaned closer, his lips nearly touching hers. "Even back then you were beautiful, *ma chère*."

"Impossible. I was thirteen. Little more than a child."

"And I was seventeen, not much more than one, as well." His husky words left his lips and landed on hers like a warm caress. "You popped up from behind those tumbling merchant's barrels looking like a frightened angel, your dark eyes big as saucers, your hair a wild mass of curls. I bought you a *cala*, do you remember?"

His one hand lifted from the wall and trailed along her cheek, then into her hair, sending a shower of pins pricking her skin. She sucked in a breath.

"I came back later, looking for you." His lids lowered, along with the timbre of his voice. "Did you know that?"

He had? Speechless, she shook her head. What had just happened? He'd been a bellowing lunatic mere moments ago. When had the powerful force emanating from him shifted into something far more dangerous than unleashed anger?

She could barely find her voice. "You need to . . ."

One muscled leg slid in between hers, forcing her thighs apart.

Her dressing gown fell open.

She gasped.

"Need to do what?" His bare, raspy murmur shot pure lust through her, dissolving her bones.

He pressed snugly against her. His thick manhood at her belly grew rigid with pulsating urgency. With only the thin silk of her nightgown and the fabric of his trousers separating them, they may as well have been naked.

His mouth took hers, his tongue sweeping inside, tangling with hers.

A little moan, and coherent thought fell to the wayside. Of their own accord, her hands slid under his jacket and found his muscled chest beneath the soft fabric of his shirt and vest. Smoky heat emanated from him, reached inside her like vaporous tentacles, and stroked. All the familiar places where every memory of him had ever lurked ignited.

God help her, she had to find strength enough to send him away before she lost herself completely. But all she could manage to mumble along with her pathetic little shove was, "Stop."

He took a step back, stared at her for a brief moment,

then wiped his mouth with the back of his hand. "Why the devil can't I leave you be?"

He pivoted and left her standing there, his long, rapid strides taking him down the hall toward the staircase. "We cannot engage in this kind of conduct when we have a young girl to consider. Any further exchange between the two of us will be on her behalf, and done with others present."

Shock swept away the fog in her brain. She pressed a fist to her mouth as a jumble of disparate thoughts fell into place like scattered pieces of a jigsaw puzzle. The man she'd held in her heart and in her dreams for years had just made a pledge never to return unattended. And in ten days, he'd be gone from her world forever. Unbidden, the idea of suffering through yet another long, lonely night gripped her, breathed down her neck, and made her call out in a small voice. "Don't leave."

Her soft-spoken words could have been a blast of cannon shot. Cameron stumbled to a halt at the top of the stairs. Stomach churning, he raked his fingers through his hair. "You don't want me to stay, Josette. You know what would happen, and we'd only be sorry."

The air shifted around him. Silk rustled as she moved slowly toward him. "*We* would be sorry? How could you possibly know that of me?"

The vise around his chest squeezed tighter, forcing a groan from his lips. Something inside him broke. He suddenly grew weary. He gave up and plopped onto the top step with a soft thud, burying his head in his hands. "Each of us would have regrets, Josette, but for different reasons."

Old guilt closed in on him, merged with the new. If not for him, his wife and Josette's sister would still live. He had no right to seek out pleasure for pleasure's sake alone. Especially with this woman. Yet, he couldn't bring himself to complete his walk down the steps and out her door. Not just yet, anyway.

She'd moved closer. Electricity sizzled between them, the energy like a prelude to a summer storm. Her light, elegant scent came next, followed by another rustle of silk. She sat beside him, saying nothing.

In the long silence that ensued, an odd sort of comfort settled in his bones, despite the lust still ravaging his soul. Her allure became an enigmatic force holding him in place. He was unable to gather enough fortitude to make a graceful exit, but, as time ticked by, he no longer wished to. Heaving a heavy sigh, he swiped his hands over his face. "You're too good for what happened back there. I beg your pardon."

"Forgiven." She wrapped her arms around her waist and focused on her toes peeking out from under her nightclothes, wiggling them about a bit.

A punch of hunger—a perilous kind—slammed into his gut. Why the devil did he find her bare feet so sensual? He clasped his hands together to keep from reaching for her, and draped them between his legs, his elbows resting on his knees. "I'm surprised Vivienne or Régine hasn't come to your aid and knocked me over the head with a lamp or two."

"They're not here."

Merde. "You're rattling around alone in this monster of a house?"

She nodded.

"When do they return?"

"Tomorrow. Late afternoon, I would guess. They went off to visit Régine's father. He has a small farm outside of town."

"Do you always leave the upstairs lit up at night like Christmas? Or is it because you're alone?"

Her cheeks flushed. "The latter, I would suppose."

What the hell did he do now? He couldn't very well leave

when she admitted being uncomfortable by herself. But to remain would only serve to complicate things.

Wouldn't it?

He could sleep on the sofa downstairs to keep guard. What he needed to do was change the subject while he decided what best to do.

"Why did you put that voodoo doll on my pillow?"

Her brows stitched together. "Voodoo doll?"

He nodded.

"I left no such thing."

Apprehension snaked through him. "Then who the hell else is crawling through my window? On second thought, how did you get in? You never answered me."

A touch of humor flitted across her features. "I picked the locks on your gate and entry door. What did this doll look like?"

He stretched his thumb and index finger apart. "About so big. With a bunch of pins at the crotch. And one in the middle of a strange looking little heart, I might add."

"Really?" She shifted her position, leaned her back against the banister, and tilting her head, studied him through those unfathomable eyes of hers. "How many pins in your manly parts?"

Feeling suddenly foolish, he shrugged. "I don't know . . . five, I suppose."

"And the heart? Describe it to me. It's important you remember details."

"It was a padded heart with red threads dangling from it. I figured whoever made the thing meant for the threads to represent dripping blood."

"Were there little knots tied at the end of each thread?"

"I think so."

"Did you keep it or toss it out?"

"I held on to it."

"Why?"

He frowned. "What do you mean, why? Wouldn't you

hold on to something an intruder left on your pillow until you figured out who the devil broke into your home and planted it there? And what kind of message was being sent?"

A mysterious light flashed through her eyes. "At least I'd be curious to know the intended message."

"You know something, don't you?"

"Perhaps," she said. "I'd need to take a look at the doll before I make any comment."

She studied him for a long while. What was she thinking? There was no mistaking the desire that lingered about her like an amatory mist. Bloody hell, with the craving for her still running rampant through his blood, he couldn't sit here much longer and manage to keep his hands to himself. What to do? He still couldn't come up with a viable solution other than spending what remained of the night on her parlor sofa.

"What are you thinking?" she asked, her voice soft as velvet.

He'd be damned if he'd tell her what had just run through his mind. Instead, he said, "René told me you had unwanted visitors today. Would you care to elaborate?"

A frown creased her brow. She wrapped her arms tighter around herself. "It'll be good when you get Alexia out of here. Before Lucien can get his filthy hands on her. This morning was too close a call."

"What happened?" Christ, René hadn't mentioned their cousin had paid Josette an unwanted visit on top of Vennard leaving his calling card. Then she'd made the shocking discovery of Bastièn's livelihood—in public, no less. And here Cameron was in the middle of the night, thrusting himself upon her like some randy schoolboy.

Josette swept a mass of curls off her cheek. "Lucien was here at sunup trying to trick Alexia into running off with him to the bayou. He gave some shallow excuse about showing her a new litter of puppies."

Cameron clenched his jaw and giving her a faint nod,

wrestled down the urge to beat a path to Lucien's door. Wherever the hell that was. "You've had a bad day."

"You might say that." She tilted her head, watching him. "But what occurred earlier was then, and this is now, is it not?"

She was lovely sitting casually beside him, barefooted and in her bed clothes, her hair a soft cloud of curls he'd like to sink his hands into. She took on a pensive look.

"Now it's my turn to ask," he said. "What are you thinking?"

"Are you sure you want to know? Because what's got me wondering is none of my concern."

"Humph. Now you've got me curious. Do tell."

She fiddled with the closure at her neck, an unconscious gesture. "Have you been with another woman since your wife died?"

His knee-jerk reaction was to tell her she was right, it was none of her damn business, but that overwhelming weariness set in again. He swiped a hand through his hair, then with a heavy sigh, rested his chin on the palms of his hands and stared at nothing in particular. "No."

"Thank you for your refreshing honesty. I can better understand some of your reticence back there in the corridor. And earlier, in the garden."

For the first time in over two years, he realized that other than acknowledging a few condolences, he'd never discussed his loss with anyone. Or its ensuing consequences. A torrent of emotion threatened to flood him. He dammed it up and took the focus off himself. "And what of you, Josette? Have you been with anyone since losing your husband?"

She gave her head a small shake. "I haven't been with anyone since the first few months of my marriage. And there is pitifully little to tell about that. We were wed for barely a year, by the way."

Merde. He didn't know quite what to say. "You should marry again, Josette. It would be a terrible loss for someone as vibrant and lovely as you to live alone the rest of your life."

Her quiet laughter startled him.

She leaned over, and tracing a finger along the curve of his mouth, said very quietly, "Why are we having this kind of discussion after what nearly took place down the hall?"

At the kick of lust to his groin, he drew a sharp breath. He grabbed her wrist to fend off her touch. But instead of pushing her hand away, he closed his eyes and allowed her supple fingers to explore his lips.

And just like that, she stepped right into a foreign corner of his fractured heart—a place he'd never before visited. Every ounce of discipline he possessed warred with the urge to take her in his arms and ease her onto the floor. A soft groan burst from somewhere deep in his throat.

Still holding her wrist, he slid the flat of her hand to where his heart beat like a drum in his chest. He opened his eyes. "Do you feel that, Josette? I cannot take much more, so I should leave."

Her response was to slide her arms around him, and nestle against his chest. "Hold me, Cameron. Please hold me, for just a while."

A shudder ran through him. Defenses exhausted, he pulled her to him. Wrapping his arms around her, he settled her cheek against his chest. God, she felt good. Smelled good, too. He spoke into her hair. "I . . . I have to leave. I can't trust myself any longer."

"I don't see how trusting yourself has anything to do with my touching you the way I just did."

"Oh, you foolish woman. Don't sit here expecting me to keep you safe when every wicked part of me wants to seduce you. I couldn't live with myself if I acted on indecent impulses and hurt you, Josette."

She pulled back, just enough to look into his eyes, hers glistening. "I am a grown woman, Cameron. I know what I want. I instigated this because I realize I used the wrong word when I cut short what nearly took place a bit ago."

He stroked her cheek with his thumb. So soft and silken, that cheek. "You told me to stop, and I complied. What else would you have me do?"

She leaned in and touched her lips to his, her breaths uneven. "What I should have said was slow down."

He swallowed her words. Instead of heating him, they flowed through him like a soft summer rain, cool and cleansing. He'd been so lonely, so goddamn lonely.

He eased back, enough to study her face. "*Thinking* you should have said something else is a lot different from *knowing* you should have used other words."

"So I've used the wrong word again, have I?" A hint of a smile touched her lips. "Let me say it another way, then. You seduced me with your essence long before you ever touched my body."

His stomach flipped over. He should leave. Just get up and walk away and it would all be over.

Instead, it was she who stood. "I am quite certain of what I want, Cameron. You are the perfect man for me to indulge in a clandestine affair. So if you don't mind, I'd like to finish what we began back there—with no apologies or regrets afterward."

"What makes me the perfect man?" He could barely manage to get the words out.

"Because we want one another but neither desires anything permanent. You'll be gone in ten days. Once you sail away, each of us will get on with our own lives. That said, I am going to my bed. Should you change your mind about leaving, my room is the last door on the left. If not, as I said when you first arrived, the night latch is engaged so the door will lock behind you."

He didn't watch her walk away. He couldn't. But he knew she'd gone because she took her essence with her, leaving a void in her place. He sat for a moment without thought. Then Madame Olympée's words tumbled through his mind.

Your joy has been swallowed up by grief. There is a certain part of your misery that will remain with you until you eradicate it. And the only way to do so is through intimacy with another woman.

He rose and started down the steps. He could use a stiff drink before he departed. At least he knew right where Josette kept the bloody rum.

Chapter Sixteen

Josette stood on the balcony overlooking her moonlit gardens, the sultry air around her redolent with night-blooming jasmine. Had it been any other night, she might have found passing time out here a peaceful activity. Despite the warm breeze, she crossed her arms and rubbed at them in a futile attempt to chase away the lonely chill gripping her. Cameron wasn't coming. He'd had time enough to reach home by now. If indeed that was where he'd headed.

Her bedroom door opened and closed on a whisper.

Her pulse tripped.

Saints help them, he'd come to her after all. She closed her eyes and slowly let go a wavering breath.

And waited.

A subtle shift in the air told her he stood not far behind her. Yet he failed to approach. She'd told him she wished to go slow. Was this his idea of drawing out the anticipation?

Or were his emotions still conflicted?

She would not turn around. He must come to her. Her skin tingled at the idea that he was about to make love to her.

Another long moment passed.

She felt him step closer until he stood directly behind her.

She could still breathe, but no longer could she draw air fully into her lungs.

Was she imagining things or had his clean, musky scent filtered through the sweet-smelling jasmine? Pleasure washed over her in waves. He was taking his time, and she intended to savor every moment of whatever was about to transpire. Oh, how she wanted this night. And any others that might follow. But if this evening was to be their only time together, she'd be glad of it, no matter the consequences.

He touched her shoulders. His hands warmed the silk of her robe and nightgown. His mouth touched her ear. "Tell me again that you are certain of what we are about to do, Josette. I can still walk away."

The husky timbre of his voice scraped across her skin and settled low in her belly. "How many ways are there to say yes, Cameron? Without doubt, I know what I want. Truth be told, I've lived for years both hating and wanting you. Much as I tried to erase the memory of you, I never could. Perhaps this night will finally allow me a release from the prison I've been trapped in."

Soft as a ghost's breath, his body touched hers, his heat penetrating her core. An arm slid around her waist, and his long-fingered hand splayed beneath her breasts with a gentleness that held an underlying strength. Gently, he pulled her against him, swept her hair off her neck with his other hand, and brushed a soft kiss there.

A thrill shot through her.

His shirtsleeves were rolled back, the fabric glowing white beneath the pale moon. Somewhere between the time she'd left him and when he'd stepped behind her, he'd cast off his jacket and vest. She slid her hand over his bare forearm. Fine hairs feathering his arm tickled the pads of her fingers. As foreign as this kind of intimacy was to her, with him it felt natural and right.

A ragged exhalation left him, a sweet breeze across her cheek. "You're being honest with me tonight. I like that."

With a gentle touch, his fingers stroked lightly along the curve of her neck and jaw, sending a thousand sparks exploding within each nerve.

She closed her eyes and leaned against him, allowing the delicious sensations to expand. "Mmm, that feels good."

His lips settled on the curve of her neck again. She leaned to the side, exposing her throat. His tongue flicked along her skin.

She moaned.

And then he nibbled. "I could spend all night in that one spot." He eased her chin toward him. His tongue touched the sensitive corner of her mouth while his hand slipped from her neck and cupped her breast.

Her nipples peaked and a broken, breathless sound escaped her lips. Wordless, she turned in his arms to face him. With trembling fingers, she worked free the buttons at the top of his shirt. Her palms ran slowly down his hard, flat stomach, and his muscles bunched beneath her touch. Her hands met the waistband of his trousers. Tugging his shirt-tails free, she caught a glimpse of his bare feet. When had he divested himself of shoes and stockings?

He reached one hand over his shoulder, grabbed a handful of material, and drawing the shirt over his head, tossed it somewhere behind him.

Moonlight danced over the hard planes of his chest. She ran quivering fingers ever so lightly over his skin. His breath grew ragged and heavy.

Instinct took over. She grasped the bulging muscles of his arms and setting her lips to a flat nipple, she licked and nipped.

He hissed, but said nothing, only stood still while she feasted on him.

Pressing her mouth to his chest, she swept back and forth

from one nipple to the other, the fine hairs on his chest tickling her face. As she tasted him, inhaled his delicious scent, she swept her arms around him and stroked his broad back with the tips of her nails.

"You're beautiful," she whispered.

A small smile hitched a corner of his mouth. "I thought I was the one supposed to say that."

She reached up and traced the outline of his square jaw. The firm masculinity of it sent another wash of ecstasy through her.

He curled a finger under her chin and lifted. When their gazes locked, moonlight shimmered in his. She doubted there could have been a more glorious man ever to walk the face of the earth.

In this moment, she floated on air.

Slipping the robe off her shoulders, he let it drop to the balcony tiles. "Unbutton me," he said in a raspy voice.

She complied and worked at the fastenings, acutely aware of the hard bulge beneath her palms. When she'd managed them all, he stepped out of his trousers and stood before her—tall, well-built, and naked.

"Now touch me, Josette."

The sound of his voice, a provocative rumble, lit yet more internal fires. Her hand went around his thick erection.

"Ah," he sighed. "Clever girl."

Whatever sacred passion was running through her, she had an unholy urge to lower her head and take him fully into her mouth. Before she had time to act, his lips found hers in a deep and hungry kiss. All the while, his hands touched and caressed. So tender he was, but with a powerful intensity that left her mind in a muddle.

With each slide of his hands along her skin, her night rail inched upward, exposing her legs and baring her hips. Deftly, he drew the flimsy piece of silk over her head and dropped it atop his discarded clothing. He stood for a long moment, staring at her. "You, *ma chére*, are a goddess. So lovely."

Slowly, he eased her to him until their skin barely touched. He swayed ever so slightly from side to side, just enough to brush his chest back and forth across the tips of her breasts.

"Oh, Lord." Her throat constricted. She lifted her face to the sky, seeking more air.

A seductive murmur rolled through him. He lifted her in his arms and carried her inside. Along the way, his mouth found her breast. He tugged the nipple between his teeth and suckled.

She cried out.

As he settled her on the bed, a dark smile lifted his mouth. "I had better keep things even here." He grasped the other nipple between his teeth and scraped lightly over it, then sucked.

At her gasp, he moved to her mouth, where he gifted her with a hot, intense kiss. "We've lost the moonlight in here," he murmured. "Is there a single candle about? I want a little light."

She tried to speak but no words came out. Finally: "On the table. Beside you."

He lit the candle and slid his naked body in beside her. Pulling her into him, he wrapped his arms around her and hugged her tight, his mouth settling down on hers for another long kiss, their tongues tangling. Through all this, he handled her with a careful touch, as if she were something precious and delicate.

But then his hand slid down her belly and to the wet, hot place between her legs. He slipped a finger inside. Then another, touching a place that made her want to beg. A strange desperation began to build within her. She wanted him now with a fierceness that demanded appeasement. Without thought, her legs wrapped around him. She bit into his shoulder. "Now, Cameron, please. I want you inside me."

"You'll have me there soon enough." As his mouth traced along her belly, he eased her legs apart. He worked his way in between them, his tongue leaving a hot trail along her famished skin. Reaching the folds of her delicate lips, he licked.

She cried out and buried her hands in his hair, tried to rock her hips to the rhythm of his tongue, but he held her steady while he devoured her. Just when she thought she could take no more, that her nerves were bound to snap, he rose over her.

Taking his own hard length in hand, he slowly guided the plump tip inside her.

He paused.

Protesting his hesitation, she canted her hips, wanting more.

A wicked smile touched his lips. "You vixen, you."

Another gentle push, and he eased his thickness into her. Then withdrew.

"Oh, please," she whimpered.

He lay still for a moment. "Are you all right?"

"Yes," she whispered, biting his shoulder again. "But you keep pulling out of me and it's driving me insane, so stop it."

"Then wrap your legs around my hips, Josette." His voice, huskier by the word, filled her with as much ecstasy as did his touch.

She complied, and he rose up, looked deep into her eyes, then plunged into her to the hilt. He withdrew and sank into her again, now slow and purposeful, never taking his eyes off hers.

"More," she whispered.

He chuckled. "Wrong word, *ma chère*. You have all of me. What you mean to say, is faster."

Steadily, he increased the tempo, driving into her over and over. She gasped and moaned, as each new level of arousal deepened with every thrust of his hips.

She met his rhythm then, over and over again until her body seized, and he swept her over the edge of sanity.

"Please, Cameron," she begged, not knowing for what she pleaded. A vibration rotated from deep within, increasing until suddenly, a powerful, overwhelming quickening radiated from her very core. She cried out his name as millions of sparks ignited flames that swirled from her loins and exploded throughout her body and in her mind.

He groaned, buried his face in her shoulder, and with a great shudder, pulled out of her, spilling his seed over her belly.

He held her then, with a fierceness that told her that somewhere inside him, Cameron was hurting. In the stillness of the moment, his ragged breathing slowed. She slid her arms around his broad, smooth back and, mimicking his prior movements, caressed his skin.

When his hold on her eased, when his taut muscles relaxed, she asked, "Why did you do that?"

"Do what?"

"Pull out of me and spill your seed on my stomach."

"Because I'll not impregnate you and then leave, Josette. But God help me, if that were to happen, wherever I have gone off to, I can be found." He lifted his head and taking her chin in hand, forced her to look into his eyes. "You would tell me, wouldn't you?"

His piercing gaze caught her off guard. "Of course."

She'd not worry about such a thing happening. She was twenty-eight years old, hardly as fertile as someone much younger, and he'd taken precautions.

His expression softened. "Good." He kissed her on the forehead. "Stay right where you are."

He rolled off the bed, and padded over to the water basin. The sleek way he moved set something churning inside her once again. His back, broad and strong, his buttocks like steel, and those legs of his, so long and graceful—that glorious flesh had been all over her and in her only moments ago. Heat coiled in her womb. Good Lord, was it possible to want him again? So soon?

Snatching the linen towel hanging on a rod beside the water pitcher, he wet one end of the cloth and returned to the bed. Gently, he cleaned her, then saw to himself.

Agile as a god with wings, he slid back into bed and pulled her to him, enveloping her in a gentle, loving hold. He simply held her, unmoving. "You're so beautiful, Josette. So incredibly beautiful."

She nestled her head in the crook of his arm, her cheek against his chest. "Will you make love to me again before the night is over?"

Rich laughter rumbled right through the bed. "We're just getting started, darling. But you'll have to give me a few minutes."

He eased her leg over his thigh and took her hand, setting it on his manhood. "You're welcome to toy with me all you like while we wait, though."

Tenderly, he combed his fingers through her hair and brushed them over her cheek. "You feel so damn good to be with. Why did we wait so long?"

To her surprise, he was growing hard in her hand. A sense of power left her feeling giddy. "Am I perverse in enjoying what I am doing to you? A great deal?"

"Am I perverse in relishing it more than you possibly could?" He covered her hand with his and helped her stroke him. "Don't stop, Josette. Drive me insane, do what you will, but pray, do not stop."

Sometime after their third round of lovemaking, she'd fallen asleep still wrapped in his arms. As much as he hated to, he nudged her until she gave a little moan. "I see a hint of morning, Josette. I had better take my leave."

She tightened her arm around his chest and snuggled closer. "Stay," she mumbled. "I don't care what the neighbors think."

He chuckled. "It's not your neighbors who concern me. I suspect at least one of your brothers lies in wait for me. If my hunch is right, it's best we clash before dawn lest the entire town bear witness to a bloodbath."

Her eyes fluttered open and her hand began to rove. Her fingers traced the scar on his shoulder. "Is this where Trevor shot you?"

He moved her hand from his shoulder. "Good God, is no one in this town ignorant of that foolish duel? Leave that piece of cheese to the mice, if you will."

Her hand slid to his thigh. "And what of this scar? What happened here?"

He gave her a hard kiss on the mouth and scooted from the bed. "Ask your brother." He shot her a wicked grin. "That is, if you dare."

Her eyes widened. "Oh!"

Laughing, he strode to the balcony to retrieve their clothing. He wheeled around to head back to the bed. His sleepy-looking lover sat in the middle of a tangle of bedding, her legs curled under her. He'd done things to her throughout the night—sinful things that made her beg him not to stop. Want rolled through his belly again.

"I wish I didn't have to go, but I must."

He slipped her night rail over her head and eased her into it, leaving a trail of kisses as he went. Then he helped himself into his own clothes, not minding that she watched his every move. If the day weren't threatening to show its face, he'd climb back in bed without so much as a blink of the eye.

She started to slide out of bed.

"Don't get up." He plumped the pillows and eased her against them. Then he leaned over and planted a kiss on her swollen lips. "I want you lying right where you are so I can hold the image in my mind for the rest of my days."

A sultry grin lit her face. "As you wish."

He moved toward the door. "Did I tell you how good you look in red? But then, you're also well-suited to wearing nothing. I'll see you soon."

He slipped from the room and moved silently along the darkened corridor. Reaching the stairs, he trotted down them on the balls of his feet. So much seemed to have changed since he climbed these steps mere hours ago. But what, exactly, he couldn't fathom.

Stepping onto the veranda, he shut the door behind him with a solid click. He paused to glance around in a silence so thick he could hear the blood surge in his ears and his lungs at work. Soon, shafts of morning sunlight would spear through the branches of the trees lining the boulevard, warning every living thing that unbearable heat was on its way. He'd not be out in the sticky stuff much. Not this day, anyway.

The hair on his nape bristled.

He was not alone.

But then he'd half-expected this, hadn't he? Still, anger shot through him at the intrusion. He slipped his derringer from his pocket and, palming it, moved through the elaborate wrought-iron gate. After latching it behind him, he strolled along the street at an easy pace, as if nothing were amiss.

Not halfway down the block, Bastièn stepped out in front of him. "Coming or going, Monsieur Andrews?"

Cameron let loose a foul curse under his breath. "Get out of my way before I lay you flat, Thibodeaux. I'm in no mood."

Bastièn crossed his arms, feet spread apart in a stance that boded ill. "That mark on the right side of your neck. Is that where my sister laid claim to you? Or is it where she tried to fight you off?"

Cameron slammed Bastièn against a tree and shoved the derringer in his gut so fast he had no time to react.

"In case you haven't figured things out, you little prick, your sister did not join a convent when her husband died. She's a widow and a mature woman who can do as she pleases. Your double standards are laughable. While Josette has spent year after year in that big house with no mate to share her life, you're like a stag in heat, busy mounting anything that so much as resembles a female."

Bastièn's jaw twitched and that irritating smirk appeared. "Ah, but you are so very wrong, monsieur. I only bed women with means. The lovely ones, that is."

Cameron squeezed Bastièn's throat a little tighter. "Your humor eludes me. If you want to meddle in Josette's affairs, try hunting down your nefarious cousin and cutting him off at the knees. Do the same with Vennard while you're at it."

"Vennard?" Bastièn stilled. His dark gaze roved Cameron's face. "What does he have to do with my sister?"

Sensing the lust for battle had just drained out of Bastièn, Cameron released him. "Ask your brother, why don't you?"

Bastièn straightened his cravat and gave his collar a tug, setting it to rights. "This is not over between us, *mon ami*."

"I am not your friend, so do *not* call me that. I'm going to walk away, but as a reminder, should you follow me, you won't have your brother at your side to stick a knife in my leg."

"You speak with such venom. A pity."

He had to hand it to Bastièn. While the man had to be furious, he appeared impressively unruffled. Hard telling what kind of revenge he'd think up.

Still, Cameron couldn't resist one last jab at the wily Cajun. "Either leave Josette the hell alone, or move out from under your *maman*'s wing and in with your sister. Try befriending her instead of skulking about spying on her as if she didn't have the brains God gave a goose."

Bastièn laughed, a soft chuckle. "You cannot be serious."

"Oh, but I am." Cameron turned and headed toward his town house. He had something that needed doing immediately.

Before the *Dianah* sailed.

Chapter Seventeen

Time to get off the ship before I delay departure.

Cameron stood on the foredeck of the *Dianah*, the restless beat of sailor's blood in his veins yearning to match the rhythmic waves of the sea. Behind him, the commotion of an expert crew readying for the journey played a siren's song to his soul. The ship's bell clanged, the sound filling him with a peculiar melancholy.

Merde, he wanted to be gone. Wanted to wake up in the middle of nowhere to the clean, salty smell of the ocean. Wanted to step onto the clipper's deck with a cup of steaming coffee in hand and greet the morning sun dancing across the water. Wanted to laugh at playful dolphins racing alongside the ship as if nothing more important in life existed.

He blew out a breath. That familiar freedom couldn't come soon enough. What the devil made him think he'd be in any position to set sail in nine or ten days? It wasn't the shipping business holding him here. There was none better to handle accounts than Abbott; and barely six months into his position, Michel had already proved capable of managing the busy office. As much as Cameron hated to admit it, any fool could see that René was an asset to the company. Not to mention Michel got on well with the shrewd Cajun.

Providing Felicité took a steamboat upriver tomorrow and forgot Thibodeaux existed.

Alexia's future was what had Cameron tied in knots. He couldn't very well leave until she agreed to sail with Felicité to England, and he saw them safely on their way.

Blast it all, that could be a month from now if Felicité kept to her plans. He glanced over at the *Simone,* and her busy crew. She was scheduled to sail in three days, bound for Liverpool. Why not haul Alexia aboard at the last minute without her expecting it? Once they reached their destination, he could see her well-situated, then leave with a clear conscience.

His gut soured.

Wasn't that the awful way he'd been shipped off in his youth? He wouldn't shanghai his worst enemy, so why would he even think to trick his own daughter? Wanting to leave New Orleans had to be her idea. And who could be more persuasive than Felicité? Alexia was already smitten with her new friend. Hell, her only friend.

But what if his cousin failed?

Bloody hell. He simply could not allow that to happen. As anxious as he was to be on his way, he couldn't leave his daughter behind to follow in her grandmother's footsteps. Or end up Lucien's victim. And if Josette couldn't handle her now, what might things be like in a couple of years?

Josette.

Images of her ran through his mind like quicksilver. He shoved them aside. Now was not the time to be thinking of her. Not when he stood on the deck of this particular ship, holding the letter he'd penned not an hour after leaving Josette's bed.

He raked his fingers through his hair. What was he to do with a daughter who deserved a better life and didn't know it? Blast it all, he could run a worldwide shipping business with his eyes closed, but couldn't begin to manage a willful child. What a pitiful excuse he was for a father.

A seagull wheeled and dove toward the water. A dip of its head below the surface and off it flew, a fish wiggling in its beak. Croxton stepped beside Cameron. "Eight bells, sir. The *Dianah* is ready to pull up anchor."

Cameron drew in a breath of salt air and dockside smells—goods, people, and decaying fish. Yes, he wanted to be well away from land. He reached inside his jacket pocket and retrieved an envelope. "You're a man I trust, Croxton. Would you do me the favor of burning this once you're well out to sea? Cast the ashes to the wind?"

Croxton glanced at Dianah's name scrawled across the envelope. His brows scrunched together. "Looks like I could've saved myself the trouble of giving you that little speech a few days back."

Cameron nodded at the envelope, but said nothing. Everything he had to say was written on those three pieces of paper. It had been hard as hell penning those words to Dianah this morning. His fingers had shaken something terrible while writing, but once it was done, the steel band around his chest had loosened.

Odd, but when he'd signed off with, *I now release you into the loving arms of God*, it was as if a lightning bolt had struck from the heavens, shot right through him and into the earth, grounding him in place for one shocking moment. A light breeze had wafted through the open window, as if Dianah were blowing him a kiss from another world, bidding him a final *adieu*.

The ship's bells clanged, pulling him out of his reverie. He turned on his heel and departed the clipper, then remained dockside, near the painted figurehead of a sylph-like lady attached to the prow. Legend had it these unique carvings embodied the ship's spirit. They were meant to appease the gods of the sea, to bring both vessel and crew safely to

the next port. He'd commissioned this particular carving—
it bore a remarkable likeness to his deceased wife.

He glanced up in time to see Croxton raise his hand in
signal. At his downstroke, precise maneuvers went into play.
A couple of sailors hauled up the gangplank while others
gathered in the ropes, set the sails and called out instructions
to one another. The grind of metal against metal screeched
through the air as the anchor cranked into the ship's hawse.

Cameron's heart kicked up a notch.

Croxton strode toward the foredeck. He paused, then
tipped his captain's hat to Cameron and disappeared to the
leeward side.

It was monumental, the clipper leaving port with Cameron's letter aboard. He lingered, waiting for the sails to
billow and catch the sea breeze. They flapped for only a
moment before those snowy-white sheets caught a gust of
wind and the sleek vessel eased away from the dock. Before
he knew it, she sailed off, a flock of seagulls her winged
escort. Cheers and shouts went up from the sailors aboard.

He remained in place as the *Dianah* grew smaller and
smaller, until she disappeared along the sharp edge of the
horizon. In her wake, an inner calm settled in, a kind of
lightness that felt like a peculiar sort of victory, if one could
call it that. The feeling took on dimension. Suddenly, he understood. His letter hadn't set *him* free. It was Dianah who'd
escaped her earthbound chains. His ability to finally say
good-bye, to truly let her go in every sense of the word, had
given her a set of wings with which to soar to the heavens.
Elation mixed with the need to stifle a sob. He had to get out
of there.

He left the dock and headed . . . to where? He stumbled
to a halt. *Merde.* He wasn't needed in the office, and he sure
as hell wasn't going back home, where Alexia and Felicité
were likely chatting up a storm over breakfast. He didn't

need to interfere with whatever progress Felicité might be making.

So what to do?

At loose ends and feeling suddenly empty, he stuffed his hands in his pockets and slowly headed for familiar territory—Jackson Square.

Soon, he found himself in the Vieux Carré amid the close-set stucco town houses and narrow streets of his youth. Lines of lacy ironwork galleries stood at attention as he ambled along. Although his father had been of British heritage, his mother had been fiercely French. She and her sister—Trevor's *maman*—had seen to it that he and Trevor adhered to old-world ways and customs while growing up in that enclosed environment. A city within a city, some had called the French Quarter, while others went so far as to label the Vieux Carré as its own country.

Once Trevor's siblings had come along, their father had bought Carlton Oaks, a sizeable plantation upriver. Cameron and Trevor, close as brothers, had divided their time equally between the French Quarter and Carlton Oaks. They'd turned into troublemakers only after both their mothers had died.

Nearing Jackson Square, he paused to purchase a *cala* from one of the strolling *marchandes*. That day long ago, when he'd bought one for Josette, flashed through his mind. Her eyes had lit up before she snatched it from his hands and ran off.

Finding a bench, he settled in to eat the confection. A faint smile touched his lips. How he'd enjoyed his childhood walks in this square with his mother, and with his aunt and Trevor beside them. And how he'd delighted in the single, sugary *cala* he was allowed during those outings.

He glanced up at the huge bronze statue of General Jackson astride his rearing horse. The city had erected the thing smack in the middle of the square after changing its name from *Place d'Armes* to Jackson Square in honor of the hero of the Battle of New Orleans. Even though the renaming had taken place when his mother was young, she'd never approved.

Life seemed so simple and carefree back then. Who would've guessed he'd one day feel like a stranger amidst his own people, and that life would become so complicated he couldn't wait to escape what was truly a lovely city?

Alexia.

How would his punctilious mother have responded to a Thibodeaux grandchild—one linked to the very reason he'd been shipped to England. An emptiness echoed through him. Maman had known nothing of that terrible time—she'd already passed away.

With a sigh, he rose from the bench and wandered in the direction of home. He turned up Toulouse Street and headed for Royal. Entering the town house, he found no one home, not even the maid. The idea of shedding his clothing down to his underwear and taking to his room held appeal. Why not spend the rest of the day reading a book and escaping the heat? He strode to the bookshelf and stared blankly at the titles gracing the leather spines. After scanning two shelves, he couldn't remember a single one. This wouldn't do.

The problem was, thoughts of Josette left little room for anything else. She'd been more than an exciting lover last night; she'd helped to free his soul. In between their love-making, they'd laughed and talked, completely at ease with each other. He discovered that aside from their powerful physical attraction, he genuinely liked her. In fact, he wouldn't mind some of that conversation about now. His groin hitched. Merely conversation. Nothing else.

Restless, he made for the stairs. Changing his mind, he headed for the door leading outside. He had no intention of dropping in on Josette unannounced. He wouldn't find her at home anyway. Not since she'd mentioned spending the day in her shop preparing creams and lotions.

The Belle Femme. Humph. Now there was a place he couldn't begin to find an excuse to visit. Besides, as much as he'd like to see her again, he needed to keep their visits focused on Alexia. He wasn't fool enough to think there'd not be another night like last night, but he had to take care not to get too involved. No sense complicating things any more than they already were.

Devil take it, he'd go see what Abbott and Michel were up to. Study a few charts and maps. Inspect the current ships in port. Hopefully, his cousin had sent Thibodeaux on some chore that would require his absence for a good part of the day.

No such luck.

When Cameron stepped over the threshold and into the office, René stood in the center of the room, crisp white sleeves rolled back, maps and charts spread across the table. He set down a ruler and pencil. The fiery look in his eyes matched the one in Bastièn's this morning.

Bloody hell if the day hadn't been hard enough as it was.

René crossed his arms over his chest and leaned a hip against the table. "I understand you had a rather enjoyable evening last night, *oui*?"

A rush of anger, and it was all Cameron could do to keep from going after René's throat. "How sweet. You and Bastièn are so close you see fit to discuss every detail in life. The way you go about it, though, one would think you were two gossipy, meddling old ladies."

He stalked past René without looking his way. "I'd like the morning reports, Abbott."

Michel, sitting at his desk, held out a sheaf of papers without turning around. "I have them. Thought you weren't coming in today."

"*Oui*," René muttered.

"I changed my mind." Cameron snatched the papers from Michel's hand and strode to the desk across the room. He sat with his back to the men, anger mounting by degrees. "In case anyone has forgotten, I co-own this rather lucrative business, which means I take command whenever I please. If anyone doesn't like it, he can leave. Now."

Abbott set his pen to his journals and, without a word, scratched away.

René snorted.

Cameron turned in his chair and, seeing René still with his arms crossed and leaning a hip against the table, swallowed the urge to scrounge up a knife and filet the bastard. Instead, he spoke calmly. "I don't give a bloody damn how capable someone is or how they might be connected to me, replacements can always be found. The one thing I won't tolerate is insolence and lack of respect for one's superiors. In the shipping business, to ignore insubordination is suicide. You, Thibodeaux, are no longer employed by this company. Abbott, issue his pay."

A half-grin caught the corner of René's mouth, the same kind of smirk Bastièn favored. "You recall the little conversation we had in front of your home the other night, *oui*? If not, allow me to give you a hint. It had something to do with two lovely ladies."

He turned on his heel and walked out.

Michel threw his pen across the room and stood. "What in God's name possessed you to release him when you'll soon be gone? Christ, Cameron, Thibodeaux is a natural at the business. He's already saved us a bundle."

Abbott glanced up. "He's only been on the job a few days and already he's more efficient than Cooper was. What will he be capable of in six months? A year from now?"

Cameron stood. He strode to Michel's side of the room and stared out the windows at the moored ships. "He was insolent. I won't stand for it."

"If you don't want him here, there's little we can do about it," Michel said. "But you'll soon be gone, so I do hope you'll reconsider. He can apologize without losing face if given the right circumstances."

Abbott set down his pen. "I agree. Once he's fully trained, he could run the San Francisco office and Cooper could be sent back here."

Cameron let go a deep sigh. He'd allowed the events of the day to fray his temper. The run-in with Bastièn, the letter he'd written to Dianah, the fix he was in with Alexia—they coalesced with the haunting idea that he didn't know what to do with himself in the long run, and he'd snapped. "Well, the upstart cannot return without a change in attitude and an apology."

Michel continued to pace. "Cameron, get hold of yourself. Either make the decision to stay here and run things or go on upriver with Felicité and Alexia until it's time to leave for good."

Michel was right. The irony that Cameron needed to leave overshadowed his anger. He let out a bemused laugh. "My own shipping company and I'm told I'm not fit to be here. Abbott, would you excuse us for a moment?"

"Now those are welcome words." Abbott grabbed his jacket and, not bothering to take the time to roll down his sleeves, made his quick exit.

When he was out of sight, Michel turned to Cameron. "What the devil has gotten into you?"

Cameron heaved a breath. "I slept with René's sister last night and Bastièn waylaid me on the way out. There was a bit of an altercation."

"You what?" Michel pivoted. "Tell me I didn't just hear that."

"I wish I could." Cameron pinched the bridge of his nose.

How could anything so wonderful between two mature and willing adults turn into such a fiasco?

Michel leaned an elbow on the waist-high maps and charts table and worked his fingers over his chin. "What was that last remark Thibodeaux made about a conversation regarding two women?"

"I think you can figure that one out on your own, cousin."

"I'm getting a glimmer, but I'd like to hear it from you."

"I told him to keep his distance from Felicité. He said he would so long as I kept away from his sister." Cameron felt sheepish now. "I think we'd better send Felicité upriver today."

Michel muttered a curse and began to pace back and forth. "You realize our supply of rum is once again at risk if Thibodeaux fails to return. Not to mention he knows his way around here, so who can say what other trouble he could stir up."

"I won't be blackmailed nor have an insubordinate employee."

Michel ceased pacing and moved to stand beside Cameron, his gaze focused on the dock. "I agree with the insubordination, but I doubt he thinks of it as such, not with his sister involved. Nor would he consider any mischief he thinks up as extortion. More like justified behavior. Why don't you take Alexia and Felicité up to Carlton Oaks? Visit with my father while things here simmer down. I'll speak with René and hire him back with the understanding that he is to show proper respect in the future."

"What if he declines?"

"He's too smart for that. The trick is to make it easy for him to return. I can handle that part."

"What if Alexia refuses to make the trip upriver?"

"You're worried she'd refuse? She clearly thinks the sun

rises and sets on both you and my sister. I doubt you'll have any problem getting her to agree."

Michel and Abbott were right. Given a second chance, René could work out just fine, and Cameron would be gone. "I appreciate your doing what you can to smooth things over and hire him back. Convince him he's got a prime position with the company and he'll not find a better opportunity. Not in this town, anyway."

Michel grunted. "I think you both have those French tempers that you let get away from you."

"Might I remind you that your mother and my mother were sisters? As much French blood runs through your veins as mine."

Michel chuckled. "And might I remind you that our fathers are brothers, and I inherited their cooler English temperament?"

"Humph." Cameron stared out at the *Simone* riding low in the water. The thought of leaving on the clipper and hauling Alexia aboard suddenly seemed more palatable. With the ship leaving port in three days, he could easily be aboard. Even with Alexia kicking and screaming. The devil could have this mess, then.

"Can you find room for me aboard the *Simone*? A cabin with two beds?"

Michel whipped around to face Cameron. "Are you serious? What of all this talk about going upriver with Alexia and my sister?"

"Leaving in three days could be a godsend. I've never looked forward to anything so much in my life as ridding myself of the Thibodeaux family. If God punishes for mistakes, he's doing a fine job of it."

Michel froze in place and stared at the door.

A chill ran down Cameron's spine.

He turned.

Alexia stood at the threshold, her face blank and pale.

Merde! Cameron stepped forward. "Alexia, I didn't mean you. I meant your uncles."

Her eyes wide and filled with . . . nothing, she turned and ran.

"Alexia, don't . . . oh, hell." Cameron started after her.

Felicité stepped over the threshold. "Now you've done it."

Chapter Eighteen

"Was that the full seven drops or merely five?" Josette stood in her laboratory, trying to recall the exact amount of tincture of polygonum root she'd added to the potion she was concocting for Madame Olympée's thinning hair.

"Drat, not another batch ruined." Unable to vanquish the image of a naked Cameron from her mind, nor the thrill her thoughts of him produced, Josette couldn't concentrate. After Bastièn's morning visit, she should be too angry with Cameron to think such impious thoughts. But there they were, tramping through her mind like lustful imps, igniting small flames in her belly and swelling her breasts.

Both exhausted and euphoric—the former caused by little sleep, the latter from a night of exquisite lovemaking that had produced a few sore muscles and a bit of tenderness in secret places—she'd have put off coming to work, but Madame Olympée's order was due today, as were several others. She forced herself to focus once again on her project.

Would two drops more or less matter so much? She huffed out an exasperated breath. The thought of cheating even one time repulsed her. Meticulous attention to detail was what gave her customers their smooth, unwrinkled skin, their lush, healthy hair—and kept them returning from as far away as Baton Rouge.

Josette loved the subtle art of alchemy. Every jar and bottle leaving her premises had been filled with a creation specific to the individual. Of late, she'd begun dabbling in *eau de parfum*. Transforming the soul of a flower or blossom into a liquid that blended with the unique oils of a woman's skin was breathtaking. It was also a challenge that caused her to lose track of time while experimenting. A pleasant loss, that. Of late, she'd been creating scents exclusive to the individual. She had a knack for it. No, tired as she was, she would never compromise her work, not even by one drop, more or less.

Another thought of Cameron washed through her. Had she compromised herself with him last night? A small smile caught a corner of her mouth. Not in the least. Good Lord, had the man cut his teeth on Casanova's memoirs? Her heart tripped in her chest and her pulse beat a new rhythm. Even her bare toes had met his deft hands . . . and tongue.

Once again, she shoved thoughts of him aside. She must concentrate. What to do since little remained of the precious herb until the next batch could be distilled? As much as she detested falling back on something Maman had taught her, she retrieved a pendulum from the silk pouch she kept amongst her beakers and vials.

Holding the golden pear-shaped bob by its chain, she suspended it over the small glass bottle and emptied her mind, her intention focused on the extract she'd introduced into the mix, and the exact number of drops she'd used. In seconds, the dowsing instrument felt weighted, as though it wanted to plunge itself into the mixture. Then it began to slowly move counterclockwise. Counting each full circle, the pendulum stopped dead at five.

Josette sighed in relief, added two more drops to the

potion and went about correcting the remaining batches she'd botched.

The pendulum had been the only thing her mother had ever given her, presented on her fourteenth birthday. She hadn't known at the time that Maman had far more in mind than presenting Josette with an instrument she could use to dowse for anything from the depth of a well to potions for the ill. As it turned out, after Solange died, Maman had decided to train Josette in the voodoo arts. But Josette had refused to have anything to do with that aspect of her mother's work.

There was a tap on the door, a signal that Josette's lead shop girl sought entry. "*Entrez vous*."

Elise slipped inside. Shutting the door behind her, she leaned her back against the panel, her cheeks blotched pink.

"Good heavens, what is it?"

"I beg your pardon, Madame. It's Monsieur Vennard. He's gone straight to your office without permission. I told him you were not in, but he called me a liar and marched right past me. There was little I could do to stop him."

"It's not your fault. The man is an arrogant cur." Josette removed the work apron covering her green gown and pushed the completed bottle toward Elise. "Paste Madame Olympée's special label on this, if you will, and see she gets it. Leave the other bottles for now. I'll tend to Monsieur Vennard."

Leaving her laboratory, Josette paused in front of the closed door to her office and drew a breath. She could do this. She could stop this man from trampling over her like a runaway horse. The idea of his attempting to purchase Belle Femme under veiled threats grew more ludicrous by the day. If worse came to worst, she would have to speak to her brothers. But that would be her last resort. She had other solutions in mind.

Pushing the door open, she marched straight to her desk

and sat. Not bothering to glance up, she removed her pistol from a drawer, along with a small bag that jingled. She emptied the bag of bullets. Slowly, one-by-one, she loaded the six-shooter.

"Monsieur Vennard. Not only did you offend my employee by your crude behavior, you broke my rules by entering my private space without permission. I'll not have you coming in here again. Nor will I have you approach my home."

The slide of steel against steel caused her to glance up. Vennard sat in front of her, a malicious glimmer in his eyes . . . and a sword pointed straight at her.

She managed not to flinch. Instead, she propped her elbows on her desk, and wrapping both hands around the butt of the gun, directed it straight at his heart. "I had a hunch that cane of yours afforded you more than a walking stick. You do realize you've placed yourself in jeopardy by exposing your little secret."

A low chuckle left his throat. "Tell me, Madame LeBlanc, how have I endangered myself?"

"I can pull the trigger right now, and claim you came at me with your weapon. My employee will confirm you forced your way in here. My shop is not for sale. Leave at once."

He lowered his sword and tapped it against a knee. "You amuse me. I did not come here about your business. If you recall, I said I'd be back in two weeks to discuss the sale. Which I will do."

"If you are not here to discuss Belle Femme, then why are you here?"

"My daughter was recently married."

Her hands were getting tired, but she refused to lower the gun. "You know I am well aware of that fact, Monsieur Vennard, seeing as how you saw me in Antoine's. What is your point?"

He brought the sword up in a half-salute. "Please, Madame

LeBlanc, do set the pistol down before you accidentally pull the trigger."

Behind his calm demeanor lurked malice. He was having a difficult time keeping it from showing. A sinking feeling ran down the back of Josette's throat and settled in her stomach. She set down the gun but kept her hand wrapped around the butt, just in case he came at her with the sword. She'd use it if she had to. Wouldn't she? For pity's sake, what was the man after?

"Go on," she said. "You have two minutes before I send for the police . . . those you have not paid off, that is."

He lifted a brow. "My daughter is eager to live in the new and elite section of town where you reside. She is determined to have the largest and finest home around, but she is too impatient to have one built. I believe the most opulent residence at present would be yours, Madame."

He retrieved an envelope from inside his jacket and slid it across the desk. "This will more than compensate you. I expect you to be out by the end of the month."

A high buzzing sounded in Josette's ears. Had she actually heard him right? He wanted her residence as well as her shop? Was he out to ruin her entirely? She steeled herself against the tremors shooting through her and tried for as much calm as she could muster.

"Not only do I have no intention of selling my shop to you, but the idea of vacating my home so your spoiled daughter can take up residence is laughable. Now, before I either call the police or take this gun in hand, I'm curious as to why you are trying to get rid of me. Because obviously, you are."

He stood and, sliding the sword back into the cane, looked her over with disdain. "Why? Because you are nothing but trash, Josette. Illegitimate Cajun trash who dares to walk the streets of this town pretending to be a lady. You belong back in the bayou. I'll not have this town sullied by your presence in the grandest home in the wealthiest district. Nor will I condone your owning a shop between the finest jeweler in town and the finest couturier. You do not fit in here. You are an embarrassment, and I'll not have it."

That old familiar feeling took hold. All her life she'd never fit in, at home or otherwise. And she didn't know why. Perhaps men like him had reinforced those terrible feelings that she was no good. Instilled them in her long before she was old enough to discern what their sideways glances meant. Or perhaps it was the common knowledge that she and her siblings were a bunch of thieving bastards that had filtered through early on.

Heaven knew she'd worked hard to clip her roots. Had steered so far from being the subject of gossip, she now existed in a kind of solitude that threatened to drive her mad at times. No matter what she did to improve her lot in life, she was still an outcast.

Oh, why was her heart pushing back and forth against her chest so? Her home, her shop—she'd acquired them through sacrifice and pure grit.

She could not lose them.

They would be all she'd have once Alexia was gone.

"Get out," she said, so softly even she barely heard the words, but there was no mistaking the threat in them. She stood, tossed the envelope in his face, marched to the door, and yanked it open.

Elise stumbled in. Josette caught her before the girl tripped and fell. Elise glanced at the gun on the desk and at Vennard. "I . . . I was concerned, Madame. I heard raised voices."

"Monsieur Vennard was just leaving, Elise. Please see him out, then return immediately." A click of heels down the hall and Josette returned to her desk. She shoved the loaded gun into a drawer and bent over, holding her stomach and swallowing bile.

Elise returned and shut the door behind her. "I am truly sorry, Madame. I . . . I was afraid for your safety."

"I should send you away," Josette said, feeling that much sicker inside. She'd trusted Elise.

The girl paled and began to tremble. "Please, Madame. I am responsible for the care of my parents and younger brother. I am trying to get him educated so he can have a better life."

"Have you listened at my door before, Elise?" Was there no one Josette could rely on but herself?

Elise lowered her gaze and picked at a nail. "Your brother is very concerned about you."

Josette couldn't contain the shock that swept through her. "Which brother?"

"René." Elise raised a fluttering hand to the cameo at her throat.

"And you've been spying on me for him?"

A tear slid down Elise's cheek. She nodded. "I'll collect my things and leave immediately, Madame."

The girl had to be taken with René to have stooped so low. She'd been a devoted employee since the day the doors opened for business. "I'm not going to let you go, Elise."

Elise's head snapped up. "You won't?"

Josette shook her head. "Since you've snooped in my affairs, it's only fair you answer my question. Have you been sleeping with my brother?"

Another tear ran down Elise's cheek. "Please don't think badly of me. I love him."

"Oh, you fool. Every woman he touches thinks she's in love with him. He'll not return your feelings in the long run."

Elise wiped her cheek with the back of her hand and met Josette's gaze. "I know there will never be anything permanent between us, but I'm certain he cares for me. At the moment, anyway. I am content with that."

"But he will use you and toss you aside. I know my brother well."

"You do not understand, Madame. I will not leave my parents so long as they live, nor will I forsake my sibling. It is what I am committed to doing. I know perfectly well I am unlikely to find a man who will take on such a burden, and also be capable of loving me with the kind of tenderness and expertise your brother has shown me."

"Good heavens." Josette remembered to breathe and sucked in air. "I know both my brothers have a way about them that women adore, but I've never allowed myself to dwell on the . . . well . . . their personal lives."

She paused, as thoughts of Cameron invaded her mind once again. Wasn't she up to the same thing as Elise? Cast no stone.

"I know you do not approve, Madame," Elise said. "But tell me, what is wrong with giving myself the opportunity to feel love? What is love anyway?"

Josette frowned. "I'm not certain what you are getting at."

Elise began to fiddle with her cameo again. "When someone loves you, you can see it in their eyes, the way they care for you. But the love of which I speak? Isn't it in reality what only I am feeling inside? Ushered in by the way René showers me with his tender affections? I'm no fool, Madame. You may think he's using me, but in a sense, I am using him as well. Rest assured, I know how to take things one day at a time."

Josette looked away. How could she argue with Elise when Josette was doing the very same thing?

The color had returned to Elise's cheeks, and her trembling ceased. A wisp of a smile touched her mouth.

Josette smiled back. "By the look on your face, I'd say you are thinking of René as we speak."

Elise's grin widened. "*Non*, Madame. You came in this

morning looking all dewy-eyed and refreshed, as if you'd taken a lover."

Now it was Josette's turn to feel heat in her cheeks. "I won't go so far as to answer that. At least not today. Perhaps one day."

"I know I speak out of place, but you have the advantage of being a refined lady who also lived a life in the bayou. You are a unique mixture of loveliness and grit that I have always admired. There are many men, not only in New Orleans, but throughout the world, who would want to give a woman like you what she requires. Not what she needs, but what she requires. Right now, your brother gives me what I require."

A knock sounded on the door and Elise stood. "I'll answer that, Madame."

She opened the door and stepped back with a gasp.

René walked into the room. Two uniformed police officers followed him.

Josette shot to her feet, her heart in her throat. "What is it? What's happened?"

René glanced from Elise to Josette. "Alexia has been seen stealing. Her actions have been so blatant, it's as if she's on a mission to be caught."

"How do you know this?"

One of the police officers stepped forward. "She pilfered a flour sack from one of the merchants without trying to hide the fact. By the time he located me, several merchants were after her, along with a number of pedestrians. That's when my colleague met up with me. We chased her, but even with her bag of goods, she outran us. We'll find her eventually, and she'll be arrested."

René turned to Josette. "We know where our niece is, *oui*?"

Unable to find her voice just then, she nodded.

"I'll go after her," René said. "I'll see that everything is returned."

The officer shook his head. "Returning what she stole will certainly make things go a bit easier on her, but let's face facts, Thibodeaux, she'll only do it again. If she can break the law like an adult, it's time she paid the price like one."

"I give you my word," René said. "I'll collect her and bring her to you before noon tomorrow."

"Very well." The officer gave a derogatory snort. "You, of all people, would know where to find the district station. God knows the number of times you were dragged there once you were old enough to pick pockets."

When they'd gone, Elise took her leave as well. Josette slumped into a chair opposite her desk. "What in the world could have prompted her to terrorize the Quarter?"

René swiped his hand over his face and sat in the chair beside her. "It would appear we've all had a bad day."

"What do you mean?"

"You already know Bastièn got into it with Cameron. Then Cameron and I butted heads. Suffice it to say, we both lost our tempers, and he sacked me. I then departed the shipping office, but not before leaving behind a few choice words."

"Oh, for God's sake, René! But what in the world does that have to do with Alexia?"

"While Michel was busy reinstating my position, he told me that Alexia overheard Cameron telling his cousin to arrange for passage on the next ship out so Cameron could be done with the Thibodeaux family once and for all."

Josette's fingers went to her lips. "Oh, no. Did Cameron go after her?"

René propped his elbows on his knees and couched his chin in his hands. "He did, but with no luck, so he retreated to his town house while I went after her."

"No matter how he feels about us, he should be horse-whipped for being so careless with his words."

"Josette, you sound like Maman. Cameron only meant Bastièn and me, but you know Alexia. Hurt her feelings, and she reacts with a blank stare and coldness that could freeze the Mississippi. Then she turns hot, and only God knows what she'll do in retaliation."

"Perhaps I had better go collect her."

René stood. "You know Maman will side with Alexia if you show up. I'll go."

He was right. In fact, if Josette went after Alexia, it would only worsen things. She stood as well. "I'll see you out."

"Don't bother. Go home, Josette. You look fatigued."

She rubbed the knots at the back of her neck while she stood at the door until René had gone. Then she fitted her green hat on her head, grabbed her matching parasol and a reticule that held the blasted articles Bastièn had presented to her.

She marched out the door and headed straight for Cameron's town house.

Chapter Nineteen

He should be guzzling lemonade in the middle of this sultry afternoon, not sipping brandy. What the hell, it might help relax his tight neck. Cameron untied his cravat and gave it a toss. He smiled to himself when it landed neatly over the stair's banister. After all these years, he hadn't lost his touch.

Heaving a sigh, he removed his jacket and vest, rolled back his sleeves, then sprawled on the sofa. He glanced around the dimly lit parlor. The housekeeper must have drawn the heavy velvet curtains before taking her leave.

Merde. What a day. Every bloody muscle ached.

He didn't like admitting it, but that blasted confrontation with Bastièn had unnerved him. Then there was the good-bye letter to Dianah that had nearly torn a hole in his heart. By the time another Thibodeaux had given him the what for, he was ready for a spot of brandy. But what topped the cake was that wretched chase after Alexia in this deplorable heat. What he wouldn't give to take back his words. That look on her face before she'd run off would likely haunt him for the remainder of his life.

He kicked off his shoes and stretched out his legs. What remained of his day would be spent right where he sat. He picked up the brandy snifter, gave a slow swirl of the amber liquid and stared into its amorphous depths. Perhaps it would be best if he slept on the idea of leaving town in three days. Or at least waited to see what transpired after Alexia returned. His gut burned, but not from the spirits. Doing the right thing by her was vital—whatever the right thing might be. He knew for certain leaving her in New Orleans wasn't an option. Something Josette had known all along.

Just thinking Josette's name, and that inexplicable craving ran through him again. For pity's sake, hadn't last night been enough of a romp to slake his lust? The lingering need had to be the result of his lengthy celibacy. What else could it be but his body wanting to make up for lost time?

But oh, hadn't she been something?

No.

Hadn't *they* been something?

She'd made it clear he'd left her well satisfied. At least he'd given her his all. That wasn't quite right, either. What transpired between them seemed as natural an act as breathing, so it hadn't been a matter of him *trying* to do anything. They'd been in unison with their wants and needs, as if they'd been together before, yet every nuance of their coupling, every taste of her flesh had been a new awakening.

A shuffling noise caught his attention. He sat up straighter, his hearing turning acute. The sound came from the rear of the house. Hadn't the housekeeper left yet? She was supposed to come mornings only.

A familiar figure from the past appeared.

"Marie?"

"Sure 'nuff, *Mischie* Cameron." A wide grin broke out on the maid's face. "I fell asleep back there so I didn't hear you come in, beggin' your pardon."

An old, comfortable feeling slid inside him. She still called him *mischie*, her pet name. He relaxed back into the sofa and took up his brandy. "Did Uncle Justin send you down from Carlton Oaks once he learned I was here?"

"No, sir. I been working at *Mischie* Michel's place here in town for a while now. My mama is there, so he thought it best I tend to her and him both."

Egads, her mother still lived? The woman had been ancient when Cameron was a child. So the old lady would live out the rest of her days with her daughter by her side. Good.

He grinned. "Aren't you a welcome sight?"

She folded her arms over her chest and sized him up. "You got yourself quite the daughter, I been hearing."

He held the brandy glass to his lips and watching her over the rim, took a swallow. "You've had a little tête-à-tête with Miss Felicité."

Marie's eyes twinkled. "Can I talk you into some of my beignets you used to hanker for? Haven't lost your taste for 'em, have you?"

He saluted her with the snifter. "Miss Marie, the day I have no appetite for your beignets is the day you can cart me off to the nearest cemetery because I'll have died."

Her light laughter settled around Cameron like a well-used blanket. "I got to fetch me some eggs, *mischie*. But I'll hasten right back." She eyed his brandy. "I'll be fixin' you some of my good café au lait to go with them beignets."

So here she was, back in his life after he'd been gone years, and already she was taking control. "It's sinfully hot out there. Are you sure you want to brave the heat for a few eggs?"

She scurried down the hall, her lilting laughter trailing behind her. In moments, she returned with an empty wicker basket on her arm and wearing a crumpled brown hat. Jesu, she still prized that old thing? The least she could do was toss the scraggily feather.

She was out the door, only to return moments later. "Pardon me, *mischie*, but there's a lady here to see you."

"Who?"

"A Madame LeBlanc. A right pretty lady, but she's in a temper."

He mumbled a curse. "She's my daughter's aunt, and she's not happy with something I said. But then, neither am I, so send her in."

Mischief flashed in Marie's eyes. "Lawdy, it's like you ain't never left. Always one thing or another going on with the ladies." She exited the house humming to herself.

Cameron didn't bother moving. Not yet, anyway. He'd do the gentlemanly thing when Josette appeared, but until then . . . he drained his brandy.

The door opened. Then slammed shut with a loud bang.

"Oh, do come in," he muttered. He set down the empty snifter and stood. "Welcome to my home, Josette. At least I'm here to greet you so you won't have to pick locks."

She trooped in, a firestorm in a froth of pale green, the large brim of her matching hat bouncing in rhythm with the womanly sway of her hips. Damn, she was beautiful. Even her flashing eyes added to her allure.

His pulse tripped, and for a moment, his awareness contracted to a fiery place low in his belly.

"I know, I know. I said something Alexia shouldn't have overheard, and now René's gone looking for her. He'll bring her here, at which point I shall apologize until I am blue in the face. That said, good afternoon."

He shouldn't want to kiss her. He really shouldn't.

She leaned her parasol against the wall, then set her reticule on a side table. Opening the string closure, she peeked inside the bag, then gave it a little shake and yanked the cords tight.

"Hmm. That was an interesting exercise in I don't know what. Have a seat."

"I won't be staying, you lout. Are you aware the police are looking for your daughter?"

A shock wave hit him, draining away whatever pleasure the sight of Josette had brought him. "What the devil for?"

Her eyes flashed, dark and ominous. "She's gone on a rampage, that's what the devil for."

He pinched the bridge of his nose while he struggled to arrange his muddled emotions into some semblance of order. "Because of what I said?"

"So it would seem."

Josette moved closer to him. He caught her scent, that wonderful, light, feminine essence that coated her skin. He knew, because last night he'd licked every inch of it. "What Alexia overheard was regrettably worded. I tried to apologize, but she took issue with me and ran off. What kind of rampage?"

"After she left you, she went from store to store stealing things." Josette paused to let her words sink in.

His jaw clamped shut. "Go on."

"She stole from people on the street. Blatantly stuffed her bounty into a flour sack—one she'd filched—and ran off."

As Josette stared at him, her eyes began to shimmer. His heart gave a squeeze. Hell, she was near tears. He took a step toward her.

She stepped back. "Don't touch me."

He spread his arms out, palms up. "Fine. I won't touch you. I'll retrieve Alexia and whatever items she stole. Do you have any idea where she might have gone?"

"Where do you think?" Josette fisted her hands on her hips. "Alexia is likely bestowing her ill-gotten gain on Maman as we speak. Thank you very much, Cameron. You delivered your daughter right into her grandmother's greedy hands."

He swiped a hand over his brow. "Then show me where your mother lives and I'll collect Alexia."

Josette crossed her arms around her waist. "René has gone after her."

Cameron watched the shadows in the room play across her stormy eyes and gorgeous face. "One thing I've recently learned about your brother is that he's a man of his word. He'll bring her back, and when he does, I'll see to righting the wrongs."

"He won't bring her here, you fool." Amidst their shimmering, her eyes flashed renewed fury. Her foot tapped a rapid rhythm. "He's to deliver her to the police by noon tomorrow along with all the stolen items."

Cameron's breath froze in his lungs. "Good Christ, that can't be. She's a child."

"Oh, I can assure you, I know of what I speak. The officer who marched into my shop behind René said he intended to treat Alexia as an adult." Josette turned her head from Cameron's gaze, as if fighting for more control. "With her family background, she'll likely play scapegoat for all our sins."

Now Cameron's temper went to flame. "Are you forgetting she has another family? The Andrews name means something around here. I'll see to having things in order with the law before René turns her in."

That bit of news didn't do what Cameron had expected. Instead of growing calmer, her fury grew.

"Damn you, Cameron. Using your name to settle matters only sends a message that she can do whatever she wants and her papa will take care of it."

Right then and there, he made his decision—he would definitely leave on the *Simone*. "It will sure as hell resolve a few things until I can get her out of here. Which will take place in three days, at most. In the meantime, she's in good hands with her uncle, and there's no need for either one of us to worry over her. At least for the rest of the day."

Josette lips parted. "You're leaving so soon?"

He swore he saw panic and confusion flicker in her eyes, but whatever he'd seen was gone before he could ponder it. "I hadn't made a firm decision until now."

"Did I hear you right? You're taking Alexia with you?"

"Yes." He shoved his hand through his hair. "In the meantime, you have no need to concern yourself with her well-being. René has likely found her by now. She'll listen to him."

"But he gave his word he'd deliver her to the police."

Cameron blew out a breath so heavy it filled his cheeks. "If you don't want me to intervene, then the little thief can jolly well rot in a jail cell for a couple days. Perhaps she'll learn a lesson or two. At least she won't be running off where I can't find her."

"You can't mean that."

"Of course I don't, but I'm her father so I can think it, can't I?"

Josette's lips twitched. "What if she refuses to go with you?"

Some of the ire had filtered out of her voice. Cameron relaxed a bit. "At this juncture, I'm not so foolish as to introduce the subject to her. It would be best to let her think she's going upriver with Felicité for a while. You can pack some of her clothing in a small bag. At the last minute, have the remainder sent ahead of us to the ship. When it's time to sail, I'll collect her, even if I have to carry her over my shoulder like a sack of flour."

Annoyance flashed again. "She'll hate you."

"Do you have a better idea?"

Josette shook her head. "Then I'll hate you."

He nearly choked on bemused laughter. "That's your better idea? And no, you won't hate me, Josette. You're angry and worried, and I can't blame you."

He settled his gaze on her, his own anger dissolving like so much salt in water. He tamped down the urge to put his arms around her and offer comfort. "You've had a fright. We all have, but I promise, everything will be all right."

Whatever went through her mind just then, her expression shifted. He frowned. "Is there something else besides Alexia that has you bothered?"

She took in a long breath, exhaled, and straightened her spine. "You had no right to order Bastièn to move into my home."

What the hell? Cameron let go a contemptuous grunt. "He said that, did he?"

"Said it? He's already moved his things out of that bordello and into one of my rooms upstairs. Says he'll get the rest of his belongings from Maman's tomorrow."

Cameron gave a rude laugh. "Isn't he the right clever bastard? He thinks I'm not leaving for ten days, so he's decided to beat me at my own game and move in immediately. Pray do not tell him I'll be gone in a mere three."

The way she held herself, her head tilted back, a new fire in her eyes, told Cameron she hadn't finished with him.

"And how dare you give him information about my personal life? You had no right."

This, he was not expecting. "I did no such thing."

She nodded toward her reticule. "Then why did he give me a variety of . . . of *things* and say to tell you they were gifts from a Mr. Goodyear, and the Earl of Condom?"

"Oh, good God!" Cameron burst into laughter. "That ass plays one hell of a game of retribution."

"What do you mean?"

"He's moved in with you and given you a selection of condoms. You do know what they're meant for, don't you?"

Her chin lifted. "Of course. Ladies whisper all sorts of secrets in my shop. I just didn't know there was an earl named after them. How humiliating for him."

Cameron grunted. "Since the good earl's been dead a couple hundred years, I doubt he gives much thought to anything. However, I suspect the item of discussion was named after him, not the reverse. As for humiliation, that is exactly what your brother is up to."

He studied her. "You don't understand, do you? You're being manipulated by Bastièn."

Confusion ran rampant in her eyes. "I am not."

Whatever anger Cameron had left in him was pushed out by a powerful urge to wrap his arms around her and bury his face in the curve of her neck. "We both are."

His voice rasped, and his breathing took on an unsteady rhythm. "First he moved into your home and insisted that I ordered him to do so. And then he intended to shame me by sending along his personal stash of goods."

Just saying the words had heat crawling up his neck. "You haven't a clue how impossible it would be for me to slip one of your brother's godforsaken *gifts* on my person with thoughts of bedding you. Believe me, Josette, there would be a certain part of my anatomy that would shrink in horror."

Her entire demeanor shifted. Was that a smile working at a corner of her mouth? Her tongue took a small swipe at her lower lip, and her eyes glittered. "I still think I might hate you."

Cameron hadn't missed any of it, even the fact her voice had taken on a smoky quality. He took a step closer, his skin heating. This, he could handle. "Is that so?"

His blood churned, sending his heart pounding out a chaotic rhythm. How could just being near her stir him like this? "In that case, I don't like you, either."

She took a step back, but the smile working at one corner of her mouth blossomed into a sultry, crooked grin. "That's not true or you wouldn't lust after me."

He took another step closer.

She raised her hand between them as if to push him away, but instead, her fingers splayed across his chest.

The touch of her hand went right through him. Suddenly,

all he could think of was sinking deep inside her. "I believe you just crossed a line into trouble."

Her lips parted and she gazed at him, her eyes smoldering.

He had her up against the wall now and could plainly sense the want in her. Her breath came in shallow pants, sending hot, jagged messages along his nerve endings.

"You've had a bad day, *chère*."

"*Oui*. I've had a bad day."

"I know just the remedy."

"Do you, now?"

He dipped his head. "Indeed."

He wasn't sure who made the next move, but suddenly they were tangled in one another's arms, mouth to greedy mouth.

She yanked his shirt out of his trousers.

His hand slid under her skirts.

He growled. "Why the devil do you wear so many clothes?"

"Take them off me if you don't like it." She fumbled with the buttons on his trousers, her nails scraping his skin in a good kind of hurt.

They sank to the floor in a jumble of skirts and petticoats, her hat disappearing somewhere beneath them, hairpins flying.

"You devil, Cameron. You drive me insane." She shoved his trousers down and wrapped her hand around his erection.

He fought for breath, sucking in her sweet scent, watching her eyes burn with desire. He grasped her drawers and pulled them off, then shoved her skirts to her waist.

When they were skin to hot skin, he tried for a deep breath, but her mouth found his again. Her tongue swept inside and moved in a matching rhythm to her hand massaging his cock.

He cupped her wet softness, opened her with his fingers.

"Let go of me," he said, his words a bare rasp against her mouth. "I want inside you. Deep inside you."

A low moan and she released him, only to grab hold of his buttocks with both hands and cant her hips. He thrust inside her hot, tight body. A raw, naked edge of need blurred his thoughts and he was lost in that ancient, pounding rhythm of erotic pleasure.

"Don't stop," she cried, as the first pulse of her orgasm squeezed tight around him.

He drove into her over and over, holding back his own climax until her final contraction eased. The intense pleasure sent him over the edge and he withdrew, spilling his seed on her belly, his groan vibrating through them both.

He lowered his forehead onto the carpet, waiting until his rapid breathing slowed. He rose on his elbows and gazed into her eyes. Lifting a hand, he stroked her hair, and brushed his lips back and forth across hers. "I ended up in your bed last night because I arrived at your door in a foul mood. Now you've ended up on the floor of my home because you rushed in here like a termagant. We ought to stop fighting like this."

Josette's laugh sounded low and wicked in her throat. "You can't be serious. That was the most enjoyable fit of temper I've ever had."

He lifted her shoulder, pulled out her crushed hat, and tossed it across the room. "I doubt you'll be wearing that again."

She gave his earlobe a nip and giggled. "Whatever will people think of me walking through the streets with a bare head?"

"I'll send you home in a carriage." He planted kisses along the curve of her neck. "God, you're a wildcat."

A bell clanged, signaling someone was at the front gate.

"*Merde*. I forgot about the maid." He scrambled to his feet, buttoning his trousers as he went, then gathered Josette off the floor. "At least she has enough sense to alert us that she's returned. I'm taking you upstairs."

He swiped her mangled hat off the floor and hooked it over the finial atop the newel post.

"Why did you do that?" Josette grabbed her discarded drawers and reticule.

"I'm letting her know I have company so she won't intrude."

"My hairpins." Josette managed to gather three off the carpet before Cameron clamped his hand around her wrist.

"Madame, your lips are swollen, your hair is in a wild state and your gown is not only wrinkled, but the front is undone. Would you care to join me above stairs or do you wish to remain in place so as to greet my gossip of a maid?"

Chapter Twenty

Brandy, beignets, and a beautiful woman. Despite earlier events, the day couldn't get much better if someone offered Cameron the moon.

Dressed only in trousers, he lazed on the bed with his back propped against a stack of pillows, watching Josette examine the voodoo doll that had been left on his pillow the other night. She sat with her legs curled beneath her, wearing nothing but his white shirt, which reached her knees, the sleeves rolled to her elbows. He wouldn't mind seeing her dressed like that for the next three days.

Somewhere in the distance, a church bell pealed five o'clock. One would think they'd both be overheated by what they'd engaged in these past few hours, but afterward he'd cooled their naked bodies with water from the pitcher on the dry sink. At least for now, they were comfortable. He'd even opened the heavy curtains covering the balcony doors and left the sheers to blow in the breeze. Living in darkened rooms during the hottest part of the year irritated him.

"Have you figured out the doll's meaning?"

Josette squinted at the padded heart with knotted strings dangling, her cheeks flushed. "I . . . I need to think about this. At any rate, the doll did not come from Maman or my brothers. The design and manner of cross-stitching is not theirs."

"Don't tell me René and Bastièn play with dolls." Oh, the wicked ways Cameron could twist this bit of news.

She glanced up. "Careful. Do not misinterpret my brothers' ways with a needle and a few scraps of cloth. Have you forgotten who our mother is?"

"Ouch, you wound." Cameron reached out and lightly brushed his fingers back and forth across the bent knee peeking out from under her shirt—his shirt. Lord, she was lovely. Even lovelier during these private times when she was uninhibited and clearly living in the moment. "What kinds of lessons did your mother teach the lot of you?"

She set the doll on the bedside table and exchanged it for her reticule. "Bastièn took a keen interest in the use of herbs and roots. He turned out to be an excellent *Guérisseur*."

"Bastièn a healer? Huh. Who would've thought?"

She shoved her thick hair over her shoulder. "Don't most people have a secret world inside of them? He's not inclined to show that aspect of himself unless it's needed, so his healing ways are not public knowledge."

Cameron stroked the inside of her thigh. Just touching her satin skin soothed him. "So tell me, what's in your secret world?"

A vague smile drifted across her mouth. "I thought we were discussing my brother. I know you don't care much for him, but he does have his principles."

Cameron grunted. "Yes, but they are very small and well-hidden."

She ignored his comment and opened the reticule, then lifted out a folded packet.

"What the devil are you up to?"

"What do you suppose this one is made from?"

"Josette, put those damn things away."

"Bastièn says he prefers to use sheep's intestines over what's in here."

"Well, I do hope the old boy removes them from the sheep first." Cameron laughed at his own joke.

"That's not funny."

"In my mind it was hilarious. The least you could do is placate me with a smile. Better yet, set your bag aside and come crawl all over me."

Her eyes widened. "You want to make love *again*?"

He grinned. "I would if I was fully able, but at the moment one part of me refuses to cooperate." Too lethargic to move, he stretched out his arm and beckoned her. "Come, *mon chaton*."

She set her reticule on the table and worked her way over to his side. "You called me a wildcat a bit ago and now I'm your little kitten?"

"Mmm." He eased her splendid length fully atop him.

His entire body thanked him.

A different kind of pleasure flowed through him. Unlike the blaze that had run rampant these last few hours, having her lying on him was like a soothing, slow-moving river of desire. No lust. No searing need. Only silken, sensual comfort.

He kissed the top of her head, ever so lightly. Acting less on thought and more on instinct, he set his fingers to her back, brushing the tips over the soft fabric of his shirt, barely touching her skin beneath it.

"Mmm, that feels so good, Cameron. Please don't stop." She pressed light kisses across the span of his chest, then rested her cheek there. "I can hear your heart beat. It's slow and steady. Strong. As if you could live forever."

His hand swept through her hair, along her back and over her pert rump. "You have the smoothest, tightest, most exquisite bum in existence."

She laughed softly and drew a nail over his skin. His

muscles rippled. "When I saw you that first time at my door, I never would have guessed you were a man who likes to cuddle."

"Is that what we're doing?" Whatever it was, he wasn't about to quit. In its own way, holding her like this, stroking her with a light touch, seemed as intimate as what had transpired earlier. He kissed the top of her head again, then took care in folding his arms around her. A kind of sigh ran through him.

"I've never been held," she said, the slow cadence of her words sounding drowsy. "It feels rather special."

"Not even when you were a child?"

"Never," she murmured. "Maman would have nothing to do with me, so René took charge. He held my hand to keep me from doing dangerous things like falling out of the pirogue or off the porch and into the bayou, but that was about all. He was so very young to take on such a heavy burden—what did he know about nurturing back then? Still, I always knew he cared, and that he did his best by me."

Cameron didn't know what to say. As a child, he'd never wanted for affection. He couldn't imagine what life would've been like without his mother's benevolent care. Josette had never been held? Gads, she must have lived a cold and dispassionate married life. An urge to remedy that filtered through his thoughts. He slid the fingers of one hand into her hair and massaged her scalp and the back of her neck in slow-moving circles.

She gave a sleepy moan. He was going to miss her when he left. But doing so in three days was definitely for the best. Not once had she brought up anything regarding his imminent departure, despite the obvious fondness growing between them. But to linger in New Orleans would only make it harder for both of them when it came time for him to leave.

And leave he must.

There was nothing for him here any longer. Even with the

streets bustling with traffic, pedestrian and otherwise, the place seemed empty with no family but Michel around. And Felicité would soon be gone, most likely taking her father with her. Eventually, he'd find a place in the world to settle down, one that felt right. He had no idea how to go about finding it other than take to the seas. He was a privileged man to be able to wander the earth in search of . . . in search of what? A place to land? In search of himself?

Josette's breathing grew steady until suddenly, the muscles in her body gave way and she relaxed against him completely.

She'd fallen asleep.

He smiled to himself.

For a long while, he lay there, not thinking, not moving. Only feeling the length of her body against his, her breath falling softly against his bare chest. Though the morning had been particularly miserable, Josette's appearance had certainly improved his day. And after he hadn't thought the afternoon could get any better, it just had.

He didn't know how long they remained in one place, her asleep, him halfway there, when a light tapping sounded on the door.

Oh, hell.

He tried easing Josette off him without waking her, but her eyes fluttered open. "Stay where you are," he murmured in her ear.

He made his way to the door and cracked it open.

"*Mischie* Cameron," Marie said. "Monsieur René Thibodeaux is downstairs asking for you. He has your daughter with him."

"Bloody hell."

"What is it?" Josette called out.

Marie tried to peek around Cameron.

He blocked her view with his body. "I'll be down in a minute. Do not tell them I have company."

She stared at his bare chest. "Of course not. What you take me for?"

Closing the door, he strode to the wardrobe and pulled out a fresh shirt. "*Merde*. I thought you said René wasn't due back until tomorrow. He's below stairs, and he's got Alexia with him."

Josette pressed her fingers to her lips and laughed through them. "Oh, dear."

"You didn't think my sheep joke was funny, but this is?" He stuffed his shirt into his trousers and grabbed a vest, only to toss it aside. They worked in shirtsleeves in this heat at the office, so who'd expect him to be dressed otherwise in the privacy of his own home? "You won't find it so funny when he puts a bullet through me."

He opened the door to make his exit and glanced back at her. "Lock the door behind me and don't make any noise."

He couldn't help but grin. She practically had her fist stuffed in her mouth. Her hair hung wild around her head. Her eyes sparkled.

"Oh, for heaven's sake. I can take care of myself. But as for you—good luck wheedling your way out of this one, *Mischie* Cameron." She rolled over and buried her face in a pillow, her shoulders shaking with laughter.

He shut the door behind him and descended the stairs. Halfway down, Josette's bonnet caught his eye, hanging like a bloody flag on the newel post. *Merde*. Well, he wasn't about to pick it up and draw further attention to it.

A flour sack stuffed with God-knew-what lay atop the sofa.

His temper flared.

A few more steps and he spied Alexia standing in René's shadow, her hand clutching his. Dirt smeared her face and stained a dress torn in too many places to count. Fine lace that had edged the collar now hung in grimy tatters. What had she been through?

Cameron had never seen dread in her eyes before, but he saw it now. Good God, she was afraid of what he'd do to her!

An urge to fix everything, to wipe away her distress overshadowed his anger. But she'd crossed a line, and he couldn't let her off so easily just so he could remove the tension from his own gut. He trotted the rest of the way down the stairs. "Why didn't you take her to your sister's home for the night?"

Raw fury snapped in René's dark eyes. "You are her father, *oui*? Then why make my sister handle your responsibility? I am leaving Alexia with you."

He glanced past Cameron to the balustrade and Josette's hat. Then his ominous gaze traveled up the stairs. Alexia's curious observation followed suit. Recognition lit her face. Surely the man wouldn't be so foolish as to do or say anything with Alexia present.

Marie rolled a tea cart into the parlor holding a plate of hot beignets and three cups of café au lait. "Would anyone care for some of my famous sweet treats? They's hot and fresh as a morning sunrise. Coffee's fresh-made too."

Alexia's attention shifted from the hat to the beignets. Her tongue darted out to lick her bottom lip.

Good old Marie—she'd honed her impeccable sense of timing over the years on both Cameron's and Trevor's youthful escapades. She'd kept them out of trouble more times than he could count. He nearly laughed at the absurdity. Here he was, thirty-two years old, and she was interrupting with yet another distraction.

René bent down and picked two hairpins off the carpet. He inspected one of them before returning his overt gaze to Josette's bonnet. Cameron swallowed a laugh. If the bastard thought to intimidate him, he could jolly well forget it.

Marie hustled across the room and grabbed the hat off the finial. "Beggin' yer pardon, Monsieur Andrews. I done left my hat out here. Didn't have no business being so careless."

A cynical smile curled a corner of René's mouth. He held out one of the hairpins. "Would this be yours, as well?

"I reckon so." Marie snatched it from his hand and scurried down the hall toward the rear of the house.

He slipped the other into his pocket and fastened his flinty gaze on Cameron.

In another minute Cameron was going to ask Alexia to take herself into the kitchen with Marie so he could kick René's arrogant arse out the door.

Alexia shoved a beignet into her mouth, her wide eyes shifting back and forth between René and Cameron. She started toward the stairs. "I need to get me something clean to wear that's in the bag *ma tante* sent over."

As she tried to pass him, Cameron grabbed her around the waist and in one smooth move, swung her around next to him. "I want you in the kitchen with Marie while your uncle and I discuss a few things."

René lifted a brow. "Why don't you want her going upstairs for a change of clothing? Look at her, she's filthy."

Enough was enough. Cameron would be damned if René would control Alexia or this household. "Because while I'm here with you, she'd be gone over the balcony in a flash and down the street stealing again."

"*Non*, Papa. I won't be stealing anymore. It's a promise."

Still holding her around the waist, he curled his fist under her chin, lifting it. "Look at me, Alexia. Didn't you make that same woeful promise not long ago?"

She turned her face from his scrutiny and bit her bottom lip. A familiar stubbornness filled her countenance.

Damn it.

The entry door opened and closed. Felicité marched in. Cameron let go of Alexia and, fisting his hands on his hips, sucked in a breath. "Has the entire blasted town decided to barge in on me unannounced?"

"Good afternoon to you, cousin." She promptly turned to René. The air fairly sizzled between them. She tilted her head and offered him a coy smile. "And good day to you, as well."

René returned her smile and lifting her gloved hand, kissed it. "Mademoiselle Felicité. So good to see you."

It was all Cameron could do not to wipe that sin-filled smile off René's face. The way he looked at Felicité, there couldn't be a pure thought running through the bloody bastard's mind. "Why are you here, Felice?"

She tugged a hat pin free and removed a fancy blue bonnet that had likely cost a small fortune. "To check on Alexia." She lifted her gaze to the stairwell.

Cameron turned and spied Alexia sneaking up the steps. Hell, she'd have the lock picked on his bedroom door faster than he could get to her. "Damn it, Alexia, get back here."

"Gots to change, Papa!" She ran the rest of the way up the stairs and disappeared along the corridor.

"Tsk, tsk. Cursing at your daughter," René said.

Cameron pivoted back to where the Cajun stood. "Don't you have gainful employment that needs tending, or are you bound and determined to further rile your superior?"

"Indeed, I do have duties needing my attention. Regrettably, your daughter has kept me from seeing to them. Had her parent been in proper control of her—"

"Get the hell out of my house before we come to blows." Cameron turned to Felicité. "When Alexia returns—if she hasn't already climbed off the balcony—I want you to convince her to accompany you upriver for a spell. Tell her you'll be making your departure in three days."

Felicité's eyes narrowed. "I smell a rat. What are you up to?"

"Since you won't be leaving here for another month, I intend on sailing for England aboard the *Simone* in three days. I'll be taking Alexia with me."

René sucked in a breath.

Cameron ignored him. "I don't want her knowing anything until the clipper is ready to haul up anchor. That way she won't slip away from me."

"And then what?" René asked, all arrogance and combativeness gone from his voice.

Cameron thought of telling René it was none of his business, but it was. . . . He was Alexia's uncle, and she adored him. "She'll become a part of my family. She'll have a better life than she could have here. I'll see she receives a good education and will want for nothing. Felicité will be there as well. Alexia trusts her."

Felicité's expression grew taut. "She won't trust me if I betray her by lying."

René exhaled a heavy sigh. "He's right, Felicité. This is no place for Alexia. It's important we all work together to see that she leaves without incident."

He looked to Cameron. "Perhaps we shouldn't say anything further in front of Felicité. That way, she won't know anything that could leave Alexia feeling betrayed."

René's abrupt change of sides surprised Cameron. He picked a beignet off the cart and took a bite. Why he was eating yet another one, he hadn't a clue.

Alexia trotted down the stairs wearing a crisp yellow dress, her smile bright enough to blind. Had Josette helped her into it? Surely Alexia would keep a secret for her aunt. And why the silly grin?

"Aren't you the lovely one," Felicité said.

Alexia looked at Cameron as if waiting for a response from him. He nodded. "Indeed. You look decent once again, but you and I have a few things to discuss this evening before we make our visit to the police tomorrow, so don't think you are out of the woods."

Alexia's face fell.

Felicité stepped forward. "Have you ever been on a plantation, Alexia?"

She looked at Felicité as though she'd grown another head. "I ain't never been out of the bayou or out of this town."

Cameron laughed. "Except for a rather tedious trip to San Francisco."

"*Oui*, that."

Felicité worked up a pleasant face. "Would you like to be my guest at Carlton Oaks? It's a splendid plantation that sits right on the banks of the Mississippi. We have some fine riding horses there as well."

That had Alexia's attention.

"Have you ever ridden a horse?" Cameron asked.

"Just Satan," Alexia said. "But he's so old and snake bit that a ride on him means going from one end of the yard and back, one slow clop of a hoof after the other. When would you be going and for how long?"

Felicité shot a nervous glance at Cameron. "We can leave in three days and stay until it's time for me to sail for England."

Alexia shook her head. "I can't be doing that. My birthday is coming up next week and Maman has plans for me."

René paled. "You are to go with Felicité."

Alexia's cheeks turned red and her eyes flashed fury at her uncle. "*Non*. I have to go to Maman's for my birthday. She said so."

A muscle twitched along René's jawline. "You will do no such thing."

Cameron watched the argument unfold. What was this about? René hadn't bothered to hide his concern. He shot a speaking glance at Cameron.

"Well." Felicité grabbed her bonnet and placed it on her head. "Alexia, would you like to accompany me to the bookseller? I have a couple of items on order. We can go to the soda shop afterward."

Alexia's face lit up. "Can I, Papa? I promise not to run off or steal anything."

"Don't think for a moment that I trust your word any longer, Alexia. But understand this—you have lived in the bayou and with your aunt in town, nowhere else. Therefore, should you do anything other than accompany Miss Felicité, I know where to find you. And believe me, if you run off again, the end result will not be a pleasant experience for either of us. Which would make me all the angrier."

René stepped forward. "Have I ever broken my word to you, Alexia?"

She shook her head. "*Non*."

He gave her a stern look. "Then rest assured, should we have to go looking for you, I will be right beside your father."

"Come along." Felicité slipped her arm around Alexia's shoulders. "I could use some fresh air, and the bookseller awaits."

On the way out the door, she turned and, behind Alexia's back, shot both men a murderous glance that told Cameron she didn't appreciate either man's way of dealing with Alexia.

Alone, Cameron turned to René. "What the devil is going on?"

René's brow furrowed. "This birthday coming up will be Alexia's fourteenth. From what I just heard, Maman has decided to take Alexia through a very dangerous rite of passage, one in which she will join her grandmother in all aspects of her work. Including the dark side. I don't approve of her intentions. Neither do my siblings."

The two men stared at each other for a moment while Cameron's blood turned cold.

Marie appeared out of nowhere. "I'll see Monsieur Thibodeaux out, if you please. Felicité knows where the latch is that unlocks the gate, but I doubt you would."

René turned to leave but paused at the door leading from the parlor to the front entry. He sent an overt glance up the stairwell. His lip curled into a sardonic smile. "Enjoy what's left of your day."

Cameron swallowed a sharp retort. When the door closed behind René, Cameron raced up the stairs.

The room was empty.

"Josette?"

He examined the bed where pillows were in place and the counterpane held nary a wrinkle. Checking every corner of the room and not finding her, he stepped onto the balcony.

Nothing.

He peered over the railing and laughed.

Below him, a scrap of pale green fabric clung to a climbing rosebush. Apparently, Josette could indeed take care of herself. Or she'd had assistance, which would explain Alexia's silly grin when coming down the stairs.

And he was supposed to teach his daughter to walk the straight and narrow?

Chapter Twenty-One

Josette shot up in bed, gasping for breath. Damn that blasted nightmare. Would it never leave her? She'd floated in dark space, the earth a million miles away. Not a sound filtering through the terrible emptiness. In a flash, she'd landed back in the murky waters of the bayou, her family huddled together and staring at her in horror. Then they dashed off. She tried to catch up to them. She ran and ran until she awoke, breathless and perspiring, her heart galloping in her chest.

And breaking in two, yet again.

But this time she'd heard someone call her name.

Hadn't she?

That part seemed frightfully clear.

Wait.

Did she just hear it again? Shaking off her brain fog, she strained her ears.

"Josette!" Vivienne rushed through the door.

"What's wrong?" Josette grabbed her robe and sprang from the bed, shoving her arms through the sleeves as she went.

"It's René and Bastièn. They've been hurt."

"Oh, dear Lord." Josette ran out the door with her cousin limping behind, her bad hip slowing her. "Where are they?"

"In the kitchen," Vivienne huffed.

"What happened?"

"I don't know. Bastièn fairly dragged René into the house, blood all over both of them. Bastièn said he only got knocked upside the head, but René needs stitches. Régine put water on to heat. I've laid out your supplies."

"What time is it?"

"The hall clock struck two when I came for you."

"How did you hear them when I didn't?"

"I couldn't sleep so I was downstairs brewing a pot of tea when they arrived."

Josette reached the kitchen ahead of Vivienne. She dizzied at the sight of René laid out on the long metal table, his forehead bloodied, the white enamel beneath him looking as though someone had butchered a pig. Bastièn and Régine worked at cutting René's jacket and vest off him.

Dark stains marred the front of Bastièn's once white shirt. A crimson line trickled from a gash to the left of an eye already bruised and swelling. He swiped at the wound with the back of his hand. It came away smeared with blood.

Josette edged him aside. "Sit. You need attention as well."

He gave a grunt and kept on laboring. "I can look after myself later. I only got a punch to my face."

"Hush. This is no time to argue. Vivienne, give him a cloth to press against his cut. Régine, grab a lantern and collect some ice for both their faces." Josette's voice grew calmer as her orders became more assertive. "Pull up a chair, Bastièn. You can oversee me until it's your turn."

He muttered a litany of French curses, and something about not telling him what to do. Nonetheless, he discarded his jacket and vest, then swept a chair to the head of the table, where René lay immobile.

Heart hammering, she shot Bastièn a glance. "Remove your shirt as well so Régine can wash out those stains."

She leaned over René and spoke softly. "Can you hear me?"

He groaned. "*Merde*. I still have my ears attached, don'cha know."

"Good," she said, not feeling at all as chipper as she tried to sound. At least he wasn't unconscious. But she knew René. As quiet and still as he lay, he was in pain. "Vivienne and I will have to cut off your shirt."

His lids fluttered open, confusion dulling his eyes. "*Non*. Do not ruin my good jacket and shirt."

Well, the jacket was in ruins and already discarded, but apparently he'd not been fully aware when that occurred. "I'll see to replacing whatever is beyond repair."

She nodded to Vivienne, who stood on the opposite side of the table. Together, they proceeded to cut away the bloodstained shirt. "Careful. Some of the fabric is already sticking to congealed spots."

They eased away the linen. Several short gashes and five long slits still spilling blood marred René's body. A chill slid down Josette's spine. She bit her tongue to keep from uttering an oath. Every one of his wounds had been inflicted by a razor-sharp knife. She signaled Vivienne to press cloths to the active lacerations while Josette wiped down his torso with witch hazel.

Completing her examination, she heaved a sigh of relief. "You've been slashed in several places. Some veins were nipped, which accounts for the copious bleeding, but the lacerations aren't all that deep. Your new jacket might have actually gotten in the way of the knife and saved you from something far worse."

"My new jacket, she can be saved, *oui*?"

"For pity's sake, René. The condition of your clothing should be the least of your concerns."

Bastièn turned sideways and, resting his elbow on the

chair's back, pressed the folded cloth to his wound. "You do not understand a man's way of handling dire situations, *ma soeur*. Ah, but wait. Could it be you have been plying us with your clever repartee not to placate us, but as your own way of coping?"

She shoved an errant curl behind her ear and swallowed a curse. "You should know since this isn't the first time you two have shown up during the devil's hours in need of repair."

"And likely not the last," Vivienne muttered.

"Humph." Bastièn gave her a sidelong scowl.

Josette swiped her forearm across her damp brow. "Hush, you two. René, the stitching will take a while, which means you'll need a dose of laudanum so your muscles don't tighten up when things get tedious."

He tried for a smile, but it came out as more of a grimace. "Is that your way of saying you are about to inflict even more pain upon my person?"

She decided to ignore his comment. "We'll need to turn you over to inspect your back. I don't think any ribs are broken, only bruised. Your trousers need to come off so we can assess the full damage."

René's hand slid to the buttons on his pants. "*Non.* They did not get me below the waist or at my back. Their intent was to gut me."

Josette's breath froze in her lungs. She looked at Bastièn, who still held the rag pressed to the side of his own head. He gave a nod.

Régine scurried in with a small bucket of ice.

"Crush some and wrap it in a square of cloth, then hold it to Bastièn's face," Josette said. "Are you injured anywhere else?"

"*Non.* I was behind René when they came at him from the front, so they couldn't have got at his back."

"Who are *they*?" She needn't have bothered to ask.

Vennard had called his henchmen into action. Just as he'd promised. She bit at the inside of her mouth. Oh, she should never have threatened to shoot that awful man. What a rash and reckless thing to have done. And here she was, looking at the consequences of her actions.

Shoving the disturbing thoughts to the periphery of her mind, she concentrated on her tasks. "Vivienne, will you wash Bastièn's face with witch hazel and get him ready for me, *s'il vous plaît*?"

At Bastièn's grumbling, Josette shot him a frown, then caught herself and went back to light banter. "Would you like to know a little secret, *mon frère*?"

He winced at the solution Vivienne dabbed on his cut. "Unless you can tell me who is so eager to send René and me to the cemetery, I am in no mood to play your guessing game."

Josette forced herself to maintain a breezy monologue. "My secret is that I have never been able to decide which of my two brothers is more handsome. But if you won't allow me to stitch that cut at the side of your face, then you'll have an ugly scar and René will win."

Bastièn grunted. "A horse could trample me, and I would still remain better looking than my brother."

Now it was René's turn to grunt.

At least Josette's chitchat had managed to lighten their mood. "Vivienne, give Bastièn a dose of laudanum before I stitch him."

"*Non*," he muttered.

She clamped her jaw against a fierce bid to snap back at him. "Tsk. Tsk. So stubborn and hardheaded you are. It's a wonder anyone managed to break your skin."

Vivienne finished cleaning Bastièn's wound. Régine handed him the clean cloth filled with ice, and all three women settled in to work on René in silence. Every so often, he flinched at the needle Josette ran in and out of his flesh, but otherwise said nothing. Oh, how she hurt for him. This was all her fault.

Filled with guilt, she offered him a small smile and a tender touch on his arm. "You've a nasty cut on your forehead that's going to require a few stitches, as well."

He managed a half-grin. "Don't mar my face or Bastièn might win your favor."

She chuckled softly. "I'll use the finest catgut, and with my special creams, the scar will fade to nearly nothing—like the other over your eye. Soon, the ladies will be falling at your feet."

"*Merci*, because they do not end up there now."

"Liar," she teased. "I hear Mademoiselle Felicité Andrews is so taken with you that her brother is having conniptions."

René lowered his lids from Josette's gaze and turned his head.

Oh, dear. Did her brother covet something beyond his reach?

Foolish man.

Hadn't he learned from what she endured that he'd never be accepted by polite society? Old hurts coalesced with her anger over what had taken place tonight—an assault instigated by a man of high social standing. A man who'd recently called her trash.

She needed to change the subject before René sensed her agitation. "I don't imagine I have to tell you that you'll be spending the night here so I can keep an eye on you."

"I doubt I'd be able to make my way home, anyway."

Good grief. Was he traveling in and out of the bayou every day for work? She hadn't considered that part of his new situation. Well, if Bastièn intended to reside here, why shouldn't René as well? A curious lightness swept through her. The idea of having them both live with her on a permanent basis carried a certain appeal. Especially with Alexia about to take her leave. But would that bring Maman calling on them? Josette doubted it. The boys were faithful. They'd continue visiting their mother regularly.

"Régine, can you soak some strips of cloth in my lichen infusion? I'll wrap René's torso with them to keep his wounds from getting infected." She pointed to the most serious injury. "This one will need a bit of the pine resin and baking soda mixture first."

Régine only nodded and joined Vivienne in tearing cotton sheeting into strips. Régine had been efficient but closed-mouthed throughout this ordeal. Was her silence because of the boys? It wouldn't do to have her retreat to her father's farm, back to a life of drudgery. She enjoyed cooking and taking care of the kitchen as though it were her own. Josette would have a talk with her in the morning.

"Some of Louis's nightshirts are packed in a trunk upstairs," she said. "We should dress René in one." She glanced over at Bastièn.

He shook his head. "None for me."

Vivienne set down the linen cloth she'd been tearing into strips and limped toward the kitchen door. "I know right where they are."

René wrinkled his nose. "*Non*. I will not sleep in one of those ridiculous things."

Exhausted, Josette lost her temper. "Then sleep naked for all I care. You have no other clothing here, you stubborn ass. I hope you know your shirt is in shreds, so you'll have nothing to wear tomorrow. At least until I can send to the tailor for something."

"We're the same size," Bastièn said. "He can wear one of my shirts until I can get a few of his things from Maman's. I'll be going there first thing for the remainder of my belongings, anyway."

René struggled to sit up, gritting his teeth. "I must go to work tomorrow. I'll need to borrow a cravat and vest as well."

Josette sat in stunned silence for a moment. René, who'd quit most every job he'd ever held within a week of starting, was intent on going to his workplace so soon? She'd never seen him so dedicated to anything. "You will not. I don't see how anyone can object to your missing a few days while you heal. I'll send along a note to the shipping office in the morning. Now lie down and have a bit more laudanum while I see to Bastièn's cut."

She worked on Bastièn amidst a flurry of curses and complaints that he'd have done a better job on himself while looking in the mirror. Bastièn's grumblings left René begging for a shot of rum in order to tolerate his brother's insufferable peevishness.

Once she'd finished tending to Bastièn's wounds, he stood and assisted René off the table, but not without a snide remark regarding René's complaints. Josette followed as Bastièn escorted laudanum-drugged René up the stairs, halting at the first bedroom they came to.

Bastièn cocked his head at Josette. "Unless you wish to observe while I rather crudely help René dispense with his trousers and drawers, I suggest you take to your own room."

"Humph." She opened the door for them. "Sleep well, René. It will aid you in healing faster."

"*Merci*," he mumbled.

Josette closed the door behind them. She leaned against the wall and waited for Bastièn. He'd refused the laudanum so he'd be alert enough for what she had to say. She let go an exhausted sigh.

In moments, he reappeared and walked beside her to his room. "This wasn't an accidental encounter," he said. "I think those three men were after René. Or whichever one of us they stumbled upon first."

Guilt flooded Josette again. How she despised that feeling. "What makes you say that?"

"Because I heard, 'There's one of them.' I don't think they expected me to come around the corner just then. René and I were meeting up to get something to eat."

The tight knot in Josette's stomach twisted. "You should have dined here and not been wandering the streets seeking food."

They reached Bastièn's bedroom, but instead of saying good night and leaving him, she halted. "I've decided to ask René to move in here as well."

Bastièn paused with his hand on the door handle. "Why is that?"

With the flood of emotions running through her, it was all she could do to keep from wringing her hands. "He seems dedicated to his new job. He doesn't need to be making tedious trips back and forth to the bayou every day. Nor should he be running around at all hours looking to fill his belly."

His piercing gaze penetrated her. "Tell me the truth, Josette. Are we invading your life?"

"Of course not."

The blue in his sapphire eyes softened. "I'll admit I marched into your home to spite Cameron Andrews, but I cannot remain if I end up hurting you."

She shook her head. "I don't know why we never thought of this before, but with Alexia leaving, it might be good for me to have you both living here." *And with Cameron soon gone, there'll be no need to feel deprived of the freedom to have a man spend the night.*

He studied her for a good long while through lowered lids. Then he twisted the handle on the door, swung it open, and stepped inside. "It makes good sense to have René live here as well. Good night, *ma chère*."

"Good night, Bastièn. Sleep well."

Once back in her room, Josette sat on the balcony for a long while. The conflict with Vennard had escalated into a dangerous situation. She must do something. But what?

How could she stop someone so powerful? If she said anything to her brothers about Vennard's threats on their lives, there would surely be bloodshed of the worst kind. And when all was said and done, quite possibly a hanging. Or two. Telling them would never do.

A thought that had threaded through the fringes of her mind while she stitched up her brothers sprang forward. What if she went to Cameron with the problem of Émile Vennard?

Cameron would be gone in three days—or was it merely two now—but at least he might be able to offer some rational advice. Her heart lurched at the idea. Who else could she confide in? She could not tell Vivienne. Her cousin was wary enough of Lucien returning to do damage or steal Alexia away. Josette couldn't add Vennard to the mix. Régine was definitely out of the question.

As that old and familiar loneliness struck, tears stung her eyes. She wrapped her arms around her waist, tucked her feet under her, and stared at the sliver of moon. She could think of no one else but Cameron. Yet, he despised her brothers.

Heaven help her.

Morning arrived too soon. Josette crawled out of bed, her back aching from having hunched over René for so long. She dressed in her favorite shade of pale blue, caught her hair in a simple chignon at the back of her head, and made her way, barefoot, as usual, to Bastièn's room.

She knocked. When he failed to answer, she opened the door. "Bastièn?"

Ever the tidy one, Bastièn had made his bed without a wrinkle in sight. His personal items—brush, comb, shaving paraphernalia—were lined up just so. He'd be no trouble to have around. As long as he didn't meddle in her affairs.

She left his room and moved to René's. As she expected, with the amount of laudanum he'd ingested and the beating he'd received, he still slept soundly. At the thought of what he'd suffered, guilt twisted her insides once again.

She tiptoed to his bedside. How handsome he was, even with the stitches on his forehead and the deep shadows under his eyes. A pang of compassion touched her heart. Some kind of change had definitely taken place in him of late. Who would've thought he'd one day be associated with Cameron Andrews and his mighty shipping company?

Josette's stomach grumbled. There'd be fresh eggs and ham downstairs. And tomatoes. Juicy, ripe tomatoes sliced and fanned out alongside her eggs. She'd breakfast with Bastièn and then have that talk with Régine.

But downstairs, Bastièn was nowhere to be seen. Neither was Vivienne.

Régine sat by herself in the morning room sipping a cup of café au lait. The two pots, one of steaming coffee, the other warm milk, sat in the center of the table along with two sets of cups and saucers. "They left before the rooster crowed. Vivienne went with him to your *maman*'s to help him carry everything since both brothers are moving in with you."

Josette slid onto a chair across from her cousin and reached for a cup and saucer. "I haven't actually asked René yet, so I wonder if it's wise for Bastièn to bring all René's belongings."

She paused, trying to gauge Régine's reaction. When she failed to respond, Josette poured herself the rich coffee and milk mixture. "How do you feel about my brothers residing here permanently?"

Régine's cheeks blotched. She took a slow sip of her brew. "It's time I got over some of the things I find disturbing about being around men. René and Bastièn, they ain't never been nuthin' but good to me." Her gaze dropped to the grounds lacing the inside of her cup. "What one person went and done shouldn't make it so I can't trust any others. I'll be making an effort to converse with your brothers."

Josette leaned over, set her hand atop Régine's, and gave it a squeeze. "I am so terribly sorry for what happened to you. I wish I could wipe your memory clean of all that took place. I only hope living here gives you some feeling of security and peace."

Régine's woeful eyes settled on Josette. "I won't ever speak of this again. All I will say is Lucien is a very bad person. Even when he wasn't a fully grown man, he was pure evil."

A blaze of fury shot through Josette. She dropped her gaze to her cup while she collected her thoughts. Her being angry wouldn't help Régine any. "I thought as much. Now we need to keep him away from Alexia, don't we?"

Régine drew a breath and exhaled, as if relieved to have finally uttered the words she'd held in for so long. "I aim to be doing just that around here. I think it'll be good to have your brothers with you. Even with Alexia gone, Lucien could bring trouble."

René wandered in, barefoot, wearing his trousers and one of Bastièn's white shirts. The tails hung loose, the collar open, and his hair looked as though he'd combed it with his fingers. Yet, he was clean shaven.

Catlike, he eased into a chair, as though he'd not a weary bone in his body. "I smell coffee."

Régine managed a smile and slid a cup his way, then indicated the two pots sitting at the center of the table. "I have ham, eggs, and croissants. For dinner I'll be making étoufée. Bastièn's gone off to collect your things. Said he'd bring back some fresh crawdads. How many eggs you be wanting, René?"

"Three, *s'il vous plaît.*"

René stared at the doorway Régine disappeared through. He glanced at Josette. "That's the most I've heard our cousin speak since she was Alexia's age."

"Exactly," Josette said. "She has her reasons."

René frowned. He winced and touched the stitches on his forehead. "I have long suspected it had something to do with Lucien."

"She won't talk about it, so don't ask. And leave your head alone. After breakfast, I need to check the bandages under your shirt. You slept well?"

"*Oui.*" He offered her a casual grin. "It was the laudanum, *non*?"

Josette wrapped her hands around her coffee cup and brushed her thumb back and forth over the raised flowers on the delicate china. "Bastièn left early to collect his things from Maman."

"And some of mine, as well. I remember the conversation."

"Not *some* of your belongings, *mon frère*. His intention was to bring back *everything*."

René paused his cup in midair, his expression unreadable.

She reached over and covered his hand with hers. "I can see how intent you are on making something of yourself with the shipping company. It won't do to have you traipsing back and forth to the bayou every day. This is a big house, René. There are six bedrooms upstairs. If you do not care for the one you were placed in last night, choose another."

He brought the cup to his lips and watched her over the rim. "After Louis died, I offered to move in with you, but you wouldn't have me."

"I . . ." She shrugged. "People change. I didn't want anyone telling me what to do or how to conduct my life. At least I think that was the reason I objected."

"This would not be an imposition?"

She shook her head. "Bastièn asked the same thing. I'm looking forward to having you here. Perhaps it will take a bit of the sting out of losing Alexia. Heed my warning, though. I will not tolerate either one of you trying to run my life."

René sat back in his chair and, with a tilt of his head, studied Josette. Then he laughed, but it was aborted with a small hiss as his hand splayed over his bandaged torso.

Josette refilled her cup. "What do you find so humorous?"

"Think on it. I shall be living not only in the grandest area in all of New Orleans, but in the finest house around. Me, bayou trash."

Josette's mind searched frantically for something to soften the shock of his last words. But before she could respond, Régine carried in a platter filled with ham, croissants, eggs, and fresh sliced tomatoes. She set it on the table, collected two plates and proper silverware from the sideboard, and after setting them in front of René and Josette, promptly disappeared.

A corner of René's mouth lifted. "I guess she said everything that needed saying when I first came in."

Josette snapped a serviette across her lap and began to fill her plate. "She's trying, René. We all are."

Following breakfast, Josette checked René's bandages. Even though they were stained with blotches of dried blood, they were otherwise clean. She decided to hold off changing them for another day.

At half past noon, Bastièn joined them in the parlor, where they sat chatting and sipping iced lemonade. Vivienne disappeared somewhere in the house.

Bastièn poured himself a glass of the chilled liquid and spread himself out on the sofa. "Have you made the decision to live here, as well?"

"*Oui,*" René said.

"*Bien,* because I brought all your belongings."

"Humph. Everything?"

Bastièn nodded. "But Maman, she be powerful angry with us for deserting her." He cocked his head toward Josette. "But she be most furious with you for stealing us away."

Josette pulled a ragged breath into her lungs. "I did no such thing. I do hope you told her you marched in here on your own. I did invite René, but he's been injured, and he has a new position in town requiring long hours, so I had good reason."

She'd not thought of Maman's reaction. How pitiful. She'd only thought that perhaps, at last, this feeling of never belonging would wear itself thin with her brothers in residence. And with Maman a good distance away.

Bastièn took a swallow of lemonade and slung his arm over the back of the sofa. "She knows about Cameron Andrews courting you."

"He is not courting me, Bastièn."

"Well, bedding you, then."

"Stop." Josette narrowed her eyes. "Why is it you two can sleep with whomever you please, whenever you please, but I choose to invite one man into my bed, one time, and you hold it against me?"

René cocked his head. "One time?" He reached into his pocket, withdrew a hairpin and tossed it to Josette. "This is yours, *oui*? I found it on that *one* man's parlor floor. Not in his bed. Not in your bed. Tsk. Tsk."

"Oooh, you are impossible. I should send you right back to Maman's. I thought it would please you to live here so close to your work."

He leaned his head back against the overstuffed velvet chair he sat in. "*Oui*. It be pleasing me."

"Then apologize."

A wicked grin creased the corners of his mouth. He placed his hand over his heart. "Ah, *ma chère*. Forgive me?"

Josette gave a shake of her head at René's antics and

turned to Bastièn. "So was Maman having a tantrum when you left?"

"*Non*. By then she was focused on boiling frogs' toenails and lizard testicles. She's fixing to level a curse on you that will turn you to stone."

René laughed.

"That was not one bit funny. Bastièn is probably closer to the truth than we might think."

Bastièn grew serious. "Lucien was there when I arrived. Beware, Josette. Maman is truly angry with you, and that pleases Lucien. He's always had an ax to grind."

A knock sounded at the front door. Josette's heart fell to her toes.

Pray don't let that be Vennard.

Chapter Twenty-Two

Josette opened the front door. Felicité Andrews stood before her looking bandbox fresh in a pale yellow cotton day gown trimmed in crisp white lace. Her hat, parasol, and reticule matched. Obviously, the girl frequented the same fabulous dressmaker as did Josette. "I'm surprised to see you here, but pleasantly so. Do come in."

"Thank you." Felicité snapped her parasol shut and returned Josette's smile. "Forgive me for arriving unannounced, but when my brother received your note that René was unwell, I grew concerned and thought to pay my respects."

Oh, didn't this hold a promise of entertainment? "Bastièn and René are in the parlor. Please, join us."

Josette escorted Felicité down the corridor, then stepped aside and allowed her to enter first. She stumbled to a halt when she saw the boys and their battered faces.

"Good heavens! What happened to the two of you?"

Bastièn and René stood in greeting—René somewhat more slowly than his brother.

"He hit me," Bastièn drawled, not bothering to hide his obvious appreciation of Miss Felicité's notable good looks.

René's eyelids lowered to half-mast as if he, too, reveled in her beauty. "He struck the first blow, don'cha know."

Josette stepped next to Felicité. "Don't listen to my mischievous brothers. They were set upon by thugs last night, and I stitched them up. Please, have a seat. Would you care for some lemonade? It's iced."

Felicité leaned her parasol beside the door. "Lemonade would be fine, thank you. Were the culprits apprehended?"

"*Non*," both men said in unison.

To Josette's surprise, when her brothers reseated themselves, Felicité went directly to Bastièn and sat beside him. She perused his bruised face. "Gracious, but that looks terribly painful."

René shifted in his chair, stretched his legs in front of him, and crossed them at the ankles. He rested his head on the chair's back and, with an elusive smile, regarded Felicité. "And mine does not?"

Felicité's gaze darted from René's bare feet, to Bastièn's, then to Josette's. She blinked fast a few times, as if not believing what she'd seen, but made no comment. Instead, she turned her attention to René's bruised and stitched forehead. "Yes, of course. But Bastièn's face is terribly swollen right along here."

She made to touch his face, but snatched her white-gloved hand back and clasped her fingers together.

"You can touch me if you like." Bastièn's words came low and throaty, loaded with innuendo.

Felicité's cheeks turned pink. In an instant, she collected herself and the color dissipated. She picked up the glass of lemonade and lifted it to her lips.

René and Bastièn scrutinized her every movement.

Despite her brothers' pain and injury, Felicité's high-spirited manner elevated Josette's mood. She doubted either one of her brothers had met such a woman as this Miss Andrews. Furthermore, Josette was confident Felicité had never before encountered the likes of René and Bastièn.

René studied Felicité through smoky eyes. Then that

sultry expression Josette had seen so many times settled over his countenance. "Ah, but I have more hurts, *ma chére*, so come, have pity on me."

Felicité squinted at René. "Bastièn looks the worse for wear. Besides, he's on this large sofa while you sit in a chair made for one."

A slow, easy grin slid across René's mouth. "I can easily make room."

Josette couldn't help it; she laughed. "René is right about his wounds, Miss Felicité. Were you to see beneath his shirt, you'd find all manner of cuts that required a good number of stitches."

Felicité gasped. "What in the name of all saints took place?"

The boys shot speaking glances at Josette. "As I said, my brothers were set upon by thugs. I'll spare you the nasty details." She moved to the low table near the sofa. "Would you care for another glass of lemonade?"

The front door opened and closed. Josette's heart hit the floor once again. But it was Alexia coming in, a frown on her face that would've frightened off a storm.

Cameron followed behind her, wearing an equally mulish scowl. Felicité leaned forward and peered down the corridor. Spying Cameron, she excused herself and went to him.

Alexia marched into the parlor and to René. "How'd you get that cut on your head, Uncle? Scoot over, so's I can fit in."

Josette bristled. "Alexia, where are your manners?"

René leaned over and whispered something in Alexia's ear. Her cheeks mottled. Instead of responding, she shot over to where Bastièn sat with his arm over the sofa back. She plopped down close to the inside curve of his shoulder, and scowled at his bruised and cut face. "Plain to see you been in another fight."

"Please, come in," Josette said to Cameron as he and Felicité approached. Whatever had been exchanged between the two cousins, some of the anger seemed to have dissipated from Cameron.

"He's already in." Alexia crossed her arms over her chest and, refusing to look at her father, began to pick at her bottom lip.

Oh, dear.

Cameron glanced from Bastièn to René. "What the blazes happened to you two?"

"They were set upon by thugs," Felicité said when Josette hesitated.

Cameron stepped closer to Josette but he eyed René. "That looks like a nasty cut on your forehead, but surely not enough to keep you from work."

René raised his shirt and exposed his torso wrapped from waist to underarms in strips of cotton stained with blotches of dried blood. "There's more than meets the eye. An old saying, *oui*?"

At the sight of her uncle's condition, Alexia's eyes widened. She let loose with French curses.

Felicité murmured something to Cameron, who nodded. She turned to Alexia. "Dear, how would you like to spend a couple of days with me at my brother's home?"

"*Non.*"

"Have you ever driven a buggy?"

"Now where would I be gettin' one of those?" She shot a grin at Bastièn. "Steal it?"

Not returning her smile, he leaned to her ear. Whatever he said, her cheeks blotched a deeper shade of red. She sprang from the sofa and headed for the door. "I'm off to my room."

Felicité stepped in front of her. "Please don't leave just yet. How would you like a turn around town in my buggy? I have it parked right outside. We can take our sweet time getting to Michel's. Stop wherever you please. I'll even let you have a hand at taking the reins. In the morning, we can ride over to the lake for a picnic. If you're any good at handling the horse and buggy today, then tomorrow you can do all the driving you care to."

Alexia's face lit up. She turned to Josette.

"Don't look to me for permission. Ask your father."

Alexia's mouth tightened into a grim slit.

A sigh, which Josette doubted anyone but she heard, left Cameron's lips. "Go on with you," he said. "Pack a few things and I'll see you in two days."

Alexia raced from the room toward the stairs. "I'll be right back."

Josette's stomach did that awful flip again. Two days and they'd both be gone from her life. She turned to Cameron and swept her hand toward the doorway. "May I have a word with you in private?"

The silence that fell over the room was laughable. He slid his gaze from one brother to the other. With a sardonic grin, he turned and followed her.

She led him across the corridor to the library and closed the double doors. Cameron, hands clasped behind his back, perused the room. His discerning gaze captured everything, from walls lined with books to the leather furniture, a world globe on a stand, and her oak writing desk. "Is this your collection, or was your husband an avid reader?"

A kind of sadness rolled through her at the reminder. "Monsieur LeBlanc was not much for books if they did not concern finances. I've spent a great deal of time alone in here."

"Impressive." Cameron turned to face her. "I meant the sheer number of books, not your time spent alone."

She hadn't asked him here to discuss her taste in reading or the quantity of her books. "I take it by the way Alexia stormed in that things did not go well with the authorities."

"At least not for her. I decided you were right, that I shouldn't try to waltz her out of the situation so I took a more severe course. Suffice it to say, my daughter now despises me."

Josette motioned for him to sit on the leather sofa. She took a chair opposite him. "What happened?"

Cameron rested an elbow on the sofa back and pressed two fingers to his temple. He discreetly rubbed in small circles. "I escorted her to the police station this morning. It seems the officer who visited your shop sent notice to those pedestrians who'd reported the thefts. They were all waiting for Alexia when we arrived."

"Oh, dear."

He nodded. "I sat beside her, but did not involve myself. She did a lot of squirming while she returned everyone's items and offered a round of apologies. The officer and I agreed that while I would see that she personally returned the remaining goods to the individual shopkeepers, I would wait outside each establishment while she went in and made her amends on her own."

"And she acquiesced?"

"Yes, until we left the station and got to the first place of business. Alexia marched in, slammed the candlesticks on the counter and said, 'Bugger off.'"

Josette pressed her fingers to her lips in a failed attempt to suppress a maverick bubble of laughter. "Pardon me. Please go on."

"That's when I decided I had better accompany her inside from then on, which I did. Other than telling me she hated me and wanted to come back here, she hasn't spoken to me since."

"Oh, Cameron, she's merely angry. And exceedingly embarrassed. She adores you."

"I do believe the last words she directed at me sounded distinctly like, 'I hate you.' How else am I to interpret such a vehemently delivered statement?"

"Give her time."

"Time? I only hope Felicité's brilliant idea to keep Alexia occupied until we sail proves successful. Mark my words, once I haul her aboard ship, she'll find a hundred different ways to express her loathing of me."

Guilt hammered at Josette. She pushed aside her own emotions to deal with Cameron's obvious hurt. "I'm so sorry you landed in this mess. It's my fault she went after you."

He stared at her for a long moment. "You actually admit to being the instigator?"

She gave a shrug. "Once I learned that you were living in San Francisco, I wrote a letter telling you about your daughter. Before I had a chance to mail the blasted thing, Alexia found it, which was how she knew where to find you."

Their gazes locked.

"Do you forgive me?"

His features softened. "I would not have known a child of mine existed had you done otherwise. There is nothing to forgive."

Tension squeezed her forehead until pain shot through her eyes. She worked at letting go of the tightness in her stomach. "Thank you, but I didn't ask you in here to privately discuss Alexia. That could have been done with my brothers present."

"What then?"

She clasped her hands in her lap. "I need a bit of advice, and I have no one to ask but you."

"Not your brothers?"

"Especially not them." She took in a deep breath and exhaled slowly. "René could've been killed last night if Bastièn hadn't met up with him. I know who ordered the attack."

His hand dropped from his temple. "Who?"

"Émile Vennard."

Cameron stilled. "You're certain?"

She nodded and told him the entire story. When finished, she said, "So you see, I dare not whisper a word of this to my brothers lest they hunt the man down. Then what would happen to them? René and Bastièn may be misguided at times, but they are not killers. Even if Vennard met with a so-called accident, my brothers couldn't live with themselves."

Something changed in Cameron. Whatever concerns he'd displayed regarding Alexia disappeared, replaced by a formidable force Josette had yet to encounter. A kind of shock wended through her at the sheer power he exuded. He stood and made his way to the wide expanse of windows overlooking her flower garden. His back to her, he said nothing for a long while.

Then he turned, his sober, businesslike demeanor in sharp contrast to the worry he'd worn when he'd first entered her home. "Vennard is a big man in a minuscule part of the world, Josette. He's not dealt with anyone used to working on a much larger scale. I've a simple solution."

She stood as well, clasping her hands in front of her to keep them from shaking. "What kind of solution?"

"Sell both your home and your shop to my shipping company."

She gasped. "What? How?"

"No money will be exchanged other than the mandatory dollar. It's merely a matter of paperwork." He pulled his watch from his vest pocket and checked the time. "It's barely two o'clock. I have time to get to the bank and to my solicitors to have the papers drawn up at once."

It was as though his commanding vitality swallowed up the entire room, taking her along with it. Heart hammering in her chest, she took a step back. "But . . . but these things take time, and you'll be leaving in two days."

He gave a quick shake of his head. "Once everything is in order, I'll sign whatever I can before my departure. Michel will act on the company's behalf for anything else."

Oh, the tears were ready to fall, and she desperately did not want that to happen in front of him. "I don't see how . . ."

Twin lines appeared between his furrowed brows. "Is there a problem?"

She closed her eyes against the wetness gathering in them. "The truth is, I have worked so hard to become a woman of independent means, Cameron. Your plan would be brilliant if only it didn't steal my freedom."

The air left his lungs in a great whoosh. He stepped forward and clasped her shoulders. Suddenly, he was two people at once—the formidable businessman whose power nearly made her tremble, and her concerned lover, touching her with protective yet gentle hands.

"Josette, darling, these kinds of things are done all the time. This entire transaction will be in name only. Everything will still belong to you. When enough time passes, or whenever Vennard himself passes, everything can revert back to you at your say-so."

Was this truly the answer? He could save her brothers? Save her shop and her home? Hope threaded through her fears. "This could work?"

He gave her a slow nod. Then heat gathered in his gaze. She stared into his dazzling amber eyes, fire igniting in her belly.

"I was lonely on the sofa, Josette." The timbre of Cameron's words shifted to a low huskiness. "I didn't care much for you sitting in that chair across from me."

An easy, deliberate smile tipped a corner of his mouth. He nudged her shoulders with his fingers. "Come closer."

She took a step forward, desperately wanting him, yet not wanting to lose a part of herself—the part she'd struggled so hard to mold into autonomous strength.

"Not close enough," he murmured and eased her against

him. Slipping his arms around her, he used his fingertips to massage the back of her neck.

She moaned as tension drained out of her. Why be concerned about losing something of herself? She'd not surrendered anything to him she hadn't wanted to. He'd soon be gone. Until then, she'd not let worry cause her to miss a moment of what they might enjoy together.

He swept a loose tendril behind her ear, then brushed a soft kiss on either side of her mouth. "That bastard must have been scaring years off your life."

He kissed the outer corner of each eye. "You'll never have to fear him again, Josette. Nor do you ever have to see or speak to the scum. My solicitors will take care of everything henceforth."

She gazed into Cameron's eyes while the full meaning of his words sank in. "But I should be there when he's told. At least I'd like to see the look on his face."

Cameron shook his head. "There'll be more power in your silence, and in the complete removal of yourself from him. I'll see to having papers drawn up forbidding him to enter your home or place of business."

She closed her eyes and rubbed her cheek against his. Here was a man she could love. But she held no illusions about him—about them. About love itself. Perhaps one day someone would come along and fill her with the same wondrous feelings.

She doubted it.

Curling a finger beneath her chin, he lifted it. "Open your eyes, Josette."

She did as he bid.

His gaze swept slowly over her face as if drinking her in. "Will you spend the night with me?"

Her heart kicked up a notch. "My brothers—"

"Can remain here while I take you to my home." He brushed his lips over hers. "Do me the honor of saying yes."

She felt him tense as he waited for her answer. Here was her first test at living an independent life alongside her brothers.

"Yes," she whispered, and felt the tension in him dissipate.

"I should make my way to my solicitor's before the day draws to a close, but before I go, is there anything else you might want of me? Any favors I might have the power to grant?"

Her knees had gone soft, but not her reasoning. "A favor, yes. Will you break bread with my brothers tonight?"

He pulled back his head and frowned. "Don't tell me you want me to dine with those scoundrels, then waltz you out the door with a jolly good night?"

She planted a kiss of promise on his mouth. "Well, not the jolly good night, but yes, I'd like you to join us. After all, they are Alexia's uncles. Cameron, please grant me this favor before you and Alexia leave."

The lids over his amber eyes lowered. "You manipulate me."

She gave him a sly grin. "We're having étouffée. Bastièn brought fresh crawdads home from the bayou this afternoon. Could we see you at eight?"

Laughter rumbled in Cameron's chest. He pulled her tight to him and wrapped his arms around her in a great hug that buried her cheek against his chest again. "I'll agree to this insanity, but only because Régine makes the best étouffée in New Orleans."

She grinned to herself. How comfortable they were with one another. How easily they conferred.

He lifted her chin and settled on her a deep and long kiss that harbored a promise of things to come. He released her, but the electricity traveling between them left its mark. "As I said, I need to visit my solicitor if I'm going to get anything accomplished."

He kissed her again. "Your lips are swollen, so you'd best stay behind while I see myself out."

Reaching the door, he paused. "Michel has a stable of horses, and I am in dire need of a good long ride to rid myself of what's built up inside me these past few days. Would you mind if I arrived a bit late?"

That hot pulse beating low in her belly ratcheted up. She gave him a sultry grin. "This is an informal evening, so if you were to show up in your riding clothes, we'd just have to be sure you bathed afterward, wouldn't we?"

A deep chuckle rose from his throat. "I do like the way your clever mind works."

Cameron was a decidedly handsome man who easily turned heads when dressed in his finery. But with his hair still wind-tousled and wearing tall black riding boots and tight britches that outlined muscled legs and hips, and a smile filled with promise, he was a fallen god.

A god Josette was about to spend an entire night making love with.

They'd finished dinner, and he sat relaxed in a chair, bantering with her brothers and, Josette swore, actually having a good time. Perhaps it was the sinful intention of carting her off to his home right in front of René and Bastièn that had him in a particularly fine mood. Or maybe it was that he was leaving soon and could afford to call a truce for one evening. Whatever it was, he'd granted Josette her favor. She could have crawled right over the table and kissed him for the way he interacted with her brothers.

And surprisingly, they with him. Oh, the banter was

acerbic, to be sure, but that was half the fun as far as she was concerned. She'd had to buy her brothers' good graces by promising them each a new suit of clothing if they could manage to be civil to her guest. Following a lengthy discussion regarding Vennard's attempts to purchase Josette's shop and home, Cameron introduced the idea of his shipping company making the acquisitions as a way to foil Vennard's plans and protect Josette. Both René and Bastièn were in robust agreement, which lent a celebratory atmosphere to the evening.

Adding to her pleasure, René moved about easily, showing few signs of stiffness. Oh, he had to be sore, but her herbs and creams were working wonders. A week from now, his stitches could be removed.

A pounding sounded at the door.

Josette's heart responded to the beat in kind. "Oh, dear. Could word have traveled so fast? Could that be Vennard ready to pounce on me?"

The three men stood. Cameron turned to Vivienne. "You should be the one to get that. If it is Vennard, do not let on that we are here. Tell him you'll collect Josette straight away."

Vivienne nodded and scurried off as the pounding increased.

In moments, Felicité rushed into the room, so out of breath she had to bend and hold her sides.

Cameron went to her. "What the devil happened? Where's Alexia?"

"G . . . gone."

Every part of Josette froze—muscles, brain, heart, breath.

Cameron held Felicité by the shoulders. "Take a slow, deep breath. That's it. Another one. Good girl. Now tell me."

"We no sooner got home when her uncle came to call—"

"Uncle?" they all said.

"A man named Lucien."

René stepped forward. "He's not her uncle. He's my no-good cousin. He took her?"

Felicité nodded. "Since Alexia was so pleased to see him, and he seemed congenial enough, I saw no harm in letting him in. I offered him tea. He said he'd come to take her to her grandmother, that her grandmother had a party planned for Alexia tonight."

Bastièn and René cursed.

"She went with him?" Josette cried.

"She wanted to, but I said no, we should wait and ask her father. Lucien seemed fine with my explanation, but suddenly I grew dizzy and the room swirled around me. He must have put something in my tea when I went for a few sweets, because the next thing I knew, I woke up all these hours later, lying on my bed, and with a servant watching over me."

"You were otherwise unharmed?" Cameron demanded. "Where the devil was Michel all the while?"

"I wasn't set upon in the way you are inferring. I doubt Lucien would have done anything to frighten either Alexia or the servants, and have them refuse to allow Alexia to accompany him. Likely he made some kind of excuse such as I had suffered the vapors. The man can be quite convincing. As for Michel, he has a lady friend. Said he wouldn't be home all night. But I knew that when I invited Alexia."

"What time did Lucien show up?"

"Around four. Teatime."

Cameron pulled out his watch. "Bloody hell, it's near midnight."

Bastièn cursed. "That's why Maman wasn't so upset when I left. She was making plans to move her initiation up to spite us."

"*Oui,*" René said and turned to Cameron. "Maman intends to take Alexia through that terrible initiation I told you about. Lucien practices the voodoo as well—that's why she sent him."

Josette could barely manage to get her terrible words out. "What . . . what if he was lying and had no intention of taking Alexia to Maman?"

Dead silence permeated the room.

Bastièn was already halfway out the dining room door when he paused. "If Maman issued orders, he would not go against his priestess. If it be the voodoo ceremony, I know where to find them. I only hope we're not too late." He shot a glance at René. "Are you up to coming with me?"

"He cannot," Josette said. "He's full of stitches that would surely tear open. I'll go."

"No!" all three men shouted.

Cameron stepped forward. "Josette, you stay here. Felicité, do what you will, but you both might benefit from each other's company."

He turned to the brothers. "I'm Alexia's father. I'll be going."

René shook his head. "*Non.* You do not know the bayou. You will only slow us down."

That same formidable power Cameron had demonstrated in the library swept over him. "Damn it, that's my daughter we're talking about, René. I'm coming along. I know how to handle myself, and I know when and how to take directions. In this case, your directions."

Chapter Twenty-Three

Bastièn guided the pirogue deep into the bayou through waters black as ink. Cameron sat on a wooden slat affixed to the middle of the flat-bottomed boat. Behind him, René perched on a similar plank.

Fireflies glimmered along the banks like nomadic stars floating down from the heavens. A noisy chorus of resonant bullfrogs, croaking toads, and high-pitched peepers filled the air. A soft splash sounded to Cameron's left. He jerked. An alligator sliding into the water? A fish jumping for mosquitoes?

Had the situation been less dire, Cameron might have found this place rather enchanting in the midnight hours, but from among the amphibians' songs, the vibrating hum of cicadas, and the occasional hoot of an owl, a murmur of distant drums raised his hackles. His daughter was out there in the middle of that gripping beat. But what if she wasn't? What if Lucien had lied about taking her to her grandmother? What if . . .

Cameron shoved the alarming thought aside. He couldn't allow such unnerving contemplations. The drumbeat grew louder. Wherever Bastièn was taking them, they were nearing their goal.

Bastièn turned to Cameron and spoke softly. "Now is the time to pay attention to that little lesson I gave you when we started out, *mon ami*. You follow what I say and do, *oui*? If you do not, we could all die."

Cameron nodded. God help him if he had to find his way out of this place alone. When they'd first entered the bayou, he'd wondered how Bastièn could navigate in the darkness, but to Cameron's surprise, after his eyes adjusted to the moonlight and fireflies, he could see well enough to follow any commands. Still, he had to be missing most of what the two brothers were acutely aware of.

They rounded a bend and an acrid scent of woodsmoke filled with a mélange of food smells tainted the air. Bastièn had said there'd be pigs roasting on spits, but had mentioned nothing about anything else. Cameron caught the distinct scent of the holy trinity of Cajun fare—bell peppers, onions, and celery. He'd recognize those and the other heady spices anywhere. The mysterious, shadowy world of the bayou was a pristine environment. These strong odors stood out like foreign invaders and grated against nature's purity.

The drums grew louder until the sound vibrated across the open waters. The rhythm of Cameron's heart kicked up. He squinted through heavy underbrush, past the cypress and cottonwoods. He caught sight of a large bonfire, its flames licking the sky. Odalie's followers danced around the perimeter of the blaze. Another kind of smoke stung his nostrils, this one sickly sweet. Surely that wasn't opium?

Bastièn used the long pole to push their pirogue past a number of others that lay empty along a flat shoreline. In the shadows, they could've been a congregation of gators waiting to attack. A twist of the pole and Bastièn eased into a narrow inlet. He brought the boat to a halt at a horizontal angle to the festivities. They straddled the planks and sat side by side, barely a foot apart.

René leaned over and spoke softly. "Hidden in the brush

like this, we will not be seen because everyone is either dazed or staring into the fire. With all the noise, they cannot hear us either, but they could sense our presence if we are not careful, so we must remain in the shadows and speak softly."

Cameron slapped at a mosquito on his neck. "Where the hell is Alexia?"

"Likely around the other side of the bonfire in a peristyle," Bastièn said.

"What the devil is that?" Cameron's patience had run out.

"A temple. A makeshift one out here. Maman's female assistants are preparing Alexia for the initiation. Have patience."

"There's Maman." René pointed to a dark-haired woman who was dressed in a thin white robe and shaking an *asson*, the sacred rattle of the priesthood. She danced a full circle around the inferno, eyes closed. An albino snake, as thick as Cameron's arm, was wrapped around Odalie's waist and trailed up her arm. Despite the sultry air, a shiver ran through him.

"She uses the rattle to release the power of departed spirits," René said. "She intends to bind Alexia to the lineage connected to Maman. That is why it is important to halt this initiation. If it goes past the point of no return, Maman will consider Alexia her true child, and own her like no other. She will become another priestess."

"Christ, she's only thirteen years old." Cameron shot a glance at René, who sipped rum from a flask. Gosling Brothers, to be exact. But Josette had given it to him to ease his pain, so Cameron refrained from caustic remarks.

"There's Lucien." Bastièn indicated a near-naked male dancing around Odalie. Cameron set his jaw until his teeth ground together. Even from where they sat, it was easy to catch the glazed look in the man's eyes. He wore a pair of white cotton trousers, the fabric so thin, his muscled legs stood in silhouette against the bonfire. The reflection against his sweat-shiny chest sent flames licking over him. His hair fell loose to his shoulders and swung about as he gyrated. The other similarly clad men twirled around the fire and chanted. The women wore colorful thin skirts and tops.

Bastièn removed his shirt, ready to make his move. The plan was for him to sneak around the edge of the group once they'd worked themselves into a hypnotic frenzy and lost awareness of their surroundings. He'd ease into the crowd, escape with Alexia into the woods, then wind his way back around to René and Cameron.

Cameron's head was beginning to pound to the beat of the drums. "Blast it all, where can she be?"

Lucien handed Maman a glass bottle filled with clear liquid. She took a mouthful and, cheeks puffed, spat a stream into the fire, where it hissed like a snake. The flames shot higher.

Alcohol.

Lucien's brew?

Wooden cages filled with white chickens lined the outside perimeter of the circle. Lucien reached in and pulled one out. With a sharp twist, he snapped off its head. Holding the sacrifice upside down over his chest, he hopped in circles, blood spurting over him, a grin on his face that looked sickeningly like someone in the throes of ecstasy.

Cameron's stomach curdled.

Another chicken left its pen and met the same fate over another chest, then another. The drumbeats increased as did the fever pitch of the gyrations and the sacrifices of the fowl. "Good God, does this go on all night?"

He turned to René and nearly flinched at the stony look on his face. Cameron didn't have to ask what Odalie and Lucien planned next for Alexia—René's countenance told the tale.

Heart pounding, Cameron glanced at Bastièn, who must

have read his mind. "Do not move. You must leave her rescue to us."

Lucien careened around the circle, tearing heads off chickens as if it were child's play. He chanted and whirled, then disappeared behind the bonfire. When he reappeared, he had a wide-eyed Alexia in tow.

Cameron cursed and made to rise.

"*Non.*" Bastièn shoved him back onto the bench. "They will kill you if you invade their sacred circle. René is too injured to go after her, so he will guide the pirogue. As another of the high priestess's sons, I must rescue your daughter. Maman is already in an altered state. Loa—the spirits from the other side—have entered her and taken over. Once the ceremony is finished and they exit her, she will not even know I was here, only that Alexia disappeared. But Lucien, he has not yet received the loa into him. We must wait."

Lucien began a series of twirls and high-kick jumps around Alexia, the lustful expression on his face unmistakable. He held the bottle to her lips. She took a mouthful and spat it into the fire. He laughed, sang something to her, and moved around her in rhythmic agitation.

He grabbed another caged chicken, snapped off its head, and lifted it to Alexia's chest. Blood splattered onto her white blouse. Fear blazed in her eyes. She struggled to pull away. Lucien grabbed her around the waist, yanked her against him, and set his mouth to her neck.

"That son of a bitch." Cameron bolted out of the pirogue.

"Stop." Bastièn reached for him.

Suddenly, the water around Cameron boiled. "Christ! Something bit me."

"Snakes!" Bastièn and René lunged for him.

Another sting, and as they yanked Cameron back into the boat, something heavy dragged at his left leg. He peered down at the writhing water moccasin clinging to him. "That bloody thing is still attached. Get it off!"

"*Merde*." Grabbing the snake behind its broad head, Bastièn squeezed, forcing its jaws apart. He lifted the wriggling creature off Cameron and flung it back into the water. "You stepped in a nest of moc'sins."

Pain shot up Cameron's leg, making him groan. "I think I got bit twice."

"Sit up," René ordered. "Keep your head above your leg so the poison doesn't reach your heart."

"We have a sudden change of plans." Bastièn reached for Cameron's boots.

He pulled back. "What the devil are you doing?"

"Your leg is about to bloat up like a dead horse in the sun. Won't be long and I'd have to cut it off you." He yanked off the boots and tossed them in the bottom of the boat. Cameron's knife fell out of one and clattered across the wood.

A kind of pain Cameron never knew existed racked his leg.

Bastièn turned to René. "I know you're in bad shape, *mon frère*, but can you go after Alexia? If we leave her here, Lucien might get to her before Maman realizes anything is amiss. If I go after her, her father is likely dead. You know what has to be done."

"You'll need this." René tossed Bastièn the silver flask containing the rum and grabbed the long guide pole, digging it into the muddy water. He pushed the pirogue out of the inlet and over to where the others were lined along the shore. He removed his shirt. Clad in only trousers and the bandage around his torso, he waded to shore.

Bastièn turned back to Cameron. "Take a few easy breaths and remain as calm as you can. Keep them shallow."

"Christ, this hurts."

"*Oui*. It be the worst kind of pain." Bastièn dug into his trouser pocket and withdrew a pocket knife. He flipped it open. "I have to cut those bites open and suck out as much poison as I can, so hold on to the sides of the pirogue."

"Why couldn't René have taken care of me while you went after Alexia since you're in better shape?"

"Because I am the trained healer. My brother wouldn't know what to do." With a quick slice of the knife, Bastièn slit the right leg of Cameron's breeches to his hip. "Good thing you were wearing high-top riding boots or a good dozen snakes would've latched on to your ankles. Not much I could've done but watch you pass over to the other side. And it's another good thing that biggest snake didn't bite into you much higher or you'd surely be a dead man."

"Why is that?" The knife cuts Bastièn made didn't hurt near as bad as the severe pain shooting up and down Cameron's leg.

Bastièn sucked and spat. Then he took a mouthful of rum from René's flask and rinsed out his mouth. "Because I wouldn't be sucking anything much higher, don'cha know."

"Christ, now's hardly the time for jokes."

Bastièn continued to suck, spit, and rinse. Finally, he stood and wiped his mouth with the back of his hand. He grabbed hold of the pole and eased the pirogue into the main waterway. "Stay still as you can and keep your breaths shallow."

Cameron glanced back at the ceremony. "What the devil? We need to wait for René."

"*Non*. He'll borrow one of those other pirogues and take Alexia to Josette, where she'll be safe. I'm taking you to Maman's."

"What?"

"Her place is closer. She has things there to take care of snakebites. I know what to do."

Cameron fought the panic trying to rise along with the escalating pain. He had to keep talking just to maintain his sanity. "How will we know if René is successful? He's all stitched up and can barely move around."

"Fair interesting what a person can accomplish when

circumstances require, *oui*?" Despite Bastièn's display of calmness, he moved them quickly through the water, his face a mask of concern.

"No matter what it takes, René will rescue your daughter. He is Maman's oldest son, so no one will harm him unless she commands it. And she won't. Josette will have some repair work to do on him, though."

The pounding in Cameron's head increased. A dirty, raw taste coated his mouth and tongue, as if the swamp and snake had both crawled inside him. "You can't take me to your mother's. If Odalie recognizes me, I won't last five minutes."

"*Non.* Above all else, she is a high priestess healer. Because of what has happened to you, René has halted the ceremony and Maman is lucid once again. You hear no more drums, *oui*? At this moment he stands in front of her and her following—her voodoo family—telling her of your plight and asking for help. Maman has her dark side, which has nothing to do with her spiritual practices, but with René challenging her in front of the others, she will not dare cast you aside. Nor can she refuse to allow Alexia to go with him if she so pleases. You saw the look on your daughter's face. She will leave with René."

"Good Christ. I should never have climbed out of the bloody boat."

"*Oui*, but that is in the past. If we are going to save you, or save your leg, you need to stop talking, stop thinking, and breathe very gently."

The pain in Cameron's leg traveled to his belly. Nausea roiled. He leaned over the pirogue and vomited. Perspiration flooded his skin, and then his flesh ran icy cold. A trembling set in that made his teeth rattle. "You don't think I'm going to live through this, do you?"

Before Bastièn could answer, Cameron leaned over the boat and vomited again, unable to halt the retching.

"There are two reasons why you should not lean too far over the water, *mon ami*. One is that you need to keep your heart above your leg. The other is you do not want some fat gator springing up out of nowhere and taking your head off."

Cameron sat back and cursed the pain running through him. As if profanity would be of any help. Of all the ways to die, this one had never crossed his mind. Old age, perhaps? Being thrown from a horse? A debilitating disease? Not the bite of a goddamned water moccasin. No, two of them. And judging by the size of the snake that had sunk its fangs into him and pumped poison into his leg, he'd gotten a hell of a dose.

His mind was beginning to fog, and his head pounded out a powerful rhythm that felt like trumpets heralding death. He hung over the side of the boat again. Clutching his gut, he heaved nothing but bile.

"You're fortunate it wasn't a rattler, *mon ami*. Rattlers steal your breath. Shut your lungs down until you suffocate. One that size would surely have killed you by now. This way, if you don't die, we only have to worry about saving your leg."

Had Cameron imagined things or had Bastièn's voice taken on a hint of compassion?

Bastièn eased the boat alongside a dock and tied it to a crude post. "Can you stand?"

Cameron tried. "Legs don't work right."

"Then I'll have to push you up until you hang over the side of the dock. Once I get you there, do not move or you'll slide into the water. As big as you are, I won't be able to haul you out."

"No more snakes," Cameron mumbled.

"*Non*," Bastièn said. "We keep them cleared from around the house. When I give you a shove, grab the post where I hooked the rope and slap your belly onto the planks. Then hang on until I get to you. Don't you let your head drop even with your leg, you hear? Let me do the work so your heart won't beat so hard."

As soon as Cameron got his upper body into position, Bastièn jumped onto the dock. With a grunt and a groan, he heaved Cameron to a standing position. "Lean on me."

Once inside the house, Bastièn eased him onto a straight, armless chair. He lit an oil lamp. "Sit up. Just keep upright for me. I'll be right back."

Between the pain and his muddled brain, Cameron had no idea how much time passed before Bastièn returned with two small bowls.

He sat beside Cameron and cut deeper into the two bites. He poured a tall glass of clear liquid. Each time he sucked and spat, he rinsed out his mouth. "Moonshine. Keeps the snake poison from getting into me."

He dipped his head, and again sucked and spat. "Judging from the distance between the puncture wounds, this here bite right above your knee came from a smaller snake. Doesn't mean it wasn't loaded with poison, though. Young ones can be just as dangerous as the older ones. But the one moc'sin that didn't want to let go was one damn big snake."

He sucked and spat again. "No telling when she ate last, so no telling how much poison she had in her when she sank her fangs into you."

Cameron shivered from the pain. "She?"

Bastièn's sharp blue eyes fixed on Cameron, assessing him. "You can tell by the tip of the tail."

Cameron tried to focus on the words being spoken. They sounded far off, and the lamplight seemed to dim as his vision blurred. But the pain in his leg . . . "I need to vomit again."

Bastièn held a bucket next to the chair. "I doubt you have anything left in you, but it's good to get it out if there is."

He set down the pail and picked up one of the bowls. Holding it against Cameron's lesions, he poured what looked like blood into the cross-cuts and smeared it into the wounds.

"What's that?"

"One of Maman's tricks. I opened a vein in Satan out back. That old horse has been snake bit so many times, Maman swears his blood acts against the poison."

Cameron shook his head, trying to clear it, trying to remember what Bastièn had said. It wasn't worth the bother. He closed his eyes.

"*Regarde-moi*." Bastièn nudged Cameron's good leg, urging him to look at Bastièn. "Are you still with me?"

It took a moment for Cameron to put Bastièn's words into any kind of order. He nodded.

"You cannot keep your mind straight, *oui*?"

Talking took too much effort. Cameron nodded again.

"I know you want to sleep, but you have to work with me." Bastièn spread something cool over Cameron's leg. Although it didn't halt the inner agony, the terrible stinging stopped.

"What was that?" he mumbled.

"Catfish slime. Steals the surface pain. Maman will be here soon. She is bound to do what she can to save you. I don't know about saving your leg, though."

What was worse, lose a leg or die outright?

Cameron no longer cared.

Chapter Twenty-Four

The clock had barely struck four in the morning when footsteps on the veranda sent Josette running to the door. A bloodstained and disheveled Alexia huddled close to René.

Josette grew dizzy at the sight. "Oh, dear heavens, you're wounded."

She reached for Alexia, but the girl shrank back and clung to her uncle.

"It's only chicken blood," he said.

The frantic buzz in Josette's brain dissipated. She'd been privy to Maman's practices in the past, so she knew Cameron and her brothers must have reached Alexia near the end of the initiation. At least Lucien hadn't stolen her away for his evil purposes.

René and Alexia stepped inside.

Josette collected herself and took care in choosing her words. "Would you like me to help you with a bath?"

Alexia burrowed into the crook of René's arm.

Was she ashamed? "Sweetheart, you can talk to me about anything. But if you choose not to breathe a word of what happened, I won't inquire. There is one thing I want you to know, though—no matter what, I will always love you."

The suggestion of a smile touched René's otherwise stoic expression.

The three of them stood in the entry for what seemed an eternity. Suddenly, Alexia's face contorted and a great sob escaped. She pulled away from René and fell into Josette's arms. "I'm sorry, *ma tante*. I . . . I di . . . didn't know how awful it would be."

"You poor thing." Josette held Alexia tight to her bosom and swayed back and forth, planting kisses atop her head. "You're safe now."

Once Alexia relaxed a little, Josette held her at arm's length and conjured a smile. "Shall we get you cleaned up and off to bed? You must be utterly exhausted."

Alexia sniffed, wiped the back of her hand across her nose, and, ignoring the tears on her cheeks, eyed the staircase as if it might be the only safe haven in the land.

Josette glanced over René's shoulder, then back to him. "Where are Bastièn and Cameron?"

René broke eye contact and stared down the corridor. "See to Alexia and then we'll talk."

Josette's heart leapt to her throat. Something had to have gone terribly wrong. She noted René's sullied and torn shirt hanging loose from his trousers. "Remove your top, René."

Without a word, he pulled the stained garment over his head and let it drop to the floor. The bandages covering his torso seeped fresh blood.

The hairs on Josette's arms stood on end. "The last thing you need is for an infection to set in."

She addressed Alexia. "Can you wake Vivienne—?"

"I'm here." Vivienne descended the flight of stairs with Régine right behind her.

"Thank heavens. I'm going to need some help, ladies. Alexia, you go with Vivienne for a bath and change of clothing. Régine, hurry and heat some water, then set out my supplies."

Taking René by the arm, Josette guided him toward the kitchen. "What happened?"

He shoved a hand through his hair. "See to what needs fixin', then we talk, *oui*?"

A seed of terror sprouted in her. "You know I cannot tolerate this kind of tension. Tell me what's wrong."

He set his jaw and said nothing. She knew better than to prod, but blast it all, her thoughts were all over the place and setting her nerves jangling even worse than they'd been all evening.

They reached the kitchen, where René boosted himself onto the worktable with a grunt and a curse. "Get this done as fast as you can. I need to return to the bayou."

She held her shaking hands before him. "Look at me, René. I've been pacing the floor for hours, sick with worry. Now you tell me to take care of you, and then we talk? Do you think keeping whatever you have to say until I've finished sewing you up is going to help either of us?"

He turned his face to the ceiling and closed his eyes. "Bastièn is fine, but Cameron got bit by a couple of water moc'sins."

Josette's heart tripped and pain gripped her stomach. "Oh, no! Is he still alive?"

"He was when I left them, but he's in a bad way. Bastièn took him to Maman's—"

"Maman's? That's insanity. You know she hates him." The irony of her words struck her like a slap. What would there be left to hate if he was already dead? A moan left her throat.

René tried for a deep breath, but winced and held his side. "I halted the ceremony in front of Maman's followers and demanded she help him. She didn't dare refuse or she would've been called a hypocrite. Besides, if Cameron's still alive, Bastièn will protect him. Now, stitch me up, *s'il vous plaît*."

Régine moved to where René perched on the table and began dabbing water on his bandages to ease their removal. She glanced at Josette's quaking fingers. "Would you prefer Vivienne or I do the repair?"

Josette wrapped her arms around her waist, and walked to the back door. Flinging it open, she gazed out at her garden, lit only by the waning moon.

If he's still alive.

This nightmare could not be happening. Some mistake had been made.

Of course, that was it . . . a terrible mistake.

Cameron might have been bitten, but that didn't mean the snakes were poisonous. Hadn't she been attacked by a plain old water snake once? Yes, that was what had gotten him. After all, it had to be black as pitch out there, so how could they have known the creatures were venomous?

A strange, stoic calm settled her nerves. Her hands ceased their trembling. She marched back to the table and, standing to René's left, spoke to Régine. "As soon as you finish removing the bandages, I'll take over."

Her cousin shot Josette an odd frown, then went back to her task.

René shoved a bent arm beneath his head as a pillow and studied Josette through half-closed lids, the tops and bottoms of his thick, sooty lashes tangling together at the outer corners. "What did you go and tell yourself that makes you so calm all of a sudden, *chère?*"

She picked up the needle and threaded it with catgut. "Don't look down your nose at me. Concern yourself with cooperating, not wondering what I'm thinking."

Régine finished removing the bandages, then went about tending to the wounds with witch hazel.

"You need to hurry." René's words to Josette were suddenly gentle.

She sank the needle into the flesh of the first cleansed wound.

René winced.

"Sorry. I had better slow down and do this right."

She paused a beat, then began to babble. "Those were likely nothing but water snakes. Remember when I got bit by one while we were digging for crawfish and my hand swelled up something awful? Maman said the infection set in because their mouths were so dirty from all they ate, mice and things. It was painful to be sure, but not from poison. Simple water snakes. That's what bit Cameron."

"*Non,* Josette," René said quietly. "It was a nest of moc'sins he stepped in. There be no mistake."

Good Lord, Cameron could very well be gone already! No, it simply was not possible. She had to clear her throat to get her words out. "Régine, would you please fetch Alexia? And some fresh clothing for René so he doesn't have to climb the stairs in his condition."

When her cousin exited the room, Josette went back to sewing. "That's Alexia's father we are speaking of. She'll need to know what's happened."

"*Oui.*" René reached out and touched her cheek with the back of his hand. "And you are in love with him, *non*?"

The needle slipped.

René hissed.

"Beg your pardon." She concentrated on her task. "This is hardly a discussion to be carrying on right now. As you said, we can talk later."

"I think now is the right moment for this particular discussion, *chère*."

She drew a hard breath to channel her frustration. "Not that it's any of your business, but we were two adults attracted to each other. We knew our time together was limited, so we simply took advantage of the circumstances. Is that such a sin?"

Her hands began to shake again. The needle dropped from her fingers onto René's stomach.

He looked down at it. "You should ask Régine or Vivienne to finish."

She stepped back and shoved an errant curl behind her ear. "I . . . Perhaps you're right. I can't seem to stop this blasted trembling."

"So you let him treat you like he did Solange? You wish to end up in the cemetery next to her?"

Annoyance rubbed against years of raw hurt, and a flood of emotions poured forth. She pressed her palms against her temples. "Stop berating me, René. Solange tricked Cameron into getting her with child. She did it ruthlessly and without shame. And I'll have you know, she tore my heart to shreds while she was at it."

A puzzled look ran over René's countenance. "What do you mean?"

"More than anyone, I trusted Solange. I was fascinated with Cameron back then. When I was thirteen and he was seventeen, I pointed him out to her and told her how wild I was about him. At the time, her target had been Cameron's cousin. It was her way out of life in the bayou, but Trevor was far too busy with Madame Olympée's favorites to pay any attention to our sister. That's when she got the idea to bargain with the madame over Cameron."

Josette paced now, rubbing her sweaty palms on her skirts. "How do you think I felt when Alexia was born? Solange broke my heart, René. She did it without giving it as much as a second thought."

"So you are in love with him and have been for many years."

"You're confusing love with desire, but I doubt you would know the difference."

"Do you?"

She marched over to him. "Oh, I would shake you if you

weren't so injured. Love builds, René. It nourishes a warmth that lasts throughout the years. Cameron—if he is alive and makes it through this awful mess—will leave. We desired each other; that is all. Certainly you, with your many conquests, can understand what the heat of desire can do to a person."

René studied her for a long moment. "If you ask me, you don't believe he could love you, so you won't let yourself think about your feelings as anything more than desire."

"I didn't ask you." Tears flooded the backs of her eyes. "We are speaking of a man who may already be dead. If he is not, and he makes it through, he'll sail off. He's told me on more than one occasion that he is a lost soul and needs to find himself. For God's sake, can't you leave this be?"

René said nothing, only watched her.

She picked up the needle. Her fingers still shook. She dropped it back onto his stomach. "Where the devil is Vivienne? Poor Alexia. She has been through so much. If we get there and it's too late, and she's lost her father—"

René frowned. "We? I alone am taking Alexia to her father."

Josette's mind froze, then cracked into a million pieces. "Of course. I only thought to go along in case she . . . she might need me." Her knees were shaking now. "Oh, dear. We need to get word to Cameron's cousins, as well."

She rubbed at her forehead and paced again. "Who can we send at this hour? I suppose I should—"

"Stop, Josette. You are in love with him." He reached out a hand for her. "Come."

She shook her head, refusing his gesture. "I cannot, or I will fall apart and be of no help to anyone."

Was he right? Did she love Cameron? She had thought she did when she was far too young to know what the word meant. But perhaps her naïve heart had recognized a simple truth back then. Perhaps her infatuation had been a seed that now sprouted. With that revelation, she was through lying to herself. She had to go to Cameron.

"René, I insist you take me with you."

Vivienne hurried in with Alexia in tow. Régine followed with a stack of fresh clothing for René.

"Vivienne, you'll have to finish what I started. Régine can assist while I observe." Josette clasped her hands together to halt their shaking. She faced Alexia. "Dear, your uncle has given me some rather bad news. It's your father. When he went with your uncles to collect you, he was . . . he was . . ."

Oh, God help her, she couldn't say the words.

Alexia took a step back. Fear shot through her eyes, then her face went blank.

René took over. "Your papa, he got bit by moc'sins."

Some transient, wild emotion flared in Alexia's eyes. Just as quickly, it was gone. "My papa, he be dead?"

"We don't know. He was bitten more than once."

Alexia looked away. "He be dead then for sure." Cold as she appeared, her bottom lip slid in between her teeth and her fists clenched and unclenched.

Josette found her voice again. "It happened right before Bastièn went to rescue you, which was why René went instead. Bastièn took your father to Maman's to treat him."

"Maman has no use for Papa. If he's not already dead, she'll make sure of it."

The expression that passed through Alexia's eyes turned Josette's blood cold. "As soon as René is repaired, we'll take you to him."

Alexia paled. "*Non*. I will stay here."

René sat up slowly and lifted his arms so Régine could wrap the lichen-soaked bandages around him. "We will fetch the two Andrews cousins. Five of us cannot fit in the pirogue."

Inch by inch, Josette fell apart inside. She could not be left behind. "But—"

"Hush." René shot Josette a speaking glance. "If Alexia does not wish to go, we will not force her."

Alexia stood before everyone, fists clenching and un-clenching, her jaw working. Suddenly her eyes glistened. Before Josette could reach her, Alexia turned and ran.

Josette's hand went to her breast. "Oh, my word. Even if he's already departed, she will never forgive herself if she refuses to go to him. Especially after what transpired between them when he forced her to return everything she stole."

Vivienne helped René on with his shirt. "I'll go to her."

"Leave her be," he said. "It isn't what happened between her and her father that has her acting this way. Maman spat on Alexia and leveled a curse on her when she chose to leave with me. She's scared to death of her grandmother now. And of Lucien."

Josette stilled. If she could strike one person from this earth, it would be Lucien. "What did he do?"

"It was what he was about to do." René cast her a mean-ingful glance that needed no further explanation. "I think I broke his jaw."

"Good," Régine said, and left the room.

He slid off the table and reached for the fresh pair of trousers. "If we are to try to fit four people into a pirogue, I suggest you figure out something else to wear. But hurry, *chère*. We need to locate Cameron's cousins."

By the time they reached Maman's, dawn had washed the sky in shades of pink. René guided the pirogue to the dock, tied it to the crude post, and held it steady while Michel stepped from the rear of the boat. Together, the men helped Josette and Felicité make their exit.

Josette shook the skirt of the thin gardening dress clinging to her ankles. The bit of water at the bottom of the pirogue had soaked her hemline. Felicité, dressed in riding boots, men's britches and a white blouse, appeared fresh and composed despite her choice of clothing. How much more comfortable those garments would be than what Josette wore.

The four steps up to the veranda were the longest and hardest Josette had ever taken. Felicité clutched her hand and murmured something that sounded like, "Dear God, help us all."

The door stood open and a green curtain made of strips of cloth, meant to keep out bugs and mosquitoes, rippled in the faint breeze. From inside, a deep moan rolled through the house.

Josette's breath caught. She squeezed Felicité's hand. Michel's footsteps paused behind them.

"He's alive," René said quietly. "But I do not recommend rushing in. I have a feeling we must tread very carefully so as not to offend Maman. I suspect she might not be in the best of moods."

René parted the drape and stepped inside. Cameron's cousins and Josette followed. Maman sat at the table in the large, open room, coffee in hand. And that awful pet snake of hers wrapped around her shoulders.

"*Bonjour,* Maman," René said.

She did not dignify him with a reply. The albino snake lifted its head and stared at them with its glassy red eyes, its carmine tongue flicking in and out.

Felicité gave a little yip and stepped back.

René slipped his hand around her elbow. "I assume Bastièn and Cameron are in the bedroom?"

Maman turned her cheek.

"Follow me," René said. "But I should warn you that what you are about to witness might not be so pleasant. For Cameron's sake, please try to keep your emotions to yourself."

"Heaven help us," Felicité whispered.

They only had to follow the groans to the short hall that separated the bedroom Bastièn and René had shared all these years from the one Josette had once shared with her mother and Solange. Bastièn had Cameron propped in bed with pillows behind him and quilts wrapped around him. His eyes were closed, but his cracked lips moved as if he tried to speak, and his throat muscles rippled convulsively, as if he were attempting to swallow.

"Can he hear us?" Michel asked.

"He's out of his mind right now, and loaded with laudanum, so I don't know," Bastièn said. "But the good news is that he's not going to die, and I doubt he will lose his leg. There were two bites. It seems the big snake gave him a dry bite. The smaller one let loose the venom."

Very carefully, Bastièn unwrapped the blanket from around Cameron's leg and exposed the wounds. The left side of his britches was slit to his waist. His leg was discolored and swollen from toes to hip. Two ugly gashes marked the spots where the snakes had attacked.

"Lord, have mercy," Josette murmured.

René shook his head and pressed a finger to his lips.

Felicité stepped forward, pale and shaken. "How do you know the larger snake didn't carry any poison?"

Bastièn looked Felicité over from head to toe, then pointed to Cameron's leg. "This is where it bit. You can see it is red and messy, *oui*?"

They all nodded.

"That's because it's been cut into. We'll need to keep infection out, but more than likely, the snake thought Cameron was a gator and was defending its territory. She was saving her poison for food. They do that sort of thing. But look at this one."

He pointed to two puncture wounds not nearly as wide apart as the others. "This bite is all discolored and the surrounding flesh has died off. There was a good dose of poison in that little snake. Lucky it didn't hit a vein."

Josette hung back, giving Felicité and Michel room to stand beside the bed. This was Cameron's family surrounding him. She had no place with them. But oh, how she wanted to go to him. And oh, how alone she suddenly felt just watching them.

"What of Maman?" René asked. "Has she been of any help?"

Bastièn shrugged. "Reluctantly. His heartbeat dropped so low I gave him some herbs and spices along with a lot of strong coffee to get it pounding again, but I don't trust her to give him anything. I only take advice, and little of that."

Josette could stand it no longer. She went to Cameron and bent beside the bed. She stroked his brow. "He's running a fever, so why do you have him wrapped in all these blankets?"

Bastièn nodded. "To make him sweat the poison out of his pores."

Maman stood at the doorway. "He needs to drain the poison out the bottom of his feet, too. Just like a horse heals through its hoofs and sends the sickness into the earth. Dat's why you don't wear no shoes." She eyed Felicité as if to make a point. "Them fancy boots will keep poison in you."

Josette ignored her mother's rude intrusion. "How long before we can move him?"

"He's in too much pain right now," Bastièn said. "Perhaps in a week or two."

"*Non!*" Maman spat. "You get dat man out of my house today."

She made certain to look every person in the room in the eye. "And dat goes for all of you."

Felicité paled and slipped her hand into her brother's.

Maman's eyes narrowed at Josette. "You get your lover what killed Solange off my property, you hear? You worthless—"

René stepped forward. "Do not speak to your daughter like that, Maman."

The snake wrapped around Maman's shoulders grew agitated and shook its rattle-less tail. "From now on, she can call me Mademoiselle Thibodeaux."

Josette took a step back. "Oh, for heaven's sake, Maman, you cannot disown me just because—"

"Look at me." Odalie slipped the agitated snake back into his cage and whirled on Josette. "Take a good last look at me. I am *not* your mother!"

"But . . ."

Her eyes spit fire at Josette. "You are someone else's bastard child I was forced to take in."

The room stilled.

Josette didn't have to hear another word. With unshakeable certainty, she knew she'd heard the truth. No wonder she'd never felt as though she belonged. "But what . . . what of my siblings? Am I not related—"

"Oh, you all have the same father, to be sure. He just dumped his brat on me from some whore what died birthing you. Said I had to raise you or he'd . . ." She clamped her mouth shut.

"Or he'd do what?" René asked.

Odalie looked from Bastièn to René. "They are your half brothers. That's all I have to say. Now leave."

"And Solange?"

"Your half sister."

Then another truth struck her. "You said *Mademoiselle* Thibodeaux, not *Madame* Thibodeaux. So you and our father were never married?"

"He already had a wife."

"Is he still alive?"

A slow, wicked twist of Odalie's mouth formed a smile so cold it was a wonder her face didn't crack. "*Oui*." She laughed—a harsh, cold sound that grated on Josette's ears.

Odalie swept her hand around the room. "Where do you think all these fine furnishings came from over the years? You think we stole it all?"

Tears pinched the backs of Josette's eyes, but they remained dry. She pulled a ragged breath into her lungs, and just as she'd done as a child when she faced Maman's . . . no, Odalie's wrath, she hid her fists in the folds of her skirt, and held her head high.

René slipped an arm around her. He shot Bastièn a dark look and nodded toward Cameron. "He may be filled with laudanum, but that doesn't mean he cannot hear all this. We must remove him from here at once. Can you find a way to make that happen?"

Bastièn's gaze fixed on Cameron. "*Oui*."

Chapter Twenty-Five

Mind blank, Cameron opened his eyes. Angels hovered above him in a sky so blue as to seem surreal. A cherub sat on a cloud peeking down at him. . . . Wait. This was a painted ceiling. A familiar painted ceiling. And he was lying in an equally familiar bed. Balcony doors stood open. A sultry breeze swept through the treetops, green leaves rippling. He was in a room on an upper floor of a house.

But where?

A movement to his right caught his attention. He turned his head. A fastidiously dressed man of impressive bearing sat in a chair near the bed. He watched Cameron through startling blue eyes framed by black hair and a close-cropped beard. A beard so meticulously sculpted it looked like a work of art. His clothing befitted a proper English gentleman out for a ride—fine leather boots polished to a soft sheen, fawn-colored britches, and a dark green jacket.

A corner of the man's mouth tilted upward. "You have finally decided to join the living, *oui*?"

Bastièn? At the sound of that deep and lilting Cajun accent, memory flooded in with a vengeance. Good God, how long had Cameron lain here for the man to have grown such facial hair?

Cameron went back to staring at the angels and cherubs while he collected his thoughts and tried to string them together in some semblance of order. This was Josette's bedchamber. He'd been snake bit. He remembered now—foggy moments of terrible pain. Ensuing sickness. Rough hands jostling him. Soft hands touching him. People urging him to eat. Feet soaking in strongly scented water. Relentless vomiting. And more and more pain.

His daughter.

"Where's Alexia?"

"At the moment, she is with your cousin, learning to drive a carriage. I was along for the ride earlier. She's getting good at it."

"How long have I been here?"

"Nearly two weeks. Taking up space in my sister's bed." Bastièn withdrew a fancy knife from his boot. "She insisted you take this room."

Surely she hadn't slept here. Cameron knew better than to pursue the subject of Josette with this damn fool.

A flick of Bastièn's fingers and the knife's narrow blade snapped into place. "She's been sleeping alongside Alexia. Not with you."

"Bugger off." Cameron squinted at Bastièn's feet. "Are you wearing my boots?"

Bastièn grinned and tossed the knife in the air, catching it by the hilt. "*Oui*. They carried many fang marks but I managed to polish each one out. You would have been dead for sure had you not had them on."

"Well, you'll soon be dead if you don't take them off." He shoved the pillows against the headboard and inched his upper body into them, shocked by his lack of strength. Pain pinched his left leg. He winced. "Damn it, that's my good knife you're playing with."

He looked closer. "Blast it all, those are my clothes, aren't they? You actually broke into my home and stole from me, knowing I was lying here helpless? You bastard."

Bastièn chuckled and flipped the knife again. "Bastard, *oui*. Thief, *non*. Michel let me in to collect some of your belongings. As for what I wear, I needed something to go with the fine boots you gave me."

"I gave you no such thing."

"Ah, but wouldn't a man of your upbringing insist on rewarding someone for saving his life? Besides, you have another pair like this, and also in brown."

"That gold vest is one of my favorites and is not meant for riding."

Bastièn shrugged. "Good, because I do not own a horse." He examined the blade of Cameron's prized *navaja*. "This be one mighty fine knife. Fell out of your boot when I removed it from your rapidly swelling foot. Where did you get such a beautiful weapon? Not from around here, that be for sure."

"I acquired it in Spain, and you're not keeping it."

Bastièn folded the thin blade into the tapered pearl handle and slipped it back inside his boot. "You think so little of your worth that you intend to offer me no recompense? For rescuing you, I would think you'd want me to have all that I wear plus one of your ships, *oui*?"

Damn if the man didn't sit there looking proud as a popinjay and acting as if he owned the place. "I'm surprised you haven't tried to steal one."

Bastièn crossed one leg over his knee and slowly swept a hand back and forth over the boot as if caressing a favored pet. "Speaking of your ships, I have decided it would be to our advantage if your fine company were to employ me."

Christ Almighty. "When a donkey plays the cello. Now, go away and send someone up with food. I'm hungry."

The door opened. Josette stepped into the room carrying a tray. At the sight of him sitting up in bed, a broad smile brightened her face. "You're awake. How wonderful."

God, she was lovely.

Even burdened with a salver, her movements were graceful and light of foot. She wore that soft pink dress he favored. He especially liked that it was cut so low. Every nerve in his body danced a little jig.

Bastièn cocked a brow. "As you can see, a Thibodeaux can read minds. And since I am also a Thibodeaux, you should be very careful right now about what is going through yours." He speared Cameron with a knowing look, paused a beat, then chuckled deep and low in his chest. The bloody dolt.

"Your pathetic stab at humor is neither funny nor appropriate, so why do you laugh?"

"Ah, so there won't be an awkward silence afterward. I am very thoughtful in that regard, *oui*?"

"Do get out, Thibodeaux."

"Only because you ask so nicely." He stood and headed for the door.

Oh, hell. "Thibodeaux," Cameron called after him.

Bastièn paused at the threshold and turned. "*Oui*?"

"Thank you for saving my life. You can keep the bloody clothes and boots."

"And the knife?"

Shit. "Yes, damn it."

Even from where Cameron lay, he could see amusement sparking in Bastièn's eyes.

"Let my sister know what time you wish for me to report to work, *s'il vous plaît*. She can inform me over dinner." He saluted Cameron and closed the door.

"The damn fool."

Josette set the tray on the bedside table and pulled a chair next to the bed. She lifted a silver cover off a bowl. "So you have hired him?"

"I didn't say that, he did. Your brother stole my boots, the beggar." Wouldn't he like to pull her onto the bed and wrap his arms and legs around her! If only he had the strength.

She placed a serviette over his bare chest, her touch a gentle whisper that sent provocative chills skittering along his skin. "Why would you want those boots, anyway? Wouldn't they always be a reminder of what happened?"

She was right. "Then what makes you think I would want to see him walking around in them?"

"You won't be here much longer to see any such thing. If you like, I'll ask him to refrain from wearing them while you're still in town. He did save your life, you know."

Cameron took a deep breath and exhaled with a groan. "He made me very well aware of the fact."

"For your information, he has quit Madame Olympée's. And as we speak, he is off to join René in swimming lessons."

"What the devil for?"

"I believe it was you who informed René he is required to know how to swim before sailing on one of your company ships. Obviously, Bastièn has similar plans." She brushed a wisp of hair behind her ear.

Cameron took note of her unconscious act. He'd kissed that ear, trailed his tongue along that lovely neck. "Well, good luck to Bastièn. I need to get out of this bed and check on business with Michel."

"You can't possibly think you'll be fit enough to do anything other than walk around this room for a few days. You've been in bed going on two weeks, filled with laudanum, and nearly at death's door. We've been lowering the dose for three days, but it still hasn't fully worn off. I can see it in your dilated pupils. You also need time to gain back your strength. Besides, Michel visits daily. So does Felicité."

"Oh, yes. Bastièn said he was out riding with Alexia and my cousin in the carriage. All dressed up in my clothing, he was. I'll just bet he wasn't there for my daughter alone, the cur." Cameron lifted the covers just enough to see he wore only his drawers. They appeared clean and fresh. He dropped the blanket, choosing to ignore the bandage around his leg and the discolored skin. Odd, but after so long in bed, he didn't feel as though he needed a bath. He sniffed at the back of his wrist. It smelled of herbs and lavender. Someone had been bathing him. One swipe across his jaw told him he'd been recently shaved. He looked to Josette in question.

She laughed softly. "While I've been allowed the privilege of shaving you daily, I was not privy to your baths. Bastièn saw to those."

"Oh, good God!" Cameron squirmed at the idea of one of his worst enemies bathing him, and one of Josette's brothers to boot. Pain shot up his leg. He winced.

She tilted her head and studied him. "He was here for you every day, and throughout many a long night."

Bastièn was there through the entire ordeal? Cameron heaved a sigh, as if that would dispel any guilt for resenting the man all these years. "I didn't even recognize him when I awoke. I guess it must have been his beard. That was a surprise."

"Oh, but doesn't he look absolutely dashing?"

"That's not a question you ask a man, Josette." Especially about someone who'd been giving him baths, for pity's sake. "It must take him the better part of a morning to get it looking like that. Whatever possessed him?"

"At first he didn't take the time to shave because you required around-the-clock attention, but when that eased up, he set about creating the finest beard in town."

"What's he trying to prove now?"

"If you were to take the time to get to know my brother better, you'd soon learn he is meticulous about his person and surroundings. I know he's been misdirected in the past, and he can be a vile enemy when crossed, but he's also loyal and honest to those he respects. I do wish you'd consider having him work for your company. I believe he is sincerely out to better himself."

Guilt could actually make Cameron's bones ache. He'd

had enough of that in this lifetime. He let loose another exasperated breath. "I suppose I'll have to bloody well hire him." A pause, then he shot her a wicked grin. "The Thibodeaux brothers working as a team. Serves Michel right for all those frogs in my bed."

"Thank you," she murmured.

He would have hired Bastièn for saving his life anyway, but why not let her think she played a hand in his decision? So sweet she was, but filled with an inner strength that fascinated him—and enough heat and sensuality to satisfy a man for a lifetime. He imagined tracing the smooth, creamy curve of her neck with his mouth. Parting her full pink lips.

Their gazes locked.

A pulsing urgency thrummed through his veins. He bent his knee to raise the thin blanket off the mounting proof of his ardor.

She glanced at the action. Her lips twitched. "Do you have an appetite?"

"A ravenous one."

"Then let me feed you." She picked up a spoon and dipped it into the bowl.

Well, hell. He peered at the contents. "Not only are you wicked with your double entendre, but what is that foul-looking stuff in the bowl? Dishwater? I'll not have it."

"It's beef broth." She set down the spoon. "Do you think you can manage to feed yourself if I hold the bowl?"

"I'd rather have jambalaya."

"Now who's the fool? You'll need to be careful while you build up to solid food or you'll sicken. We've barely managed to get liquids and a bit of bland rice into you."

He grunted.

"You certainly can grumble a lot."

"Didn't I hear you say I was near death? As sick as I was, I doubt even the Pope would find himself in a particularly jolly mood."

"Indeed, you were near to dying, but once that crisis passed, in between doses of laudanum, you were quite demanding. You used up my entire supply of tooth powder, by the way."

"Tooth powder?"

She nodded. "Every time you roused enough to speak, you demanded to have your teeth brushed."

"I was trying to rid myself of the taste of snake and mud. I doubt I ever will."

Without warning, she leaned over and brushed a light kiss across his mouth, then sat back. "Mmm. Nice, with a hint of mint. Not a trace of mud or snake."

He folded an arm behind his head and studied her smiling face. Something very warm, very comfortable, and very enjoyable washed through him. His mood shifted. "What makes you so cheerful today?"

"You're awake and alert. That's something to celebrate."

"How is Alexia doing?"

"As well as can be expected. She went through quite an ordeal. Odalie has rejected her with the same vehemence as she has me. And then there's Lucien. He frightened her silly."

"The bastard."

"René broke his jaw."

"Humph. Your brother was far more lenient than I would've been, so in the end, perhaps the right person went after Alexia." Damn if he didn't miss the little hoyden. "Has she been in to check on me?"

Josette nodded. "But not while you were awake. I'm afraid that's going to take a bit of time. She feels responsible for what happened that night. Feels as though she nearly caused your death. I don't think she knows quite how to face you. One good thing that came out of all this is that she seems cured of wanting a life in the bayou with her grandmother. At least for now. But knowing Maman . . . excuse me. Knowing Odalie, she will not accept Alexia back again."

He cocked a brow. "So you call her Odalie now?"

Josette gave him a faint smile. "I forgot, you were barely among the living when she informed me that although we siblings share the same father, he merely deposited me on Odalie's doorstep one day and ordered her to raise me. Why she agreed to his demand, I can't imagine. Obviously, she didn't like it much."

A short silence told him she wasn't going to elaborate further, so he tried to draw her out. "How do you feel about the news?"

She shrugged. "Actually, I find it rather freeing. At least I now know why I never felt like I fit in or belonged anywhere. Although I have to say, I was touched by the way my brothers stepped forward and halted Odalie's tirade against me. Half brothers or whole seems to make no difference to them—they denounced her for the way she's treated me all my life."

"And now you have a house so full you're forced to share a bed with Alexia."

Something came and went in her expression. A small smile touched her lips. "Truth be told, I rather enjoy having so many around. Régine is in her glory doing all the cooking. She said to tell you when you awoke that she's looking forward to preparing all your favorite dishes. My brothers seem to have settled in rather nicely. Vivienne bustles about making certain everything is in order, and Alexia . . . well, as I said, she is doing as well as can be expected."

"And tell me about you, Josette. How are you in other ways?" The desire licking through him like flames wouldn't hold off much longer, but he wasn't ready to halt this conversation.

He suddenly knew why—he cared about her.

And he wanted her properly situated before he left. "With

the way Odalie treated you, I can understand why you felt you never belonged, but you now have a large family under your roof. You're free to leave your past behind—cast it off like an old overcoat. That's what I intend to do."

She sank her teeth into her bottom lip. "But I imagine you intend to board another ship as soon as you are able, and Alexia will be leaving with you."

Lord, it was going to hurt her when he took his daughter with him. He didn't know quite what to say. "In the meantime, there's nothing holding you back from enjoying every moment of her while she's here, is there?"

Josette placed her hands in her lap and dropped her gaze to them. "I know."

His chest tightened. Damn it, no one deserved to be treated the way she'd been all her life. The impulse to reach out to her, to hold her tight, grabbed hold of him. But that wasn't all of it. He wanted more. Much more. He wanted to make love to her. He should want to do so in a slow, sweet way, but a raw edge of desire cut right through that thought. And he was no fool. She wanted him as well. He'd seen it in her all the while she'd been sitting there. This time, however, it would have to be her taking the lead. Her on top. He was too weak for anything else.

"I'm hungry."

She lifted her head and fastened her gaze on his. "That's a good sign."

He gave her a slight nod. "But not for that damnable broth."

The pulse at her throat quickened. "Then what, pray tell, might you be hungry for?"

He grinned, slow and easy. "You, my dear."

Chapter Twenty-Six

Josette fairly sailed out the door and down the stairs, filled with an energy that hadn't expressed itself since before Cameron's injury. Making love could do that to a person, he'd said as he laughed and watched her dress. But while their lovemaking had had her practically floating on air as she'd left him, he'd lounged beneath the covers, lassitude his bed partner.

Pausing just outside the front gate, she snapped open her ruffled black and white umbrella, one that complemented the pattern in her hat and dress, and marched down the tree-lined street toward St. Charles Avenue. He'd asked her to return to his bed tonight. Oh, indeed she would. Tonight, and as many other nights as possible before he left to sail the seas.

Her heart squeezed at the thought. He'd be leaving soon. Far too soon. And taking Alexia with him. She was his daughter. He had the right to do so. But oh, how Josette would miss them. For now, though, she'd live every precious moment she had left with them to the fullest.

She intended to store enough memories of her private times with Cameron to last far into her winter years. She smiled to herself. Her young-girl infatuation had blossomed into something she'd once only dared to dream of. Other women should be so fortunate.

"He is my paramour."

She grinned at the magical sound of her words floating in the air around her. Imagine that, Cameron Andrews, her lover. And a magnificent one, at that. Even today, incapacitated as he was, he'd still managed to loosen all the tight knots in her muscles, melt her bones with every exquisite stroke of his fingers and tongue. Had she cried out his name? Oh, she had, but he'd muffled the cry with his mouth over hers and then proceeded to take her over the edge and into oblivion.

She sighed.

Once she returned this evening, she ought to show her gratitude.

Indeed, she'd do just that and she knew exactly how.

She laughed softly.

There were other things to thank him for as well. She was a stronger, more confidant woman because of him. On her own, she'd been tough. Had to be to survive. But she'd always lived in fear that something or someone would come along and take what was hers, then toss her back into a dismal life in the bayou. Now, because of Cameron, her business and home were secure.

And he'd been right about having a family under her own roof to dispel her sense of not belonging. That sorrowful feeling had vanished—along with that awful recurring nightmare. Odalie was gone from Josette's life. The truth of her parentage—the fact that she was not tied by blood to the woman who'd always hated her—was incredibly freeing and left her with a deep sense of relief.

She wiped the back of her gloved hand across her damp brow and hurried along. It was much too hot to be out in the blazing sun. The empty streets told her that much. Well, she had her place of business to oversee so there was no way around it—she had to be out and about.

Belle Femme.

Trying to focus on the mounting backlog in the shop had been nearly impossible with all that had gone on at home. But once she arrived, she'd be able to set her mind on what needed tending to. She was good at doing that, remaining focused.

Thank goodness for Elise, who kept the shop girls in line and everything running smooth as silk. However, the girl's note yesterday practically begged Josette to make an appearance. They were nearly out of Madame Olympée's special creams and Madame Vennard's . . .

Madame Vennard.

How Josette would like to tell the rude woman to take her business elsewhere. Wasn't that a laugh? There was no other place like Josette's to recommend. No one came close to what she offered. But why couldn't she refuse to do business with rude people? Madame Charmontès did. Whatever had changed in Josette, the truth of the matter was now glaring. She had allowed women such as Madame Vennard to treat her like a peon, all because she had been afraid to lose business. From now on, if anyone treated her girls or herself with rudeness, she would inform the person politely, but firmly, that such behavior was unacceptable and not allowed on her premises. Madame Charmontès would be proud of her.

Her decision felt quite good, actually. *She* felt quite good. Removing herself from Odalie's life had had a startling effect on Josette—and her brothers. She doubted she'd ever forget the look on Odalie's face when both her sons stepped forward and denounced her for her lifelong treatment of Josette. But something Odalie had said, or was about to say, after she'd ordered everyone off her premises, nagged at the back of Josette's mind. She gave a mental shrug and walked on. Whatever it was would surface when she least expected it. Wasn't that the way it always went?

She reached the Vieux Carré and, deciding to take a different route, turned up Rue Iberville. Halfway down the block, the hair on her nape prickled. A feeling that she was being watched gripped her.

She glanced about. No one dallied on the street in this heat. She paused, only to meet silence. Nonetheless, her heart beat like a rabbit's. Refusing to turn around, she hurried on. It was broad daylight, for heaven's sake—she was perfectly safe.

Footsteps sounded behind her.

Her breathing faltered. She glanced over her shoulder just enough so her peripheral vision caught the silhouette of a tall man. She swallowed the dry knot in her throat and quickened her pace. Blast it, she was nearly upon a *ruelle*, a narrow alleyway that could prove dangerous.

The footsteps behind her beat a faster cadence.

Oh, Lord! She pivoted to cross the street to avoid a trap. Too late!

Strong hands grabbed her, shoved her into the narrow passage, and pushed her against the wall, knocking the wind out of her. Her hat tumbled to the ground. Her cheek chafed against the rough brick.

Catching her breath, she cried out.

A gloved hand covered her mouth. "Hush!"

Frightened out of her wits, she nodded and obeyed while she tried to get her brain to function.

One hand held her pinned against the wall, the other slid from her mouth.

Think. She had to think. Stay calm. "What do you want? My reticule? Take it."

The familiar scrape of steel against metal grated against her ears.

A sword being drawn.

Émile Vennard!

Her heart jumped to her throat, and for a moment, words failed her. Then anger set in so raw, it left her cold. "You, Monsieur Vennard, are required to keep a distance of at least fifty feet from my shop, my home, and my person. Release me at once."

He swung her around and shoved her back against the wall so hard her head cracked against the bricks. Stars danced before her. She blinked to try to bring him into focus.

Pure hatred sizzled in his eyes. "You little witch. You think you outsmarted me? You think your lover has outdone me? You and your brothers are in for one very big surprise."

She'd spent a lifetime as an outcast, tormented by a woman she thought to be her mother. She'd had years of Vennard bullying her. By all the saints, he would plague her no more.

Steeling herself, she glared at him. "I will see you punished for this."

His face lowered to hers, so close she caught the scent of liquor on his breath. "I don't recommend it."

Something shifted in her. A sudden thrust of courage suspended all fear. "Don't think to threaten me any longer with regard to my brothers. I will say this only once, Monsieur Vennard. Should any harm befall either one of them, your daughter will never again find herself safe on the streets."

He laughed, his eyes cold and ruthless. "You wouldn't live to see the next sunrise."

"Are you actually saying you would do me in?"

"My daughter does not concern you. See that it remains that way."

"Then see to it my brothers do not concern *you*." She tried to move, but he held her fast against the wall. Her head was beginning to pound and her mouth could have been filled with cotton as dry as it was. "What could you possibly want from me? I no longer own my home, or the building where my shop is located. None of it is for me to hand over to you. There cannot possibly be anything you can take or want from me. So why did you drag me in here when you should know by now I am not only under my brothers' protection, but I have a powerful family backing me?"

His fingers dug into her shoulders, so deep she winced. He grew so livid even his beard quivered. "You still run the shop. Close it down and leave. Go back to the bayou where you belong."

Despite the pain he inflicted, she refused to back down. She returned his bold gaze in equal measure. "I am beginning to see how things are with you. I managed to crawl out of the swamps and marry well. And because of my husband's standing in the community, you were forced to swallow your prejudices and act with civility toward me. No wonder you wanted Louis's holdings after he passed. You thought to be rid of me, but then I opened the shop, which has women clamoring for appointments, including your wife and daughter. But you are quite aware of their patronage, aren't you?"

She stared at him, into those steel blue eyes and . . .

She froze.

The gray hair. The gray beard. Had they been black, had the blue in his eyes not faded somewhat with age . . . oh, dear Lord in Heaven, why had she not seen the resemblance before?

As the terrible realization set in, Vennard loosened his grip and stepped back.

"It cannot be," she whispered and closed her eyes. To her horror, what she saw against her closed eyelids was a reverse image of him. The hair and beard framing his face appeared black. Had Bastièn not recently grown a beard as well, she never would have made the connection. Both brothers had Vennard's height, the breadth of his shoulders.

Sick to her stomach, she turned from him, her knees weak. Planting her palms against the brick wall, she steadied herself, her breath quaking in her lungs, perspiration clammy on her brow.

She waited until the air in her lungs found a rhythm that allowed her to speak. Slowly, she turned back to him. "Bastièn has your eyes."

A heartless smile curled one corner of his mouth, but he said nothing.

The past registered in flashes across her mind. "I don't understand. Why would you want to harm your own sons?"

He took another step back. Shadows swallowed his features. "Because their damnable mother was supposed to have kept them in the bayou where they belonged. I should have drowned them like the litter of stray cats they were."

A shudder ran through Josette. "But you stayed with her long enough to give her three children. Why?"

He gave his head a small shake. "I tired of her shortly after Bastièn was born. I did not know Solange existed until I brought you to Odalie, but there was no mistaking the brat came from me."

A sudden realization struck Josette as to what Odalie had been about to say when she'd ordered everyone from her home. Just as he'd threatened to harm Josette's brothers if she didn't sell to him, he'd threatened to harm Odalie's precious sons if she didn't raise Josette as her own.

A shudder ran through her. "Who was my mother? Odalie said she died giving birth to me and that she also lived in the bayou."

"Who the woman was does not matter. She's dead."

A fireball of fury rolled from the marrow of Josette's bones and burst into flame. "She doesn't matter? Another one of your illicit affairs gone bad doesn't matter? Well, she was my mother, and she matters to me!"

"Keep your voice down."

"I shall not!" she yelled.

"Hush your mouth. Your mother was Lisette Laurent, a friend of Odalie's. When she found out Lisette had given birth to my child, Odalie gave her a cup of tea laced with the roots of the maudit tree out of Africa."

"My God! She poisoned her?"

Vennard shrugged. "Who am I to judge? Imagine Odalie's surprise when I dumped Lisette's little orphan on her and told her she either took good care of you or her boys would suffer."

"I think you match Odalie in pure evil."

"Not quite. Unlike you, Solange was Odalie's flesh and blood, yet she thought nothing of gifting her with the same kind of tea."

Josette staggered and braced her hands against the wall for support. "Even Odalie wouldn't have done such a cruel thing."

He tsk-tsked. "Solange was such a disappointment to her mother, wasn't she?"

The horror of Vennard's words hit Josette so hard, a cry of pain tore from her lips.

"Ma'am, are you all right?" A stranger stood at the entrance to the alleyway, his umbrella raised as if intending to defend her.

Vennard stepped farther into the shadows, grabbed his sword from where he'd leaned it against the wall, and held it behind his back.

Josette had no doubt he'd use the blade on the stranger if need be. "I am not all right, but I shall be in a moment, so please wait there if you will."

"Yes, ma'am."

She stared hard at Vennard. This beast of a man, one of

the wealthiest merchants in all of Louisiana, was her father.
How very ironic. Not only had she been raised in near
poverty, but what she had managed to obtain, he wanted to
destroy. "You truly underestimate me. I cannot tell you how
much stronger this little revelation has made me."

She bent and snatched up her crushed hat, brushed it off,
and plopped it atop her head. With as much dignity as she
could muster, she marched to where the stranger stood.
Pausing a few feet short of him, she picked up her umbrella,
shook off the dirt, and moved to stand beside the man.

"Thank you for coming to my aid, sir." She turned to face
Vennard. A peculiar humor suddenly ran crazy patterns
through her and she called out, "I picked your pockets a time
or two in my youth, don'cha know, Papa?"

He remained in the shadows, his face invisible from
where she and the stranger stood.

"Can I be of further assistance, ma'am?"

"Yes, thank you." She used quick strokes to brush off
the front of her skirt. "If you'll offer me your arm and walk
me to Rue Dauphine, I can make my way from there on
my own."

The young man presented his bent elbow, then reached
into his pocket and withdrew a white handkerchief. "Your
cheek, ma'am. It's bleeding."

"Oh." She took the folded fabric and touched it to her
face. It came away dotted with blood. How utterly calm she
managed to appear, but the cracks in her façade were beginning to take shape. "It's not bad, merely a scrape, but I
fear I've ruined your good handkerchief. I'll see you get a
new one."

"That won't be necessary, ma'am. I have others. Can I
escort you somewhere? I hope I'm not being rude, but I
overheard you call the man Papa, and after what I just wit-
nessed, I doubt you should go to wherever he lives, beggin'
your pardon."

"I have other family. They'll take care of me."

I have family.

The words struck a chord deep in the recesses of her heart. She blinked hard at the tears trying to gather and withdrew her hand from the man's arm. "Well, here we are, Rue Dauphine. I can manage from now on. Thank you so very much, Mister . . . ?"

"McCabe, ma'am. Ethan McCabe, from Dallas. I'm in town on business and staying at the Saint Anthony. If you change your mind about needing anything, just send a message. It ain't right to treat a woman so harsh, daughter or not."

What an insane conversation they were having when she'd just been mauled and threatened by a father she'd never known existed but had plagued her since Louis's death. Dear God, her legs were about to buckle. "Thank you, I'll keep that in mind. Now if you'll kindly excuse me, I have appointments to keep."

Head held high, she hastened to her shop before her knees gave way. Closing her umbrella, she placed her gloved hand over her marked cheek and peered through the window. Thank heavens there were no customers, and except for Elise, the staff must be on their lunch break.

Elise had her back to the door, straightening bottles in a cupboard. Josette let herself in. At the jingle of the door's overhead bell, Elise turned. Her professional smile faltered. "Madame?"

Josette hurried past Elise. "I'll be in my office. I want no interruptions."

She barely made it to her desk before her knees gave out. Her hands shook so terribly, she could hardly remove her gloves and hat.

Émile Vennard was her father. The revelation was both stunning and laughable. She and her brothers were the progeny of one of the pillars of society. Yet he was a philanderer who took up with women from the bayou and thought never to see his bastard offspring in town. No wonder he wanted her shop closed. His wife and legitimate daughter were Josette's best customers!

She wept then, leaned her head against the chair's back and let the tears slide down her cheeks, the salt from them burning the bloody side of her face. All this time she'd pampered Miss Louisa Suzette Vennard, applied facials, mixed special blends of perfume until they were just right for each season, she'd been catering to her own sister!

All at once the fog in her brain dissipated, and the satire of her life prevailed. How little she'd thought of herself all these years. Well, no more. How dare Vennard try to force her to give up her beloved home so he could present it to that spoiled girl? The man must be mad. He probably despised Josette more than Odalie did.

A light tapping on the door told her it was Elise. "Are you all right, Madame?"

"Please put Madame Olympée's order ahead of the others and leave them in my laboratory. I'll be along in a moment."

First she had to take care of herself. Closing her eyes, she covered her face with her hands. What to do? Bastièn and René had to be told. Usually, she could gauge their reactions, intervene when necessary, and leave them to their own devices when the situation called for it. But this time . . . this time, she didn't have a clue what the right thing to do might be.

Cameron would know. Hadn't he helped her with her home and business? Oh, if only he'd had the information that Vennard was her father, things would likely have gone another way entirely. Yes, she would go to Cameron before she told her brothers about their father. First, she'd have to give Cameron time to regain his strength. A few days, perhaps a week, and he'd be up and around. She'd better check with Michel to see when their next ship was set to sail.

Her tears finally dry and her breathing back to normal, she stood and made her way to the rococo armoire where she kept her personal items. Opening the top doors, she peered into the mirror attached to the inside of the left panel.

"Oh, dear," she muttered. "Won't this take some explaining?"

Her hair was a mess. Not only was her cheek scraped raw with blood already drying, but it was also swollen and bruised. What she needed was the scant supply of ice that remained in storage at home. And a clean spider web from her garden. The spider's healing silk laid across her wound would be just the thing. She hoped there'd be one about; they'd been using them on Cameron's wounds.

Rifling through a small drawer, she found nothing to treat the bloody scrape. The only thing left to do was to go to the laboratory and hope she didn't run into Elise along the way. The last thing she needed was to have her asking questions.

She headed for the door.

It opened and René stepped in. His piercing gaze scanned her face. His jaw clenched and a muscle rippled alongside it. "What's happened, Josette?"

"Elise sent for you, didn't she? I'm going to fire that busybody."

"No, you are not." He came forward and, curling his finger beneath her chin, he lifted it and turned her head so her damaged cheek faced him. He scowled as he studied her. "What you are going to do is tell me exactly what happened."

Her heart tripped in her chest. *And have you murder your own father? I think not.*

She jerked her head away. "For heaven's sake, René, must you watch every move I make? I was hurrying to get out of the heat and not watching where I was going. I tripped stepping onto the boardwalk and fell."

Before he could see the lie in her eyes, she turned and stepped past him to stand in front of the painting behind her desk. She bent to where she'd dropped her hat on the floor, picked it up, and wiped it off, studying the artwork as if she could actually see it through the tears threatening to spill over once again. "A clumsy move on my part, that is all. What I can't take care of here, I'll see to at home. Now please excuse me. I have let things slide so long here that any further delay and I will lose customers."

Her teeth clenched at his silence. She needed time to figure this out so he and Bastièn didn't go off half-cocked. She had to speak to Cameron. But he first needed time to heal.

"You lie through your teeth, *ma soeur*. Who are you protecting?"

You and our hot-tempered brother! There went the sick feeling churning in her stomach once again.

"Speak up, Josette. You know I cannot abide harm coming to my family."

Family.

That word again. She bit back a sob and drew in a shaking breath while she scrambled to get her throat to work. "Thank God you are in my life, dear brother. I cannot begin to tell you how much you mean to me, but please, give me a few days and I will tell you everything."

She turned to face him. At the sight of his worried frown and his set jaw, she nearly gave in. Not yet. She had to do this the right way and keep him and Bastièn safe. "I am asking you to trust me in something that is exceedingly important. Something that is about to change all our lives. One week, René, give me one week."

He studied her for a long moment. And then, despite the sharp look in his eye that told Josette he wasn't necessarily compliant, he gave her a brief but stern nod. "*Oui, chère*. One week. Now come, let me take you home."

Chapter Twenty-Seven

Three glasses of wine failed to ease the tight band around Cameron's chest. Maybe a fourth would do the trick. He poured another and leaned back in the dining room chair, observing everyone present. Five days had passed since he'd awakened from his two-week nightmare. Five days since Josette had made sweet, uninhibited love to him. Five days since she'd then traipsed off to work with a promise of bedding him again, only to return withdrawn, her face bloodied, refusing to say what happened until he was further healed. Thereafter, she claimed the long hours spent at her shop were necessary to meet her clients' demands. During what little he had seen of her, she'd remained pleasant but aloof. And always with René or Bastièn in the room, pacing the floor like caged animals.

Then there was Alexia. She sat directly across the table from Cameron. Not once had she addressed him or looked him in the eye. Instead, she clung to René, as she'd done since that terrible night in the bayou. She'd even taken to spending her days at the shipping office, following her uncles around, or so Michel said. Which left Cameron to while away the hours with only Josette's two cousins in residence.

What the devil was he doing living amongst the infamous Thibodeaux family anyway? How had his life managed to become even more twisted than the months following Dianah's death? Hell, being stranded on a remote island wouldn't leave him feeling any more alone than sitting here surrounded by this anomalous clan. In fact, lolling under a palm tree somewhere in the South Seas was beginning to sound a damn sight better than putting up with this agony.

He downed his wine and poured yet another glassful. Josette shot a quick glance his way, then continued conversing with Bastièn and Vivienne regarding some new healing technique.

Alexia said something he didn't catch. Josette apparently had. She smiled and turned her attention to Alexia and René. As he watched them interact, a muscle in Cameron's jaw twitched. Without doubt, he knew what he had to do. As soon as Alexia went to bed, he'd say his piece.

Alexia yawned. René murmured something in her ear. With a nod, she bid everyone good night—again without eye contact. Damn it, there went that pinch in his chest again.

Vivienne rose and escorted Alexia from the room. Régine collected the last of the dishes and disappeared in a cloud of silence.

Cameron took a sip of wine and cleared his throat. "Bastièn, you indicated the discoloration in my leg might take a few months to dissipate, and the pain could come and go for a lifetime. Otherwise, I am now perfectly able to return to my town house, which I shall do in the morning. Also, Michel brought me the current shipping schedule, which piqued my interest."

Josette frowned at Cameron's last remark. Instead of looking at him, she fiddled with the serviette next to her plate. Bastièn, in the middle of a swallow of wine, paused.

René unbuttoned his jacket, pulled over an empty chair and slung one arm across the back. His lids lowered lazily as he focused on Cameron.

"The *Colette* brings another shipment of rum tomorrow from Bermuda," Cameron said. "In a little less than a week, she'll return to the island. Since the ship is named after my mother, I thought it rather fitting I climb aboard when she sails."

Josette's face blanched.

Bastian and René shot speaking glances at one another.

Despite the discomfort shooting through Cameron at voicing his intent, he practically laughed out loud. "Gentlemen, and I use that word loosely, I realize you were expecting Michel to assist you on your first training voyage, but since the *Colette* sails back to the Gosling Brothers distilleries, I thought perhaps I should be the one to escort you." Cameron grinned. "In case you have it in mind to steal the poor men blind."

Bastièn swore softly.

René chuckled.

Josette dropped her gaze to her lap. "Which means Alexia will sail with the three of you to Bermuda. I suppose I should consider that a good thing, but where will you and she go from there?"

Cameron drew in a long breath and took a deep swallow of his wine. God, what he'd decided pained him more than the ache in his leg. He took his time making eye contact with the brothers, but Josette kept her head bowed.

"Look at me, Josette."

She lifted her chin.

Was that pain in her eyes?

His chest tightened all over again. Lord, a week ago she would have let him draw her into his arms to comfort her. Now, he didn't dare try. Of late, she seemed a stranger to him. "My daughter belongs here. With all of you. Since she no longer desires a life in the bayou, and to all our relief, wants nothing further to do with Odalie or Lucien, we are free of that worry."

René studied Cameron intently while Bastièn drained his wineglass and refilled it.

A pale Josette took to staring at the floral centerpiece and twisting the serviette in her hands, her knuckles white. "What changed your mind?"

Cameron swiped a hand across his brow. Blast it, why was this so hard to put to words? "I may be her father, and I may care about her, but she has a stable home here. As different as your lives are from mine, you are her family and what she has always known. A stronger, more cohesive clan I have not encountered since growing up with my own relatives."

He paused a moment to make his point. "My decision has been harder for me than you might imagine. Alexia belongs here, Josette."

At the sound of her name, Josette ceased staring at the flowers and locked gazes with Cameron. Were those tears shimmering in her eyes? His fingers tightened around the wineglass stem. "My own daughter, and she hardly speaks to me any longer."

"Give her time, Cameron. I told you she's filled with guilt and blames herself for what happened."

He shook his head. "If I were to force her to leave with me, she'd likely detest me for the rest of her days. Perhaps this way, when I return to call on her now and then, or if she agrees to visit me once I've found my place in the world, time will have matured her and hopefully healed her heart."

That said, he settled his gaze on Josette's cheek. "Speaking of healing, you seem to have done so quite nicely. I think you can attribute it to your own expertise. You have quite the talent."

Josette set her serviette on the table and rose from her

chair, a portrait of unyielding restraint. "If you'll excuse me, I had a rather long day and have the same due tomorrow. I wish to retire."

"Not quite yet," Cameron said. "When you returned here five days ago with your face cut and swollen, you gave me your word you'd tell me what happened once I was up and about. Well, here I am, Josette, up and about. And since tonight will be my last evening in your home, and in a little less than a week I'll be leaving New Orleans, it's time you did a little talking."

"*Oui*," René muttered.

Josette glanced from one brother to the other. A look of panic crossed her face. "Oh, dear. I . . . I meant that I wished to speak to you in private. Before . . . before I mentioned anything to them."

René positioned his chair toward Josette, a cold, hard glint in his eyes. "No need to repeat your words when we are all here. Speak to us, Josette."

She closed her eyes and took in a deep breath. "I did not trip and fall on the banquette."

René snorted. "Tell me something I do not already know."

Her shaky fingers shoved a stray curl behind her ear. "I was on my way to Belle Femme when I decided on a different route from my usual one, so I turned onto Rue Iberville. Halfway to Dauphine, I realized the street was deserted. Soon after, I became aware I was being followed."

"Did you see who it was?" Bastièn asked.

She raised a hand. "Please, allow me to tell this my way."

Cameron nodded. "Fair enough."

"At first, I thought whoever it was merely meant to pass me by, but my instincts said otherwise." She began to pace. "That was when I spotted a *ruelle* up ahead and made to cross the street to avoid any danger of being drawn into it. But I was too late. Someone grabbed me, shoved me into the alleyway and forced me against the wall."

Cameron uttered an oath under his breath.

She touched her fingers to her cheek, as if oblivious to her action. "That's when my face scraped against the brick."

René focused on her wound. "Were you able to see who it was? Could you identify him?"

She nodded, and continued to pace from one end of the room to the other.

It took all Cameron had in him not to go to her side. "Who was it, for God's sake?"

She stared past the three men, her white-knuckled fingers clasped together. "Émile Vennard."

The sensation of a fist punched Cameron's gut. "That bastard! He's got legal orders to stay well away from you."

René and Bastièn glanced at each other. Both stood.

"What did he want?" Bastièn demanded.

She ceased her pacing and looked at Cameron. "Not only is he a man filled with scorn, he is also someone used to having his way. He has not taken kindly to your intervention on my behalf. Even though I no longer own my home or the building where my shop is located, he demanded I shut down Belle Femme and leave New Orleans at once."

Bastièn headed for the door. "René, are you coming along? I feel a need for fresh air."

"*Oui.*"

"No." Josette rushed over and splayed a hand across Bastièn's chest.

He halted, his face red with rage. "Do not stand in my way, *ma soeur.*"

"Whatever you think to do to that man, you cannot." She looked at Cameron, pleading in her eyes. "Prevent them from doing Vennard harm."

Ignoring the pain in his leg, Cameron rose and moved to Josette. "Why, when I want to tear him limb from limb myself? Perhaps it's not such a bad idea if Monsieur Vennard gets a taste of his own medicine."

Cameron glanced at René and Bastièn. "Just don't do anything that requires a coffin."

"Stop it, all of you," Josette cried and started pacing again. "You must not harm him."

René took Josette by the shoulders and held her steady. "Give me one good reason why I should show leniency to a man who not only threatens a woman, but harms her? Especially if that woman is my sister?"

She stared at him for a long moment, as if she saw something in his face that frightened her. Then she shrugged his hands off her shoulders and backed away.

René followed, his brows scrunching together. "What is it, *chère*?"

What the hell? Cameron stepped toward her as well.

She held up a hand, stopping Cameron and her brothers from coming any closer. "I learned something in the *ruelle* that has changed my life." She looked from one brother to the other. "And what I have to say is about to change yours."

She paused for a beat, then lifted her chin. "It seems Monsieur Émile Vennard is our father."

The tomb-like silence that followed seemed to suck the very air from the room. If Cameron's head grew dizzy at the news, the brothers stood like pillars of salt.

Bloody hell. Once pointed out, the resemblance was plain as day. Both men had Vennard's physique and, in one way or another, carried his features. When Cameron had met the man in the attorney's office, he'd noted those striking blue eyes. Why had he not connected the unusual color to Bastièn? No wonder Josette, who'd once thought Bastièn's beard dashing, complained of late and hounded him to shave it off.

Bastièn was a younger version of his father.

Damn.

* * *

Despite the trauma of having to tell her brothers the truth, in the silence that followed, a kind of peace settled over Josette. She decided against telling them what Vennard had said about Odalie poisoning Solange—at least for the moment. Learning about their father was enough for now. "I would imagine Vennard has grown quite uncomfortable with his legitimate family doing business with his secret family. Enough so as to threaten me, but if you were to bring harm to our father, you would prove yourselves no better than he. Perhaps you should sleep on this revelation before you run off to do damage."

She turned to Cameron, her heart stopping when she saw that he was ready to come to her defense yet again. "René and Bastièn need time to let the news sink in, just as I have required time these past few days. I do hope you can help them to see things my way."

She drew in a deep breath and on the exhale said, "Now if you will excuse me, I really should like to be alone. I, too, have much thinking to do."

Her heart now in shreds, she walked away. She knew Cameron wanted her. She had seen it in his eyes all evening—had seen the way he'd looked at her the few times she'd visited him these past five days. She'd used working late as a feeble excuse to stay away from him. Strange how circumstances could so easily alter a person's life.

Before her encounter with Vennard—she couldn't bring herself to think of him as her father—she'd had every intention of spending as much time with Cameron as possible until he departed. What dangerous foolishness, playing games with her heart. When had she started depending on him? Better that she pulled away when she had. Going to him for advice meant going to him for solace as well. She knew darn well seeking his comfort mattered more.

Footsteps sounded behind her. "Wait, Josette."

She stopped in her tracks, her heart caught in her throat. "Please, Cameron, I need to be alone."

"I've decided to leave your home now, not in the morning, so I'd like a moment, if you will."

The reality of his words, deep and husky in his throat, stunned her. "It's nearing midnight. It's too late for you to be leaving. The morning will have to do."

"I'm not a boy, Josette. I've walked the streets of New Orleans at all hours. You must know why I'm leaving tonight and not in the morning."

She turned to face him. This beautiful, strong, kind man who'd strolled through her dreams for years would soon be gone. Her knees weakened and her insides trembled. She doubted memories of him would be enough to fill her life after all. She wanted to ask him why he had to leave New Orleans at all, but she had no right. "I don't know why you cannot wait until tomorrow, but I suppose whatever choice you make shouldn't much matter."

He frowned. "You can say that after what we've shared? Look at me and tell me the truth. Try telling me that what we've had together doesn't matter. The reason I am leaving tonight is because I can no longer lie in your bed night after night waiting for you to vacate the bed you share with Alexia. Waiting for the door to open. Waiting for you to slide in beside me and—"

"Cameron, don't." She laid a hand against his chest. She shouldn't have. His heat, the beat of his heart, coursed right through her. She dropped her hand. Now wasn't the time to pretend. She had to speak the truth. "I . . . please understand that it was foolish of me to feel I could make love with you every day and think nothing of it. Truth be told, I've ached for you day and night knowing you were just down the corridor. What we shared grew more wonderful with each rendezvous. So much so, I feared if we continued, it would be unbearable to watch you climb aboard a ship and sail away. While you'll be gone, off to a new life, to who knows where or what, I'll be left here with nothing but an empty bed and a few memories to keep me warm."

Emotions flashed through his eyes like a kaleidoscope, shifting and throwing off indecipherable patterns. Oh, she could barely breathe now.

He reached out and drew the backs of his fingers down her cheek, tucked a strand of hair behind her ear, his amber eyes filling with sadness. "You're right. It is wrong of me to want as much of you as I can get before I leave. I've been selfish. Forgive me."

"Why can't you make a life for yourself here in New Orleans?" Good Lord, had she actually asked him to stay? Requesting a future with him when she'd known all along it could never be? Not because of who they each were, not because of how very different their lives had been, but because, in the end, she was Solange's sister.

Cameron shoved his fingers through his hair. "I don't know who I am anymore. I'm even more confused now than before I left San Francisco. One thing I do know is that New Orleans is no longer my home. I may have been born here, but I sure as hell don't belong here anymore. At least I don't think so. Maybe sailing around the world will change my mind, I don't know. In any case, I'll be back now and then to see Alexia. I will look forward to seeing you, as well."

"Will you be so anxious to see me again if you have a wife by your side?" At that precise moment, at the thought of him with another woman, she knew a simple truth—she was in love with him. But he did not share her feelings.

She had to get rid of him before she blurted it out or before a flood of tears left her a hopeless mess. "In all honesty, I could not tolerate seeing you with a wife, Cameron. Please, let's say our good-byes now and leave whatever we had to our memories. It will be easier on me."

He stared deeply into her eyes for a long moment. "Of course. How very sensible you are." He took a step away from her. "I should never have acted upon my desire for you, but for the love of God, Josette, I couldn't help myself."

She managed a small nod. "I wanted what we had as well, so please, never be sorry. If I felt you left regretting our time together, it would break my heart. I hope we can at least give ourselves that much."

His gaze flitted back and forth from her eyes to her mouth. "Will you kiss me good-bye, then?"

Oh, please, yes! He read her thoughts and moved closer, until their bodies touched. He stroked her cheek again, then lifted her chin and settled his mouth on hers. This wasn't the harsh, demanding kiss she'd expected. Instead, the kiss was tender, whisper-soft and gentle—and far more painful than if he'd ravished her.

He turned and was gone.

Cameron rolled out of bed around noon, wishing he'd not awakened at all. He'd drunk more rum when he'd returned to the town house, but it had done nothing to obliterate the emptiness inside him. His bedding lay in a heap on the floor, proof he'd tossed and turned the night through. Six days and he'd be gone. Sooner if another ship was on the schedule to leave port. The *Arabesque* would set sail tomorrow. He could be on it. Get the hell out of here so he wouldn't be tempted to tear down walls to get to Josette.

Anger settled in his bones at the way life had turned on him. Disjointed thoughts rattled around in his head. What of Vennard? Josette was under her brothers' protection, and whatever cunning measures they took to see that their father caused her no harm before they left for their training voyage was of little concern to Cameron.

Tell that to his heart.

Alexia.

Today, he intended to let her know that she would remain here. She'd no doubt be glad of it. The thought curdled his stomach. At least his sour gut told him he wasn't completely numb to life.

He bathed, dressed and made his way to the docks, where he watched the *Colette* pull sleekly into port. By nightfall the rum would be unloaded. Then she'd be inspected and readied for her next trip—with him and the Thibodeaux brothers aboard. Was that such a good idea after all? Would he look at them and constantly think of his daughter? Of Josette?

Fresh pain shot through him at the idea of not seeing either one of them for God knew how long.

He turned, and there stood Alexia beside a loaded dray, holding Abbott's cat in her arms and acting as though Cameron didn't exist. He knew better. She was wily as they came.

He walked over to her. "Good afternoon, Alexia. You've Midnight in hand, I see."

"*Oui.*" She stroked a little harder at the cat's fur. The little beast wiggled. She paused. "Gotta go. Abbott will be wanting his cat back."

"Wait." Cameron crossed his arms over his chest and nodded toward the *Colette*. "Do you see that ship there?"

"A body would have to be blind not to."

"Your uncles are going on a training mission aboard her next week."

"*Oui.* I read the ship's manifest."

He had to grin. "Did you now?"

"*Oui.*" She went back to petting the cat.

"Then you know someone will go along to train them."

"*Oui*, Michel."

"No, Alexia, plans have changed. I will be the one to

show them the ropes. I'll be going as far as Bermuda and then changing ships. They'll return without me."

She stopped petting the cat.

"Your uncles will return and once again, your family will be intact. I won't be asking you to go with me because I have finally realized you belong here."

Her head shot up and he swore he saw a glimpse of panic in her eyes. But as usual, it was gone before he could pinpoint anything

"You won't be back?"

"From time to time," he said. "I know you haven't wanted to be around me of late, but I'm hoping things will change so that when I do return, we can enjoy a visit with each other. In time, perhaps you might want to come to me."

"Humph. Wherever that might be." She dropped the cat and marched back into the shipping office. "Abbott, your damn cat scratched me."

Wasn't she something, though? Despite the pain her rebuff had caused him, he loved her. God, the realization hit him like a punch to the heart. *Huh.* He adored the little scamp. Too bad he hadn't succeeded in getting her to love him back, but if it wasn't in her, he couldn't force things.

At the thought, it was as if a cloud of sadness descended upon him. He watched the door she'd disappeared through for a long while, then he set out on foot to walk the Vieux Carré one last time.

Near dusk, he climbed aboard the ship, looked back at the city and imagined how it would feel to leave it all behind on the morrow instead of waiting until next week.

"Are you all right?" René came up behind him.

Cameron nodded. "I'm fine."

"Josette, she is not so fine today."

"She's got a lot to be concerned about."

"*Oui.*" René looked Cameron over for a long moment, then settled in alongside him. In the silence that stretched between them, they watched the city lights blink and come to life, one by one.

Cameron squinted at a woman running toward them. "Isn't that Josette's shop girl?"

"*Oui*, Elise." René frowned and stepped to the ship's railing.

"Hurry, René! Oh, please hurry!"

He was already running down the gangplank. "Did something happen to Josette?"

Elise nodded frantically. "The shop. It's on fire!"

Chapter Twenty-Eight

"Let go!" Josette cried, wrestling with René's iron-fisted grip.

"Don't be a fool," he shouted.

Something exploded inside the shop, shattering the store-front window. Orange flames shot out, licking the night sky like a dragon's tongue. A roar went up from the crowd of bystanders.

"Get her out of here!" the fire warden bellowed above the clamor.

René dragged her away from the hot blaze. She fell into his arms, grabbing fistfuls of his jacket. "Oh, God, my very life was in there."

The fire brigade frantically hosed water into Josette's shop and along the sides and upper floor of the building, trying to keep the fire from spreading to adjacent structures. Trained volunteers scurried on and off ladders, shouting orders to one another. Others seesawed the long handles on water pumps, keeping the hoses gushing.

Bastièn squeezed through the crowd and rushed to her. "*Merde*, Josette. Your hand. You've been burned. We need to get you home."

Her flesh registered not a lick of pain. All she felt was the shock and horror of what was happening before her eyes.

René tugged at her arm. "Come along. You're only in the way."

Dazed, she turned and looked into his eyes, the sinuous flames reflecting in their grave depths. Suddenly, the thick fog in her head cleared. Tears trickled down her cheeks and her knees went weak. What had she been thinking, trying to get back inside a burning building when all was lost? Had she been insane?

She scanned the crowd, knowing full well she sought Cameron. Instead, Vennard came into sharp focus. Their gazes locked. A wicked grin broke across his face before he turned and melted into the throng.

"Are you satisfied, Vennard!" she screamed. "No more Belle Femme for your darling daughter and wife to frequent. No more bayou Cajun trash to cater to them like royalty!"

Onlookers stared at her through eyes gone wide. Narrowed lips began moving in a telltale manner that meant gossip now flowed as rapidly as water from the firemen's hoses.

Bastièn grabbed her chin and forced her face to him. "Did Vennard start the fire?"

Her nostrils stung from the acrid tang of charred wood coalescing with the sweet scent of what had once been her exclusive fragrances. Oh God, the insanity of it all. Hysterical laughter threatened to overwhelm her. She choked it back with a strangled sob, and shook her head. "My sleeve caught on a candle. It tipped over onto a beaker of alcohol that spilled across the table and floor. It only took seconds before the fire went out of control."

Anguish quickly replaced the edge of hysteria. "I did this to myself. Dear Lord, I destroyed my own life."

René slipped an arm around her and squeezed. "You are not ruined, *ma soeur*. You can rebuild. We will help you."

In that instant, she knew she would do no such thing. She was finished. Finished fighting for acceptance in a community that shunned her. Finished wanting something out of life that was never hers to have.

Alexia wiggled through the crowd and clung to Josette, her face streaked with dirt and tears. "*Ma tante*, I thought you were inside. I thought you were dead."

Josette's brain fogged once again, blurring the horrid scene before her. She hugged Alexia to her breast. "You're right, René. I don't need that shop. I don't need anything as long as I have my family. Please, take me home."

Her brothers and Alexia surrounded her as they attempted to guide her through the horde of spectators. Cameron and Michel appeared and pushed ahead of them, clearing a path.

Once they reached the outside perimeter of the crowd, Cameron and Michel stepped aside to give her room to pass. At the sight of Cameron's severe and aloof expression, a strange chill ran through her. Despite the commotion, she heard him say to Michel, "I'll lend a hand with the hoses and ladders, then I'll head home. I've decided to leave in the morning, so make room for me on the *Arabesque*."

Another shock jolted her. *He's leaving so soon?*

In less than an hour, she'd lost most everything dear to her.

Covered with soot, his emotions about as hollow as Josette's burned-out shop, Cameron headed for the town house, his wounded leg cramping and feeling as though it had been set aflame.

Smoke curled in the night sky, making a mockery of the stars and the moon. What the devil had happened to him back there? A vision of the Thibodeaux clan huddled together and protecting their own, to the exclusion of all others, sliced through him like a piece of broken glass, leaving bloody shards in its wake. He'd have reached Josette first had he been able to move faster, curse his throbbing leg. Even Alexia had beaten him to her—only to leave the scene clinging to one of her uncles with nary a glance Cameron's way.

Damn it, Josette might not want anything further to do with him, but Alexia was as much his kin as she was theirs.

Who was he fooling? He was irrelevant now. He didn't belong amongst them. Never had. Never would. He knew that as clearly as he knew his own name. So why should their dismissive actions wound him?

What the hell was wrong with him? Had he lost his common sense when it came to them? He should never have gotten involved with Josette in the first place. And what good was he to Alexia when she had a tight-knit family to depend on? What moral right did he have to whisk her off to God knows where just because she was his offspring? Of late, she might as well have been a stranger for the way she ignored him.

Could he blame her?

Leaving her behind shouldn't be so difficult. Besides, she'd be nothing but trouble—hadn't a lick of sense most days. He pushed down a knot of guilt and confusion before it wound too tight.

He'd have a trust set up for her. One day he'd return. Or give it a few years, and he could invite her to visit him— once he knew where the hell he'd end up and what he wanted out of life. One thing was for certain—he wouldn't settle in New Orleans. After seventeen years of living in cool climates, the sultry weather alone threatened to do him in. He swiped a hand over his face, up into his hair. His brain felt as though it were awash in mud.

He thrust his hands in his pockets and picked up his pace, breathing hard against the crushing pressure in his lungs and the fire in his leg. Christ, how had he ended up in this mess?

Come morning, he'd be gone. Two days at sea and he'd be a new man, the nightmare behind him. His thoughts in a tumult, he concentrated on his feet hitting the ground, driving him toward the town house. With every step he took, he shut down a little, just as he'd done after Dianah died. Soon, he'd feel nothing. He ought to be damn glad about that part, at least. He always coped better that way.

Head down, he stepped inside the town house and nearly ran into Marie.

"Lawdy, you look like you been rolling in dirt, *mischie*. What's happened? And where be the rest of your clothing?"

He glanced at his stained shirt and vest. "I have no idea what happened to my jacket and cravat. I think I might have handed them to Felicité. She'll be along in a bit if she has them. Those fire bells you likely heard had to do with Madame LeBlanc's shop. It went up in flames tonight."

Marie's hand shot to her mouth. "That nice lady you had here at the house?"

Cameron nodded. "I tried to help. We all did. At least we saved the shops on either side, but her place is in ruins." He glanced down at his stained shirt. "Would you mind running a bath for me? Then pack my things. I'll be leaving on the first ship out in the morning."

"What?" Her brows dipped together. "But I thought you weren't leaving 'til next week."

"There's been a change in plans." Blast it, the last thing he wanted was Marie's questions. Nothing much got past the old bird.

Slowly, she eyed him up one side and down the other. "What be the matter, *mischie*? I don't see you smile anymore. Only once, and that be when Madame LeBlanc was here. You sweet on her?"

A noise left the back of his throat. "I doubt I've thought of things quite that way, Marie. The bath?"

"Yessir. Coming right up, sir." She headed for the bathing

chamber at the rear of the house. "But if'n you ask me, which you ain't, of course, you ought to be doin' some hard thinking while you be doing some hard scrubbing."

Cameron climbed the stairs to collect his robe, but decided on fresh clothing. What he needed was a few drinks and some food—and no conversation from nosey Marie. He'd go to Antoine's. He stripped himself bare and rinsed off most of the soot before sinking into the tub.

Josette.

Nothing he did seemed to cast her out of his mind for long. At the mere thought of her, remembered sensations of their lovemaking flooded his every nerve ending. Desire washed over him like a sudden rain. He grew hard but ignored his rebellious body. The absurdity of what he'd been through since landing in New Orleans hit him like a slap to the face. He'd let himself become tangled up in an affair where everything turned out to be an illusion.

While he'd introduced her to pure physical gratification, she had somehow managed to instill in him a vulnerability he'd not known he possessed. What in God's name had happened to him? He couldn't possibly be attached to her.

Could he?

He knew the answer before the thought had fully formed. He'd let his guard down. Just a few short weeks ago, he'd had no idea he'd be taking a lover when he landed in New Orleans. Now look at him, pining away like some schoolboy. He'd been a damn fool for getting involved with anyone, let alone his daughter's aunt. A few days at sea and this would all be behind him. His head would clear and he could think straight once again. He'd had enough pain in his life.

God, he missed the sea.

He scrubbed himself clean with a fury, as if doing so might wash away his painful thoughts. Little good that did. The image of Josette walking away tonight with barely a glance his way had been burned like a cattle brand on his mind. He climbed from the tub, dressed, and wandered into the parlor lit by a lone gaslight. He poured himself a brandy and sat on the divan, where he leaned his head against the back and stared at the ceiling, lost in thought.

The outside door opened.

He stilled, his hearing suddenly acute.

Marie rustled around in the back of the house, so it couldn't be she.

"Papa?" Alexia peeked around the corner, her face drawn, her movements hesitant.

"Alexia?" His heart pounded a few extra beats. "What are you doing here?"

"I came to see you, Papa."

What the devil? He drew in a slow breath, unsure how to react. "Then come in and *see* me, don't just peer around the corner like a timid mouse. How's your aunt's hand?"

Slowly, Alexia sidled around the corner, her face obscured in shadows. "It be fine. Bastièn said it's only raw and not burned after all. She must've scraped it on something."

"I see."

"You still plan on leaving in the morning?"

He lifted his head off the back of the sofa and studied her. "How'd you know that?"

"We heard you. Or *ma tante* did, anyway. Why can't you wait until next week, like you had planned?"

What did he have to lose by being honest? "Because I can't think straight any longer, Alexia, so I need to get away. I've been here far longer than I expected. And I've disrupted your life. You need to carry on without having to be afraid of a father who might drag you off at any moment."

"Nawlins is a mighty fine town. Why can't you live here?"

She stepped farther into the room, her fingers nervously working the fabric on her dress. *Her dress?* Bloody hell if she wasn't wearing a clean and proper gown. With matching blue ribbons in her hair. He glanced at her feet peeking out from under the gown. She wore the shoes he'd bought her and only seen her in one other time. Why now? The idea that she'd dressed specially for him tore a hole in his heart.

"The weather is too hot and stifling for me, Alexia. Cousin Michel is in charge of the shipping company, so there's nothing here for me . . ." He paused at the way his last words sounded. "Except for you, of course."

He swallowed against the odd sensation thickening his throat. "But you and I both know I'm only in your way. I don't want to be that kind of burden on you."

"Take me with you, Papa."

He stilled as the shock of her words rippled through him. He lifted his head from the back of the sofa. "What?"

She blinked and a tear rolled down her cheek. "I . . . I just found you. I can't be losing you now."

An ache unfurled in his chest. He slammed his eyes shut and took a deep breath. When he opened them, he saw she'd ventured a little closer, looking as though he might be some kind of puzzle she needed to solve.

He stared at her, his jaw slack.

Her chin quivered. "Say something, Papa."

A sensation of warmth tinged with a bit of pain flooded his chest and fought with the myriad of emotions churning up from his gut. "Come here, Alexia."

She stepped close enough for him to catch the scent of Josette's special soap.

"I'm too damn big to crawl on your lap, ain't I? But I sure do want to."

A bubble of laughter smoothed out the lump in his throat. "I suppose if you're old enough to curse like a sailor, then you're too old to be climbing onto my lap." He patted the cushion next to him. "But come, sit with me."

She slid onto the seat, and said nothing, as if she'd decided anything else that needed saying was up to him. He reached for her hand and rested it across his broad palm. For a long stretch, he said nothing.

"What'cha thinkin', Papa?"

He had to clear his throat to speak. "I'm thinking your hands must have been quite small and chubby when you were a babe." He tapped his finger along each knuckle on the back of her hand. "You likely had dimples right here, and here, and here, they were so fat."

She giggled.

He drew in a ragged breath against the heavy pressure in his chest and looked away.

"Are you weeping, Papa?"

He turned back to her. "In my own way, I suppose I am," he said, not recognizing his own voice. "I've missed out on so much of your life, and that's something I can never get back. I surely don't want to miss out on anything else."

A smile, the color of sunshine, lit her face and eyes. "Then you'll be taking me with you?"

"Are you sure? Have you discussed this with your family?"

Her head bobbed up and down. "*Ma tante* said I should come tell you right away. She said I should stay the night so you don't leave without me. She'll have my things sent to the ship first thing."

"Is that so? I doubt your aunt would send you here on your own. Allow you to wander through the streets by yourself at night."

Her bottom lip slid between her teeth. "René brought me. He said you'd appreciate him doing the escorting, and that you'd appreciate *ma tante* sending my belongings to the ship direct. He also said to tell you that he and Bastièn would be there to see us off in the morning. I know what I'm doing, Papa. I done said my good-byes to everyone else, don'cha know."

An odd jolt ran through Cameron. That was it? Nothing more from Josette? But why should he expect any farewells sent his way? "You don't say."

They looked at each other for a long while, as though they'd both finally decided to venture over a bridge that had needed crossing for some time. Only now, they'd walk it together. "You'll miss your family, Alexia. You need to know that."

As quickly as her smile had come, a cloud passed over her face. "You don't want me coming along?"

"Of course, I do." He slid his arm around her shoulder and gave it a squeeze. "After all I've gone through to make sure you have a better life, how could you think otherwise? But it's important you know how serious your decision is. We can't be a week at sea and have you changing your mind."

"Oh, my heart and mind, they be feeling the same. I been giving this lots of thought." There went her lower lip between her teeth again. "So can I stay here tonight, Papa?"

Something deep in his own heart clicked into place. "You may, but I want you to go to bed and stay put, because we'll be leaving right before dawn."

She stood and, stretching her arms above her head, contrived a yawn. "Well, I best be getting' to bed. I'm powerful tired."

They both laughed.

"Come along, you little scamp."

Together, they climbed the stairs. He waited in the corridor while she donned the nightgown she'd left behind after her overnight stay with Felicité.

"*Entre*, Papa," she called out in a light and airy voice.

He opened the door and stepped inside to find her already in bed, the covers pulled to her chest. He grinned and moved to the side of the bed. "Why do I have a feeling we're in for quite a time of it once we sail?" He bent and planted a kiss on her forehead.

"Papa?"

"What?"

"Can I take Midnight with me?"

"Abbott's cat? I should say not." He headed for the door, then halted. "How about we find you a kitten when we reach our first port? It can go along with us on all kinds of adventures, on every ship we decide to sail on."

"Truly?"

He nodded, then turned once again to leave.

"I love you, Papa."

He nearly stumbled. He raised his head to the ceiling to keep from choking on unspent tears. He struggled to find his voice. "I love you too, Alexia."

He walked out the door, then stuck his head back in. "Alexia?"

"Yes, Papa?"

"I'm glad you're in my life."

Chapter Twenty-Nine

Instead of facing east, in the direction the *Arabesque* was heading, Cameron stood aft, watching the early evening sun turn the clouds in the west a luminescent orange and vibrant purple. Three days at sea and the solace and comfort he usually found aboard ship had evaded him. The peace of mind he'd always found on the open seas had escaped him entirely.

No matter what he did, he couldn't seem to erase Josette from his mind. He glanced over his shoulder at Alexia, who stood starboard observing the sea. She had Abbott's damn cat in her arms. Not once had she mentioned what or whom she'd left behind, but he knew she missed her family because he'd heard her talking to the little beast. No wonder she'd secreted the cat aboard; it was her only connection to New Orleans.

The thought pinched his chest. Would she get over the melancholy he could read in her eyes? Should he have insisted she remain with her family? It seemed as though instead of being clear in his goal to sail the world, Cameron was only more confused.

He'd been taking a hard look at his past since they'd set sail. Today he'd come to the conclusion that he'd been avoiding living life to its fullest these last three years. Standing not far from his daughter, and with an entire crew aboard, all he felt was loneliness. He hadn't been able to shrug off the hollow feeling that had settled inside every part of him.

"Papa, look!"

He turned to where Alexia was pointing. A school of dolphins jumped and cavorted not a hundred yards away, drawing closer to the ship as they swam. He joined her. "Would you look at that?"

"Are they trying to keep up with us?"

"So it would seem."

"Do they do that sort of thing?"

"Indeed, they do," he said. "I've seen them swim alongside a ship for miles on end."

Suddenly, several dolphins shot out of the water right beside the ship. Alexia squealed. "They see me, Papa! They looked right into my eyes. It gave me goose bumps, don'cha know!"

Josette should be here to see this. He drew in a ragged breath and stepped away from Alexia, who was so focused on the dolphins, she took no notice of his movements. Returning aft, he went back to watching the color-play in the clouds.

He missed the hell out of Josette.

A memory of the day he'd caught her working in her garden flashed through his mind. The way the light had shone around her like a nimbus, her anger at him that had only served to fire his blood. Then there was the game they'd played that had nearly landed them in bed together. And what of the times when they had? After hours of making love, she'd curl her lithe body against his and fall asleep in his arms. Damn it. He didn't just miss her. He ached for her. And he missed everything about her. He loved that she was bold enough to have faced all those women who'd shunned her and built a business around them. He loved that she'd had the courage to find her way out of the bayou and away from the abusive woman who'd raised her. He loved her tenacity, even her stubbornness.

Hell, he loved *her*!

He had to lean against the rail while the realization seeped through his bones and made him weak. He didn't just *think* he loved Josette, he *knew* it from the depths of his soul. He wanted her in his life, and he wanted to be a part of hers. Damned if he didn't want to grow old with her curled up beside him every night. The idea of spending the rest of his life looking at the same face over breakfast every morning held a sudden appeal. He wanted to be one of those old couples walking along a beach at sunset, collecting seashells.

His mind tracked back to Trevor and Celine's wedding day and how they'd had that look about them that said thirty years from now they'd still be holding hands and laughing together. That's what he wanted; he wanted to love and be loved forever. And he sure as hell did not want to travel the seas alone only to end up in some beautiful spot on earth as a recluse.

Why had it taken him so long to see that she'd become an essential part of his life? God, how could he have been so stupid as to have left her behind? Her sister had once stolen her dreams, and here he was, sailing off and stealing yet more.

He wanted his old humor back so he could whisper wicked things in her ear to shock her and then make her laugh. He wanted to share secret glances with her in a crowded room, an exchange that could only take place between two lovers who knew each other intimately.

He wanted to play more risqué games with her, wanted to watch her try to best him. Hell, he even wanted her to try to out-drink him on those occasions.

He wanted . . . no, he *needed* her as his best friend, his lover, his mate. She deserved someone who could love her with everything he had in him. And by God, he was the very one!

A prickly feeling shot through him and landed in his gut. Had he done so much damage, leaving the way he had, that she'd closed her heart to him? God, he hoped he wasn't too late. Well, he'd bloody well go begging if he had to.

Turning on his heel, he headed for the stern, meeting the ship's navigator and captain midway. "Turn the ship around."

The navigator cupped his ear as if he'd not heard right. "Say what, sir?"

Captain Creesy stepped forward. "Sir, we're halfway to Bermuda."

"I'm well aware of the fact, Josiah. Nonetheless, we're heading back to New Orleans."

The captain sputtered. "But, sir, I've a contract to fulfill."

Cameron chuckled and slapped Josiah on the back. "Might I remind you that it was my contract you signed? My shipping company employing you?"

The captain cleared his throat with a small cough. "May I ask the reason, sir?"

Alexia sidled up to Cameron, the poor cat in her arms being petted half to death during the girl's intense scrutiny of Cameron. "That's what I want to know."

As if he were about tell her exactly why he was turning back and have her beat him to Josette's door. "Let's just say I have some unfinished business that requires my immediate attention."

"Yes, of course," the captain said, but stood before Cameron in stunned silence while the navigator waited for his orders.

"Captain Creesy," Cameron said. "If you will hasten to order the ship turned in the opposite direction, once you reach New Orleans, you and your entire crew shall be paid in full. Then, when you immediately turn this little money spinner around and reach Bermuda, you will all receive double pay. So if you'll give James here your direct order, we can pick up the afternoon westerly and sail into the sunset."

The navigator's eyes lit up as he took survey of the crew's whereabouts.

"You heard the man," Josiah said. "Let's get this bloody ship turned around."

Alexia's hand slid into Cameron's. He looked down into eyes filled with a mixture of trepidation and excitement. "Why we going home, Papa?"

Home. Didn't that tell him something about her? "We need to return Abbott's cat." He gave her hand a tug and headed toward the foredeck. "Come along, *pouchette*. Let's get right up front while the ship turns about."

Alexia had to trot alongside him in order to keep up with his long strides. "You wouldn't go ordering the captain to turn back just because I stole Abbott's . . . oh, you be fooling me." She grinned up at him. "Whatever you're turning back for, I'll be seeing *ma tante* and my uncles again. Oh, and *Tante* Vivienne and Régine. That will be nice. Very nice. Maybe we can have us some étoufée soon's we get there."

He bit the inside of his lip to keep from grinning. "Is food all you can think about?"

"*Non.* I been thinking about lots of things, Papa. I been thinking *ma tante* must be missing you something terrible."

"What makes you say that?"

"She loves you. And I can tell you love her, so maybe you be missing her, too?"

Sweet and painful, those words. Especially coming from a child too old for her years, yet innocent as a babe when it came to some things. "How could you possibly know such a thing?"

"I see it in your eyes, the way you look at her when you talk to her, and how you keep watching her when you think she isn't looking."

Maybe not so innocent, after all. "And she does the same? Is that your thinking?"

"She told me she loves you. She said she would miss you because you're the best thing that ever happened to her."

Stunned, he drew in an audible breath that trembled. "She told you this?"

Alexia nodded.

"When?"

"When I told her I was sure I wanted to leave with you. She said she'd miss us both and her heart would break a little."

Apprehension washed through Cameron again. Would she turn him away? Damn if Josiah couldn't get this ship turned around fast enough. Josette was worth going after no matter the cost to his company. She was worth everything he could manage to give her—including his heart and his soul.

And his promise to love her forever.

The *Arabesque*'s towering rigging, as tightly tuned as a giant violin, thrummed and keened as the ship made her wide turn. Her masts creaked as she took the wind on her portside until at last, fully turned, she began to pick up speed. Twin white waves curled away from her sharp bow in high, arcing plumes, filling the air with a salty spray as she headed full-speed for New Orleans. Cameron grinned and licked the tangy water off his lips.

Finally, this journey felt right.

Josette stood on her bedroom balcony, gazing into the darkness and ignoring the bellow of male voices rising up from the open window below. She swiped at the tears trickling down her cheek. Enervated, she couldn't concern herself with whatever René and Bastièn might be arguing about. If they were even quarreling, that is. For all she knew, they could be having a devil of a good time over nothing more than wagering on the precise moment the sun might rise tomorrow morning.

She rubbed at her folded arms through the thin silk of her robe as if she'd grown cold, but it was nothing more than emptiness chilling her bones. She still couldn't remember much of what had transpired the night of the fire—from the time the flames engulfed the pool of alcohol to when she'd found herself at home. She couldn't even recall how she'd managed to get out of her laboratory. By rights, she should have been trapped. All she knew was she'd suddenly found herself in the street, clinging to René for dear life.

She clearly remembered Cameron, though. He'd watched her leave the scene, his face a stone mask. Mixed with his coldness was a pain so tangible she could've reached out and touched it. Why had she been so foolish as to tell him she didn't want to set eyes on him before he left? What she'd said to protect her breaking heart now seemed unduly harsh. Worse, her dictum had left its mark—he'd taken her at her word and not come to her. Had left town without the goodbye she'd secretly hoped for.

He and Alexia had only been gone for a little over a week, but it felt more like months. Two people she loved erased from her life. Just like that. Shouldn't she be glad he cared enough to take his daughter with him? Wasn't this what she'd wanted for Alexia all along? The girl desperately needed her father's influence. And when she hadn't returned the night Josette had sent her to Cameron, she knew he had accepted his daughter. Of course he would have. Josette had never doubted it for a moment.

René and Bastièn had held different opinions. They'd laid odds on Alexia returning the same evening, along with a side bet as to whether it would be of her doing or her father's. But the next morning, they'd returned home with downcast eyes after seeing Alexia and Cameron off.

Her brothers' questionable activities hadn't angered

Josette. She knew them well. They wagered on just about anything, and acted as though they were celebrating something by imbibing a good supply of rum. Such behavior was their way of coping with the loss of a young girl they'd both helped raise.

Stark reality settled in the pit of Josette's stomach like spoiled fruit. Alexia was destined to grow into womanhood in another part of the world. Under the guidance of a cultured, educated father armed with wit and intelligence—a man Josette loved but could never have. The thought gave a stiff tug at her insides.

Someday, she and Alexia would be reunited, and Josette would be able to see how her niece turned out. As for Cameron, Josette might never meet him again. A soft moan, nearly a sob, tore loose from her throat. There had to be only so many scars a heart could endure before it gave up and crumbled to dust.

She had nothing now but a house filled with two cousins and two brothers—two brothers who were planning to leave on a voyage that had this evening caused an argument between her and them. She hadn't a clue as to how much time had passed while she'd stood on the balcony and stared out at the moon.

Her life was empty now. All that she'd worked so hard to achieve was gone. In an instant, her life had changed. Who was she now? What did she have to look forward to but tending to her garden and stitching up her brothers' wounds now and then? Whenever they were in town, that is. Another shaft of pain lanced her heart. Next week even they would be gone on a journey. What if they decided to take a permanent assignment elsewhere? If one brother went, the other was sure to follow.

A light tapping sounded on the door. She ignored it. Whichever brother it was, he'd soon let himself in after she failed to respond. When it came to respecting her privacy, those two weren't always the most discerning of men. And tonight, she was desperate for seclusion.

Another tap.

She drew in a heavy breath but couldn't find the energy to summon her voice and send whoever it was away. The snick of the door produced half a grin. She waited for some kind of remark that would initiate a conversation. The silence lengthened, then stretched out so long, it irritated her.

"What is it?" When she got no response, she turned.

Cameron!

Her heart beat a drumroll in her throat. She pressed her hips against the railing for support. Dear Lord, he'd returned! "Where's Alexia? Is she all right?"

"Indeed. She's asleep in my town house." His voice rolled through the night, deep and husky.

"Have you returned for good?"

"No. The *Arabesque* sails again tomorrow."

A sharp, sweet pain sliced open yet another piece of her heart. "Will you be taking Alexia with you?"

He nodded and, lifting his shoulder off the door frame, moved fully out of the bedroom and into the shadows on the balcony. It didn't matter that she couldn't see him clearly. She knew his features well enough in any light.

"Why in the world did you return?"

"She'll need a tutor while we sail around the world, so I returned to find one. She'll learn a lot more than books can give her in our travels, but she'll still need someone to teach her mathematics, that sort of thing. Might you have anyone to recommend?"

She stiffened. He was here to find a tutor? Good Lord, why not just cut out her heart and be done with it. She glanced over his shoulder, at the bed they'd once shared, her mind in a whirl. "I haven't the foggiest notion whom to recommend."

Clouds cleared from the sky and moonlight poured down

like a message from the heavens, illuminating his features. He followed her gaze to the bed, then back, and stepped forward. Raw lust smoldered in his eyes.

Her throat tightened and the air left her lungs. Her hand came to her breast as if the gesture itself might bring back her breath. His eyes followed her movement, then scanned her face as if he sought answers in her countenance. She turned her back to him and stared out at nothing again, trying to gather her wits.

"Have you ever swum in the ocean, Josette?" He'd moved close enough so that his voice was a deep, seductive rumble across her skin. "Have you ever sat beside a crystal-clear lagoon under a palm tree and drunk milk from so many coconuts you can't manage another sip?"

The fine hairs on her arms prickled and sent a shiver down her spine. Her belly heated, and her nipples tightened. A tangle of confusion and desire knotted her insides. "You know I have not."

"Would you like to?"

She could feel his heat now, and heaven help her, she wanted to lean back against his chest and have him hold her in his strong arms. "What are you asking of me, Cameron? To become your daughter's tutor? I have a life here."

He swept her hair off her shoulder and leaned to whisper in her ear, sending a thousand sparks shooting through her. "Do you, Josette? Have a life here? You have a house is about all I can figure."

Enough of trying to think straight. She wanted this. Wanted him. Tomorrow she'd likely be sorry, but for tonight, she'd lie with him one last time. She bent her head to the side, exposing her neck. An invitation. "It must be sweltering in the tropics. Hotter than here. So why would you want to sit under a palm tree and sip on a coconut?"

His hand came to rest on her opposite shoulder as he settled his body against hers, the mass of hot energy running through her like lightning. His words vibrated against her throat. "On the other hand, the Alps are lovely this time of year."

He ran his tongue along the curve of her neck. She hissed in a breath. "I cannot go with you when you leave, but we can give each other this night."

"Tell me something, Josette," he murmured, his voice a husky rasp. "Do you love me?"

Oh, indeed she did, but to speak the words aloud would only lure her into yearning for a future that could not be had. "What good would it do if I did?"

"Quite a lot, actually."

He slipped her robe and gown off one shoulder, nipped at her skin, and turned her around to face him. "You love me. I know you do, but I need to hear you say it."

He'd discarded his jacket somewhere and his sleeves were rolled. A glimpse of those muscular arms and she longed for his embrace. "What gave you that idea?"

He took a quick taste of her lips and then pulled back. "It took me three days at sea to figure out that I can't live without you—that I won't live without you—and about two minutes to realize you'd been sending the same message to me in ways that I was too stupid to perceive. Another two minutes and I had the captain giving orders to turn the bloody ship around."

Her throat got tight and her lungs froze so she could barely speak. "You . . . you did?"

He nodded. "Tell me you feel the same, Josette."

She opened her mouth, but no words came out.

He grinned. "I already know you love me, but I need to hear it from your own lips."

"My own lips? That sounds like you've heard it from others."

He nodded. "Alexia told me so."

"And how would she know this?"

"My dear, did you not, the very night before Alexia and I

sailed off, tell her you loved me and that your heart would break a little at my leaving?"

She scoffed. "I said no such thing."

His hands, hot and large, grasped her shoulders. He peered deep into her eyes, momentary confusion washing through his. "Are you serious? You never told Alexia that you love me?"

"Not a word."

He paused, his eyes searching hers. Then he lifted his chin to the sky and laughter rolled out into the night. "Why, that fibbing little scamp."

"Shush, or you'll have my brothers up here."

He lifted a brow as he lowered his mouth and lightly brushed his lips across hers. "Is that so?"

What did he mean by that? The silence struck her. "It's awfully quiet downstairs."

His fingers slipped to her breast, their movement atop the silk nothing less than a heated, delicious message that went straight to her womb. "I kicked your brothers out of the house."

She laughed softly against his mouth as his gentle fingers whipped up a firestorm in her belly. "So that was the ruckus. Obviously, they didn't go quietly."

He kissed the corners of her mouth. "René left saying that under the circumstances, it was only fitting he locate Felicité and even the score."

His other hand swept around to the small of her back and he moved even closer, surrounding her with his essence. "When I climbed the stairs saying I was going after a wife, I told René if he was off to do the same, then he had my blessing. I think that's when he changed his mind about getting even and hied off somewhere with Bastièn."

"A wife?" Her heart stuttered in her chest. "I thought you said you needed a tutor for Alexia."

"That, too."

For a brief moment, an almost painfully shy smile touched his mouth. "You've bewitched me, *ma chaton*. You are the most genuine, uninhibited, and natural woman I have ever encountered. If you won't have me, I want to thank you from the bottom of my heart for what you have given me."

"What did I give you?"

"You gave me the courage to care again."

Her breath left her lungs. She planted her forehead against his chest to steady herself. "You're asking me to leave New Orleans forever, aren't you?"

He caressed her back. "Forever is a very long time, darling. Who knows what will happen five years from now? Ten? They say when one reaches one's winter years, a desire to return to one's roots grows strong. We were both born here, if you recall."

"But what would become of Vivienne and Régine? I've taken care of them for years."

"They can live here and enjoy your gardens while they cater to our shipping line's captains. Those men would be thrilled to stay in a fine home instead of yet another lonely hotel room. Think of how proud Régine would be of her delicious cooking. Your brothers have agreed that this is a good and flexible plan. They want to try their hand at experiencing a bit of life outside New Orleans, but they'd like a home to return to whenever they please."

"You ask a lot of me if you seek an immediate answer to such a life-changing question."

A subtle stiffening of his muscles told her she'd struck a chord. "Be my wife, Josette. Come along with me to places you've only read about. The house will be here if we should ever choose to return. Don't be the only one who refuses to find her wings. Come with us . . . come with your family next week on the first leg of our journey. After that, we can sit on the beach in Bermuda and watch glorious sunsets while we decide which ship we want to take and where."

Could it be? Could she actually do this? She pulled her head back and looked up into eyes now filled with uncertainty. "I can't think straight. Those are all good and sound reasons, but somehow not enough to convince me."

"Then let me give you the best reason. I love you. And I know you love me. We've been fools not to recognize it weeks ago. Marry me, Josette."

His words pierced her heart, then shot straight to her brain, setting it abuzz. He deserved nothing less than the truth of what she was capable of doing. Her hands shook at the thought of exposing her secrets. Setting her trembling palms against his hard chest, she pushed away from him. "There's something I need to give you."

His brows knitted as she swept past him and into the bedroom. She went to the glass-shelved étagère and to the box sitting on it. He followed along behind her and watched over her shoulder as she opened the container and removed the false bottom.

Lifting out his diamond stick pin, she turned and handed it to him. "Here. I stole this from you the night you bedded my sister for the first time. That's when I swiped your pocket watch as well. Before we go any further, I think you should know how deceitful I can be and what foolish things I sometimes do when angry."

He held the pin in his palm, turning his hand a little so the light from the wall sconce caught the stone's dazzling facets. She waited in the dead silence, her heart pounding in her ears. Was this the moment he changed his mind and walked away? She wouldn't blame him if he did.

He kept his focus on the pin for a long while, seemingly fascinated by its brilliance. "You were quite the little thief, weren't you?"

"More than that," she said, "I have been a liar, as well."

He looked up, the sharpness of his glance stealing her breath. "How so?"

She had to wait a beat before she was able to respond. "I lied when I told you I didn't know about the voodoo doll."

"So you did sneak in and place it on my pillow. You must have been truly angry with me to want me castrated and my heart bloodied."

She felt the heat crawl up her neck and bloom in her cheeks. "You are wrong on both counts. That was a voodoo love doll. I made it when I was thirteen years old and with stars in my eyes. The strings on the heart had knots on the ends, meaning your heart would forever overflow with love for the maker of the doll. The circle of five pins in your . . . well, they were meant to make you want to father five children one day."

Cameron lifted a brow. "I'll have you know, the sight of them had the opposite effect. What made you place it on my pillow after all this time?"

"I didn't. Alexia went snooping in my things and found the doll at the bottom of a trunk I had stored in the attic. She understood the voodoo ways enough to comprehend the doll's meaning. When I figured out how the blasted thing ended up on your pillow, I realized that Alexia wanted us together. I said nothing to either one of you because I didn't know what to do. I thought her wishes to be as foolish as mine had been at her age."

"Perhaps yours were not so foolish, after all, my dear. Look where we stand today."

"I don't know why I kept the doll since it caused me a great deal of pain. When I found out that Solange carried your child, I was devastated. I figured I had made that happen. I also believed that my manipulations had caused you to fall in love with her."

Just saying the words sent a sharp pain lancing through Josette. She broke eye contact with Cameron and stared at the floor.

"My dear, you never cease to amaze me." Cameron set the diamond stick pin on the shelf and grasped her shoulders. "Look at me, Josette."

When she continued to stare at the floor, he curled a finger under her chin and lifted it, his amber gaze filled with a depth that startled her. "I never loved Solange. Trevor and I were wild youths, carousing day and night. By the time we managed to stagger into Madame Olympée's every night, our eyes were blurred and our brains were sotted. Had it not been your sister, it would have been anyone else the madame had presented to me. I'm sorry your sister died because of my careless behavior. Truly sorry. I would give anything to change that part of my life and have her walking the earth to this day, but I did not love her."

Josette closed her eyes and pressed her forehead to his chest. "Dear God, Cameron. Solange did not die in childbirth. Odalie poisoned her well after Alexia was born."

Cameron's body jerked. And then he stiffened. "You know this for a fact?"

"Vennard told me."

"And you trust his word?"

She nodded. "I believe him, yes."

"But it was because she gave birth to my child that Odalie poisoned her."

"Solange was determined to carry a wealthy man's child. She was convinced it was her only way to escape a sorry life in the bayou. Had she not chosen you, she would have tricked someone else. Do not blame yourself for her demise. Odalie is deranged. Not only did she murder her own daughter, she poisoned my mother, as well. It seems she got rid of whomever or whatever displeased her. I now have my suspicions about how my grandmother suddenly took ill and died."

"Good Christ! Odd that Odalie spared you."

"Vennard said she didn't dare do me harm or he'd have had René and Bastièn done in."

When Cameron said nothing, Josette slid her arms around him and held him, rubbing at the taut muscles in his broad back. God help her, whatever came of this, at least she'd told him the truth.

They stood together for a long while, silently holding each other. Finally, he took in a deep breath and let go with a great sigh. She felt him relax, as though he'd come to terms with what she'd told him.

He backed away enough to tug at the tie to her robe. Easing the fabric off her shoulders, he let it fall to the floor. Grasping a handful of his shirt, he yanked it over his head, tossed it aside, and swept his arms around her once again.

"I know of a wonderful sidewalk cafe in Paris that serves the most incredible desserts." Despite his half-smile, his husky words rumbled from somewhere deep in his chest. He cleared his throat and continued. "Much to the owner's chagrin, I sometimes toss crumbs to the pigeons. Care to join me?"

Oh God, she'd go anywhere he wanted to take her! "I've thought many times I'd like to see Venice one day."

The sight of the hard planes of his belly, his well-muscled chest, sent a rush of selfishness through her.

He's mine.

All this is mine.

His fingers traced small circles around the tips of her breasts. "Venice is best in October when it's not so hot. There's a little restaurant off St. Mark's Square that's been open since the sixteen hundreds. Believe it or not, they still serve many of the same recipes. Their saffron ravioli is worth the trip."

"If my mind was frazzled before, you're making me dizzy from all you propose."

He ran the back of his fingers over her cheek. "We can travel the world, darling. We'll have a myriad of choices as to where we end up settling. Some you will never have thought of until you stumble across a place that feels at once like home."

He swept his tongue over the curve of her neck. "You are a beautiful woman who makes my soul ache when I'm not with you, so you may as well decide to marry me and end my misery."

His fingers traced the outline of her lips, his nostrils flaring with the force of his breath. "I want you," he said hoarsely. "Not just your body, but all of you. I want you by my side as we move forward in life. I need you, Josette. Say yes."

This was all real. He was real. This beautiful, wonderful man who'd haunted her dreams and who'd left a vacuum in her heart when he'd been sent away in his youth, had returned. And he wanted her in his life. *Forever.* His countenance, so sweetly filled with devotion, caused her words to catch in her throat, her tongue to swell.

At her silence, his lips grew taut. Suddenly, he looked shy, unsure of himself. "Say something, for God's sake."

Swallowing hard, she opened her mouth to speak but nothing came out. She drew in a breath, ready to scream her response if she had to. Suddenly, her throat relaxed and one soft word escaped. "Yes."

A wave of pure pleasure lit his countenance as if the moon had become the sun and shone brightly upon him. He pulled her tight to him and wrapped his arms around her, resting his chin on top of her head. "Thank God."

He was quiet for a moment, simply holding her. Then he said, "We have a wedding to plan aboard ship, so instead of leaving tomorrow, I'll give you a week."

She pulled back and met his eyes. "Aboard ship? You want to marry aboard the *Colette*? Why, Bastièn and René are scheduled to sail on her."

He nodded. "Did I tell you that my parents married aboard ship? It's an Andrews family tradition. I doubt it's customary to haul along the bride's entire clan, though. But it's only for a little over a week, so I guess I can manage to put up with your brothers until we reach Bermuda."

She laughed and cried at the same time. He loved her. He cared for her. He'd wrapped up her doubts and misgivings in a neat little package and handed it to her tied with a ribbon of promise. And in a week he was going to take her with him to see the world.

She had to be the luckiest woman alive.

He reached into his pocket and tossed a packet onto the glass shelf.

"What's that?"

A mischievous grin lit his eyes. "A French envelope. You can add it to that crude collection Bastièn gave you. I bought it some time ago, but we won't need it."

"We won't?" She ran her fingers along the front of his trousers, coming to a stop at the hard ridge against her hand. She squeezed.

He sucked in his breath with a hiss, and sweeping her up in his powerful arms, he headed for the bed. "Not as my wife."

He set her down so the backs of her knees touched the mattress and placed his hands on either side of her face, directing her mouth to his. His breath fell against her lips— sweet, warm, and laced with rum. "I love you, Josette."

As the words she'd once thought never to hear left his mouth in a husky rasp, she stilled. A gentle peace flowed through her like holy water raining down from the heavens. She wrapped her arms around him and reveled in the exquisite moment. "I love you, too, Cameron."

He touched his forehead to hers and held her face between

his strong, gentle hands. "Do you have any idea how good it feels to say and hear those words?"

Nothing spoken could possibly convey how very much she loved this man. She settled for a simple phrase. "I think I do."

Epilogue

Three years later

Josette and Cameron stood on the bridge of the *Alexia,* watching the ship's namesake at the helm as she guided the clipper up the Mersey River into Liverpool Harbor and along seven miles of docks. Even though it was Alexia's first time bringing a vessel into port on her own, the captain who stood beside her had little more to do than stand with his hands clasped behind his back and nod every now and then to Cameron, indicating the girl was doing a fine job.

"She handles a ship as if she'd been born at the wheel," Josette said. "I suppose all her years guiding pirogues through bayou waters gave her a certain level of confidence. Nonetheless, I find her skills amazing."

"Ah, but look closely, my dear. Her grip on the wheel is so tight, her knuckles have drained of blood."

Josette leaned back against Cameron's chest. His hand slid around to rub her swollen belly. The babe kicked.

Cameron stilled. "Did you feel that?"

She laughed. "If you felt it, then surely I did, as well."

Covering his hand with hers, she gave his a squeeze. "I'm going to miss the seas during my confinement."

"It's only for a while, darling. We have the rest of our lives to go wherever we wish. It means a lot to me to have you with family until well after the child is born. Besides, Celine will have plenty of good advice to offer."

"Who would've thought I'd get with child at my age?"

He kissed the top of her head. "Are you calling thirty-one ancient? You may think you haven't changed much, but honestly, darling, you look younger than when we married. And more beautiful, if that's even possible."

"Shimmying up palm trees can do that to a person."

"God forbid, don't remind me," he grumbled. "I'm fortunate I didn't turn gray overnight. You were worse than Alexia when it came to such folly."

Her soft laugh was accompanied by another squeeze of his hand. "I was intent on gathering my own supplies. Coconut oil does wonders for the skin."

Alexia turned, and with a grand smile, gave her father a brief wave. She stood barefoot, dressed in sailor's trousers, with her raven hair in a long braid hanging down the middle of her back. The captain wasn't tall for a man; Alexia nearly met his height.

Cameron waved back. "Do you think Prince Albert had any clue when he commissioned Albert Docks that one day a beautiful seventeen-year-old girl would be maneuvering one of the world's fastest ships into port?"

"Might I remind you once again, that despite her penchant for that damnable outfit she insists on wearing, your daughter wishes to be referred to as a young lady, not a girl? If you expect to remain on speaking terms with her, you had better heed her wishes. Can you guess what she wants for her twenty-first birthday?"

"Egads, Josette, she's barely seventeen. Whatever she

thinks she wants now will have been long forgotten by the time she reaches her majority."

"I sincerely doubt she'll change her mind in this regard. Not after today, anyway."

"Humph. Then do tell, since I now find myself on veritable tenterhooks."

"You're such a tease. She wants command of this ship, Cameron. How do we convince her it would be impossible?"

Even with the sway of the ship and the wind ruffling Josette's hair and skirts, she felt Cameron's energy shift. "We don't. She'll make an excellent captain."

Josette sucked in her breath. "I was afraid you'd say that. Besides the fact that no sailor worth his salt would agree to sail under a woman's command, would you want your daughter alone aboard a ship filled with only men?"

"Thank God her last tutor taught martial arts."

"Oooh, you're impossible. I worry that her fierce independence will cause her to do something silly, and you're not helping matters. She's already balking at having to spend time in Liverpool. Whatever is to become of her? She's beautiful, intelligent, wealthy, and scares the daylights out of any man who even thinks to be her suitor."

Cameron chuckled. "As her father, I do not find that last part problematic. Not in the least."

"Lord, Cameron, she's so world-wise, yet still thirsty for knowledge and more time on the seas."

"Mmm." He rested his chin atop Josette's head and rubbed slow, comforting circles on her belly. "Would it be fair of me to hold her back? I've lost count of the number of clippers we've boarded since we first set sail, but not Alexia. She's kept detailed records of all the ships' activities, cargo, and ports of call. She can spot a thief or liar in under a minute. She's learned every seaman's job, and can outperform most. So far, she's picked up Portuguese and Dutch from the deckhands, and is learning Italian. You know yourself she'll never be content trying to live a life others would call normal."

Josette sighed. "I give up." She glanced at Alexia's bare feet and at her brogans set neatly off to the side. She called out to her. "Alexia, change into a proper lady's gown before we dock. And put on some decent shoes."

"It's too late, *ma tante*. We're nearly there."

"Alexia, do get going," Josette said. "We don't want your grandfather to see you dressed in that garb the first time he lays eyes on you. We'll wait for you before we disembark."

Cameron lifted his chin off Josette's head. "Good God. Would you look who's gathered dockside with my family? Did your brothers know we would be staying here until you gave birth, or are they on another one of their bloody *inspection* tours?"

Josette bit her bottom lip to keep from grinning. "I may have written to them once or twice." Oh, she had, but it was to beg them to be here to greet their new nephew or niece, whichever gender the babe turned out to be. Besides, they hadn't seen Alexia since last year in Hong Kong.

The ship bumped up against the mooring. Ratlines flew through the air and the gangplank was quickly lowered. Josette's heart tripped a beat. Would Cameron's family accept a Cajun? Of course they would, she told herself. Odd how those familiar misgivings still haunted her every now and then. She picked out Trevor among the group. He was hard to miss because he and Cameron so greatly resembled each other.

Boldly, Alexia perused the gathering on the dock. She squinted for a brief moment, then squealed and took off down the gangplank, her bare feet slapping against the wood. "Uncles!"

"So much for greeting your side of the family in a ladylike

manner," Josette grumbled. "The least she could've done was had the decency to don her brogans."

Cameron, grinning from ear to ear, grabbed Josette's hand and started for the gangplank. "Don't blame life aboard ship for that little quirk. I do believe she got into the habit of not wearing shoes from your side of the family. Come, *chère*, it's time to meet this goodly lot."

ACKNOWLEDGMENTS

Thank you, Gwen Brunet, for sharing your spine-tingling story of having been bitten on the foot by a copperhead (and having it remain attached, like the water moccasin on Cameron's leg). Without the modern-day antivenin and being airlifted not once, but twice, to specialized hospitals, you'd likely not be around to give me the details that I passed on to Cameron. Copperheads and water moccasins carry the same kind of deadly poison. His run-in with the snakes and his painful recovery truly was your experience fictionalized, Gwen. Old Satan represented the antivenin made from horse and sheep blood that is in use today but wasn't developed until 1895.

Thanks go to those members of the Voodoo Society of New Orleans who were willing to share their sacred knowledge with me. Odalie was a deranged woman who stepped far beyond the rituals that were taught in the old tradition of Voodoo Queen Marie Laveau. Odalie, who created her own dark and deadly world, is purely a figment of my imagination.

The little restaurant in Venice Cameron mentioned, the one that serves recipes from the 1600s, does exist. I've tasted that awesomely delicious saffron ravioli many times, and I thank the chef for keeping it on the menu. Visiting Nawlins—especially the French Quarter—at any time of the year, except during the oppressive heat of summer, is a treat for me. I researched the town so thoroughly that when I arrived, I walked around as if I'd once lived there—well, in my heart, I guess I had while writing this series. Many thanks to the management of Antoine's for taking me on a historical tour of the fabulous restaurant. Antoine's really has existed since 1840. It really is that large, with fourteen dining rooms, and the French-Creole food really is very good.

Thanks to my critique partners, Tara Kingston, Ashlyn Macnamara, Barbara Bettis, Tess St. John, Lane McFarland, Averil Reisman, and Renee Ann Miller. You are wonderful authors in your own right. Without you helping me keep my story on track, I doubt Cameron and Josette would've had a chance at a happy ending.

Jill Marsal, as always, you are my superagent who knows just what an author needs. Thank you for believing in me.

To the Kensington crew working diligently behind the scenes, especially my publicist Jane Nutter, editorial assistant Elizabeth May, and production editor Ross Plotkin: You are all beyond wonderful. To my editor, Alicia Condon, there is an inherent grace about you that elevates how I perceive myself as a writer. I thank you.

And thank you, dear reader, for picking up this book. Without you, I'd be writing for my own entertainment. I love hearing from readers. You can contact me on Facebook, Goodreads, Twitter, or through my website at www.kathleen bittnerroth.com.

Authors appreciate and need reviews so if you'd care to leave one, I'd be grateful.

Don't miss any of novels in the When Hearts Dare series!

CELINE

Kathleen Bittner Roth

"The sexual tension barrels ahead right to the end."
—*USA Today* bestselling author Leigh Greenwood

*He stepped off a jewel of a sternwheeler onto
one of the most beautiful plantations in
all of Louisiana. And into her life.*

Celine's breath caught in her throat. Heat smoldered
in her belly. What a sensual man. The scion of
the Andrews family carried an aura of
personal magnetism so powerful, a sensation close to
fright swept through her. She stood still and aloof,
masking her emotions. His intense gaze seemed
almost a physical touch. She held her head at a proud,
haughty angle, not flinching from his bold scrutiny.

In seconds, Trevor regained his cool, casual air.
A lusty grin caught at the corners of his mouth,
and fire danced in his eyes as he bent ever so slightly
at the waist, tipped an imaginary hat,
and strode casually into the house.

She would never be the same . . .

*From plantation-era New Orleans to the
untamed American West, here is the sweeping,
unforgettable tale of a headstrong young beauty
and the man she is destined to love.*

ALANNA

Kathleen Bittner Roth

"Gripped me from the opening page . . .
kept me reading long into the night."
—Jodi Thomas

Wolf caught the faint scent of cinnabar and roses.

The girl turned her head and stared boldly at him,
her cool demeanor at odds with the fire in her look.
And then her lips parted, as if she needed more air.
A punch of lust hit Wolf's groin.

There was pure sin in his startling blue eyes.

The moment hung suspended between them,
and then expanded as his feral gaze held hers.
Stranger? Not to Alanna. He went by the name of Wolf,
and he was a legend in these parts,
known from San Francisco to Boston as a
relentless tracker of lost persons. His quest
to find his mother's killer would lead him
to Alanna . . . and his destiny.

In his arms, she would never be lost again . . .

"Ms. Bittner Roth weaves a tale of mystery,
seduction, and love. A must read!"
—Ashlyn Macnamara, award-winning author

Books by Bestselling Author
Fern Michaels

More by Bestselling Author
Hannah Howell

__Highland Angel	978-1-4201-0864-4	$6.99US/$8.99CAN
__If He's Sinful	978-1-4201-0461-5	$6.99US/$8.99CAN
__Wild Conquest	978-1-4201-0464-6	$6.99US/$8.99CAN
__If He's Wicked	978-1-4201-0460-8	$6.99US/$8.49CAN
__My Lady Captor	978-0-8217-7430-4	$6.99US/$8.49CAN
__Highland Sinner	978-0-8217-8001-5	$6.99US/$8.49CAN
__Highland Captive	978-0-8217-8003-9	$6.99US/$8.49CAN
__Nature of the Beast	978-1-4201-0435-6	$6.99US/$8.49CAN
__Highland Fire	978-0-8217-7429-8	$6.99US/$8.49CAN
__Silver Flame	978-1-4201-0107-2	$6.99US/$8.49CAN
__Highland Wolf	978-0-8217-8000-8	$6.99US/$9.99CAN
__Highland Wedding	978-0-8217-8002-2	$4.99US/$6.99CAN
__Highland Destiny	978-1-4201-0259-8	$4.99US/$6.99CAN
__Only for You	978-0-8217-8151-7	$6.99US/$8.99CAN
__Highland Promise	978-1-4201-0261-1	$4.99US/$6.99CAN
__Highland Vow	978-1-4201-0260-4	$4.99US/$6.99CAN
__Highland Savage	978-0-8217-7999-6	$6.99US/$9.99CAN
__Beauty and the Beast	978-0-8217-8004-6	$4.99US/$6.99CAN
__Unconquered	978-0-8217-8088-6	$4.99US/$6.99CAN
__Highland Barbarian	978-0-8217-7998-9	$6.99US/$9.99CAN
__Highland Conqueror	978-0-8217-8148-7	$6.99US/$9.99CAN
__Conqueror's Kiss	978-0-8217-8005-3	$4.99US/$6.99CAN
__A Stockingful of Joy	978-1-4201-0018-1	$4.99US/$6.99CAN
__Highland Bride	978-0-8217-7995-8	$4.99US/$6.99CAN
__Highland Lover	978-0-8217-7759-6	$6.99US/$9.99CAN

Available Wherever Books Are Sold!

Check out our website at
http://www.kensingtonbooks.com

Romantic Suspense from
Lisa Jackson

Absolute Fear	0-8217-7936-2	$7.99US/$9.99CAN
Afraid to Die	1-4201-1850-1	$7.99US/$9.99CAN
Almost Dead	0-8217-7579-0	$7.99US/$10.99CAN
Born to Die	1-4201-0278-8	$7.99US/$9.99CAN
Chosen to Die	1-4201-0277-X	$7.99US/$10.99CAN
Cold Blooded	1-4201-2581-8	$7.99US/$8.99CAN
Deep Freeze	0-8217-7296-1	$7.99US/$10.99CAN
Devious	1-4201-0275-3	$7.99US/$9.99CAN
Fatal Burn	0-8217-7577-4	$7.99US/$10.99CAN
Final Scream	0-8217-7712-2	$7.99US/$10.99CAN
Hot Blooded	1-4201-0678-3	$7.99US/$9.49CAN
If She Only Knew	1-4201-3241-5	$7.99US/$9.99CAN
Left to Die	1-4201-0276-1	$7.99US/$10.99CAN
Lost Souls	0-8217-7938-9	$7.99US/$10.99CAN
Malice	0-8217-7940-0	$7.99US/$10.99CAN
The Morning After	1-4201-3370-5	$7.99US/$9.99CAN
The Night Before	1-4201-3371-3	$7.99US/$9.99CAN
Ready to Die	1-4201-1851-X	$7.99US/$9.99CAN
Running Scared	1-4201-0182-X	$7.99US/$10.99CAN
See How She Dies	1-4201-2584-2	$7.99US/$8.99CAN
Shiver	0-8217-7578-2	$7.99US/$10.99CAN
Tell Me	1-4201-1854-4	$7.99US/$9.99CAN
Twice Kissed	0-8217-7944-3	$7.99US/$9.99CAN
Unspoken	1-4201-0093-9	$7.99US/$9.99CAN
Whispers	1-4201-5158-4	$7.99US/$9.99CAN
Wicked Game	1-4201-0338-5	$7.99US/$9.99CAN
Wicked Lies	1-4201-0339-3	$7.99US/$9.99CAN
Without Mercy	1-4201-0274-5	$7.99US/$10.99CAN
You Don't Want to Know	1-4201-1853-6	$7.99US/$9.99CAN

Available Wherever Books Are Sold!
Visit our website at www.kensingtonbooks.com